THIS BOOK IS
IN THE CARE OF

_____

_____

THE MONSTER
IN THE HOLLOWS

ANDREW PETERSON

THE WINGFEATHER SAGA

SAGA

BOOK 3

THE MONSTER
IN THE HOLLOWS

First published in Great Britain in 2021 by Hodder & Stoughton
An Hachette UK company

Published by arrangement with WaterBrook, an imprint of Random House,
a division of Penguin Random House LLC

3

Text copyright © 2011 by Andrew Peterson
Family tree illustration copyright © 2011 by Andrew Peterson
All other interior illustrations copyright © 2020 by Andrew Peterson

First published by Waterbrook in the United States in 2020
Interior illustrations by Joe Sutphin
Cover art by Nicholas Kole
Cover design by Brannon McAllister

The right of Andrew Peterson to be identified as the
Author of the Work has been asserted by him in accordance
with the Copyright, Designs and Patents Act 1988.

A CIP catalogue record for this title is available from the British Library

Trade Paperback ISBN 978 1 529 35985 5
eBook ISBN 978 1 529 35986 2

Printed and bound in Great Britain by Clays Ltd, Elcograf S.p.A.

Hodder & Stoughton policy is to use papers that are natural, renewable
and recyclable products and made from wood grown in sustainable forests.
The logging and manufacturing processes are expected to conform
to the environmental regulations of the country of origin.

Hodder & Stoughton Ltd
Carmelite House
50 Victoria Embankment
London EC4Y 0DZ

www.hodderfaith.com
www.hodderfaithyoungexplorers.co.uk

For Jamie, my bride,
who knows me best and loves me still.

Contents

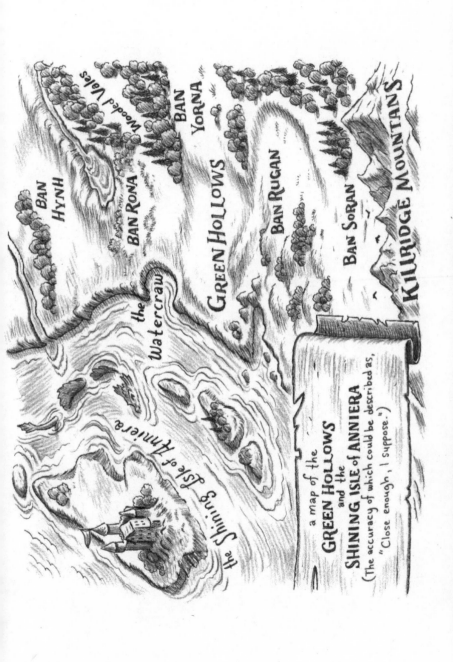

BAN HYNH

Wooded Vales

BAN RONA

BAN YORNA

GREEN HOLLOWS

BAN RUGAN

BAN SORAN

KILLRIDGE MOUNTAINS

the Watercraw

the Shining Isle of Anniera

a map of the
GREEN HOLLOWS
and the
SHINING ISLE of ANNIERA
(The accuracy of which could be described as,
"Close enough, I suppose.")

1

A Smoldering Silence

It wasn't a sound that woke Janner Igiby. It was a silence.

Something was wrong.

He strained into a sitting position, wincing at the pain in his neck, shoulders, and thighs. Every time he moved he was reminded of the claws and teeth that had caused his wounds.

He expected to see the bearer of those claws and teeth asleep in the bunk beside him, but his brother was gone. Sunlight fell through the porthole and slid to and fro across the empty mattress like a pendulum, keeping time with the rocking of the boat. The other bunk's bedclothes were in a heap on the floor, which was typical; Kalmar never made his bed back in Glipwood, either. What wasn't typical was his absence.

For weeks, Janner and Kalmar had lain in their bunks all day, Janner recovering from his wounds, Kalmar keeping him company. Every time Janner woke, he found his furry brother in his bunk, usually with a sketchbook in his lap. The *skritch-skritch* of Kalmar's quill each morning was as comforting as birdsong. Janner liked to lie awake for a few minutes before he opened his eyes, listening to Kalmar's breathing, reminding himself that the creature beside him was, in fact, his little brother. He still wasn't used to the way he looked, covered in fur, or to the husky growl at the edge of his eleven-year-old voice. But his breathing was the same, and so were his eyes. If ever Janner doubted, he just had to look at those bright blue eyes to know that beneath the wolfish fur was a little boy.

Janner took a deep breath and swung his feet to the floor. His wounds stung. His thighs were wrapped in bandages, and he winced when he saw the dark stains there. Nia and Leeli would have to change the dressing again, and that meant more pain. Janner took a moment to muster the energy to stand, something he had seldom done alone since he'd been wounded. He shuddered at the cold memory: the shock of the icy water when he plunged in after Kalmar; the hot sting of claws digging into his thighs as the little Grey Fang kicked against his embrace; claws scraping against his back and tearing his shirt to shreds; and, worst of all, the sharp teeth as they bit into his shoulder and neck—his brother's teeth.

The ship creaked and fell silent again. Since the day they had sailed away from the Ice Prairies, the ship had seemed like a living thing. It groaned like an old man sleeping; it coughed when the sails luffed; it sighed when they tacked into a happy wind. The crew shouted and laughed at all hours of the day, and even at night Janner was kept company by the slapping of waves against the hull and the murmur of sailors keeping watch.

And then there was the heartbeat of the ship: Podo Helmer. Janner's peg-legged grandfather marched from fore to aft, starboard to port, the steady *tap-clunk, tap-clunk* of his footsteps beating deep into the night, keeping the ship alive and all its passengers with it. The old man's voice boomed and bellowed, a presence so constant that if Janner ever wondered where Podo was, he had but to listen for a moment to hear either a barked command, a burst of laughter, or the beat of his wooden stump on the deck.

But now the ship's heart had stopped beating, and that was the silence that had woken Janner. Neither the odd calm of the waters, nor the silence of the crew, nor even Kalmar's absence was as troubling as the utter stillness of Podo Helmer. It was as if the old man had disappeared.

Then, as if to confirm Janner's sense of dread, there came to his nostrils the unmistakable smell of smoke. Janner stood, too fast, and the pain in his legs, neck, and back made him dizzy. But he didn't care. He had to find out what was happening on deck, even if just to be sure that he wasn't stuck in a nightmare.

Janner took three steps toward the stairs and the hatch flew open. Light poured into the hold.

"Janner! My boy, what are you doing out of bed? In the words of Mildresh Enwort, 'You've been badly wounded by your brother's clawful attack!'" Oskar N. Reteep's round form filled the hatchway, blocking the sunlight like an eclipse.

"Mister Reteep, what's wrong? Where did everybody go? Why do I smell smoke?" Janner took a step forward and winced as another pang shot up his leg.

Oskar jiggled down the stairs to Janner's side. "Easy, there. That's it, lad." He took Janner by the arm and helped him forward.

Janner asked again, "What's happening?"

Oskar pushed up his spectacles and wiped his sweaty pate. "Everything's all right, lad. Everything's all right." Oskar, who used to spend all his time puffing on a pipe at his desk in the rear office of Books and Crannies, who had only ever read about real adventures, and who had never been on a ship before, was as close to being a sailor as he would ever be. He was barefoot, his breeches were cut off at the shin, and he wore a sleeveless shirt, which allowed him to proudly display his new tattoo. And though he was no smaller and no less squishy, he seemed healthier.

"If everything's all right, why do I smell smoke? Are the Fangs back?"

The seven Fangs they'd subdued on the ship when they escaped Kimera had gotten rowdier by the day. They had howled and scratched at the stowage walls until it became clear that they wouldn't stop until they scraped their way out. The Kimerans wanted to execute them, but Nia wouldn't allow it. Weeks into the voyage, Podo decided to set them adrift on a little skiff with a jug of water, assuring everyone that it was as good as an execution, and that if the Maker wanted them to survive, it was up to him to arrange it. Janner had lain awake many nights, imagining that they'd somehow catch up to them, slip aboard, and kill the crew in their sleep.

Oskar waved his hand as they mounted the first step. "No, no. Those wolves are long gone. Your mother sent me to bring you topside." Oskar's face turned grave. "There's something you need to see."

Janner had always been impatient when it came to getting answers. With

his legs hurt, the eight steps to the deck were likely to be an arduous journey, and he didn't want to wait that long. "What is it? Please, Mister Reteep!"

"No, lad. This is a thing to see, not to hear about. Now bear up and come on."

Janner took his old friend's arm and eased his way up the steps into the sunlight. When his eyes had adjusted, he saw the open sea for the first time since they'd set sail. He had seen the ocean from the cliffs back home, stretching out forever east, and he had seen it when they escaped the Ice Prairies, with the frozen crags at his back. But now it surrounded him. The effect was dizzying. The Dark Sea of Darkness was vast and terrible to behold; it quickened his pulse and took his breath—and he knew in an instant that he loved it.

He thought of the little sketch of his father sailing alone on his twelfth birthday and how he had gazed at the picture for hours and longed to do the

same. The smell of the sea, the sun on the water, and the knowledge of his father's love for sailing rushed at Janner like a rogue wave and sent his heart spinning.

The exhilaration faded when the breeze shifted and the sharp smell of smoke invaded his thoughts again. He pulled his eyes from the ocean and noticed that everyone on the ship was on deck, standing at the port rail, looking silently south at a cloudy sky. Standing among the crew was a tall, beautiful woman, her left hand on a little girl's shoulder and her right on the shoulder of a little Grey Fang. Beside them stood Podo, shirtless and strong with what looked like a club in one hand.

"Come on, lad," Oskar said, and Nia, Leeli, Kalmar, and Podo turned to greet him.

Seeing them together gave Janner strength. He pulled away from Oskar and limped into his mother's arms. His legs, neck, and back stung but he didn't care anymore. He had seen each member of his family over the weeks of his recovery, but never all at once. He felt Podo's hand on his head, Leeli's cheek against his shoulder, his mother's arms enfolding him without jarring his wounds—and Kalmar's hand on his forearm.

Then he felt Kalmar's claws, and though he didn't want to, he cringed—only a little, but enough to break the happy spell of his family's welcome.

"Good morning, son," Nia said, taking his face in her hands. She smiled at him, but there was grief in her eyes. Janner could see she'd shed tears recently. Leeli didn't say a word but held Janner's hand and looked out at the gray horizon.

"Mama, what is it?" Janner asked. "Why won't anyone tell me what's happening?"

Nia helped Janner to the railing and pointed at the horizon. "Look."

But Janner didn't see anything unusual. The waters were eerily calm, as if the Dark Sea were holding its breath. It felt like their ship was trespassing. But that wasn't anything to look at, was it? Everyone on the ship was staring at something, but Janner saw only clouds—then he remembered the smell of smoke, and he knew.

"Those aren't clouds, are they?"

Podo shifted on his wooden leg and shook his head. "No, laddie, they aren't."

"It's smoke," Janner said.

All the maps Janner had ever studied sped through his mind. He saw continents and countries fly past, with their rivers and borders and forests. He saw Skree and the Phoob Islands and the wide expanse of the Dark Sea of Darkness, and then he saw in his imagination their ship approaching the Green Hollows in the east. There, just to the south of where Janner guessed they might be, was a little island off the northwestern coast of Dang.

"Anniera," said Janner. "The Shining Isle."

"Aye, lad. Nine long years," Podo said, "and it's still burning."

2

A Haven in the Hollows

If Janner had ever wondered if Anniera was a real place, now he knew.

He didn't just know by the awful smoke choking the sky or its scent on the wind, but by the look in his mother's eyes. It was as if the churn of the Dark Sea had abandoned the waters and left them calm, only to inhabit the eyes of Nia Wingfeather. When Janner looked up at her, he saw sorrow, anger, pain, and fear passing over her face like colliding waves, stirring the deep waters of remembrance. More than ever, Janner believed. He believed because Anniera wasn't just a story to his mother; it was memory. She had walked there with the man she loved. She had given birth to her children there. For a while, she had lived and breathed the legend of the Shining Isle.

Janner looked out at the gray sea and the black smoke that hovered above it and grieved for her loss; he grieved, too, for his own. He had lost his home, just as she had. When he thought of the Igiby cottage standing empty and dark, and of the Glipwood Township, now just a ruined village at the edge of the cliffs, he felt a stab of homesickness. How much more, he thought, must his mother long for her kingdom, her city, her people—and her husband?

Since the day they had fled Glipwood, they had been on the run, moving from place to place. From Uncle Artham's tree house to the East Bend of the Blapp, from Dugtown to Kimera, and now across the Dark Sea toward the Green Hollows, which lay somewhere just beyond the horizon.

Janner was tired of running. He wanted a place to call his own, a place where Fangs didn't roam, where Stranders didn't want to cut his throat, and where he and his family could finally be at peace. He wanted rest. He had even entertained the idea that perhaps reports of Anniera's destruction had been wrong. Maybe they would find a way to live in the land of his dreams; maybe he and his family could even live in Castle Rysen again, where he'd been born. A castle!

Janner's cheeks burned at his foolishness. He was only twelve, but he was old enough to know that life usually didn't turn out like it did in the stories he read. Still, until this moment he had allowed himself the tiny hope that the white shores of Anniera might be waiting for him. Now that hope burned up and floated away with the smoke on the horizon.

"Mama, how could it still be burning?" Leeli asked.

Nia's lips stiffened and her eyes filled with tears. When she didn't speak, Podo answered for her. "I don't know, lass. I suppose if you were determined to cinder everything in the land, it could take years."

"Nine years?" Kalmar asked.

Nia wiped her eyes. When she spoke, Janner heard the tremble of anger in her voice. "Gnag has hate enough in his heart to melt the very foundations of the castle, down to the bones of the isle itself. He won't rest until Anniera sinks into the sea."

"But why?" Janner asked. "Why does he hate it so much? Who is he, even?"

"Who knows? When hate rages long enough, it doesn't need a reason. It burns for the sake of its own heat and devours whatever, or whomever, is set before it. Before the war, rumor came to us about an evil in the mountains— but Throg is a *long* way from Anniera. We never imagined it would come to us." Nia closed her eyes. "By the time we realized the Fangs were after Anniera, it was too late. Your father believed the Symian Strait would protect us—or at least give us time to mount a defense." She shook her head and looked at the children. "The point is, Gnag seemed to come from nowhere, like a crash of lightning. He wanted Anniera. He wanted us dead."

"But he doesn't want *us* dead, Mama," Leeli said. "We only got away because he wants us alive."

Nia sighed. "You're right. I can't make sense of it, except that he knows what I've known since you were born." She dropped to her knees, turning her back on the smoky sky and looking up at the children's faces. "He knows you're special. You're more precious than you can imagine. It seems that Gnag built his army of Fangs out of people." Kalmar looked away. His wolf ears lay back like the ears of a frightened dog, and Nia pulled him closer. "But when he attacked Anniera, I saw monsters so awful I can't describe them. Gnag has uncovered old secrets. Secrets about the stones and songs, secrets I think Esben—secrets I think your *father* knew something about."

Every time Janner heard the name Esben, his stomach fluttered. It was still hard to believe his father had been a king. But all this talk about power and secrets and stones was frightening.

It was true that the three children could do things Janner couldn't explain. When Leeli sang or played, Janner had heard the sea dragons in his mind. Their words had buzzed in his head like bees in a hive. Sometimes Leeli's song connected the siblings even when they were miles apart, and Kalmar seemed to be able to see—to really *see*—what no one else could, especially when Leeli sang.

Several times now something had awoken within them, something they couldn't explain. Nia had told them it was a gift of the Maker, something they couldn't—and shouldn't—control. But if they couldn't control it, how could Gnag? And why did he want to? How could he know something about them that was mysterious even to their mother?

"I wish he'd leave us alone," Leeli said, resting her chin on the rail and looking down at the water.

"I just want things to be normal again," Kalmar said. "We'll be normal in the Green Hollows, won't we?"

Nia put her hand on Kalmar's furry face. "I hope so."

"How do we know the Green Hollows is still safe?" Janner asked.

"The Hollowsfolk are strong, and they've never liked outsiders. If anyone has kept Gnag and his armies out of their country," Nia said with a smile, "it's my kinsmen."

"And once Gnag figures out we're there?" Janner asked. "What then?"

"I don't know. But the more Gnag seeks you, the more convinced I become that he's afraid of you. *Afraid,* children. So take heart. After the battle in Kimera, I have a feeling Gnag might have finally learned to leave the Jewels of Anniera alone."

"And if he isn't finished with you," said Oskar, "he'll look everywhere but right under his nose. If I were Gnag, I'd imagine you three ran west, past the edges of the maps, or south, past the Sunken Mountains—as far away from Dang as possible. But here we are, slipping right into his own backyard."

"The Green Hollows is Gnag the Nameless's backyard?" Kalmar asked.

"The southern border of the Hollows is the Killridge Mountains, where they say Gnag sits among the peaks in the Castle Throg and broods on the world's destruction," Oskar said.

"But the mountain range is huge," Nia said. "And treacherous. There's no way through. The only people crazy enough to live there are the ridgerunners."

"Ridgerunners! Pah!" said Oskar, trying to sound like a sailor. He spat, but instead of a nice, dense, seaworthy glob plopping into the sea, it was a spray of white spittle, some of which landed on Podo's arm.

"Keep practicin', old friend," Podo said, wiping it off. "Make sure ye get the bubbles out before ye spit. And remember, it helps if ye snort. Improves the consistency. Watch."

Podo reared back and snorted so long and loud that the whole crew took notice. They watched with admiration as Podo launched a dollop of spit that sailed an astonishing distance before splooshing into the waves. The Kimerans nodded and murmured their approval.

Podo wiped his mouth. "Sorry, lass. Ye have to seize the teachable moments, you know. Carry on."

"As I was saying," Nia said with a withering look at Podo, "the ridgerunners are the only ones who live in the mountains."

"But the ridgerunners serve Gnag the Nameless, don't they?" asked Leeli. "Zouzab does."

"The ridgerunners serve themselves," Nia said. "The only reason Zouzab was in Skree at all was because Gnag captured him. Or maybe bribed him with fruit."

"They do have a thing for fruit," Oskar said.

Janner thought about Mobrik, the ridgerunner in the Fork Factory. If it hadn't been for three apples, Janner would never have been able to bribe the little man, and he'd probably still be covered in soot at the shearing station with Sara Cobbler and the others.

The thought of Sara Cobbler made his heart skip a beat. Every day since he had escaped the factory, he had thought of her bright, courageous eyes. He was haunted by the memory of her trapped behind the portcullis, in the clutches of the Overseer and Mobrik, while he clattered into the night on the carriage. But what could he do? He was on the other side of the world now. Even if he were still in Dugtown, he wasn't sure he could help her.

"But couldn't Gnag just go around the mountains?" Kalmar asked Nia.

"You don't have to worry about that either. The rest of the Hollows is surrounded by a deep, twisted forest. They call it the Blackwood. As far as we know, no one's ever survived it. It's thick with ancient trees, and terrible things live there. The sheepherders who wandered close enough to see the forest's edge always returned with the most awful stories. Stories about monsters."

Leeli shuddered.

"What kind of stories?" Janner asked.

"What kind of monsters?" Kalmar asked.

"The Hollowsfolk call them the *cloven*. Split and twisted things. The scarytales said that Ouster Will was a cloven." Nia shivered. "The point is, Gnag won't come through the Blackwood, either. Not even Fangs would be so foolish. The Green Hollows is as safe a place as we'll ever find."

"If there's anything left of it, lass," Podo said. "Maker knows you're right—the Hollowsfolk are a wiry bunch and more than capable of keeping the Fangs at bay. But it's been nine years. The world has changed. No one ever thought Anniera would fall, either."

Podo looked south with a surly eye. Janner wondered if the old man was troubled by memories of Anniera, where Wendolyn—Janner's grand-mother—had been killed by the Fangs of Dang.

One of the Kimeran crewmen shouted, "Captain! Something's coming!"

All eyes turned to the sailor at the foredeck, who pointed at the smoky southern sky.

"Somebody get me the 'scope!" Podo snarled, and in an instant a sailor handed him a long cylinder. Podo propped his elbow on the rail and squinted into the telescope.

A moment later, Janner saw a shape speeding toward them like an arrow out of the smoke.

"No fear, lads," Podo said. "It's the birdman."

3

At the Helm
of the Enramere

Artham circled the mast of the ship once before landing lightly on the deck. His transformation from Peet the Sock Man to a powerful, winged being gave Janner hope that the world wasn't just full of terrible surprises but wonderful ones too.

Artham's wings stretched as wide as he was tall, with dark feathers and bright red and white eyelets. His torso and chest were lean and muscular, like any other chest and torso except for the reddish, almost scaly skin—like a rooster's comb, Janner thought—and the dark little feathers that swept up his sides and swirled over his shoulders. Artham's face was hawkish and his hair shot out in several directions in a way that complemented his lanky frame. When his boots touched the deck, there was hardly a sound but the windy flap of his wings and a leafy rustle when he folded them.

Janner beamed with pride when Artham's bright eyes fell on him first of all. He forgot his wounds and found himself standing straighter.

"Janner. I'm glad to see you alive." Artham's voice was rich and refined, the voice of a Throne Warden—nothing like his high-pitched gibbering weeks ago. He gave Janner a smile and a quick nod, and then he turned to Podo with a serious look. "We've been spotted. Three ships are sailing straight for us from the south. I planned to fly over and get a look at—at the Isle, but I saw the ships coming and turned back. We don't have much time."

"What kind of ships?" Podo asked.

"Not sure."

"Fangs?"

"Probably. There was plenty of movement on the decks, but I couldn't get close enough to tell whether it was the slithery sort."

Podo scowled. "There's little chance we can survive a fight against three ships."

"What can we do?" Janner asked, feeling at once that he'd spoken out of turn.

"The only thing anyone can do. Press on and pray the Maker brings us safely to port." Podo winked at Janner, then turned his full attention to the crew. "You men, trim the sails and get us to the Hollows! If there's not wind enough, we row!"

The crew snapped into action, and the ship came to life.

"Janner, you're bleeding!" Leeli said.

Janner looked down and saw a trickle of blood slipping along his left shin. As Nia and Leeli bustled him downstairs into the hold, he cast a glance over his shoulder at Kalmar and Artham, the little wolf and the birdman, wishing he could stay with them on deck.

Then the wind began to blow. The crew shouted as one, and Janner heard Podo above them all, whacking his old bone club on the mainmast and bellowing praises to the Maker and curses on the Fangs with the same breath. Wind filled the great sails and tensed the mast, and like a waking giant, the boat groaned as it heaved ahead.

Their ship, Janner had learned, was called the *Enramere*. She was a relatively new vessel, built not ten years before the Great War according to Podo's reckoning, which made her under twenty—not long enough to have many of her own stories but long enough to prove herself seaworthy. She'd been used first as a fishing boat, but in the years after the Great War, she'd been recommissioned by the Fangs for use in transporting troops and supplies to and from Dang. Gammon, the leader of the Kimeran rebellion in the Ice Prairies, along with a company of his warriors, had seized the ship during a raid of the Phoob Islands years ago and had kept her ready ever since.

Janner felt like he knew the *Enramere* intimately, having lain so long in her hold like a baby in a crib, listening to her hum, feeling her nod, watching the colors of the wood change with the angle of the light coming through the porthole. Now, with the crew's footsteps thumping overhead and the wind pushing her east, he imagined the ship's pleasure as she cut through the waves at a fast clip. He had read about ship captains in books like *Scourge of the Sea* and *Before the Western Wide,* how they named their ships and treated them like true loves. He thought about his father's affection for sailing and wondered if his own keen impression of the *Enramere*'s mood and manner was due to Esben's blood in his veins. He hoped so.

When Nia was satisfied that Janner's injuries were properly tended, she allowed him on deck to help however he could. Janner didn't want to be in the way, so he stood with his back against the door of the captain's cabin and waited for the right moment to ask someone what he could do. Moments after he climbed into the late-afternoon sunlight, he was caught up in the business of sailing and forgot all about his wounds.

The crew shimmied up the mast and hauled fat ropes and skittered to and fro for no apparent reason, while Podo bellowed orders from the helm with one hand on the wheel and the other waving the bone club around his head.

"Look at him." Kalmar's furry head appeared at Janner's shoulder. "Sad to think this is his last ride."

The wind whipped Podo's white hair into a fury, and at the edges of his mouth curled a terrible, grizzly grin, but his eyes were bright and calm, pools of still water that wouldn't ripple for all the winds of Aerwiar. Podo Helmer was made for the sea and for danger and for the clash of wills, and so the fierce love in his heart for his family bolstered his strength even as their peril rose. It was a thing to see. But whatever the day's outcome, whether they were sunk by the ships or they slipped safely into the port in the Green Hollows, this would be Podo Helmer's final dash across the waves. The dragons had allowed their old enemy this final passage across their waters.

"Looks like he means to make it a good one," Janner said.

Artham swooped down and landed on the prow. He pointed south and shouted, "They're gaining!"

Kalmar helped Janner limp between the burly Kimerans to the port rail. Janner spotted three ships in the smoky distance. They were a long way off, but they were pointed farther east on a course to intercept the *Enramere* before it reached the Green Hollows. Janner didn't know much about sailing, but he could tell the other ships had the advantage of the wind.

Podo strode to the rail and squinted at the horizon, making a sound between a snarl and a laugh. He shook his fist in the air, threw a fiery curse across the waves, whirled around, and stomped back to the helm.

"Come here, lads!" he barked.

Janner and Kalmar exchanged a glance and dashed to the wheel.

Podo grabbed Janner's hands and placed them on the handles. "Hold here and here." Podo knelt, put his scratchy face beside Janner's, and pointed. "See that little hump in the distance?"

Janner did. A thin, dark shape on the eastern horizon. "Yes sir."

"That's where we're headed. That's the Green Hollows. It's farther away than it looks. Now keep her nose pointed just to the left of that spot and she'll sail straight for it. Kalmar, yer job is to keep Janner company and to fetch me if the wind changes. Clear?"

"Yes sir," Kalmar said.

"But where are you going?" Janner asked, hating how frightened he sounded.

"I forgot me pipe. If this is my last voyage, I aim to enjoy it."

Podo marched away, humming a happy tune as he disappeared into the captain's quarters, leaving Janner feeling very small at the helm of a very big ship. The wheel tugged back and forth with a will of its own. It was harder to hold steady than he expected. He felt the slow rise and fall of the sea beneath him, the thrilling tension of wind and water, and the way sail and keel and rudder harnessed that power to drive the *Enramere* through the waves.

Janner took a deep breath, squinted one eye, and aimed the ship as Podo had instructed. He was conscious of the crew watching him, but he tried to focus all his attention on the hump of land and did his terrified best not to look anywhere else.

After a while, he realized he was smiling so wide his cheeks hurt. For the first time in his life, he was sailing.

4

Fresh Wounds

Several minutes later, Podo emerged from his cabin with a pipe between his teeth, and though Janner was thrilled to be steering the ship, he was relieved that Podo was back. But the old sailor only nodded at Janner and moved to the bow to speak with Artham. Janner's arms were getting tired, but he already knew he would miss the feeling of the wheel in his hands.

He glanced to his right and his smile vanished. The ships in the distance were gaining. They were close enough now that Janner could make out movement on their decks. More than once Kalmar had to remind him to keep his eyes on the land at the horizon because the nose of the *Enramere* was drifting to port or starboard.

"Can you see them?" Janner asked.

"Yeah," Kalmar said.

"How many?"

"It's still hard to tell. The weird thing is . . ." Kalmar's voice trailed off. His ears twitched, and his face looked troubled.

"What is it?" Janner asked.

"I can *smell* them." Kalmar wrinkled his nose. "Lots of them. And it's not just that I can smell them. I can smell their numbers. If I wanted to, I think I could probably count how many there are, just by sniffing."

"You should tell Grandpa," Janner said. "I'm sure he and Uncle Artham would want to know how many we're up against. And, Kal? I'm sorry."

"Sorry for what?"

"Your new sense of smell," Janner said gravely. "It must be awful. I'm so sorry."

"What do you mean?" Kalmar asked.

"Grandpa's toots must be unbearable."

They exploded with laughter.

"I know!" Kalmar said. "I didn't want to say anything, but I can hardly breathe! And it's not just Grandpa—it's everybody." Kalmar lowered his voice. "Especially Leeli!"

Even as he laughed Janner was fascinated by the way the old Kalmar seemed to peer out through the Grey Fang, as if he were only wearing a costume.

"Look out, you're off course," Kalmar said, wiping his eyes with his furry forearm.

The nose of the ship had drifted south again, and Janner tugged at the wheel until the ship straightened. Podo glared at him from the forecastle and pointed just left of the land in the distance, then jabbed his pipe back between his teeth and resumed his pacing.

Kalmar clapped Janner on the back, right on one of his bandages. Janner hissed and jerked away. The cold, painful memory of Kalmar's claws raking his skin returned, and Janner felt a flash of irritation. At first it was just irritation that Kalmar had smacked him, but beneath it lay a seed of anger, a deeper wound that worried Janner. He didn't want to be angry. He was glad Kalmar was back, and he knew that the Fang who had thrashed in the water was only a shadow of his little brother. But still. It had been those same claws. Those same teeth.

"Sorry," Kalmar said. He wasn't smiling anymore.

"Don't worry about it." Janner tightened his grip on the wheel and shrugged. "Just keep those claws to yourself." He meant it as a joke, but it came out bitter.

Before Janner could apologize, Kalmar shrank away and padded across the deck. Janner wanted to follow, but he couldn't leave the wheel. Artham, deep in conversation with Podo on the other side of the ship, saw Kalmar leave. He gave Janner a questioning look, and Janner replied with a shrug and a heavy sigh.

"Captain Helmer!" cried a sailor from the rigging. "Captain!"

Janner craned his neck to see a Kimeran sailor clutching a line and leaning precariously from the mainmast, a scope up to his eye.

"What is it, sailor?" Podo answered without taking his eyes from the oncoming ships.

"They're not Fangs! It's men on the decks!" A cheer went up from the crew.

Janner spotted Kalmar at Podo's side, speaking to him and pointing at the ships. Podo nodded and patted him on the shoulder.

"Kalmar here says there are more than a hundred sailors on yonder ships, and that they're cooking henmeat with totatoes and butterroot. That's a meal I ate many a time in the Green Hollows, boys! They're Hollowsfolk on them ships, and that means we've got ourselves an escort to Ban Rona!"

The crew cheered again. Then something splashed into the water a short distance away. Before Janner had time to wonder what it was, he spied commotion on the deck of one of the distant ships, and a tiny speck rose into the air, gaining in size as it arced toward them. A stone the size of Janner's head fell short of the *Enramere* by an arrowshot and disappeared into the waves with a mighty splash.

Podo ordered one of the men to run up a flag of surrender, but it did no good. More stones splashed into the water—still a fair distance from the ship but getting nearer every moment.

Why were they attacking? Surely the Hollish ships could see by now that they weren't Fangs. Maybe it didn't matter. Maybe the Hollowsfolk had become like the Stranders, so twisted that they despised not just the Fangs but everyone. It had been jarring to realize that men and women could be as treacherous as Fangs, ready to cut your throat or bind you and toss you into the Mighty River Blapp. And because regular people had it in them to treat a soul with kindness (unlike Fangs, as far as Janner could tell), theirs seemed a greater evil. But the Hollowsfolk? Janner had only ever heard good things about them—rowdy people, sure, but not evil. Not like Stranders, at least.

An earsplitting crash shook the *Enramere* as one of the catapulted rocks found its mark at last. It smashed into the deck on the starboard side, splintered the rail, and bounced into the sea. No one was hurt, but Janner shuddered to think what would happen if one of those stones hit someone.

He realized the ship had drifted off course again so he tugged the wheel around to straighten it, wondering what he was doing at the wheel when they were under attack. He was too young and too small to helm a ship during a battle.

As if in answer, a strong, familiar hand squeezed the back of his neck.

"Fine steering, Janner," Artham said. "But it's time to get below. Things are getting ugly up here."

Another stone smashed into the *Enramere,* and without a thought of either sailing or his wounds, Janner hurried down to the main deck after Kalmar, dodging frantic Kimeran crewmen and praying he wouldn't be in the path of the next stone. As he descended the steps to the hold, he heard another crash and felt the vibration in the ship.

Belowdecks on a bench built into the bulkhead sat Nia, Leeli, and Oskar, their eyes wide with fear.

"Janner! What's happening?" Nia asked. "Are we close to the Hollows?"

"No ma'am. But it wouldn't matter. It's Hollowsfolk in the ships, not Fangs."

"What?" Nia asked, narrowing her eyes.

"They started launching stones at us as soon as they were close enough."

"But—"

"Your highness, even the people of the Green Hollows are corruptible," Oskar said.

"Nonsense," said Nia. "These are my people. And it's time they knew it." She stood and straightened her dress, showing no concern when another stone shook the ship. "Come with me, Leeli."

5

"The Boatwright's Daughter"

Nia marched up the stairs, flung open the hatchway to the deck, and waited for Leeli to catch up. Beyond her, Kimeran crewmen made ready for battle as Podo ordered Artham to bring the *Enramere* about. Janner, Kalmar, and Oskar stared after Nia in shock for a moment, then followed Leeli out of the hold. Janner had no idea what his mother was up to, but he wasn't going to cower below and miss it.

"Lass! What do ye think you're doing?" Podo said from his perch at the mainmast. "Get below before ye get hurt!"

"I'll do no such thing. Janner told me those are Hollish ships. Is that true?"

"Aye," Podo shouted, "and it's Hollowsfolk sailin' em. But they've given us no chance to parley and won't stop their launching though we've waved and whooped like cowards. They aim to sink us and I don't aim to be sunk. So it's a fight, kinsmen or no." He winced as another stone crashed into the sea just beyond the bow.

The look Nia aimed at the three Hollish ships was enough to make Janner want to hide. She marched to the prow and pulled Leeli with her. "Leeli, get out your whistleharp and play us a song, dear. Play it loudly. How about 'The Boatwright's Daughter'?"

The three Hollish ships were near enough now that Janner could make out the sailors' burly figures and catch the glint of swords, axes, and hammers in their hands. Behind the sailors crowding the rails stood a line of archers. They drew back their bows as another sailor lit the end of each. In moments, the *Enramere* would be burning.

Leeli pulled her hair from her face and lifted the whistleharp to her lips.

She bobbed her head, remembering the melody, then loosed the song into the winds.

When she played, the air itself changed. The sails luffed and the very waves seemed to pause in their dance as this new music flew over them. Janner's ears tingled, and a now-familiar sensation filled his head. He could hear words—ancient words in an ancient tongue—and though he didn't understand them, he could sense the memory and mood of the speaker as if he were eavesdropping on a conversation through a wall.

He was listening to the sea dragons. The knowledge came to him that there were scores of them swimming below their ship in great loops and whorls, a herd of serpents as aware of him and the *Enramere* as he was of the clouds in the sky.

Kalmar whimpered, closed his eyes, and flattened his ears. Janner's mind swam with voices, and he knew that however vividly he heard the dragons, Kalmar *saw* them, and with that thought came fleeting images of ruddy scales and shimmering fins, sharp teeth and bright eyes in the murky deep.

He blinked away the vision and pulled his attention back to Leeli, who stood at the forecastle as she had stood at the icy crags of Kimera, playing her whistleharp and swaying with the song.

The Hollish sailors froze and stared across the water at the *Enramere*. The only movement was the sea. Then, beginning with one voice and growing to many, these words came from the Hollish sailors:

> I'll come to you in the wintertime
> When the fruit of the fall is fading
> I'll bring a barrel of apple wine
> As long as your love is waiting
>
> But oh the sorrow a sailor sees
> Whenever he meets your father
> He's mean as a swarm of deadly bees
> He'll cut off your legs right at the knees

It does no good to beg him please
To marry his only daughter

So I'll come to you in the spring of the year
When the bud and the bloom is growing
And I'll drive an ox to plow, my dear
And furrow the field for sowing

But oh the sorrow a sailor knows
Whenever he meets your father
He reeks of the sweat between his toes
The roaches gather wherever he goes
And never a man will ever propose
To marry his only daughter

So I'll come to you in the summertime
When the grass in the hollow is swaying
We'll nibble the grapes and clementines
And look at the children playing

But oh the sorrow a sailor weeps
Whenever he meets your father
He picks his nose when he's asleep
He's big as a cow and smart as a sheep
I pray the Maker my soul to keep
I love his only daughter

So I'll come to you when I'm old and gray
I'll sail from over the water
I'll lay a rose at your father's grave
Then I'll marry his only daughter

When the song was over, Leeli lowered her harp and looked up at Nia. "Was that right, Mama?"

"Perfect," Nia said. "Look."

The Hollish ships drew near, but no arrows were shot and no stones were launched. The Kimeran crewmen drew their weapons and gathered around Podo at the port rail like a wall. The Hollish assault had stopped, but it would take more than a shanty to ease the tension. The *Enramere* had been damaged, and some of her men were wounded.

"Highness." Oskar took Nia by the arm. "Highness, you and the children should take cover. If the Hollowsfolk have come under the sway of Gnag the Nameless, it's best if they don't know the jewels are on board."

"If anyone in Aerwiar despises Gnag, it's the people of the Green Hollows," Nia said. "My children will be quite safe."

"Oskar's right," Podo said, his eyes still trained on the approaching ships. "It's been a long nine years. A lot can happen, even in the Hollows. You should get below. Artham, you too. There's no sense trying to explain those wings of yours just yet."

After glaring at the two old men for a moment, Nia herded the children below. Artham followed with his wings folded tight, ducking behind the Kimerans and into the hold.

"I felt them again," Janner said when the children had settled around the table. "The dragons, I mean."

"Me too," said Leeli. Her voice trembled. "I thought they were coming again. For Grandpa."

"They were already here," Kalmar said. "Hundreds of them. They're swarming the water below the ship, and I think they've been with us the whole time."

Leeli grabbed Kalmar's hand and looked at him with tears forming in her eyes. "Were they angry? Are they after us again? They'll take him. I know it."

"They weren't angry," Janner told her.

"How do you know?" Leeli said. "What did they say?"

"I don't know what they said, but it was nothing like before. I don't think they'll betray their promise. Grandpa's safe till he gets to the Hollows. Don't worry."

Leeli studied Janner's face for a moment, then relaxed a little.

Janner glanced at Artham, remembering that he, too, could hear the dragons speak, but he only stood at the top of the steps with one hand on the door and the other on the hilt of his sword, ready to fling open the door and rush to Podo's aid if things with the Hollish sailors went badly.

The *Enramere* thudded into the Hollish ship, and Janner heard first the thump of feet on deck as they lashed the ships together, then voices. Nia stopped her pacing and listened, tense as a bowstring. Leeli still gripped Kalmar's hand and stared at the floor of the ship as if she could see the herds of dragons congregated below.

After what seemed a long time, the door at the top of the steps opened and Podo peeked his grizzly head inside. "Artham, you and the children keep out of sight for now. Nia, dear, your people would like to see you."

Nia drew a deep breath and climbed the steps without a word. Before the door closed behind her, Janner caught a glimpse of a few Hollish sailors. They stood a head taller than the Kimerans and had broad, hairy chests, red and gold hair, and beards so thick and bushy they looked like bears. When they saw Nia, their eyes widened, and Janner heard gasps.

The door shut and Artham winked at the children. "This is going to be fun," he whispered, and he beckoned the children closer. They scrambled to the top of the steps and put their ears to the door.

"I am the daughter of Podo Helmer and Wendolyn Igiby," Nia said in a strong voice. "My husband was Esben Wingfeather, and with him I ruled the Shining Isle until Gnag the Nameless waged war on the free lands of Aerwiar. You may have thought me dead and my children with me, but by the Maker's hand we live and sail from Skree to the Green Hollows for refuge. My name," she paused, "is Nia Wingfeather, Queen of Anniera, daughter of the Hollows."

After a dumbstruck silence, a rowdy cheer exploded on the deck. The

Hollish sailors clapped in time and chanted, "Rah! Rah! Rah! Rah!" The chant carried to the other Hollish ships and grew in volume until even Artham and the children gave up their silence and chanted too.

Janner moved to open the door, but Artham stopped him.

"Your mother will present you when she sees fit to do so. You're not just a boy on this side of the sea, lad. You're a Throne Warden, and these Hollowsfolk know what that means. Just wait."

Janner wasn't sure what all that meant, but he didn't mind. His mother was a queen and a native daughter. These were her people. And they were a people who were strong enough to have survived the Great War and still sail the Dark Sea. They were still fighting. It meant there were yet places in the world that Gnag hadn't ruined, places where Janner and his siblings might finally make a home.

"Are we going to be all right?" Kalmar asked.

"I think so," Janner said. "Didn't you hear? Our mother is the Queen of the Shining Isle."

"Will we have a house?" Leeli asked, her eyes widening.

Artham laughed. "And a bed too."

Janner limped back to his bunk and eased himself into it, wondering where the Hollowsfolk kept their books and how long it would be before he got to settle into the nook of a tree and read.

A few minutes later, Nia appeared. Her cheeks were flushed and she looked happy. She announced that they were a half-day's sail from Ban Rona, where the people of the Hollows would give them, she was sure, a queen's welcome.

6

Through the Watercraw

"Children! Keep out of sight, but come here. I want ye to see this."

Podo didn't have to say it twice. The children had spent four long hours in the ship's hold, bursting with anticipation of their arrival at the Hollows. Janner and Leeli hurried up the steps and into the late-afternoon light, but Kalmar stayed behind.

"Kalmar?" Janner said, peeking back into the hold.

"Go ahead." Kalmar sat on his bunk, a gray shadow among shadows. "I'll be out in a minute."

"Go on, Janner," Artham said. "I'll keep him company."

Janner was too excited to wonder what was wrong, so he pulled the door shut behind him and squeezed between Nia and Leeli at the rail. He spotted the lead Hollish vessel ahead of them. The second ship was a short distance off the port side, and the third was following the *Enramere*.

"That," Podo said, pointing from the wheel, "is your new home. Ban Rona."

In the light of a fiery sunset, Janner's first look at the port city of the Green Hollows was magnificent. They were sailing into a harbor, the mouth of which was framed by towering cliffs on either side, forming a wide gateway. The cliffs were narrow, like two giant walls rising out of the water, twice as high as the mast of the ship. The walls stretched for miles, curving back to the mainland on either side of the port, as if the ships were sailing through the open end of a giant horseshoe.

The crags rose above them, sharp against the deepening blue sky; foamy waves clapped like thunder against the feet of boulders worn smooth and strange by epochs of tidal surge. At the top of the cliffs, bonfires blazed and figures stood on the brink, watching them pass, hoisting swords and axes and bows in time with the familiar "Rah! Rah! Rah!" of the Hollish warriors.

"Word has already spread," Oskar said. He removed his spectacles and wiped a tear from his cheek. "The Queen of Anniera has returned."

Janner was surprised to see that Nia wasn't smiling. Her back straight, her face stern, she was a tower of strength, fiercer with each syllable of her kinsmen's chant. She appeared both younger and older, and Janner felt a shiver of awe that this woman was his mother.

On the far side of the harbor, nestled in the arms of the cliffs, lay the city of Ban Rona. The sun was low enough that streetlamps had been lit, and firelight glowed from a thousand windows as if the buildings were watching their arrival with happy faces. The dwellings at the waterfront were connected by a maze of torchlit boardwalks. The city rested on the slope of a hill, at the top of which stood a stout gray fortress.

"The Keep," Nia said.

"Is that where the king lives?" Leeli asked.

"There isn't a king in the Green Hollows. We call him the Keeper, and he's more like a chief. The Keeper isn't part of a bloodline, like a king usually is. He's chosen by the people at the Banick Durga."

"The games," Janner said. "I remember reading about them."

"Yes. Maker willing, we'll go this year and you can see them for yourself."

As the last of the Hollish ships slipped into the harbor, Janner heard grinding metal and groaning timbers. His first impulse was to run for cover, but neither Nia nor Podo seemed concerned. Nia pointed at the precipice of the nearest cliff and said, "Watch."

There was a commotion at the top of the walls. The clank of metal grew louder and louder until at last the waters behind the ships foamed and roiled, and out of the sea rose the biggest chain Janner had ever seen. It drooped between the cliffs, and as it rose he saw more and more chain, interconnected like a giant fishing net. It stretched across the entire opening, forming a massive iron grid that nothing bigger than a rowboat could pass through.

"It's called the Watercraw," said Podo over his shoulder. "No ship, no matter how strong, can breach such a defense. No wind could blow hard enough, and no captain would be foolish enough to try."

Janner felt himself smiling. He wasn't sure about the rest of the Green Hollows, but at least Ban Rona was safe. Safe from people like the Stranders, and safe from Gnag the Nameless and his Fangs. The cozy houses that lined the streets of Ban Rona looked as warm and inviting as the Igiby cottage, and Janner hoped one would be theirs.

As the crew took in sail and Podo steered the ship toward the wharf, Janner watched a sailor from the first Hollish ship leap to the dock and confer with an assembly of men and women gathered to greet him. More people appeared and lashed the *Enramere* to the dock. The ship thudded into place and stilled.

Their voyage across the Dark Sea of Darkness had ended at last. The Kimeran crew cheered, and their joy spread to the crowd gathered ashore. People clapped and whooped and chattered.

Everywhere Janner looked he saw Hollowsfolk—men with rugged faces and bushy beards, women with long hair enflamed by the bright sunset, children peeking out from between the adults—all of them dressed in browns, deep greens, and blues, all of them smiling, all of them eager to see with their own eyes the return of their lost daughter. Podo watched Nia, who looked out over her people with eyes that shone with tears.

The crowd parted, and the biggest man Janner had ever seen moved to the front. He was dressed like the others, but his shoulders and huge arms were bare. Around his neck hung a golden chain with a glimmering red pendant. At the edges of his rusty beard were seven little braids, each beaded with a jewel of a different color. His nose was crooked in a way that made him more handsome, and his eyes were big and kind. He wasn't old, but he wasn't young, either—there was wisdom in the ruggedness of his face. Janner liked him immediately.

When the man's gaze settled on Nia, he froze. The two of them looked at each other without a word, and the crowd hushed.

The man spoke quietly, but the wind carried his voice. "Nia."

Janner felt his mother stiffen, and after a pause she said, "Rudric. Rudric ban Yorna." Her face softened. "You're the Keeper?"

"I am. And you," he said as he bowed his head, "are the Queen of the Shining Isle. Long have I asked the Maker to protect you, wherever you were. Long have we kept our hillfires burning with the hope that this day would come."

The man's face glowed in the last blush of dusk. He dropped to his knees, and like a great wave emanating outward, all the Hollowsfolk did likewise. Janner's arms prickled at the sight of a thousand men and women bowing to his mother.

Rudric stood and raised his voice. "Welcome, daughter of the Hollows!"

The Hollowsfolk cheered and the men beat their chests with fists like sledgehammers.

Rudric held up a hand to silence them as he looked past Nia at the ship's crew. "Podo Helmer, is that you?"

"Aye," said Podo. He nodded at Rudric and stepped forward. "You're even bigger than you used to be, lad."

"And you're as terrifying as ever."

"Is yer father well?"

"As well as can be for an old fighter." Rudric smiled and raised an eyebrow. "He still swears he can't smell properly out of his left nose hole because of you."

"Served him right," said Podo with a chuckle.

Rudric's eyes fell on Janner. "I don't have to ask if this is Esben's son."

Janner blushed and looked at his feet. None of his wounds hurt now.

"It is," Nia said. "My eldest. Janner Wingfeather."

"A Throne Warden, then?" Rudric said with an approving nod. "And this young beauty is the Song Maiden?"

"Yes sir," Leeli said with a curtsy. "My name is Leeli Wingfeather and I'm nine."

Rudric laughed. "An honor to meet you, Leeli. The Green Hollows is a land of music. May your songs fill the vineyards and valleys in the days to come." Rudric looked the ship over again and asked, "What about the third?"

"Janner, where's Kalmar?" Nia asked.

"He's belowdecks with Uncle Artham—"

"Artham? Artham Wingfeather is here?" asked Rudric, shocked.

"Yes, I'm here." Artham emerged from the hold and stepped to the rail. He had draped a canvas over his shoulders and wings, and clutched it at his chest in a way that also concealed his talons. The crowd gasped and many whispers filled the air as word spread along the boardwalk and into the streets that Artham Wingfeather was present.

Rudric bowed his head again, and though he was taller and broader than Artham, his eyes twinkled like a boy's in the Throne Warden's presence. "Welcome, sir. And the young king is here too?" Nia nodded, and Rudric shook his head in wonder. "All these years we feared that the last of Anniera had died. Yet here on a single ship its light shines."

The Keeper and his people stood reverently before the *Enramere* and its passengers for a moment, and then Rudric spoke again. "What am I thinking? You must be sick of that ship. Come and put your feet on steady ground again. All of you. As Keeper of the Hollows, I welcome you to Ban Rona, where no evil dwells, no ridgerunner thieves, and no Fang treads. My home"—he looked at Nia—"and *your* home."

"Thank you, Rudric." Nia gave him a smile, but it vanished as quickly as it had come. "Keeper, the youngest son of Esben has seen terrible things. I beg you to treat him with kindness. Janner, go fetch your brother. Let's get this over with."

Janner limped down the stairs into the dark hold to find Kalmar. "Kal?" he called.

"I don't want to go," Kalmar said in a small voice from somewhere in the corner.

"It's beautiful. You should see it. They can hardly believe we're here. I can hardly believe it myself. There's not a Fang in sight."

Kalmar was silent.

The silence filled the hold until Janner realized what he had said. "You'll be fine, Kal. Mama's like a queen to them. And you're—you're the High King of Anniera. It doesn't matter how furry you are."

"They're going to stare at me. And they'll know."

"They'll know what?"

"They'll know how weak I was."

Janner made his way through the darkness and stood before his little brother, trying to ignore the return of the throbbing in his legs and back. All Janner could see of Kalmar was the glint of his eyes. "But you're the High King. And I'm your Warden. You can't stay in the dark down here forever."

Janner took Kalmar's clammy, furry hand in his and pulled him toward the door. Kalmar took a deep breath when they reached the foot of the stairs, ashamed, Janner knew, of his gray fur and pointed ears and black nose, ashamed of the wolfish badge of failure he bore.

When the boys emerged from the hold, Rudric was nodding his greetings to Oskar, then to Errol the first mate, so the two brothers stood at the top of the steps for a moment unnoticed by anyone on the pier.

Then the air was split by a Hollish woman's shriek. Rudric broke off the conversation and looked around for the source of the commotion. When he spotted Kalmar with his arm around Janner, his confusion turned to shock. Someone screamed, "FANG!"

Men and women surged onto the ship, shoved the Kimeran crew aside, and lunged at Kalmar, who snarled and bared his teeth. Artham, Nia, Podo, and the Kimerans were stunned. Kalmar crouched like a dog about to pounce.

"Kalmar, no!" Janner screamed, and Kalmar's face quivered and his growl turned into a howl of anguish. He looked at Janner with unbearable sadness and curled into a ball at Janner's feet.

Janner had time to fall over his little brother to shield him as the Hollowsfolk seized them both. He wrapped his arms around Kalmar and gritted his teeth against the pain in his legs and back, clinging to his brother among screams of "Fang!" and "monster!" until Kalmar was torn from his embrace.

7

A Fang in Ban Rona

As they dragged Kalmar away, Janner saw the Hollowsfolk kicking him and pummeling him with their fists. Leeli screamed and Artham screeched Kalmar's name as the little wolf stretched out his hand toward Nia and Podo. They struggled against the onrush of Hollowsfolk, shocked by the violence of the crowd's reaction. Nia beat at a Hollish man who held her back as she screamed for order, but no one listened. Janner fought to push through the crowd, but it was too thick and too angry. One of the men grabbed Janner by the arm and held him fast. Cutting through all the noise was the heartbreaking sound of Kalmar, yelping like a hurt puppy.

Janner could hardly believe that these same people had been cheering their arrival only moments before. Their faces, once so bright with welcome, were now dark with anger.

Another sound thundered out and cut through the chaos at last. Janner saw movement from the corner of his eye and looked in time to see Rudric leap onto the *Enramere's* deck. He swung a war hammer with all his might and struck the mainmast so hard that the whole ship shook.

"I said, 'Stop!' " Rudric bellowed.

And they did.

Rudric's face was red and his eyes burned. He held the hammer in one hand and clenched the other into a fist. His chest was thrust out, and the front of his tunic looked ready to rip open. "If you would contend with Rudric ban Yorna, then so be it! Riot away." He glared at the crowd and bared his teeth, daring anyone to challenge him.

The mainmast creaked and groaned, then splintered where Rudric's hammer had struck it. It groaned again and toppled over the starboard side, pulling timber, sail, and line into the sea, leaving only a stump where Rudric stood.

"Unhand the beast and let the Queen of Anniera speak!" Rudric bellowed. "Olliver, release her!"

Nia jerked her arms away from the man and rushed to Kalmar's side.

One by one the Hollowsfolk backed away until only one man remained. He stood with his foot on Kalmar's back and held a sword over his head. "It's a Fang, Rudric," the man spat. "Would you have it loose in the Hollows?"

"If the Queen of Anniera has something to say in the matter, I think you'd best hear it before she tears you to pieces, Bunge."

The man glanced at the crowd, then down at Kalmar, then finally at Nia. She rose, fierce and defiant, and stood nose to nose with the man. Bunge lowered his sword and stepped aside.

"Queen or not, it is no small thing to bring a Grey Fang to our shores." Rudric lowered his war hammer and looked intently at Nia. "Do you understand?"

"I do."

"Then I ask you, not as your old friend but as the Keeper of the Hollows, why have you done it?"

"Because—" Nia's voice caught in her throat. She took a deep breath and lifted her chin. "Because he's my son."

The crowd gasped. Even Rudric was shaken. He looked at Kalmar, who hunkered at Nia's feet, whimpering.

"This is the son of Esben Wingfeather?"

Nia wiped a tear from her cheek, as if irritated it was there. She looked as if she wanted to speak but couldn't.

Rudric approached her and lowered his voice. "I'm sorry, Nia. But I'm the Keeper now. We have to deal with this in the council." He clenched his jaw and turned to the man called Bunge. "Don't hurt it. Take it to the dungeon."

When Bunge moved toward Kalmar, Artham stepped forward and stood between them.

Nia put a hand on his shoulder. "Artham, don't. My people have their ways. If we're going to make a home here, we have to do this by their rules. We can't keep running. We have nowhere else to go."

Artham hesitated, then knelt and whispered something in Kalmar's ear and moved away. Artham could have flung off the canvas, spread his wings,

and sent the Hollowsfolk scampering if he wanted. He could have gathered Kalmar up and flown to safety. Janner wanted to act, but if Artham was unwilling to stop Kalmar's arrest, then he must have a good reason.

Nia knelt and looked Kalmar in the eye. "Everything's going to be all right. One way or another, we'll come for you tomorrow. Understand?"

Kalmar nodded. Nia kissed his head, and then Rudric gave a signal and Bunge jerked Kalmar to his feet.

"Bunge!" Rudric snapped. *"Don't hurt it."*

Bunge scowled but bowed his head stiffly to Rudric. A Hollish sailor tied Kalmar's arms behind him, and then they led him away.

Rudric slid his war hammer back into the loop on his belt. "Nia, I know you're angry and you don't want to trust me right now. I'll make sure he's fed and well treated. The Hollows is still a place of welcome—"

"Spare us your talk," Podo said, stepping forward. "If ye have a place for me family and me crew, we'll take it with gratitude. But now's not the time for words. The only thing we have to talk about is when we're going to get young Kalmar back."

Rudric looked from Podo to Nia and back again, then nodded. "Danniby here will show you and your men to your lodgings. I'll send someone to fetch you in the morning once I've gathered the seven chiefs. Then we'll discuss the Fang." Rudric turned to Podo and the Kimerans. "Sorry about the mainmast."

He strode away.

When the crowd dispersed, a slight, bearded Hollish fellow (Janner soon learned they all had beards) in a black cape stepped forward and cleared his throat.

"Greetings. They call me Danniby. If you'll follow me, you'll find some beds, berries, and bibes."

"Bibes?" Leeli asked.

"Aye, bibes. Short for imbibes, I suppose. Stuff good for drinking, that is, like ciders, juices, milk of goat, that sort of thing. Anyone like a hot meal and a bibe?"

After some confusion, everyone on the ship raised a hand. Janner saw the worry on Nia's face, but Rudric's assurance eased the tension they all felt.

Even with Kalmar in the dungeon it was hard not to look forward to a regular bed and a good meal.

"Bibes it is, then," Danniby said. "Come with me."

The Kimerans debarked in single file, many of them pausing when they reached the dock to kiss the planks and thank the Maker for a safe voyage.

"We've got berry bibes, grape bibes, apple bibes, and cherry bibes. You name the fruit—we've likely got a bibe for it," Danniby said as he led the Kimerans away.

"Good men, those Kimerans," Podo said. "Left their homes in Skree just to get us here safe and strong. I hope they sleep well."

"Aye," said Oskar, trying to sound like a sailor again. "In the words of Boyg McKrowlin, 'Good gravy! They've earned it.' And so have I, if I say so myself. Standing around on this old broken ship isn't going to free Kalmar any sooner. Highness?"

Nia tried to smile. "You're right. It's time you children ate something other than glipper fish and old oats."

"I like that man," Leeli said.

"Rudric?" Janner asked.

"Yes, the big one. I don't think he wants anything bad to happen to Kalmar."

"I've known Rudric since we were children," said Nia, "and I think I know his heart. This will be sorted out soon."

"I'd bet my bibes on it," Podo said. "Now you all run along."

"You aren't coming?" Artham asked as he adjusted the canvas over his wings.

"I'd like to stay here for a spell," Podo said, gazing out at the dark horizon beyond the mouth of the harbor. "It's my last chance to feel a boat rocking beneath me feet. I half wish I'd been knocked overboard by one of them stones, to tell the truth. Not only would I have deserved it, but my last breath would have been seawater. That's how a sailor ought to go."

Janner watched Podo's back, wondering what was going on in his stormy old heart. All those years in Glipwood, Podo had avoided the cliffs, avoided ever looking out over the Dark Sea, especially on Dragon Day. Ban Rona was a seaside town, where Podo would be reminded with every lift of the breeze that he was banned from the waters he so loved. Now that Janner had seen him sail, it was hard to imagine him happy on land.

"Papa, you're not just a sailor." Nia put her hand on his back. "You're a father and a grandfather, and there's plenty of life yet to live. Say your good-byes and come with your family. We need you."

"Please, Grandpa," said Leeli.

Podo pulled his eyes from the waters, his bushy eyebrows trembling with emotion. Finally, he stepped away from the broken mast, picked up his leg-bone from where it lay on the deck, and let Leeli lead him down the plank to the dock.

At the last step, he paused and looked down into the black waters lapping at the hull. "There you have it, dragons," he said. "Scale Raker will trouble yer waters no more. I thank thee for safe passage."

When Podo stepped from the plank to the pier, the center of the harbor bubbled, and out of the sea rose a dark mass of serpentine shapes. They swayed and rumbled and roiled the waters, till Yurgen, the oldest one, flung open his jaws and roared. The torches on the pier sputtered in the wind of the dragon's bellow, and Podo froze with his back to the sea, eyes closed and head low.

Leeli was frantic. She took his hand in both of hers and pulled, dropping her crutch and hopping on one foot. Podo finally took another step, then another, each one bringing him closer to solid ground and farther from the Dark Sea.

When at last Podo stepped from the pier to the cobbled street of Ban Rona, the dragons disappeared as quickly as they had come.

Podo took a deep breath, smiled down at Leeli, and said, "Now, then. Let's have some bibes. Me drinker is dry and me eater is empty. Which way did that Danniby fella go?"

8

The Orchard Inn
and Cookery

It took Janner a while to realize what was so strange about Ban Rona.

As they walked the clean streets of the city, they passed wagons and clusters of people walking in conversation. Many of the houses boasted gardens in the front so that one had to pass between bright flowers and totatoes on the vine to reach the front steps. Men and women sat outside on benches, puffing pipes or munching on grapes, laughing in the cool of the night.

And every house, Janner noticed, had a dog. Not just a dog, but a *big* dog. He could see their tails waving like flags in the windows. He saw them curled up on the landings and chasing sticks, dogs of different colors and breeds, but all of them at least twice as big as Nugget had been—before the water from the First Well, anyway. More than once, one of the dogs padded out to greet Leeli as she passed, as if they sensed in her a great store of affection with nowhere else to go.

"The people aren't afraid," Janner said, finally realizing what was so different. "It's after dark, the streets are full, and there are no Fangs slithering about. Everyone's happy. I've never seen that before."

"It's the way it was and the way it should be," Artham said. "All the work has been done, dinner is on the table, and the children are alight with a final burst of energy before bed. That's when stories get told. Look."

They passed a lawn where a fire crackled in a stone ring. A grandmother sat on a bench with a book in her lap, reading to a circle of children gathered at her feet. Whistleharp music drifted to their ears, and with it the sound of singing. Janner caught the scent of something delicious as they passed a window where a family sat around a table. It reminded Janner of the Dragon Day Festival in Glipwood, where he'd seen Armulyn the Bard singing by the fire. But here, no one was afraid. There were no Fangs to be afraid of.

Janner spotted the Kimerans a few streets ahead as they rounded a corner after Danniby. The climb up the hill from the waterfront was gradual, but after their sea voyage, Janner and the others were unused to long walks, so by the time they turned the corner after the crew, they were all breathing a little harder.

Oskar, however, was spry as a thwap, grinning as he marched in front, wide eyed and looking everywhere at once. "Walking the streets of Ban Rona!" he said to himself between grunts. "Never thought in an epoch that I'd sail across the Dark Sea! Firepits! Flower beds! Oh, Maker, let there be books too."

Danniby waited beneath a shingle that read THE ORCHARD INN AND COOKERY. He smiled and swung open the door as they approached, and the smell of pumpkin and cinnamon and butter wafted over Janner. The Kimerans had already found seats around wooden tables or near the fire blazing in the stone hearth. Hollowsfolk turned and studied the sailors, but Janner sensed only curiosity, no malice or suspicion. After a moment, the locals returned to their conversations and their food, leaving the weary crew to themselves.

Oskar squeezed through the room to an open table and waved the others over. As soon as Nia was seated, he plopped into his chair and tucked a napkin into the collar of his tunic.

A fair woman with her hair in a bun approached the table and stood with her hands on her hips. "Welcome, travelers. Danniby likes my pumpkin bread or else you'd be at a different inn right now." Her eyes passed over each of them till they landed on Nia. "So is it true?"

"Is what true?" Nia asked.

"Are you really Nia Wingfeather?"

"I am."

"And you brought a Fang to Ban Rona?"

Janner steeled himself for his mother's anger, but it didn't come.

"No. I brought my son," Nia said. "He's no Fang, however much he may look it."

The woman seemed satisfied with Nia's answer and took their orders without further interrogation. Janner asked for grape cider and a bowl of henmeat stew, hardly able to believe he was eating dinner in an actual inn without a Fang in sight.

Podo stood and raised his mug of rootberry ale. "Crew of the *Enramere*!" The Kimerans roared in answer and raised their own mugs. "Maker bless Gammon of Skree, who routed the Grey Fangs at the Battle of Kimera and saw to our escape! May he and his cold soldiers fight till the land is free again. Maker bless each of ye for sailing the Dark Sea with dragons beneath and Fangs behind!" The men cheered as the Hollowsfolk watched with amusement. "Maker bless the Green Hollows, where Gnag the Nameless fears to tread!" Now the Hollowsfolk cheered. "And Maker bless Anniera." There was a respectful silence. Men and women stared at their mugs. "May that great kingdom rise from the ashes." Podo looked at Nia and Artham, then at Janner and Leeli.

"And Maker be with Kalmar tonight," said Janner, quietly enough that only his family heard.

"So be it," said Artham.

The room erupted in cheers as the kitchen doors swung open and servers carried out trays and trays of steaming food. Janner tried to eat with a glad heart, but his gladness was tinged with worry for Kalmar. He prayed that Rudric was true to his word to make sure his brother was well fed and unharmed until they could secure his freedom.

When they had finished eating, the innkeeper, a skinny, bald fellow named Norn, showed them to their rooms. He had a spring in his step because Danniby had filled his inn and promised him a vat of elderberry brew at the next harvest. Each room had two beds, so Nia and Leeli took one, Oskar and Podo another, and Janner ended up with Artham. The rooms were simple but comfortable, with soft beds, a wardrobe, and a writing desk.

Norn brought Nia ointment and fresh bandages for Janner's wounds. The ointment was in a clay jar, and when Nia lifted the lid, a bitter smell wafted out.

"What's that?" Janner asked, wrinkling his nose.

"Something I wish I had weeks ago when you first got hurt." Nia took a rag and dabbed it in the jar. "It's a mixture of gadjic shavings, sludgeberry squeeze, and sweetroot. We call it gadbalm. Not only will it heal you quickly, but it will also numb the pain. Lie down."

Janner winced with each poke, dab, and wrap, but he immediately felt his scratches tingle with warmth. He didn't know if his weariness was because of the medicine, but he found he couldn't hold his eyes open.

Nia pulled the bed quilt up to Janner's chin. "I'll wake you for breakfast," she said and kissed him on the forehead. "Get some sleep. We'll bathe and find new clothes tomorrow after the council. I won't be able to rest knowing your brother's alone in a cell."

"I'm not sleepy," Janner said with a yawn, and the next thing he knew, it was morning.

He stumbled downstairs to find everyone eating oats and milk in a heavy silence. Before they had finished eating, Danniby arrived to summon them to the Keep.

A mist lay on the harbor in the early light, obscuring everything but the tops of the cliff walls in the distance, where the tiny flicker of watch fires glowed. As the Wingfeathers walked the short distance to the Keep, the city woke. Birds sang in the boughs of trees that lined the cobbled streets. Garden gates swung open as sleepy-eyed men and women of all ages stepped out to greet the day. Dogs bounded down the front steps of the houses for their morning walks, and wagons clattered by.

Janner noticed clusters of children with leather satchels waiting at street corners. Few of them looked happy, and some looked as if they might fall asleep standing up. Some sat cross-legged on the sidewalk, mindlessly poking sticks between cobblestones, while others found benches on which to sprawl. Some of the girls stood in groups of two or three, giggling or playing clapping games.

"Mama," Janner asked, "what are all the kids doing standing around? Don't they have chores to do?"

"School," Nia answered absently, as if Janner had interrupted a deep thought.

A long wagon topped with several benches and drawn by four donkeys rounded the nearest corner and halted. The driver said, "Mornin'," to the children at the corner, and with a chorus of grumbles and yawns they boarded.

"They don't look too happy about it," Janner said, watching over his shoulder as the wagon halted a few blocks down the street to load another group.

"Why would they be?" Podo said. "Wastin' a whole morning learning when they could be out *doin'*. I'd be grumpy too."

"They *are* doing something, Papa," Nia said. "I loved school, and so did Mama. You would have loved it too if you hadn't grown up in Skree, running with those rotten Stranders."

"Well," was all Podo could say to that.

"Will we go to school?" Janner asked. He had never been to an official school. In Skree, schooling had been abandoned when the Fangs took over, so it was left to the parents. He had read plenty about schools and libraries and apprenticeships, but all he had in Glipwood was a mother determined to teach him T.H.A.G.S. (the Three Honored and Great Subjects all Annieran children studied: Word, Form, and Song). He loved reading and writing so much it was hard to imagine not enjoying a whole day of it with other students.

"All I know right now is that Kalmar is in a dungeon, and we have to get him out. We'll worry about school later," Nia said as they approached what appeared to be a main thoroughfare. Big trees grew out of a median that lined the center of a wide street running straight up the grassy hill to the

Keep. The houses here were bigger and boasted fancy cornices and even foun-
tains in their front gardens.

Danniby led them up the hill to the main gate, where guards stood on
either side of a portcullis. It reminded Janner of the entrance to the Fork Factory, and a shiver ran down his back. For the first time that morning, he felt
a hint of dread. What if that man—what was his name? Bunge. What if
Bunge had hurt Kalmar—really hurt him? What if all the Hollowsfolk on
the council were more like him than Rudric?

The guards at the gate stared at Artham as they passed. He still wore the
canvas draped over his wings, but it was obvious he was hiding something.

Just through the gate was a grassy courtyard, and beyond it lay the Keep.
It was a sturdy but beautiful structure, built of log and stone with living vines
creeping up its walls and winding around its pillars. Some of the vines were
heavy with colorful fruit, and people with long poles gathered it into baskets,
pausing now and then to pop a grape or redberry into their mouths. Janner
counted four stories, each with windows flung wide open to balconies where
people looked out over Ban Rona to the sea. Leafy branches peeked over the
edge of the roof. Janner had never heard of trees growing on *top* of a building,
but the people of the Green Hollows seemed able to grow anything anywhere
they wished.

The two main doors of the Keep stood open, and Danniby led them
through and into the great hall. It took Janner's eyes a moment to adjust to
the dim light filtering through windows in the ceiling, but he knew immediately that the hall was full of people. They sat around an enormous tree that
rose out of a mound in the center of the room. Its trunk was bigger than the
biggest glipwood oak, and its lower branches were as fat as trees themselves.
The limbs rose like strong arms, up, up into the reaches of the ceiling and out
to every wall, and Janner realized they grew *into* the walls and ceiling of the
Keep itself—which meant the branches he saw sticking out of the roof were
a part of the tree too. He couldn't tell where the tree ended and the Keep
began.

In a nook shaped by the enormous roots was a wooden throne where

Rudric ban Yorna sat in the glory of his strength. He wore a black tunic and cape. His beard with the seven jeweled braids cascaded over the expanse of his chest, where the red pendant glimmered. He should have been diminished by the size of the tree, but it served instead to magnify his station. Janner knew Rudric wasn't a proper king, but the title of Keeper seemed in this moment the greater one, and he had to resist the urge to bow.

Around Rudric gathered hundreds of Hollowsfolk, all sitting on the grassy floor. Young and old, male and female, fair and rugged, they stared at Nia Wingfeather and her companions. Janner felt that any discomfort or fear his mother carried must have been transformed into some marrow-deep power in her, for under the heavy gaze of the council, she seemed equal in bearing and strength to the Keeper across the room. They were as formidable as the towering cliffs on either side of the harbor, with some invisible chain slung between them.

"Queen Nia," Rudric said. He stood, and his voice boomed through the hall like a rolling boulder. "It is time to discuss the Fang."

9

The Council in the Keep

Come. We have a place for you." Rudric gestured toward a waist-high twist of root to the left of his throne. Nia led Leeli, Janner, Oskar, Artham, and Podo through the multitude to the tree. Janner could feel every eye in the room watching, and he was self-conscious of the way he walked, the way he held his mouth, and how filthy his clothes were. He wanted to exude the same quiet strength as his mother, but he was pretty sure he exuded nothing but awkwardness.

They approached the root, and Rudric motioned for them to sit. Beside him were the chiefs: four men and three women seated in smaller chairs. Each of the chiefs had a dog, either curled at the foot of the chair or leaning against it. Rudric's dog sat at attention beside his throne and looked big enough to swallow the others. Each woman's hair and each man's beard was adorned with a single jeweled braid that matched one of Rudric's seven braids. They frowned as the Wingfeathers sat on the root bench.

"I've been the Keeper of the Hollows for five years," Rudric began. "You fled Anniera nine years ago. It was years before that since you had set foot in our land."

"Yes, Keeper," Nia said. "It's been a long time."

"I've gathered the council today in order to hear your case but also to help you understand why things happened on your ship the way they did. I've no wish to offend the Queen of the Shining Isle."

He waited for Nia to answer, but she only lifted her chin and listened.

"When Gnag the Nameless and his Fangs overran your kingdom, we heard rumors, but we didn't believe them for days. We smelled the smoke a full day before we saw it. I was in the company that sailed to Anniera to give aid where we could, but—" Rudric cleared his throat. "But the whole city was burning. Flames scorched the sky. We brought back as many survivors as we could, but they didn't number enough to fill a single ship. It was terrible. I saw Fangs dancing in the fire and trolls everywhere. I saw other creatures too." He lowered his voice. "Long-legged things, skittering things. Things that lumbered and wailed and leapt over burning houses."

Leeli leaned her head on Podo's arm and squeezed her eyes shut. Janner looked out over the council and saw men and women with ashen faces remembering the terrors of days past.

"We fled," Rudric continued. "Anniera was a ruin, and we feared the Green Hollows would be next. So we boarded ship and sailed ahead of the smoke with Fang ships in our wake. The watchers at the Watercraw weren't prepared for a fleet of Fang ships and couldn't get the gate raised in time. The Fangs followed us right into the harbor. Thousands of them. Men, women, and children armed themselves and fought from the piers. We put out fire after fire, launched stone after stone, and when the Fangs leapt overboard and slithered through the sea, when they crawled out of the water like a plague, we fought them with swords, hammers, bows, and spears. We fought with our hands.

"Many men died, Nia. More than you would believe. Your family in Ban Rugan: Malik and the rest of the Igiby clan, the Boormyn clan, Yarley Craigh and his five daughters, your aunts and uncles, your cousins, Nia. All dead."

Nia's eyes were closed. She sat straight and still, but Janner could tell Rudric's words stung her.

"It was a terrible time. For nine years Fangs have plagued our waters. Six times they've attacked in force. A whole fleet of ships tried to break through the Watercraw and failed. Again and again we drove them back. They dared not come through the Blackwood, though over the years even the cloven have grown bolder. Lands that were once safe for sheepherders and grazers are now in danger of twisted things that rove the forest and its edges."

Rudric paused again to see if Nia had anything to say. She didn't.

"All these years, our northern borders were untroubled. The Fangs were vulnerable to the cold. We saw the way they dragged and cowered when an icy wind blew, and how they never sent skirmishers from the north hills. We were safe for a long time. But last year, something changed. A new thing came to the Hollows."

Rudric motioned to someone on the far side of the hall and two massive doors swung open. Two men entered, rolling a cage on a wooden cart. In the cage was a ragged, broken thing.

Its snout was longer than the Grey Fangs Janner had seen at the Battle of Kimera. Those Grey Fangs had seemed intelligent, more so than the snake-like ones. But this creature snarled and rattled the bars of the cage with beastly strength. Even from the other side of the hall, Janner could see that its eyes were blank with madness, devoid of anything human; it swung its head about, throwing a hungry, unthinking gaze at everything it saw. Its snout was curled in a permanent snarl, revealing long, needle-like teeth, and a dry, black tongue lolled out of the side of its mouth like a dead fish. Its fur had been torn out in patches, revealing sickly pink skin.

When it saw the array of Hollowsfolk, its thrashing intensified. It arched its back and loosed a papery shriek that was the closest thing to a howl the wretch could manage. Its black eyes roved the room, and Janner was terrified that its eyes would linger on him, as if they were empty wells into which he might fall forever. Janner would have grabbed Leeli and run had Rudric not been so calm.

"This," the Keeper said, "is only a shadow of the thing we captured. Its name was Nuzzard and it spoke quite well when our scouts at the Cullagh Orchard caught it. It was part of a company of Grey Fangs sent to test our borders for weaknesses. The others died. You know what happens when they die?"

Nia nodded. "They turn to dust. We're no strangers to Fangs, Rudric."

"Good. Then do you know what happens to them over time?"

Nia hesitated. Janner thought about the Grey Fangs in the *Enramere's* brig. They had grown more violent by the day, but what happened to them after they were set adrift no one knew. They had probably died, but as Podo said, that was in the hands of the Maker.

Nia looked at the sniveling monster in the cage and shuddered. "This, I suppose."

"The Grey Fangs are dangerous enough in their ordinary form—if it can be called that—but what they *become* is even worse." Rudric crossed the room and stood before the cage. The creature shook the bars and howled its papery howl. "They become the stuff of scarytales. I hate to imagine what would happen if this thing were loose in the Hollows." Rudric nodded at the guards, and they rolled the wagon away. "So you see, your highness, we cannot let a Fang loose in the land."

Nia stood and clenched her fists at her sides.

"You may speak," Rudric said. Janner wasn't sure, but he thought he saw, beneath his bushy beard, a gulp.

Nia spoke through her teeth. "I come to you not only as the Queen of Anniera, but as a daughter of the Hollows. I grew up here in Ban Rona. My grandfather Kargan Igiby was himself the Keeper for two seasons. I see gathered here ambassadors from Ban Hynh, Ban Rugan, Ban Yorna, and all the villages between—men and women who knew me when I was young, who have known the Igiby family for an epoch. I love this land as you do and would not put it in danger."

Janner noticed Rudric steal a glance at the assembly, and like a flicker of light a smile flashed in the brush of his beard. Janner couldn't make sense of it at first, but when he saw the faces of the Hollowsfolk gathered in the hall, he understood. They were as attentive now as they had been angry the night before. Rudric had readied them to listen.

Nia took a deep breath, turned to the assembly, who sat under the tree like children at storytime, and spoke.

10

The Queen's Tale and the Warden's Wings

The Fangs attacked Castle Rysen more swiftly than we could have imagined." Nia spoke quietly, but her voice carried through the leafy hall. "Esben, the children, and I were together in the dining hall one moment, and the next it seemed the whole world had grown scales and fangs. They poured into the castle. We ran. Esben never made it out of the castle. Mother was killed."

Podo sucked in a breath and stared at the floor. Janner heard several sniffles in the room and wondered how many of the assembly had known Wendolyn Helmer.

"By the Maker's hand we crossed the Dark Sea of Darkness, where we've hidden these many years in a little town called Glipwood, where my father grew up. The Fangs had no idea who we were until this summer. One of them recognized the Annieran crest on one of my necklaces, and they would have shipped us to Gnag himself if we hadn't had help."

She looked at Artham, and all eyes in the room followed her gaze. He sat under the drape of canvas with his head bowed. Janner saw his cheek twitch, and one of the hidden wings stirred.

"Artham P. Wingfeather, Throne Warden of Anniera, found us. He'd kept watch over the jewels for years, so when the Fangs captured us, he came to our rescue." Nia smiled at him, but he looked away. "The Throne Warden was true to his vow to protect the High King. Not even the Dark Sea could keep him from us."

Artham's cheeks splotched with either embarrassment or nervousness.

Then he made a tiny whimpering sound, quiet enough that Janner wasn't sure the assembly heard it. It was odd to see flickers of Peet the Sock Man after so many days of Artham behaving as he must have before the Great War. Before something had happened to him. Something that had left him with a shock of white hair and hideous claws that he hid under a pair of knitted socks.

In the Phoob Islands, something more had happened, and it was something Janner still didn't understand. Even as Kalmar had transformed into a Grey Fang, Artham had changed from a crazy man with claws to an elegant winged warrior. His unwieldy talons had refined into rust-colored hands with slender, graceful claws. He had become not less but *more,* and the gibberish was replaced by a strong voice and eloquent speech (Artham was a poet, after all). But just as there had been glimpses of the real Artham hidden in Peet the Sock Man, now Janner caught a glimpse of Peet the Sock Man in the real Artham. It was troubling.

"We escaped," Nia said, releasing Artham from her gaze. "On the way to the Ice Prairies, where we thought we might find refuge, Janner and Kalmar were separated from us. Then they were separated from each other. Janner braved much evil to escape Dugtown and eventually made his way to Kimera, a secret city in the snow. But Kalmar—" Nia's voice cracked. "Kalmar lost his way." The statement deepened the silence of the room. Even the great tree seemed to listen. "He was captured by Stranders—men and women with black hearts—sold to the Fangs, and in the dungeon . . . in the dungeon he—"

Janner knew the story, but he could hardly bear to hear it told. He tried to imagine what it would be like to tell a room full of strangers about his darkest moments. He was glad Kalmar wasn't there to hear it.

"He became a Fang," Nia said. Many in the crowd murmured to one another and shook their heads. "Gnag has learned to change people. He's learned to take the essence of a snake and meld it with a man or woman to create something horrible. That's why there are Fangs. Grey Fangs. Kalmar was captured by the Fang makers."

The assembly hissed with hatred. The man called Bunge stepped out of the crowd and shouted, "I knew it! It's a beast, and there's no undoing it! Kill the Fang like we have all the others! If it's not human, it's not welcome!"

Artham flung off his canvas and unfurled his wings. "Hollowsfolk," he cried, "behold the Maker's good pleasure!"

The assembly gasped.

"I was broken, I tell you, hardly a man at all! Unmade and foundering was I! But in the pit of the Phoobs I too sang the song of the stones! I became no Fang, but sprouted these." He flexed his wings and swooped them forward, blowing back the hair of those nearest him. "I cannot tell you why. All I know is that in my heart was a burning love for young Kalmar. Gnag bends things for breaking, and the Maker makes a flourish! Evil digs a pit, and the Maker makes a well! That is his way."

"Warden Wingfeather, we hear your words," Rudric said, stroking his beard. "We see your wings, and indeed we are as suspicious of you as of the young Fang in the dungeon. If I believed it were possible to bind you, I would." The Hollowsfolk murmured their agreement. "You are neither animal nor man, unnaturally transformed. How does this come to be if not by some black power?"

Janner saw on his mother's face that even she wanted to know the answer to this question. Podo's and Oskar's bushy gray eyebrows were raised thoughtfully as they watched Artham for his reaction. The birdman's wings ruffled and folded. Artham pursed his lips and nodded his head.

"The mystery runs deeper than my understanding, but I'll tell you what I believe." Artham locked his fingers behind his back, looked over the faces of the assembly, and cleared his throat. "When the Fangs took Castle Rysen, my brother—Esben—" Artham swallowed. He took a deep breath and began again. "When the Fangs took the castle, my brother Esben—" Janner saw beads of sweat form on his uncle's brow. "—Esben naid he seeded something—said he needed something. Said he needed something-thing-thing from inside. Said he would bum cack. Cack!"

Artham closed his eyes and clenched his jaw. He twitched his head.

Whispers fluttered like moths among the Hollowsfolk. The blood ran from Janner's face as he watched Artham sink below the surface while Peet the Sock Man rose. Artham opened his eyes long enough to look on Janner with a childlike panic that stabbed the boy's heart.

"I'm sorry," Artham whispered. Janner couldn't tell if he was speaking to him or to everyone. "I'm so, so, so sorry," he repeated, and the old Peet's shrill voice played at the edges of the words.

He closed his eyes again, crouched, and sprang into the air. He flapped his great wings and circled the tree a few times before lighting on a high branch. Janner saw in his uncle's wheeling eyes not just the madness of Peet the Sock Man but the frustration and grief of Artham P. Wingfeather, the Throne Warden who couldn't stop what was happening. As beautiful and strong as Artham had become, something still haunted him, something that lurked like a sea dragon in his deep waters and had lain silent for weeks, choosing this of all moments to rise to the surface.

Rudric seized his war hammer from beside the throne. The Hollowsfolk were a tumult of angry shouts, cries of alarm, and shaking fists. Nia and Podo shouted for them to lower their weapons. Oskar waved at the people and said, "In the words of Goverly Swimp, 'There's no need to panic!' "

"We have to stop them," Leeli said. "They'll kill him." She pointed across the room at a group of men stringing bows and fishing arrows from a barrel.

Before he realized what he was doing, Janner ducked behind Rudric, climbed up the back of his throne, and jumped for the lowest branch of the tree. As soon as he caught the branch, all the hours he'd spent climbing glipwood oaks, swinging from mossy limb to mossy limb, scooting after Kalmar either to catch him or to keep him from hurting himself, suddenly felt like practice for this single moment. He climbed the tree as lithe as a thwap, swinging under limbs, scooting along others, closer every moment to the upper corner of the chamber where Peet trembled and twitched like a trapped bird, his talons flexing, his wings flapping madly.

Artham was terrified, and he was terrifying.

Janner edged along a branch of the tree as thick as his waist, calling Artham's name again and again, but if Artham heard, he showed no sign. The men with bows had nocked arrows and trained them on Artham, waiting for either a signal from Rudric or a movement from the birdman. Janner was sure Artham could defeat every warrior in the room if he wanted, but these were old allies, kinsmen, people acting not out of evil but out of fear; there must have been enough of Artham's sanity left to restrain his fury—but why didn't he flee? The main doors to the hall were flung wide open, and it would be an easy thing for him to fly through and away to safety.

Janner had started climbing the tree with an idea in his head, but now that the floor was so far below he wondered what he'd been thinking. "Uncle Artham!" he cried again, but Artham only shook his head and goggled his eyes everywhere except at Janner, whimpering to himself in nonsensical words.

If Janner was going to act, he had to do it now. The archers were hungry for a reason to shoot, Rudric was shouting, Oskar was waving his hands, and Nia's head was buried in Podo's shoulder. Only Leeli saw Janner in the tree.

Their eyes met, she smiled at him, and Janner said, "Uncle Artham, HELP!"

Then he jumped.

11

Two Wardens
and a Sock Man

Amidst a chorus of gasps, flapping wings, and shouts, Janner heard his uncle's screech and felt his strong arms snatch him from the air. He felt a rush of wind, was blinded for a moment by sunlight, and before he knew it he was set lightly on the roof of the great hall.

The leafy branches of the great tree rose out of the roof like trees themselves, and though Janner could still faintly hear shouting in the hall below, birdsong filled the air. To the east as far as he could see lay green hills and valleys, dotted with trees and patches of farmland. Here and there a cottage sat under a shade tree like a sleepy dog. To the south and west were the shingled roofs of Ban Rona, then the harbor, the cliff walls of the Watercraw, and beyond it, the Dark Sea of Darkness. The sun was sailing up into midmorning, and Janner had to squint to see Artham, a winged silhouette crowned by a muss of white hair.

"Thank you, Janner." His voice quavered, but it was Artham who spoke, not Peet.

"You just have to remember," Janner said, taking his uncle's hand. "You're the Throne Warden."

"It's remembering that's the problem, lad." Artham smiled, but his tone was bitter. "There are things I want to forget, but I can't. Things I've yet to atone for."

Janner's smile faded. "What things?"

Artham shook his head. "I'd prefer that you remembered me as a good man. Not a coward."

Janner didn't understand. His uncle had saved them time and again, fought the Fangs at every turn without a care for himself. How could anyone ever think of him as a coward?

The commotion in the great hall below their feet increased, and Janner could hear people climbing the steps toward the roof. "Uncle Artham, listen! Whatever you're talking about doesn't matter. I love you. We all do."

"You wouldn't if you knew," Artham said as he moved to the edge of the roof and spread his wings. "I have to go. I'll only cause you trouble."

"Please. Don't go. We need you."

"This land, these hills might be the last safe place in all of Aerwiar. You'll go to school, you'll have friends, you'll read books—Janner, the library in Ban Rona is magnificent. I traveled here many times in my youth to study the poets. You finally have a home. Don't you see? You'll have trouble enough convincing them to free Kalmar without these ridiculous wings stirring up trouble." Footsteps thudded up the stairs, and voices rose. "Besides, I never know when I'll bart stabbling."

"Start babbling," Janner said quietly.

"You see?" Artham hung his head, and his left eye twitched. "I fear I shall never be healed."

Tears stung Janner's eyes. He didn't want to live in a world without Artham watching over him, always appearing when they needed him most. But he could see a sadness in Artham's eyes, a resolve that couldn't be shaken. "Where will you go?"

Artham drew a hand over his face and whispered, "As far from the Blackwood as possible."

"Why? What's in the Blackwood?" Janner asked.

"I'll go to Skree." Artham put a hand on Janner's shoulder and forced a smile. "Gammon and his men could use a flying birdman on their side. I'll see what trouble I can stir up on the other side of the sea, where trouble might do some good. Now that you're safe, I should go where I'm needed."

"But you *are* needed." Janner wiped his nose. "I need you."

"There's the beast!" a man shouted from the doorway. He held a battle axe in both hands and edged forward while more Hollowsfolk with weapons—men and women alike—crowded in behind him. "We'll have no cloven in the Hollows, do you hear? None!"

Artham dropped to a knee and wrapped his strong arms around Janner.

"Maker bless you, lad. Take care of your brother. Be a better Warden than I. You have Podo, and Nia, and though it may not seem so, the people of the Green Hollows are good hearted and noble in their way. This will make a fine home. Good-bye."

Janner looked into Artham's deep eyes. He thought about the day on the rope bridge, high in the trees of Glipwood Forest, when Peet the Sock Man had invited them to his castle in the boughs. Even then he had seen a great sorrow in those eyes. Why did the madness creep into his mind even now, even after his mighty transformation? And what lurked in the Blackwood that frightened even Artham P. Wingfeather? It made Janner think of his old fear of Glipwood Forest, and that made him think of their journey to Dugtown, and that made him think of the Fork Factory, and that made him think of a girl with beautiful eyes set like jewels in her soot-covered face.

"Uncle Artham, listen. There's a place in Dugtown called the Fork Factory," Janner said. "It's full of slaves. Children."

"Not for long," Artham said with a wink.

"There's a girl there. Her name's Sara Cobbler." Janner's cheeks flushed. "Will you find her? She helped me escape. Tell her—tell her thank you. From me."

Artham smiled. "You have my word. You're a precious jewel, my boy. Your father would be proud."

The Hollowsfolk rushed forward, swinging their weapons. Without taking his eyes off Janner, Artham flapped his wings and rose. He flew back and away from the great hall, swatting away arrows as if they were sticks thrown by children. Janner watched through tears until his uncle disappeared behind a cloud.

12

Turalay

Janner was astonished by how quickly the Hollowsfolk calmed down. Minutes after it was clear that Artham was gone, the mob of burly men and fierce women filed back downstairs, sheathed their weapons or smoothed their dresses, and sat in the great hall to resume the council. When Janner reached his family at the root of the tree, they huddled around him and peppered him with whispers.

"Are you all right?" Nia asked.

"Sakes alive, that was a reckless move, boy! Well done!" said Oskar.

Podo squeezed Janner's shoulder. "Yer lucky the mad bird didn't drop ye."

"Where is he?" asked Leeli.

The others quieted and looked at Janner.

"He's gone."

"Fer good?" Podo asked.

"I don't know."

There was a moment of silence while they took in this news, and Janner realized the assembly had grown quiet too.

Nia turned her attention back to the council. "Rudric, I ask your forgiveness. Artham carries a great weight in his heart, and sometimes it is too much for him."

Rudric was seated on his throne again, and Janner sensed a quiet kindness in him that he wanted to trust. "We all carry burdens, Queen. But not all of us sprout wings or grow fur. The Green Hollows has remained safe from Gnag's blackness only because of our strength, our vigilance, and our determination to empty the Hollows of anything that might threaten our peace. You must understand, highness, that we mean no disrespect to you, your station, or Anniera itself when I tell you we can't allow a Grey Fang to walk our streets."

Janner's heart sank as the Hollowsfolk muttered in agreement. Nia's speech might have swayed the ruling, but Artham's madness had ruined Kalmar's chance.

"Is there nothing I can say to convince you that my son is as safe and sane as he ever was?" Nia asked. "Are you telling me I have to choose between my homeland and my child?"

"And what assurance have we that he is, as you say, 'safe and sane'?" Rudric countered.

Janner was troubled by the shameful thought that he wasn't sure. He knew his brother's heart was healing, if not whole—but if Kalmar carried the same shadow of guilt or fear or madness that Uncle Artham did, and something triggered it, would the little Grey Fang become as wild as Artham had only moments ago? Would he hurt someone? Janner's wounds were painful reminders of what Kalmar was capable of.

"I will vouch for him," Nia said. "I declare *turalay*."

The assembly erupted in gasps. Janner didn't know what *turalay* was, but it caused the blood to drain from Rudric's face. Podo took Nia's hand and tried to pull her back to her seat, but she yanked away from him and approached the throne.

She knelt before Rudric, who shrank against the back of his chair. Janner heard him say in a quiet, urgent voice, "Nia, please! This isn't the way!"

But Nia's anger was kindled and she declared again, *"Turalay!"*

The cries of the crowd deteriorated into a cacophony of shouting. Some shook their fists and said, "Let her vouch!" Others shook their heads, saying, "Not the queen!"

Finally Rudric, with a grave expression, held up his hands for order. "The queen," he said, "has declared *turalay*. Bring the Grey Fang."

The doors swung open and another cage was rolled into the hall. At first it looked empty, but Janner spotted a little gray heap in the corner, so small it looked like a crumpled blanket. The crowd watched in silence as the cage was placed at the foot of the mound between two sweeps of tree root.

"Kalmar! It's going to be all right," Leeli said, and her voice was like music. "We're all here."

The little heap stirred and two trembling ears appeared, then two blue eyes and a wet black nose. Kalmar held himself tightly, shivering as if he were

cold or sick. When he saw Leeli, then Nia and the others, he whined. Janner's heart ached. He fought the urge to tear open the cage and flee with his brother.

Rudric dusted off an ornate wooden box beside the throne, opened it, and removed a dagger. Without a word, the seven men and women of the council came forward and flanked Rudric. Nia, who seemed to know exactly what to do, stood between them and held out her right hand, palm upward.

"Nia Wingfeather, Queen of Anniera," Rudric said in a loud voice, "you have invoked *turalay* for the sake of the Grey Fang, whom you call son."

"I do, and I regret it not," she said.

"Then before the chiefs of Ban Hynh, Ban Rugan, Ban Yorna, Ban Finnick, Ban Soran, Ban Verda, and the Outer Vales, you vouch for the Grey Fang—"

"His name is Kalmar Wingfeather," Nia said. "And I will hold you in contempt until you call him thus."

Rudric glanced at the chiefs. In all his strength, he seemed small before Nia. "Very well. You vouch for *Kalmar Wingfeather*. You hold your life forfeit for his, and should he break the life laws of the Green Hollows, from this day forward, it is not only his blood that will be shed, but yours—" He stepped closer to Nia and lowered his voice. "You mustn't do this thing. The Fang—I'm sorry—the *boy* is wild. I heard him last night in the dungeon, howling like an animal. His claws are bloodied from scraping at the stone. And that is only the beginning. You saw the other Fang! In time, the boy too will descend, I know it, and not only will he hurt someone, he'll kill, he'll be lost, and you'll be lost with him. Please, Nia! There is no changing this."

"He's my son," Nia said. Her eyes burned into Rudric's until he looked away.

"*Turalay*," Rudric said at last, and he drew the knife blade across Nia's palm. She didn't flinch. The Keeper of the Hollows took Nia's wrist and held up her bleeding hand for the assembly to see. "Hollowsfolk! Before these witnesses has the ancient law been invoked! Beneath the branches of the ancient tree has the oath been made! Let blood seal the freedom of the captive!"

"Let it be," answered the assembly.

Rudric released Nia's hand and stepped aside. She walked forward and placed her palm against the trunk of the giant tree, and Janner noticed for the first time that there were many other palm prints, faded with age, dappling the smooth bark above the throne.

Blood trickled down her wrist and flowed into the bark of the tree until she was satisfied and held her hand out again for all to see. "Now, in the name of my father, Podo Helmer; my grandfather Kargan Igiby; his father, Janiber Igiby; and in the name and in the name of the Maker himself, release my son."

The guards unlatched the cage, and the door creaked open.

"Kalmar, come," Nia said.

Kalmar blinked and cocked his head sideways, looking from Nia to the guards and back again like a scared puppy. Without a thought for what the council would think, Janner ran to the cage, stepped in, and carried his brother out. He stood with his family at the base of the tree and watched as the Hollowsfolk filed out of the hall in silence.

Rudric appeared with bandages for Nia's hand. Podo took them with a stiff nod and wrapped his daughter's wound. Rudric cleared his throat and struggled to look Nia in the eye. "That didn't go as I had hoped."

"Little does," Nia said, looking away.

Oskar shook his head and stared at the floor. Kalmar was free, but at the cost of Nia's own life, should his recklessness or foolishness or even some deeper, uncontrollable impulse get him into trouble. And trouble, Janner thought with a feeling of dread, was something Kalmar never managed to avoid. Besides all that, Uncle Artham, their fiercest protector, was gone.

"Come, children," Nia said. She helped Leeli to her feet, kissed Kalmar on the forehead, and led them out of the room.

As they stepped into the sunlight, Janner glanced back at Rudric. He slumped on his throne and watched them leave. Above his head, Nia's bloody handprint glistened on the tree.

13

Pumpkin Stew
and an Old Friend

The Igiby family walked back to the Orchard Inn under a cool sky. The day was beautiful and bright, but it did little to lift the burden from Janner's heart. He could tell from the bright orange edges of the leaves that autumn was coming to the Hollows, and he wondered how cold it got here.

The family walked in silence, happy that Kalmar was free, but the seriousness of the day hung over them like a fog. Kalmar didn't seem to be injured, though his fur made it impossible to tell if he was bruised. He was skittish, though, and kept close to Janner's side.

Janner wanted to ask his mother or Podo what they would do next, but he doubted anyone had thought past returning to the Orchard Inn for lunch and a safe place to rest.

"Look," Leeli said, pointing beyond the Keep at a field where a group of children ran barefoot on the grass. "Are they playing zibzy, Mama?"

"Something like it," Nia said.

"Probably a bit rougher than ye boys are used to, though," Podo said. "When I first showed up here, these Hollowsfolk sopped me like a biscuit. And I was a pirate, remember, fresh off the meanest ship that ever sailed."

"Didn't they like you?" Leeli asked.

"Oh, they liked me fine. But I was an outsider. Had to prove me grit, you see."

"What did you have to do?" Kalmar asked. It was the first time he had spoken since being released, and Janner was relieved to hear his voice. However he looked, however abused he had been at the hands of the Hollish guards, Kalmar was still in there.

"We'll talk over lunch," Nia said, leading them toward the inn. "There's much to discuss, and your grandfather can tell his stories then."

Janner thought it odd that his mother was in such a hurry until he noticed the way she glanced at the windows of the homes that lined the street. He spotted faces peeking out from behind curtains to watch them pass—watching Kalmar in particular. Some wore their distrust plainly; others looked frightened. Janner didn't have to try too hard to imagine he saw anger as well, and he couldn't wait to be back at the Orchard Inn.

When they arrived, the dining room was empty but for the woman who had served them the night before. She slumped in a chair before a smoldering hearth fire and gave them a look that smoldered too.

"I was afraid you'd be back," she said. "With the wolf, I see."

Again Janner waited for Nia's anger, but it didn't come.

"With my son, yes," she said. "Am I to assume that we're the cause of your empty dining hall?"

"You are," said the woman without looking up. "Word spread that the Grey Fang was freed, and that it would be coming here. People scattered like flies and left me with a pot of pumpkin soup and no one to eat it. Even your Kimeran sailors left. Said they couldn't sleep unless the beds were on the tide, so they've gone to their ship. I doubt they'll be back for dinner, either."

"I'm sorry for your trouble." Nia stepped closer to the woman and waited until she lifted her eyes from the fire and met Nia's gaze. "But we have nowhere else to go, and nothing to eat. We'll clean your kitchen, tend to your rooms, and seek other lodging—to honor your goodwill and good work. I've no doubt that once we move on, your cinnamon bread and pumpkin stew will lure a hall full of hungry bellies soon enough."

The woman sighed, brushed off her apron, and stood. She looked at each of them but Kalmar, shook her head, and disappeared into the kitchen.

"Well! That was uncomfortable," said Oskar, scratching his belly. "I'm just glad we won't have to wait for our soup." He plopped into a chair, tucked a napkin into his shirt collar, and rubbed his hands together.

Nia nodded at her children and they sat, filling every space at a table near the fire. Nia, though, walked into the kitchen uninvited. She emerged a moment later with six mugs of hot cider—three in each hand—and the hostess followed with a tray of steaming wooden bowls. She appeared to have softened toward Nia and thanked her for her help.

"You're welcome, dear. We'll help you clean up when we're finished."

"No need, your highness. My name's Elenna." The woman curtsied awkwardly and left them alone.

"Janner," Nia said, "please thank the Maker for our food." When Janner bowed his head, the steam from the pumpkin soup filled his senses so that when he gave thanks, he meant every word.

"Now! I have three questions," Oskar said. He held his spoon before his lips, ready to slurp the soup up as soon as he was finished speaking. "One—why in the Deep did Artham leave? Two—what is this *turalay* business? Three—where is the library? Kalmar! Goodness me, is your bowl empty already?"

Kalmar let out a snarly burp and wiped his snout with his forearm.

"That was four questions," Leeli said with a giggle.

Elenna glided out of the kitchen and refilled Kalmar's bowl, but she still wouldn't look at him, even when Kalmar thanked her.

"Uncle Artham's going back to Skree," Janner said.

Nia raised her eyebrows. "What does he plan to do there?"

"He said they needed him there. I think he's going to Kimera first, to see if he can help Gammon fight the Fangs. And I asked him to do something about the Fork Factory in Dugtown. Sara Cobbler is still there—"

Kalmar snickered. "Sara Cobbler, with the bright diamond eyes?"

"What?" Janner said, blushing.

"You talked about her in your sleep," Podo said.

"Almost every night," Kalmar said. "'Sara! Your eyes are so pretty! I'll come back for you, Sara!'" He howled with laughter till Janner punched him in the shoulder.

"Boys!" Nia glared at them. "Behave yourselves at the table. Kalmar, leave your brother alone. He can't help it if he's in love."

Janner stirred his soup and shook his head while everyone laughed. When they were finished and his cheeks had returned to their natural color, he said, "The *point* is, Uncle Artham's gone." There was much clearing of throats and wiping of eyes and sipping of soup. "He said he would only bring us trouble. It's like he's two people, and he never knows when Peet the Sock Man is going to take over. I wish I understood what changed him. Something happened—and I don't just mean whatever gave him the talons. He said he wanted to get as far away as he could from the Blackwood."

Nia looked up from her bowl. "I didn't know he ever entered the Blackwood. It's a terrible place."

"Terrible like Glipwood Forest?" Leeli asked.

"Worse," Nia said.

"Much worse, lass." Podo's face darkened. "Glipwood was dangerous because of toothy cows and horned hounds and all manner of critters. They were dangerous, sure, but not evil. The Blackwood is full of *monsters*. When I was a young man, I once rode west, far past the orchards, and sat on my horse atop a ridge to watch the forest edge. The spine of the Killridge Mountains in the south sloped down to the foothills where the forest began. The tree trunks were like dirty bones, and the branches were like fingers. I could see the woods movin', I tell ye. And I don't just mean the trees. I mean things in the forest were teeming about. It was like—like worms crawling around in moldy bread."

Podo slurped his soup without noticing the way everyone else at the table gagged. Nia looked at the ceiling and shook her head.

"Apt description. That's all," Podo said with a shrug.

"As long as anyone can remember it's been either haunted or populated with the cloven," Nia said. "Creatures so ghoulish they can't even be described—according to legend anyway. I can't imagine why Artham was ever there."

Janner finished his soup and wondered if he could have more, just as the innkeeper appeared and filled his bowl.

"As for your second question, Oskar," Nia said, "*turalay* is an old Hollish law. It means that Kalmar and I are bound in life and death."

Kalmar looked up from his second bowl of soup and blinked. "What do you mean?"

"If you break a law, I receive your punishment too."

"And there's no changin' it," Podo said gravely. "If you steal Danniby's sack of apples and the council decides the fitting punishment is a month in the dungeon, your mother goes along with you."

"It was the only way." Nia smiled at Kal. "And I trust you."

"You don't have to worry. I won't steal Danniby's dumb apples," Kalmar said.

"I know you won't, son." Nia leaned over and took Kalmar's chin in her hand and made him look at her. "You're the King of the Shining Isle. That means something. This fur doesn't." She held up her bandaged hand. "I don't regret this. Nor will I ever."

Janner watched them quietly, the Fang and the queen, and assured himself that Kalmar would never break the laws of the Hollows. He told himself that his mother's decision to invoke *turalay* was her only choice and that Kalmar would honor her trust. Then he wondered why he was telling himself anything, except that he was trying to convince himself, trying to quiet some smaller, secret voice in his heart—one that still wasn't sure that Kalmar could be trusted. The wounds in his legs, chest, and back throbbed for the first time that day.

Oskar had finished his fourth bowl of soup and leaned away from the table with his napkin draped across the expanse of his belly. "And what about my third question? The library. I've much research to do if I'm to translate the First Book, and besides, I've been dreaming of reading *The*

Further Excitements of Billiam Stone again and wager I could find a copy here, since Billiam Stone's exploits often involve the misappropriation and burglary of fruit and its accoutrements. A library would be most welcome."

"If you want to see a library, I'm the man to show you," said a new voice.

They all turned to see a short and very old man standing in the doorway, dressed in a finely tailored suit. His face was clean shaven, and several tufts of curly white hair burst from beneath his top hat. He was smiling so widely that his cheeks bunched into little eggs that pushed his eyes into a happy squint.

The man removed his hat and bowed low, sweeping his arms wide. "Your highness. It's good to see you."

Nia gasped. She leapt to her feet, dashed across the room, and hugged the little old man so tightly that she lifted him off the floor.

"Bonifer!" Podo cried. "Bonifer Squoon!"

14

An Inheritance
from Kargan Igiby

Janner's mind spun. A character had just stepped out of the stories he'd been told and into the Orchard Inn.

"Books and Crannies!" Kalmar whispered into Janner's ear.

Janner looked at his brother with surprise. "I can't believe you remember that."

"We found his old journal, right?"

Janner thought back to the day in Glipwood when he and Kalmar had unpacked crates of books for Oskar and discovered one of Bonifer's journals. It was the same day Kal had found Oskar's map—the map that led to the weapons chamber beneath Anklejelly Manor, which led to their escape from the horned hounds, which led to just about every bad thing that had happened since.

"Wasn't he Papa's friend?" Kal asked.

"Yeah," Janner whispered. "His advisor."

When Podo released Bonifer from a bone-crunching hug, the old man adjusted his top hat, brushed himself off, and looked the children over with what seemed like reverence. He took a step forward, checked himself, and bowed again. When he didn't rise, Janner realized that Bonifer was waiting for some signal. Nia cleared her throat.

"You may, uh, rise," Janner stammered.

But the man still didn't move. Janner wondered for a moment if he was stuck or asleep, but finally the old fellow spoke in a quiet voice. "I don't mean to offend, Throne Warden, but I wasn't waiting for you."

Janner's cheeks grew hot, and he stared at his feet.

"Kalmar," Nia said gently, "he's waiting for the king to bid him rise."

"Huh?" Kalmar looked confused, then understanding came over his face, followed by a look of terror at not knowing what to do. "Hi, sir," he said with a gulp. "You don't have to bow to me. My name's Kalmar. They used to call me Tink, but now it's just Kalmar. It's nice to meet you."

Bonifer rose at last. "I do, in fact, have to bow to you, your highness. I'm a citizen of Anniera. You're my king. It's as simple as that." He held his hat in his hands and beamed at the little wolf. "King Kalmar, we have met before, though you don't remember. I held you in my arms when you were a baby. I was in the next room when you were born, and I heard you draw your first breath. Your father was my dear friend, and though it seems you've undergone some . . . *changes,* I can see him in you yet."

Kalmar nodded, unable to meet Bonifer's kind eyes.

"And now," Bonifer said, turning his attention to Janner with a bow of his head, "it's my honor to meet the Throne Warden. Janner, you're as assertive as Artham ever was, and handsome too. The maidens of the realm will faint at your passing, as is proper for a Throne Warden."

Janner's cheeks still burned, but from embarrassment now.

"Leeli Wingfeather, Song Maiden of Anniera. How lovely you are! I am at your service," Bonifer said, stooping to look her in the eye. He patted the whistleharp around her neck. "An ancient instrument for ancient songs. How I have longed to hear them once again echo in the halls of Castle Rysen."

"An honor to meet you, sir," Oskar said, stepping forward as he smoothed a wisp of hair to his head and straightened his spectacles. "An indibnible honor! I hail from Glipwood by the Sea and have been the least of this company of heroes since our adventure began. My name is Oskar N. Reteep, bookseller, appreciator of the strange, neat, and/or yummy."

"The honor is mine, Reteep." Bonifer squinted one eye at him, taking in at a glance Oskar's belly, his sailor's tan, his tattoo, and his inability to conceal his baldness. "I wonder which of those I might be."

"Which what?" Oskar asked.

"Strange, neat, or yummy."

"*And/or* yummy, Mister Squoon. You'd be surprised how many things can be all three at once. Take frumpkin blossoms, for example—"

"And you'd like to visit the library." Bonifer pointed his cane at Oskar.

"Oh, very much, sir."

"Me too," Janner said.

"Of course you do," Bonifer said, nodding at Janner. "Your mother has had you hard at work on your T.H.A.G.S., no doubt. And as the firstborn your emphasis is limning. *Words* are your game, are they not?"

"Yes sir," Janner said. "I do like to write."

"And King Kalmar here is an artist, as Leeli is the Song Maiden. Your mother has done Anniera proud."

"It's so good to see a familiar face, Bonifer." Nia pulled out a chair so he could sit. "Things have been unpleasant since we arrived."

"Yes, yes," Bonifer said, hobbling over to the chair. "Gnag the Nameless has poisoned even the good hearts of the Hollowsfolk. They're so fierce about their borders that they don't trust anyone anymore, least of all someone with a snout."

He looked with glistening eyes into Kalmar's face and smiled. "Your highness, I have traveled the reaches of Dang and have seen terrible things. I know of Gnag's twisted ways. He has discovered powers long forgotten and has wrenched them into new horrors. I have seen many like you who, in one moment of weakness, were forever marked. But you aren't your fur any more than I am my flesh. *Who* you are runs deeper than your skin. A man may be handsome in aspect but black as death in his heart, you know."

Kalmar nodded.

"Let these Hollish brutes say what they will. Only remember that a name runs in your blood, immutable and strong. It may take some time before they trust you. I've been here nine years and only now do I feel I can walk the Hollows without their eyes on my every move."

"So you've been here from the beginning, then?" Podo asked.

"Yes. When the castle was overrun, I escaped. I sailed the strait from Anniera to Dang and followed the cliffs north to the Watercraw. A long and miserable journey for an old man. I've been here ever since, though I've managed to travel a little, as in the old days. Much of Dang is under the fist of Gnag, and those few who are not will be soon enough. The Green Hollows seems impervious even to Gnag's best efforts, though, and thus he has abandoned his campaign here. Pray to the Maker he doesn't discover your presence here or all his might will descend on the Hollows, and I fear even the strongest Hollish warrior will be twisted into his service."

Bonifer fell silent, and his warning filled the room. He winced and struggled to rise, and Janner hurried forward to help. He felt sad for the old fellow and wanted so much to ask him about Esben. Bonifer was a connection to his father and his homeland. He was proof that Janner's wildest dreams were as real as the air in his lungs.

"Thank you, lad," Bonifer said when he was standing again. "Now, on to lighter matters. I know you'd like a library. But I can offer you something even better." He turned to Nia and his eyes twinkled. "I can offer you a home. How does Chimney Hill sound?"

Nia's eyes widened and her mouth fell open, but no words came.

Bonifer removed a yellowed envelope from his breast pocket and waved it in the air. "I have here, along with a healthy inheritance from your grandfather Kargan Igiby—Maker rest his soul—the deed to Chimney Hill, your ancestral home. It was left to your mother, Wendolyn, who entrusted it to the House of Rona should any of her descendants fall into need. Since you are homeless, husbandless, a refugee from a fallen kingdom, and weary beyond measure, I think no one will contest your qualifications."

"But—but has no one lived there?" Nia asked. "I assumed that after all these years someone would have—"

Bonifer handed her the deed and smiled. "Someone *has* lived there, my queen. And that someone is me. I've kept it free of cobwebs and thwaps these nine years, have stocked the pantry with bread and a hundred jars of jam preserves, and have even this morning instructed the maidservant to make your beds. There is a fire in the hearth even now."

"Does that mean we have a home?" Leeli asked.

Nia smiled. "Yes, dear. And a fine one too."

Minutes later, the Wingfeathers sat atop a carriage that clattered through the streets of Ban Rona toward their new home. The Hollowsfolk watched them pass—some with scowls and narrow eyes, some with wonder, and some with curiosity.

Neither Janner nor any of his family cared in the least.

15

A Home at Chimney Hill

The city of Ban Rona was bigger than Janner first thought. The buildings near the harbor, like the Orchard Inn, were tall and close together with narrow alleyways between them. They were made of wood and brick, handsomely built to complement the pleasant, tree-lined streets, which were busy with city traffic.

The busiest area, the harbor district, was a place of rowdy commerce even though, Bonifer told them, the Great War had stopped the flow of ships to and from the Hollows. The harbor was large enough that fishermen could make a good living catching, filleting, smoking, and selling garp, glipper, and stonk fish—not to mention the occasional eight-eyed chabgome, whose tender side meat was famously delicious when garnished with a redberry spread. Fruit merchants and bakers from other Hollish cities still came to the waterfront market to sell their jams, pies, juices, and breads there, though their only customers now were fellow Hollowsfolk. Business wasn't thriving, but the bustle kept Ban Rona's people in good spirits.

As the Wingfeathers rode the carriage west, away from the sea, the space between the houses widened, and some yards boasted little stands of apple, dornut, and ermentine trees under which big, lazy dogs lay wagging their tails. Janner wished the Hollish people were as glad to see the newcomers as their dogs seemed to be. The dogs that weren't panting on lawns ran in the hilly fields where goats and horses grazed.

Bonifer drove the carriage up a hill to the edge of the city, where there were no side streets, there were fewer houses, and the road was no longer cobbled. The old man reined in the horses and turned to his passengers with a smile that took over his whole face. Janner couldn't help returning it.

Bonifer swept his hand before him, indicating the view without a word. The three children stood and looked past the old man at a world of green. Janner had never seen so many shades of it. There were stands of dark green trees, bright gardens bursting with fall crops, hills that lay like the grassy bellies of a thousand sleeping giants, all pocked with houses and barns and lined with fences. Janner had seen the countryside from the roof of the great hall, but now that he was out among the hills and hollows he could feel the land's living beauty. He loved it.

"That one there," Podo said, squinting one eye and pulling Leeli close so she could see where he pointed, "that's where we're going. Chimney Hill."

The lane wound down a steep incline and met with another, wider road. The new road followed a babbling creek as it swept along the valley floor; just before the road disappeared around the shoulder of another hill, a lane veered off toward a stone bridge that arched over the creek. Across the bridge, the lane twisted its way gracefully up the hill, around several old trees heavy with fruit, past a little waterfall that leapt from a boulder and splashed down to the creek, and at last to the wide, flat lawn in front of Chimney Hill.

The house was bigger than Janner expected, but it looked as cozy as the Igiby cottage back in Glipwood. Big windows opened onto a flower garden on the front lawn. A tree as high as the second story stood at the west corner, and even from this distance Janner could tell it grew *into* the house, like the great tree in the Keep. Rising from the center of the roof was a wide chimney where smoke puffed out over the hollow and whispered a welcome to Janner's heart.

"You grew up there, Mama?" Leeli asked.

"Your grandmother did."

"Aye," Podo said. "I spent many hours in that front garden tryin' to convince yer great-grandparents to let me court yer grandma."

"That's not what I heard," Nia said with a wry smile.

"What do ye mean?"

"I heard it was *mother* you had to convince."

"Pah! She loved me from the first time she saw me ruggedly handsome face." Podo struck what he must have thought was a ruggedly handsome pose.

"Indeed, how could she not?" said Bonifer with a roll of his eyes as he snapped the horses into a trot. When the carriage turned onto the bridge, Janner saw a stone marker set in the earth beside the creek. It read:

CHIMNEY HILL
Built in the 348th Year
of the Third Epoch
by Janiber Igiby
(As Far as We Know)

Lanterns flickered at the cornerstones of the bridge, and several more were spaced beside the lane all the way to the house. Janner's stomach fluttered. After nine years in the Igiby cottage living under the eye of the Fangs of Dang, then their weeks in Peet's tree house, then his long journey to Kimera only to be swept onto a ship for a voyage across the sea, he was finally going to have a home again. He had ached for a place to call his own for so many weeks that he wondered what he would ache for now that he had one.

Anniera was a pleasant dream, but Chimney Hill was just beyond the next tree, around the next turn of the lane. He hoped one day to see the Shining Isle with his own eyes, but if he had to grow old in the Green Hollows, where the fruit was plentiful, the land was green, and there wasn't a Fang in sight (except for the one sitting right next to him, of course), then he would grow old happy. All he really wanted were good books to read, a warm bed, and his family and friends near.

"Welcome home," Bonifer said. He eased his old bones down from the carriage, adjusted his lapels, and held out a hand to Nia. Podo hopped down and lifted Leeli to the ground while the boys and Oskar clambered out and stood with the others in front of the house.

Lanterns shone on either side of the big wooden door, and yellow flowers clustered in pots on the porch. The place seemed old, but it was well tended and very much alive.

"Are you all right, Grandpa?" Leeli asked.

"Aye, lass." Podo sniffled and wiped his eyes. "It's me allergies."

"I'm allergic to old memories too," Nia said. She put an arm around her father and stepped inside. "Let's make some new ones, Papa. These children should know which beds they'll sleep in, Oskar will want to know what's for dinner, and I'd like to sit by the fire with Bonifer and hear more of his story. But not before a warm bath. We all smell like fish and sailor sweat."

Janner took each step with care, looking closely at the steps, the landing, the places where the main door was worn smooth, the decoration on the flowerpots, the view from the front door; he wanted to remember every detail so he could write about it later. It felt like a silly thought, but he wanted his grandchildren to know what his first visit to Chimney Hill was like, right down to the smell of honeybloom in the autumn air.

The last to enter the house, Janner stepped over the threshold and into his new home.

The first thing he saw was the fireplace. It was as big as his bedroom in the Igiby cottage (though not as big as the fireplace in Kimera, where he had seen the dragon bones). The stonework was beautiful and drew the eye up to the high ceiling where timbers were interlaced with the boughs of the tree at the corner of the house. As in the great hall of the Keep, he saw leafy branches and even a few yellow apples dangling near the ceiling.

Before the hearth lay an enormous rug made of animal fur so deep and soft that Janner's feet disappeared when he stood on it. Bookshelves flanked the chimney all the way to the ceiling, and Oskar was shimmying up a ladder to inspect the books. Podo had recovered from his sadness and was already reclining in a chair by the fire, puffing at his pipe.

On the other side of the room stood a long dining table, and beyond that was a kitchen stocked with pots and pans and baskets of vegetables. A kettle hissed on the stove. Nia held a teacup as she conversed with a young woman in a simple brown dress and apron. The woman held a little girl, not more than three years old. Janner heard Nia introduce herself, stroke the girl's hair, and laugh kindly at something the woman said.

"A fine home, is it not?" said Bonifer. He stood beside Janner in the entryway, and Janner noticed that when the old man stooped over his cane, they were the same height. Either Bonifer was very short or Janner was getting taller than he realized.

"When I woke up this morning, I was at the Orchard Inn and Kalmar was in the dungeon," Janner said. "I can hardly believe we're here right now. It's been so long since we've been *still*."

"Indeed! I hope you'll be here for many years, my boy." Bonifer patted Janner's arm. "May you fill those shelves with books of your own."

Janner smiled. It was a nice thought, however unlikely it seemed.

He heard a snarl and spotted Kalmar chasing Leeli around a couch on the far side of the hearth. She was giggling so hard she could hardly breathe, and Janner was amazed for the hundredth time by how agile she was with her crutch. He was sure Kal could catch her if he really wanted, but she wouldn't make it easy.

Nia came out of the kitchen with a cup of hot tea cradled in both hands. "Kalmar, Leeli, listen. I want to introduce you to our maidservant. This is Freva Longhunter."

The young woman was pretty in her way, though she hunched bashfully and allowed a lock of hair to cover one of her eyes. She smiled and nodded at each of them and didn't seem to mind the presence of a Grey Fang.

"And this," Nia waved at the little girl peeking out from behind Freva's leg, "is her daughter Bonnie. They live in the servant's cottage and will assist with meals, gardening, and cleaning. This house is a lot bigger than our old cottage. It's going to require much more work."

"It's an honor to meet you all." Freva curtsied. "If you need anything, just ask. I'm good at cleanin' socks, bakin' greengrape cake, and can make a bed *real* well. I like when the sheets and the blanket sort of meld together, so they almost become one thing—ye can't understate the importance of a good blanket meld, you know." She straightened with pride. "It's my specialty."

"Thank you, Freva," Nia said. "Now. Let's see to your rooms, children."

Janner and Kalmar looked at each other and grinned. Leeli clapped her hands. They followed Nia to a wide, curved stairway to the right of the fireplace. It swooped up to a landing where several comfortable chairs were arranged around another fireplace in the same chimney. More books crowded more shelves, and Janner grinned as he skimmed the titles.

Four doors lined the wall beyond the landing, each tinted a different color and engraved with different designs. The brown one was lined with bare, wintry tree branches, the green one was leafy, the bluish one was looped with vines, and the red one was decorated with fruit.

"I haven't been here for ages, but I think this one will suit you, Leeli." Nia opened the reddish door, and light spilled into the hallway. Against the wall stood a large downy bed (the sheets and blanket of which were arranged with great care), and a rocking chair sat in the corner by the window. A tall mirror hung on the wall beside an ornate wardrobe, the doors of which were open to reveal a rack of fuzzy coats.

"This was my mother Wendolyn's old room," Nia said. "She used to sit beside that window at night, staring out at the stars and pretending to ignore your grandfather's singing. He would stand in the garden below and profess his love until *my* grandfather chased him off with a rake. This is the bed I slept in when I came to visit as a girl. What do you think?"

Leeli limped into the room, spun around with a teary smile, rushed to her mother, and wrapped her in a violent hug. They left Leeli to her new room and moved on to the blue door.

"Sorry, your highness!" called Bonifer from the top of the stairs. "That one's mine, if that's all right, and it's not terribly clean. I only found out you were here this morning, you see, and by the time I pressed my suit and hitched the horses I didn't have time to straighten it."

"It's no problem, Bonifer," Nia said, smiling. "You've taken good care of the place. You can sleep wherever you like. We'll have a look at the green one."

"I beg your pardon, highness." Bonifer looked downcast. "It's just—I haven't had any company in nine years, and I'm unused to all this commotion. Forgive me."

"Hush, old friend. There's nothing to be forgiven." She pushed open the green door. "Ah. These two beds should suit the two of you perfectly."

The boys' room boasted two desks, two wardrobes, and a bunkbed as wide as a wagon. The boys darted inside and clambered around on it like thwaps. In minutes they were wrestling, tumbling about on the floor, and howling with laughter and pain and more laughter. Janner didn't care about his wounds, and he didn't care that his brother had fur and claws. He was so happy about having a room again that he could think of nothing else.

"Now," Nia said over the racket, "I'm going to take a long, hot bath. You may fetch me only when the table is set and dinner is served." She left them to their wrestling match.

A few seconds later, while Kalmar jabbed him in the ribs and twisted his foot, Janner noticed that Bonifer Squoon was watching Kalmar from the doorway. He thought he saw a strange look on the old man's face—a look of fear.

Darkness crept into Janner's joy as he realized that he was only beginning to glimpse the troubled road that lay before his little brother. If Bonifer Squoon was afraid of him—Bonifer, who had told Kalmar only an hour ago that his fur didn't matter—then the Hollowsfolk would be an even greater problem.

As if to confirm this thought, Nia poked her head back through the doorway. "After dinner I intend to give all three of you a thorough scrubbing. I want you presentable when I take you to school in the morning."

16

Podo Helmer
Falls in Love

Janner didn't realize how tired he was until his head hit the pillow. He and Kalmar had wrestled before dinner, after dinner, and after their baths, so by the time Nia finally ordered them to bed, they were both sweaty and out of breath. Janner opened one of the windows to let the cool air in, then blew out the lamp.

"Kal, come look at this!" he whispered.

Kalmar knelt beside Janner at the window. The stars seemed close enough to touch, and their beauty was a song in the dark silence of the sky. A night owl hooted from its perch in the tree outside the window. Somewhere in a distant pasture a donkey brayed. The window faced the field behind Chimney Hill, and Janner could see beyond the fence a road rising and falling and twisting across the countryside, with lanes branching off and winding toward other homesteads and barns. Golden light glowed in the windows where people were still awake, reading or visiting or eating fruity desserts. The brothers knelt for a while in the quiet and looked out on the beauty of the Hollows.

"It smells good here," Kalmar said. "I can smell everything—the owl in the tree over there, the goats in the next pasture. They don't smell so good, I guess. I can smell apple butter on the hot bread in that house across the way. I don't know how I'm going to get to sleep."

Janner had a thousand questions for Kalmar, but he hesitated to ask most of them. He didn't want his brother to feel any odder than he already did. "Are there any other . . . changes? I mean, like being able to smell everything."

Kalmar thought for a moment. "I can see better. I feel stronger. Hungrier."

"I didn't think that was possible. You're always hungry."

"That's not what I mean."

"Then what do you mean?"

Kal's ears twitched and he shook his head. "Nothing. Never mind."

Janner heard frustration in his voice and decided to leave it alone. The silence was broken a moment later by the clop of hooves on the road and the squeak of tack and wagon.

Although Janner knew there was no Black Carriage in Ban Rona, the memory of it woke an old fear in his bones, and he sensed a shortness in Kalmar's breathing. For most of his life he had lived in terror of the Black Carriage; it was impossible not to think about it.

Two horses rounded the bend, pulling a wagon. A lantern swung from a hook jutting into the air above the driver and cast a weak yellow light. The driver was a skinny fellow in a riding cap, whistling a Hollish tune.

"It's hard to believe we're not in danger anymore." Kalmar sighed and climbed into the top bunk. "Will you close the window? Too many smells out there."

"Yeah," Janner said.

He didn't remind Kalmar of the truth, that they weren't out of danger. He had seen enough of the Hollowsfolk and heard enough of Podo's stories to know that school in Ban Rona was going to be tough. Janner tried to sleep, reminding himself that none of the Hollish schoolchildren had braved the Fork Factory, fought a Fang, or sailed the Dark Sea of Darkness. How tough could they be?

Janner woke to the smell of bacon and the sound of Kalmar bounding out of bed and down the stairs. He lay still for a few minutes, enjoying the murmur of morning chatter downstairs, the clank of dishes, and birdsong outside the window. Light fell on the hill outside and melted the frost.

He got up and removed his bandages to apply the gadbalm ointment Nia had left on his desk. There was no blood and no scabbing. The scratches were clean and pink with scar tissue. In just two days, the cuts had closed and only ached a little when he touched them.

When he came downstairs with the wad of bandages in his hand, he found Leeli already up and wearing a new dress, one of Freva's that she had hemmed and adjusted for Leeli just that morning. Leeli's hair was braided, and her face glowed from a good night's sleep. She smiled at Janner with jam on her cheeks. Podo sat at the other end of the table and palavered with Oskar and Bonifer. The presence of three old men in one house guaranteed that breakfast would be hearty every morning. Nia greeted Janner and sat him down in front of a plate of eggs, bacon, and toast with ermentine jam.

"I planned to prepare a plate of fruit and leafy greens," Nia said, "but your grandfather would hear none of it."

"Meat!" Podo said.

Nia took the wad of bandages and inspected Janner's wounds. "It looks like the gadbalm did quick work. How are your legs?"

"Better," Janner said with a mouthful of toast.

Freva shuffled out of the kitchen and offered Janner a cup of juice. "Bibes, sir?"

"Huh?" Janner swallowed his food.

"Bibes? It's tanjerade. Very sweet."

"Oh. Yes, bibes would be fine. Thank you." He watched Freva as she hurried back into the kitchen, wondering why she was so bashful and wishing she wouldn't call him "sir." He also wondered where her daughter was—and her husband too, for that matter.

"When you're finished, try these on." Nia placed a stack of new clothes on the table, along with a pair of clean, unworn boots. Janner could already tell they were finer clothes than he had ever owned.

Kalmar emerged from behind the fireplace in his new outfit. He wore a white shirt with a stiff collar and a pair of black leggings.

"What about the boots?" Nia asked, appraising him with her hands on her hips.

"They didn't fit. My feet aren't . . . normal." Kalmar's ears lay flat, which Janner had figured out was the equivalent of his cheeks turning red. "I'd rather go barefoot, if that's all right."

"It is," Nia said. "Off with you, Janner. I want to see if yours fit too."

Janner's boots were too big, but not by much. Podo said that at the rate his feet were growing he'd soon need to wear boats instead of boots. He couldn't remember ever getting new clothes; in Glipwood, clothes had always been handed down from the Blaggus boys or made by Nia out of old scraps of fabric or tattered blankets. These were sturdy and clean, and with the new boots he even felt taller.

"Now come here by the fire and let yer Podo tell you a few things about school in the Green Hollows. You need an idea of what's likely to happen today. I expect at least one of you will come home with a fat lip or a black eye." Podo lit his pipe and waited for the children to gather around him on the thick rug. "When I came to the Hollows many years ago, I sailed through the Watercraw on me pirate ship, as rascally a sailor as you could imagine. I had already lost me leg by then, had sailed the sea Maker knows how many times, had run with Growlfist and the Stranders, and had a bit of a reputation for rowdiness. I was Podo Helmer, Scale Raker, and weren't afraid of nobody. So even though I'd heard that the Hollish ways were rough and tumble, I thought nothing of it."

Podo puffed on his pipe and stared at the fire.

"When I stepped off the ship and onto the pier, the first thing I saw wasn't the piles of fruit or the crowds of traders or the horses or the dogs. The first thing I saw was a woman. A woman with long hair the color of walnut and a face to stop yer heart. She was carrying a basket of apples and was turning to greet someone. When she did, her red dress spun a bit, the sun leapt off the water and lit her face, and I felt me heart kick like a mule. I'd never felt that way before. You children remember Nurgabog."

Janner thought of the wretched old woman from the Strand, crawling across the floor of the Strander burrow without a tooth in her head, wounded by her own son. She had loved Podo when she was young, and that love was all that had saved the Wingfeathers from Claxton Weaver and his band of thieves.

"Well, Nurgabog was a good woman in her way. But when I laid eyes on this woman at the market, I knew me whole life had come to a strong cross-wind, and I had to decide whether to sail through it or let it carry me off. I decided that instant to marry her."

"And you fell in love." Leeli sighed. She lay on her stomach with her chin in her hands, looking wistfully at Podo, which was what girls were supposed to do when they heard love stories, Janner thought.

"Nope," Podo said. "I walked right up to her, bowed so low me nose scraped the cobbles, and asked her name."

"Wendolyn," Leeli said, sighing again.

"I'm gettin' there, lass," Podo said. "She smiled back at me, and I was certain I would never be happy till I married her. We talked for hours, but I never paid much attention to what she was saying. I just kept lookin' at her face, the way she walked, wondering how I'd ever been happy without her. It was magic, I tell ye. She brought me home to meet her father that very day—"

"To this house," Leeli said.

"Nope. To a house in town. Her father was a trader of fabric and wicker. Sailed up and down the coast of Dang for weeks at a time, but he happened to be home this particular day. He was a fine feller, even if he couldn't spit right, and I settled in fer the interview. I figured he'd want to get to know the man who wanted to court his daughter. As we talked, a servant girl came in and offered us tea. I declined, but the man took some. He spilled a little on the floor and got all upset at the servant. Started sayin' mean things to her, and I got right uncomfortable fast. The girl with the walnut hair came in and took up her dad's abuse. She shooed the poor servant girl out of the room and kicked her in the rump for good measure. Right before Zola May slammed the door—"

"Zola May?" Leeli scrunched her face in confusion.

"Aye. Right before Zola May slammed the door I caught a glimpse of the servant girl's eyes. They were wild with strength—like lookin' at a wall of dark clouds screaming across the sea to flatten yer ship. Her face weren't pretty, but fair enough and flushed red with the pain of her treatment. Her hair was cut short and hung sad-like around her eyes. Then the door slammed shut and she was gone. It was an uncomfortable moment. I said, 'Let's get back to talk of courtin'.' Well, Zola May turned on the prettiest smile you ever seen and sidled up to her father to cool his temper. He agreed to let me court his daughter right quick, and before ye knew it I bade farewell to me crewmates and to me life on the sea. I was tired of outrunnin' the sea dragons anyway.

"Thus began my courtship with Zola May Rubleshaw. I found lodging at a waterfront inn, got a job choppin' glipper fish, and did me best to clean up me appearance. Combed me hair. Even bathed once a week. I don't know what Zola May saw in me, but she loved me so. After a while, though, me heart stopped kickin' like a mule, and I started listenin' to her words. She talked on and on about her fine dresses, her disdain for the Green Hollows (which I was comin' to love), and her ache to get out of town and see Aerwiar. I was sick of travelin' by now, and anyway I couldn't set foot on a boat without fear of the sea dragons swallowing me up.

"All the time I spent at the Rubleshaw place, I kept bumping into their servant girl. As I said, she weren't pretty—not like Zola May—but she had a way about her. I found that I enjoyed talkin' to her more than Zola May, and after two weeks started visiting Zola May just so I could see how the servant girl was doin'. She worked hard. Suffered the anger of Zola's dad in silence, and bore up when Zola May treated her worse than the family dog.

"Then everything changed." Podo leaned forward with a big smile. "One day I was sittin' on the garden bench out in front of Zola's house in the cool of the evening. We were talkin' about whatever, and I told her outright that I didn't want to travel anymore. I didn't want to leave the Hollows. I wanted to follow the Maker's wind, and it was blowing me straight and true away from the wild of the waters and to solid ground. Zola rolled her eyes. 'That's a giant waste of time,' she said. 'Don't you find me pretty, Podo?' She stood up and twirled her dress and flung her pretty hair about because she knew I was weakened by that kind of beauty, like every man.

"But right at that moment the servant girl walked by, leading a donkey loaded with vegetables for sale at the market. Her dog was at her side, and I saw how the servant girl's hand lay on its head while they walked. She scratched it behind the ears and smiled at those who passed her. I knew in that instant that I'd be happier as the servant's dog than Zola May's husband.

"In the weeks I'd visited with Zola May, I never saw her lift a finger to work. Never saw her speak a kind word to anyone but me or her father. She never listened much to me or what I cared about. When the servant girl passed, Zola May was still standin' in front of me, tryin' to get me to stop usin' me brain and gaggle at her prettiness. And right then, right under a sweep of Zola May's walnut hair, that servant girl—I didn't even know her name yet, because all they called her was 'servant'—she looked at me and threw one of her simple smiles my way. It shot through that walnut hair and Zola's ridiculous twirlin' like a bolt of lightning. I stood up and excused myself. Told Zola May she could twirl all she wanted, but I wouldn't be around to see it."

Podo laughed and smacked his knee. "You should've seen her! She looked as shocked as if I'd just belched in her face. I limped down the road to catch up with the servant. Hers was a beauty of a better kind."

"The servant girl was Wendolyn?" Janner asked. "But this house is huge! Why was she a servant?"

"Our family always believed that good work was better than wealth or status," Nia said. "So even though they had enough money to enjoy a life of leisure, my grandfather and his grandfather before him made sure their children knew the value of good work and good rest. When I was a girl, I worked at the market for years. That's why you three have always had your share of chores."

"In Anniera," said Bonifer, "it was not unusual to see your father, Esben, pulling totatoes out of the earth beside the farmers in the field. And he was the king! Not everyone agrees with this tradition, but it is hard to argue with the *kindness* that has always marked the Shining Isle. It started with the Maker, then the kings, and it flowed down to the subjects of the kingdom like water from a river, irrigating the furrows. Everything grows better that way."

"So did you marry her right away?" Kalmar asked.

"I wish I could have," Podo said with a chuckle. "No, it wasn't as easy as I thought. I fell harder for Wendolyn than I ever did for Zola May. In fact, from the moment I left Zola on her porch and chased after the servant girl with the donkey, something strange happened to me brain and me heart. I found that all the things I believed beautiful about Zola had turned ugly. And all the things that were plain about Wendolyn shone like rubies. Whenever I saw Zola in the market, I wondered what I had seen in her. And when I looked at Wendolyn, I saw her grace and her gentleness and deep waters and strength. She was the prettiest woman I'd ever seen. And that was in her work clothes!"

"Grandpa, what does this have to do with school?" Kalmar asked.

"I'm getting to it, lad. Coming here to Chimney Hill to meet Wendolyn's parents was the start of the hardest thing I ever did. Now, I fancied meself handsome. I was proud of me whiskers, me long hair, me tattoos, and even of me stump!" Podo stamped his peg leg on the floor. "I wasn't afraid of anything. But then I met Kargan Igiby. He was as big around as a tree, and his arms were thick as sweetermelons. It was like meeting a kinder, less stinky version of Growlfist the Strander King, only this time I had to prove meself to his daughter. As soon as I walked up the lane and knocked on that front door over there, he flung it open, asked me name, and punched me in the nose so hard I didn't wake up until dinner."

"That's awful!" Leeli said. "What did you do to him?"

"Nothin'. I was an outsider. He said if I even looked in his daughter's direction he'd sock me again. I wasn't afraid, though. I just went to her window and sang me sailor songs until old Kargan woke up and chased me over the hills. Half the time he caught me, and when he did, he whopped me good. I'd wake up in the middle of a field with a bloody nose and a smile on me face. I had me affection set on Wendolyn Igiby, and nothing could change that.

"But I was mighty perplexed. I asked around at the wharf and finally learnt that it didn't do any good to mention the name of Wendolyn Igiby. They'd got word from Kargan Igiby that I wasn't to speak to her. It didn't matter so much with Zola May because she was always flirtin' with the sailors—but with Wendolyn I was an outsider askin' to court a true daughter of the Hollows. That ain't something that happens in these parts. I didn't have a chance with her. Drop it, they said. But I'd see Wendolyn and her dog in town and I'd go mad wanting to talk to her. As soon as I did, I was set upon by whole herds of Hollish men. They'd stop whatever they was doin' and jump on me. I lost seven teeth." Podo proudly showed them his gums.

"As soon as my intentions were known, I couldn't go near Wendolyn without gettin' pounded. After a year—a *year*, mind you—I finally figured out what I had to do to win her hand. I had to compete in the Banick Durga."

"What's that?" Kalmar asked.

"It's a week of poundin', wrestlin', chasin', and hurtin'." Podo winced at the memory. "Every three years the tribes of the Hollows travel to the Field of Finley as they've done for an epoch. Any man fool enough to enter has a chance to be Keeper of the Hollows. That's how Rudric come to be Keeper. Remember how big he is? He got the job because he won the Banick Durga. And that's what I set out to do."

Podo paused and puffed on his pipe, enjoying the surprise on his grand-children's faces. "That's right. I signed up. What few friends I had told me I'd better back out if I wanted to live. They weren't threatening me, mind ye—they were worried about me. But I figured the only way I could show me deep love for Wendolyn was to compete, and if I died tryin', well, that was fine with me. I loved her."

"Mother tried to stop him too," Nia said. "She came to his window one night and begged him not to go through with it. She said she would marry him and run away with him."

"But I wouldn't hear of it," Podo said. "I was done running."

Oskar had left the table and joined the children on the carpet without Janner noticing. "What happened next?" he asked. He lay on his pillowy stomach, looking up at Podo like a bald toddler. "In the words of Fripsky von Chiggatron, 'Do tell!'"

"I traveled to the Field of Finley. Alone. I set up me tent and waited for the whistleharp to signal the start of the games, praying to the Maker for strength and a sure and steady hand. But also for endurance. I didn't think I could lick a single one of these giant, fruit-happy Hollish fighters, but I could *endure*. That's something that don't take strength of arm but strength of heart, and my love for Wendolyn had given me that."

"Did you win? What happened?" Leeli scooted over and leaned her head on Kalmar's shoulder. Janner thought his brother would squirm away, but he was too interested in the story to care.

"The first games were about speed. They were races. I'm pretty good with me stump, but not that good. I fared pretty bad. The worst of it was, the Hollish don't care much for sportsmanship. If you run a race, you'd better expect to get an elbow in the ribs or a fist to the jaw, and they try to trip ye the whole run. Not just me, either. They punched each other too, and it was all part of the game.

"The second day was about strength. They had barrels of water to lift, logs to throw, wagons to push. I did all right at that, but nothing close to the Hollish brutes. I was makin' a right fool of meself. But the next three days were given to fights. I entered the field with fifty different opponents and lost nearly every fight. But I kept fighting. I could hardly walk I was so tired, but I kept swinging and dodging and getting back up.

"The last day was the toughest. It's about strength, speed, and sneakery too. It's a race to find MacDullogh's boot. Somebody hides it the night before, and the first man to return it to the dais on the Field of Finley wins the day. I hardly slept the night before, partly because me whole body was bruised, and partly because I knew it was me last chance to win the hand of Wendolyn Igiby, me heart's true love.

"I woke at dawn with the rest of the men and waited for the whistle to blow. When it did, fists flew and men bellered just to get a lead on the others, even though no one knew which direction to run. I spent the day limpin' across the countryside as fast as me stump would allow, looking in creeks and under boulders and even in big piles of horse biscuits for that blasted boot. Now and then I'd see another Hollish racer and he'd pile at me just to slow me down, whether I had the boot or not. I'd get back to me feet and traipse on, prayin' with one breath to the Maker that I'd find the boot and with the next that I wouldn't."

"Why pray that you wouldn't?" Janner asked.

"Because findin' the boot was only half the fight. Think how hard it would be to get it clear back to Finley without getting' caught and beaten! Well, the Maker seemed to curse me and bless me both, because I rounded a hill and saw MacDullogh's boot on a stone in the center of a creek. I stood there a minute, waiting for some burly fellow to tackle me, but there weren't a soul in sight. I whispered Wendolyn's name, snatched that boot, and hoofed it with all my might over the hills to the Field of Finley. When I topped the last rise, I saw the crowds all gathered around the circle of the field. From every direction giant bearded men snorted and raced at me like mad toothy cows, and I tell ye, I would have preferred toothy cows to the wrath about to set down on me. An outsider hasn't won the Banick Durga in a thousand years."

Podo stared at the fire and spoke in a low voice. "I spotted Wendolyn. She was like a white shore to a drownin' sailor. I ran for all me life for that green circle of field in the distance. A stampede of cursin', angry Hollish men followed me like thunder, and they were gaining. I didn't even see the line of sneaky ones who had circled back to ambush whoever showed up with the boot. They came at me from both sides, and more from behind."

Podo leaned back in his chair and took his time relighting his pipe.

"That's all I remember."

"What?" the three children said in unison.

"I didn't win, of course," Podo said with a wink. "They trampled me, snatched the boot, and fought over it for the rest of the day. You'll see at the

Banick Durga in the spring that all the real action happens at that moment, when some poor fool shows up at the finish line with the boot. You can imagine how rough it gets, and how big the fella must be who finally manages to get that boot to the dais. Take Rudric, for example."

"But what about Wendolyn?" Janner asked.

"I woke to her kiss on me lips." Podo closed his eyes with a smile.

The boys covered their faces and groaned. Leeli sighed with bliss.

"I was so tired and battered I could hardly walk, but she pulled me to me feet and put me on her donkey and took me home. Her father, Kargan, came to see me every day, and he became one of me best friends. We married in the bright summer, right there on the front lawn."

The story settled over the room, and Janner's heart was warm. "But, Grandpa," he said after a moment, "what does this have to do with school?"

"Because you'll all have to walk through your own Banick Durga. The Hollish children don't care if you're the Jewels of Anniera. All they know is you're outsiders. It's like that all over Aerwiar, but in the Hollows that kind of mistrust involves more roughness than usual. So be ready. I don't want you startin' a single fight. The only time you're allowed to swing first is in defense of the helpless. So stick together. Understand?"

"Yes sir," Janner said, and the children looked at one another. Kalmar looked worried, and Janner knew he had good reason. If the Hollish folk treated Podo that way, he shuddered to imagine how the children would take to a Grey Fang in their school.

"It's time to go," Nia said.

"You're going to be with me, right?" Kalmar whispered to Janner.

"I'm a Throne Warden," Janner said. "Of course I will."

Janner remembered Artham leaping into the rockroach den in Glipwood Forest, talons cutting through the air, coming to their defense, heedless of his own safety.

Janner gulped. He was scared to death.

17

The Ten Whiskers of Olumphia Groundwich

The ride from Chimney Hill was quiet in the cool of the morning, and a mist hung over the creek in the valley. When they crossed the bridge and turned left onto the main road, Janner shivered with anticipation, excitement, and anxiety. Kalmar and Leeli sat with him in the carriage without speaking. Podo had stayed behind and waved from the lawn along with Bonifer and Oskar.

"Where's the school?" Janner asked as they crested the hill and Ban Rona spread out before them.

"There," Nia said. "Beyond the field next to the Keep. See it?"

Kalmar, Leeli, and Janner huddled together and squinted in the direction Nia pointed. A rectangular lawn lay flat and green, its borders marked with flagpoles. Next to the field was a cluster of stone buildings. Janner didn't know what he expected—a castle with turrets and secret staircases? From this distance it was hard to see much, but it was still disappointing. Leeli and Kalmar "hmmphed" and settled back for the ride.

"It's where I went to school, and your grandmother too," Nia said.

"Will it be like our studies back in Glipwood?" Janner asked. "T.H.A.G.S., I mean."

"No. You'll study your T.H.A.G.S. in addition to your schooling here."

"What?" Kalmar groaned. "Do the other kids have to study T.H.A.G.S. at home too?"

"No. But the other kids aren't the Jewels of Anniera," Nia answered. "I have a feeling you'll be begging me for T.H.A.G.S. by this afternoon." Janner, Kalmar, and Leeli looked at one another nervously. "In the Hollows you'll each choose a guild. That's where you'll spend most of your time. In the morning, you'll be together at lectures, where you'll learn history and puzzles and fruitery. Then you'll move outside and learn punching—"

"Punching?" Kalmar asked, perking up.

"Yes. Punching. There'll probably be a kicking class too. All in preparation for the Finnick Durga in the spring."

"What's that?" Kalmar asked.

"The Finnick Durga is like the Banick Durga, only for guildlings. It's a full day of races and wrestling."

Janner and Kalmar grinned at each other.

Leeli groaned. "Do I have to?"

"No, dear. Womenfolk don't have to if they don't want to, though many do. Neither do the boys, for that matter, but it's unusual for a boy in the Hollows to opt out of it. Even the slightest young fellows enjoy a good tackle and smash. It's in the Hollish blood. But you'll have something else to do, if I can work it out. It'll be something you'll enjoy especially."

"What is it?" Leeli climbed over the bench and squirmed between Janner and Nia.

"You'll see. I need to make arrangements before I know for sure."

"What are guilds? How big are the classes?" Janner asked.

Nia laughed. "You'll see in just a few minutes. Now hush and enjoy the scenery. And pay no mind to these Hollish buffoons who peek through window shades and scurry like ridgerunners."

She shook the reins and urged the horses to a trot. They rode down into Ban Rona, among homes and businesses where the townspeople either studiously ignored the Wingfeathers or stared at Kalmar outright. After they passed through the busy streets, Nia drove the carriage through the shade cast by the great tree of the Keep.

Janner stared at the roofline where he had last seen Artham. He wondered where his uncle was. Had he found a boat to sail back across the Dark

Sea, or had he tried to fly the whole way? That seemed impossible, but in the last few months he had learned that *impossible* was a word that had little meaning.

The carriage followed the lane past the rectangular field and through a gate, over which a wrought-iron sign hung. It read THE GUILDLING HALL AND INSTITUTE FOR HOLLISH LEARNING. The wagon rolled past the gates and into a cobbled courtyard, which held a statue of a man mounted on a warhorse, holding his sword high. Beyond the statue stood a large stone building joined to several others by covered walkways. The buildings looked strong enough to last a thousand years, and the lichen and vine creeping up the walls suggested that they already had.

It seemed a pleasant enough place—more interesting than it had looked from a distance—but Janner was unsettled by its strange silence. It wasn't a dead silence, like the kind he felt at Anklejelly Manor or in the old Glipwood Cemetery, and it wasn't the lonely silence of a prairie or an empty house; it was a living, waiting silence, as if he had just rounded a tree in Glipwood Forest and encountered a sleeping bomnubble.

"Where is everybody?" Leeli asked.

"In class. Down you go," Nia said. "We need to speak to the head guild-master."

Janner wanted to ask what a head guildmaster was, but he figured he would know soon enough.

The three children were as skittish as thwaps in Podo's garden as Nia marched up the steps and knocked three times on the main door. It swung open immediately, and before them stood a tall, hideous woman in boots and a blue dress. The sleeves were too short, so her knobby wrists and half of her forearms stuck out past the frills. Her hair was pulled back in a bun, which made her heavy brow and jaw seem even bigger. She frowned at them with a face that boasted exactly ten curly whiskers: two sprouting from her chin, six on her upper lip, one jutting out from the center of her nose, and one on her left cheek. Janner felt bad for counting them.

"Oy! Nia Igiby Wingfeather!" the woman barked. Her voice was somehow shrill and husky at the same time. "I was expecting you. Follow." She spun around and clomped away.

Nia gave the children a surprised look and led them into the school. The floors and walls were polished stone, lit by lamps that hung from the arched ceiling. Paintings, tapestries, and framed poems hung on the walls between the many doors they passed. Behind some of the doors Janner could hear muted voices of teachers holding forth, while behind others he heard clanking, shouting, and hammering.

The ten-whiskered woman stopped and held open a door labeled HEAD GUILDMADAM. Nia thanked her with a nod and herded the children through. The room was furnished with a small desk and several chairs. A big brown dog snored on a blanket in the corner. Nia gestured for the children to sit and waited until the whiskery dame closed the door and sat at the desk.

"I figure you don't remember me," the woman said with a scowl. "I figure you're Nia Igiby who up and married a king and left the Hollows. I figure you're bringing your three pups here for a proper Hollish education. I figure you think you're *somebody* now, don't you?"

"I do, as a matter of fact," said Nia. "And I think you're somebody too."

"Oy? Then who, your highness? Who is the woman who sits before you?" The woman leaned back in her chair and folded her arms. She stared at Nia and frowned with great effort, which caused the six whiskers on her upper lip and the two on her chin to flick about like the antennae of a bug.

"Children," Nia said, still looking the woman in the eye, "I'd like you to meet the guildmadam. Guildmadam Groundwich. I knew her many years ago as Olumphia Groundwich, the Terror of Swainsby Road."

Janner's skin went cold. He was expecting the students at the school to be a challenge, but he had assumed that, like his own guardians, the adults there would at least be pleasant, even if they were firm. But this woman looked more than firm and far less than pleasant. She looked scary.

"I recall many an afternoon when children shook in their shirts as they passed Swainsby Road," Nia continued. "They took dares to dash past the row of houses between Seaway and Apple Vale, afraid they'd be pelted with dog droppings or dornuts or chased by mad dogs. But what they were really afraid of was Olumphia Groundwich. Isn't that right?"

"Oy!" said Olumphia Groundwich, and she narrowed one eye. "Your mother knows me well. So well, in fact, that she had another name for me. Didn't you, Nia Igiby? You called me something that no one else dared to call me."

"I did," Nia said after a pause.

"Tell them." Mistress Groundwich scratched at a whisker and waved her hand. "Tell them now so we can be done with it."

Janner prayed that whatever name Nia called her wouldn't lead to a fight right there in the guildmadam's office. He desperately wanted to be on this woman's good side, though he doubted she *had* a good side.

"I called you friend," Nia said with a smile. "My *best* friend."

"Oy!" Mistress Groundwich said. She leapt to her feet and towered over them. "Oy!" she said again. It startled all three Wingfeather children, who nearly jumped out of their seats.

Nia embraced Olumphia, who lifted Nia off her feet and made a noise like a growl, at which point the big dog in the corner woke and thumped its tail. Nia looked like one of the children being swung around in one of Podo's hugs.

"Nia, my heart is full of joy at seeing you again. I just knew you'd been killed or imprisoned or . . . or . . . *Fanged*." She shot a glance at Kalmar and continued. "But you didn't! You came back! And with children!"

"It's good to see you, Olumphia," Nia said, laughing. "And head guild-madam! By the hills and the hollows, I'm impressed! You hated school."

"I'm as surprised as you are. Never thought anyone would call *me* guild-madam. I'm even more surprised that I love it. I always wondered why the Maker made me so tall and lanky, and why he gave me these rogue whiskers. Used to pluck them out every other day, but I found the students more terri-fied of me with them than without. I don't have a husband—yet—so what do I care?"

"Finding a man might be trickier with whiskers," Nia said.

"Oy! Hadn't thought of that." Olumphia plucked out one of the whiskers. Janner cringed. Olumphia blinked away the water that sprang to her eyes and chuckled. "There! I'll find me a Hollish prince in no time. The blasted thing will be back by tomorrow evening, though." Olumphia held up the whisker and inspected it with a frown.

"I've come to enroll the children in school," said Nia. "We haven't had time to talk about guilds yet, so I thought you might explain the way we do things in the Green Hollows." Nia turned to the children. "Guildmadam Groundwich, this is—"

Olumphia flicked the whisker aside and silenced Nia with a wave of the hand, then advanced on the children. She towered over them with her hands on her hips.

"Up! Stand up so I can see you." The three children stood at attention while Olumphia Groundwich studied them each in turn.

She grabbed Janner's chin and turned his head left and right, saying, "Oy, oy." Then she squeezed his arms, appraising his muscles. He flexed so she'd be impressed, but she shook her head and said, "Oh, dear, dear." When she was finished, she took a step back and folded her arms. "Your name, young man?"

"Janner Igiby. Er, Janner Wingfeather."

"Well, which is it?"

"I guess it's both."

"You guess."

"Yes ma'am. I only found out I was a Wingfeather this summer. So I feel like I'm mostly Igiby."

She dismissed him with a grunt and moved on to Leeli. "Your name, young lady."

"Leeli Igiby Wingfeather."

"Very good, very good. And what is this?" The headmistress indicated Leeli's crutch.

"My leg doesn't work quite right."

"Fangs, I suppose. Yes?" Olumphia looked at Nia, who nodded.

"And you," she said to Kalmar, narrowing her eyes. She leaned close to his face and sniffed. "What are *you*? A dog?"

Janner moved to Kalmar's side and clenched his fists. He didn't care if the woman was ten feet tall, she couldn't call his brother a dog. Leeli hopped a step closer to Kalmar and pointed her chin at the woman. Kalmar stared at Olumphia with an unreadable face. No ear twitched and no muscle flinched. Janner wondered what was going on in his little brother's mind. What was the guildmadam doing? It seemed there was no end to the meanness of the Hollowsfolk.

"Olumphia, I'll not have you speak to my son that way." Nia's voice was steady, and Janner heard an edge of anger in it.

"I'm not a dog," Kalmar said. "My name is Kalmar. Kalmar *Wing-feather*."

Olumphia Groundwich held his eyes for a spell, and finally nodded. "I'm sorry, lad. I meant no offense. Nor to you, Nia. I wanted to see how he would react. And I wanted to see how his brother and sister reacted. Well done, children." She patted Kalmar's shoulder and didn't seem to notice the way he squirmed away.

"Why?" Janner demanded.

"Because you can expect that the students here will call him worse."

"Can't you do something about it?" Nia asked. "Can't you discipline them?"

"I'll do what I can. I'll make sure the other guildmasters do as well. But to be honest, they may be a problem too. At least in the beginning." She turned to Kalmar. "I was treated like I was a beast when I was a girl. Your mother here was one of the few people who were kind to me. I know how you must feel—"

Kalmar stiffened and started to speak, but she cut him off.

"I don't mean I know *exactly* how you feel. I know your situation is unique. But I can relate to your fear, your anger, and your frustration. I can even relate to your whiskers." She winked at him, and Kalmar smiled. "So listen to me closely, Kalmar Wingfeather. You'll need to be tough. Tougher than you've ever been."

"He's already pretty tough," Leeli said. The dog in the corner had crossed the room and sat beside Leeli with his head against her shoulder. "He usually wins when he wrestles Janner."

"No, he doesn't," Janner said under his breath.

"I mean a different kind of tough, Leeli. Wrestling is what I *don't* want him to do. He's going to have to bear up when they throw their words, and you're going to have to bear up with him. It's the only way this will work. There will be time to punch in punching class. Outside of that, you must give them no reason to fight you. Understand, Kalmar?"

"Yes ma'am." Kalmar nodded.

"Now. Let's talk about classes. Do any of you know which guild you'd like to start with?"

The children looked at Nia uncertainly.

"I was hoping you might show them around," Nia said. "Let them see what they're getting into."

"Oy. We'll start in the Guildling Hall. Leeli, you're welcome to bring Brimstone with you. She seems to like you."

They followed Guildmadam Groundwich out of the office and down the long hallway. Nia walked beside her, and they reminisced about their school days. Olumphia's lanky gait looked especially strange next to Nia's queenly grace, but it was easy to imagine the two as girls roaming the streets of Ban Rona. They stopped at the end of the hallway before a set of wooden doors.

"Ready?" Guildmadam Groundwich asked the children, and without waiting for an answer she swung open the doors.

Janner saw the backs of a hundred heads, all facing a man on a platform at the front of the room. The hall was crowded with children of all shapes, sizes, and ages. They sat on furs spread on the stone floor, just as the adults had sat on the floor of the Keep at the council.

The man on the platform, who held a green apple in his hand, stopped talking when he saw them. Every head in the room turned, and every eye fell on Janner, Kalmar, and Leeli.

The silence was thick with fear—Janner and his siblings' fear and the fear of a hundred Hollish children.

It hung in the hall like smoke.

18

The Further Fate of Sara Cobbler

Smoke filled the Fork Factory. It was always smoky there, but one of the pipes on the furnace had ruptured, and the children—the tools, as the Overseer called them—scrambled to repair it while black smoke spewed into the chamber.

Sara Cobbler covered her face with the front of her shirt and crawled under tables cluttered with shards of metal, past carts laden with coal and stone, around barrels of swords, forks, daggers, and arrowheads, dodging the feet of other children who were either running toward the broken pipe to repair it or away from it as Sara was doing.

Tears streaked her sooty face. She was trying to reach the bunkroom so she could lie down and rest for the first time in more than a day. Maybe the chaos created by the broken pipe would provide enough distraction that she could slip away unnoticed. If they caught her, she'd be punished—probably with even more work and less sleep, and she might be thrown into that horrible coffin again—but she didn't care. She was so tired that even ten minutes of sleep was worth the risk.

Through the smoke and the red glow of the furnace she saw the door to the dining hall just a stone's toss away. She looked left and right to be sure that none of the Maintenance Managers were watching, and then she mustered the last of her energy and sprinted to the door.

"Where are you going?" asked a flat, gravelly voice.

She skidded to a halt at the door and hung her head.

Crack! A whip snapped beside her face, and her ears rang. "Turn around, tool."

Sara Cobbler turned and beheld a short man in a black, tattered suit. A bent top hat slumped on his head, and he grinned at her with yellow teeth while he coiled his whip. He wore fingerless gloves. Behind him the smoke roiled and children ran to and fro, fetching tools and lengths of pipe and buckets of water to cool the metal they had to handle.

"You again," the Overseer said. "You're the one who helped that boy escape. What was his name?"

"Jan—"

"Wrong! He had no name. And neither do you. You have been abandoned by the Maker—if there is one—and left to me to use for my own ends.
Get back to work."

Sara sighed and tried to take a step toward the filing station where she'd
been working since the night before. But her feet didn't obey. She had been
standing for more hours than she could count and had used the last of her
strength to run for the door. She crumpled to the ground and lay there, unable to get back up.

"Tool!" the Overseer cried, grinding his crooked teeth. His eyes were
wild and wheeling with madness. He cracked the whip again, this time so
close that it rustled Sara's hair. The Overseer limped forward and howled at
her, cracking the whip again and again, seeming to enjoy the fact that the

other children in the factory had stopped whatever they were doing to watch his fury.

Sara lay in the ashes, staring through the strands of her hair at a furnace grate, imagining it was a fireplace in a house like the one she had grown up in. She ignored the Overseer and his cruel whip and floated in the music of memory: her mother singing her to sleep, her father whistling in the barn, and the sad cry of Janner Igiby calling her name while he rode out of the Fork Factory and into the torchlit streets of Dugtown. He had reached for her. Pleaded with her. His hand had been just inches from hers as he begged her to join him. Oh, how she wished she had found the courage to follow.

Crack! went the whip, and the fire was no longer in a cottage but in the red maw of the furnace grate. Janner was gone and with him all hope for— anything. Sara felt the Overseer's grip as he dragged her, dimly saw the dull eyes of the children watching her pass, and heard as if from a great distance the Overseer's voice: "Another day in the coffin for you, tool."

Good, she thought. She would finally be able to sleep.

19

A Tour of the Guildling Hall

H ead Guildmadam Groundwich!" said the man at the front of the room. "Whom have you brought to visit?"

"Good morning, Guildmaster Fahoon." Olumphia smiled, and then as quick as the turn of a page she scowled at the students. They all winced as if she had looked each of them in the eye at the same time. Her whiskers trembled like little snakes about to strike. "I came to introduce you and the guildlings to our three new students. They're the children of Nia Igiby Wingfeather, who happens to be the Queen of Anniera." She paused. "I *said,* she's the Queen of Anniera!"

Fahoon jumped and dropped the apple. "Sorry, guildmadam. It's unusual for us to have guests of such station. Guildlings! Rise and bow."

The children did so, and Nia motioned for them to sit.

"The eldest son is Janner, the daughter is Leeli, and the one who *looks* like a Grey Fang is, in fact, Kalmar Wingfeather, who is, in fact, the High King, since his father fell to the Fangs many years ago. Oy!" Again, Guildmadam Groundwich paused. When the students didn't move, she lowered her voice to a frightening tone. *"Rise. And. Bow."*

The students scrambled to their feet and bowed again, and Janner could hear whispers among them. Kalmar stared at the floor and flattened his ears. Nia nudged Kalmar, and he said, "Thank you." His growly voice carried through the hall. "You may, uh, sit."

The whispers rose in volume as the children settled on the floor again.

"Proceed," said Olumphia after another long glare, and she closed the door.

The tension vanished when they were cut off from the hall, and Janner's shoulders slumped with relief.

"There. That went better than I expected." Groundwich smiled at the children and led them out the door and down a covered walkway, Brimstone padding happily beside Leeli.

Vines wrapped around the columns and clung to the roof; grapes dangled like dollops of candy everywhere they turned. Olumphia plucked a few as she passed and told the children they were welcome to snack as well.

"Leeli, you're going to like this," said Olumphia. "Brimstone, as you can see, is already excited about it."

The dog barked and bolted ahead of them to the next stone building. The shingle hanging over the door was carved with the silhouette of a dog; HOUNDRY, it read. Brimstone wagged her tail and pawed at the entrance.

Olumphia pushed open the heavy door, and a chorus of barks, whines, and howls poured out. With the noise came the smell of dog and hay, tinged with the odor of animal waste. Kalmar winced and covered his face, but Leeli's eyes widened. She looked at Nia in disbelief. Guildmadam Groundwich's dog bolted through the door, and Leeli hurried after.

The inside of the chamber was as full of dogs as the Guildling Hall was full of children. But unlike the students, the dogs were glad to see them. They barked happy barks and circled the Wingfeathers, wagging tails and sniffing at boots and whining to be petted. Leeli dropped her crutch and hugged the first dog that approached her. It put a paw as big as a saucer on her shoulder and panted in her face. Another dog nosed his way under her other arm, and she stood supported between them, smiling so wide that her face turned pink. Then the dogs trotted forward and dragged her along. Leeli squealed with delight as they paraded her around the room, pursued by a train of barking dogs, most of which were as tall as Leeli.

Janner and Kalmar laughed. It was as if the Maker had prepared a place just for their sister. Guildmadam Groundwich and Nia left Leeli to her glory and led the boys across the room to the office door.

"Hello? Biggin?" Groundwich knocked on the door as she opened it. "Biggin O'Sally?"

"Biggin's gone. Just us." A boy swaggered into the doorway and leaned against it as if he didn't have a care in the world. He wore a white shirt without sleeves, and his pants were held up with suspenders. He tilted his head a little so the lock of his long black hair that wasn't slicked back didn't cover his eyes. A strip of dried meat hung from his mouth, and he chewed it as he observed the visitors without even a nod of greeting.

"Who is it?" came another boy's voice.

"Head Guildmadam Groundwich and some others. One's a furry kid."

The way he said it didn't bother Janner for some reason. The boy was stating a fact, not hurling an insult. Kalmar didn't seem bothered by it, either.

"I wanna see." Another boy, a little taller but dressed the same, with the same slick hair and unimpressed expression, appeared at the door and looked Kalmar over. "Oy. He's furry," he said, and then he went back to whatever he had been doing.

"These are the O'Sally boys," said Olumphia. "Where are the others?" She craned her neck to look inside.

"With Pa. Training. Out back." The first boy sniffed and swallowed a chunk of meat.

"You can tell him, then," said the guildmadam. "He has a new student. I won't hear any complaint about it. Her name is Leeli Wingfeather, and I wager she'll know dogspeak better than either of you by the end of the week."

"No, she won't," said the boy with a hint of a shrug. "Nobody can train better than me and my brothers. Not even Pa, though he won't admit it. Don't mean any disrespect, ma'am."

"I took none, Thorn. But you're wrong."

"That's always possible, ma'am." Thorn took another bite of meat and looked past them at Leeli for the first time. She sat on a bale of hay, scratching a gray horse of a dog behind the ears and singing to it. Behind the gray dog, a dozen more stood patiently in line, as though waiting their turn. "Very possible," said Thorn with a nod of surprise.

A herd of puppies swarmed into the room on the heels of a skinny man with a beard so long he tucked it into his belt.

"There's Pa," said Thorn with a lift of his chin, though it was obvious who the man was. He swaggered just like his sons, wore the same kind of sleeveless shirt and suspenders, and even slicked back his black hair.

The man leaned against the door and nodded at the guildmadam. "Ma'am," he said.

"Guildmaster O'Sally. I'd like you to meet the High Queen of Anniera and her children."

O'Sally bowed without question and stayed there until Nia released him. "Your highness," he said. "It's my honor. Welcome to the houndry."

"My daughter, Leeli, is to be your new charge," Nia said. "She'll work hard and do as she's told. I don't want you treating her differently than any other nine-year-old student. If that means she has to take her turn shoveling waste, then so be it. But don't treat her worse, either."

Leeli had recovered her crutch and joined them.

"Oy." O'Sally smiled at Leeli. "It'll be good to have a girl around. I'll put her in charge of the puppies. I've twelve this week that need tending. How does that suit you?"

Leeli's mouth hung open. She tried to say something but instead crumpled to the floor. She had fainted with joy.

When they had woken her and settled her in the puppy wing of the houndry, Olumphia Groundwich continued the tour with Janner and Kalmar. She showed them the juicery, where the various juices of ermentine, blue grape, apple, and berry were squeezed and mixed and boiled and sweetened and canned. They went from there to the woodwright's cabin where a guildmaster gave them a quick tour of the tools and projects underway. Students were building things like wagons, mallets, bowls, fences, and skullwhackers. Then they visited the rockwright class, the bookbindery (which Janner especially liked), the boatery, the cookery (which Kalmar especially liked), and the needlery, where one learned to make dresses and quilts (which both boys especially *dis*liked).

"Your father loved to sail, or so I've heard," Olumphia said. "I'd show you the sailery, but it's held at the waterfront and is reserved for our oldest students. Maybe in a few years. There's one more thing to show you. Come."

Olumphia walked them up stairs that led to the roof of the main building. From there they could see the field between the Keep and the school. The field had been empty that morning when they first arrived, but now it was crowded with children. Some were running laps, while others leapt over barrels. Some had as many as ten dogs harnessed to small wooden chariots and were racing one another down the length of the field. Another group stood in line before an instructor who appeared to be teaching them how to punch, while the opposing line was learning how to block. A whistle blew. The punchers punched, the blockers blocked, and those who got it wrong got a fat lip or a black eye. The guildmasters broke them up and repeated the drill.

Janner was suddenly unsure that he wanted to go to school. Wrestling Kalmar was one thing; fistfighting a school full of students who hated them was another.

"Do we have to do that?" he asked.

"You don't *have* to," said Guildmadam Groundwich. "But it's either that or the needlery."

Janner sighed.

"What's the matter?" Kalmar asked, jabbing Janner in the ribs. "Afraid you'll have to fight me?"

"Don't look so happy." Janner smacked Kalmar's hand away. "Those kids are bigger than you, and they'd love to punch a Grey Fang in the face."

"Ah. They're too slow."

"We'll see," Janner said. He dreaded the class, but he was glad Kalmar seemed like his usual scrappy self. Janner hoped he would stay that way. He couldn't read Kal's face anymore, so it troubled him when his brother was quiet. Deep down he feared that one day Kalmar would look at him with eyes that were no longer blue but yellow and wild. If a punching class kept the quiet Kalmar away, then fine. Janner was willing to take a punch in the face.

Somewhere a horn blew. The runners and racers and blockers and wrestlers on the field cheered and ran toward a long, low building.

"That's the horn for lunch," said the guildmadam. "The tour's over. Where would you boys like to begin? In the morning you'll have two hours in Lectures and Learning, followed by two hours on the field. After lunch you'll spend the rest of the afternoon in your chosen guild."

"Bookbindery," said Janner. His first choice would have been the sailery, but he was happy to wait till he was older if it meant he could spend his afternoons with books.

Kalmar hesitated.

"Son?" Nia said.

"Me too." He smiled at Janner. "Bookbindery. I want to go where Janner goes. If that's all right."

"No, it isn't." Nia assumed her motherly, no-nonsense tone. "I think we both know you don't care a squawk about bookbinding. You're going to have to choose something you're truly interested in or the guildmaster will make you miserable. They can tell when you're wasting their time. What do you *want* to do?"

"Well," he said, casting a glance at the field, "can I do that stuff? The racing and the—the punching?"

"There's plenty of time for that during field training," said Nia. "Two hours before lunch every day. You need to choose a guild, something that will put your skills to good use."

"But I don't have any skills. Not like Janner. Is there a drawing guild?"

"No, but your T.H.A.G.S. training will be to your advantage in any number of guilds—like the woodwrightery."

Kalmar didn't look excited about wood.

"What are your skills, boy?" Olumphia said, growing impatient. "You must be good at something."

"I'm fast. I can shoot a bow."

Kalmar *was* fast. And he could outshoot Janner and Podo both at archery. Janner had a hard time imagining his little brother sitting still long enough to enjoy binding a book or building a wagon.

"There *is* another option," Olumphia said thoughtfully, appraising Kalmar from head to foot in a new light.

"No," Nia said. "He's too young."

"I'm the head guildmadam, remember? I can make arrangements. They'll allow it if I approve."

"That's not what I mean, Olumphia. He's going to have a hard enough time with students his own age. They'll all be older." Nia took Olumphia's elbow and gave her a firm look. "And meaner."

Guildmadam Groundwich ignored her and bent low to look Kalmar in the eye. "Lad, there's a guild like the one you're asking about. But it's usually reserved for older students. How old are you?"

"Eleven."

"You'll be in a class with thirteen-year-olds. Boys and girls two feet taller than you. Are you sure?"

Kalmar didn't look sure, but he said, "Yes ma'am."

"Kalmar, you'll be hurt," Nia said.

"If what Grandpa says is true, I'm going to get hurt anyway, right?"

Nia had no answer, so Olumphia spoke.

"Oy. You're going to get hurt. But at least this way you'll know how to defend yourself. You'll learn to sneak too. The Durgan Guild is for spies and fighters. If your mother will allow it, I'll allow it."

Kalmar implored Nia with his eyes.

Finally, Nia sighed and said, "Fine."

Kalmar let out a yip of excitement.

Janner thought he was out of his mind. Hollish children were tall and strong and used to fighting. Two hours on the field every day was going to be scary enough.

Bookbinding, on the other hand, sounded wonderful. Besides, the children who chose bookbinding as a guild would probably be readers and book lovers too, which meant that for the first time Janner would have someone to talk to about books (someone other than Oskar N. Reteep, anyway). The thought came to Janner for the first time since they had arrived in the Green Hollows that he might make friends—*real* friends, not like the Blaggus boys in Glipwood, who were only good for a laugh and a game of zibzy. Friends he could read with and write with and talk with, friends he would still know when he was a grownup, like Nia and Olumphia, or Podo and Buzzard Willie. Janner couldn't wait for bookbinding.

"You may join the Durgan Guild," Nia said, holding up a finger. "But on one condition." She looked at Janner.

Janner looked back for a moment, uncomprehending. Then his eyes widened and an angry heat rose in his chest. He took a step back. "You can't be serious."

Nia didn't look surprised at his outburst.

Janner wheeled on Kalmar. "Why couldn't you just pick a normal guild? What's so wrong with the juicery? Or the cookery! You could eat all day and never get punched *once*!"

"I didn't mean to—"

"You never mean to." Janner folded his arms and turned away.

"Janner, listen," Nia said gently, "the more I think about it, the more I think Olumphia's right. It would be good for your brother to be in the Durgan Guild. If he's going to earn the respect and trust of the Hollish people, this might be the best way to do it."

"But why does it always feel like the world spins around *him*?" Janner was aware that he was throwing a fit and making a fool of himself, but he didn't care. "Why can't he go off and get beaten up without me?"

"Because he's going to need you. If he were in the cookery, he'd be fine. But the Durgan Guild is another matter."

"What about *me*?" Janner jabbed his own chest and glared at his mother.

"You're the Throne Warden," she said.

Janner rolled his eyes. He didn't want to be the Throne Warden right now. He wanted to be a kid with a book under a tree or on a boat in the harbor. He wanted to stomp down the stairs and run till he couldn't run anymore. And he *didn't* want to learn to fight, especially if it meant being thrown into a class of cruel thirteen-year-olds. He had had enough of fighting in the Fork Factory.

"But I don't want to be the Throne Warden," Janner said with all the bitterness he could muster.

"I understand," Nia said. Janner had planned to send her over the edge with that comment, but she didn't seem surprised. "Sometimes I don't want to be the queen. But what I want doesn't change what I am. You're the Throne Warden. I'm your mother. Kalmar is your brother. All your anger can't change those facts."

"Janner, I don't mind the bookbindery," Kalmar said. "Or the cookery. I'd love to learn to cook. Let's just forget the whole Durgan Guild thing."

Janner stared into the distance and clenched his jaw.

He tried not to, but he couldn't help picturing Uncle Artham looking down at him with disappointment. Janner hated to admit it, but he knew the right thing was to protect his brother—not just from the students at the Guildling Hall but from Fangs and bomnubbles and even Gnag the Nameless—and learning to be a warrior spy was sure to be a bigger help than learning to cook or bind books.

Janner's heart was still hard and hot, but he sighed and said, "Fine."

Olumphia cleared her throat. "Oy! I'm glad that's all worked out. Let's eat."

20

The Durgan Guild

The Jewels of Anniera sat at a table with their mother and Guildmadam Groundwich and ate a lunch of smoked henmeat on brown bread. The hall was long with a low ceiling and many windows. A table at the front bore several platters of henmeat along with totatoes and apples, and beside the platters were piles of crispy loaves of bread.

The line of guildlings had dwindled to just a few by the time the Wing-feathers arrived, which meant that everyone in the room watched them enter, get their food, and follow Guildmadam Groundwich to an empty table. Thorn O'Sally had already brought Leeli from the houndry and even got her a plate of food before swaggering off to eat with his friends.

Janner was so irritated he hardly noticed the students watching his brother's every move. Nia and Olumphia chattered about old times while the children ate in silence. Leeli could tell Janner was upset, so she restrained her glee about the houndry.

When the plates were clean and a horn blew, the students filed out of the dining hall and went to their guilds. Nia hugged each of the children, told them she'd pick them up in a few hours, and left. Head Guildmadam Groundwich turned to them and smiled. Janner tried to convince himself that nothing bad was going to happen.

"Well, my new guildlings," Olumphia said, wiping the crumbs from the whiskers around her mouth, "the time has come."

She led them back toward the houndry in silence.

"Leeli, Guildmaster O'Sally is expecting you for your first afternoon in the Houndry Guild," Olumphia said as they approached the door. "You'll be here for the rest of the day with a class full of guildlings. I've asked O'Sally to keep watch over you, especially in the beginning. I think you'll like him. Biggin and his boys are strange, but they know dogs better than anyone in the city. Do as he says. Call him 'Guildmaster O'Sally' until he tells you otherwise. Questions?"

Leeli shook her head and took a deep breath. She smiled at Janner and Kalmar, but Janner could tell she was nervous. He wanted to tell her to cheer up—at least *she* wasn't about to get a pounding—but he changed his mind.

"You'll be fine," Janner told her, and he gave her a quick hug. "We'll see you in a little while."

Kalmar squeezed her arm and smiled, and then Leeli stepped into the houndry. She was greeted by so many dogs that she nearly fell over. The door closed on the sound of her laughter.

The guildmadam was already striding away, and the boys ran to catch up. They followed a walkway to the edge of a flagstone courtyard, where she stopped and held out a hand for silence. Janner counted fourteen students sitting in a circle in the center of the yard, watching two other students as they tumbled about on the ground in vicious combat. A man sat among the students in the circle, pointing at the wrestlers and speaking from time to time.

"This," Olumphia said in a voice just above a whisper, "is the Durgan Guild. It's the oldest of the Hollish guilds, named after Connolin Durga. Oy!" She gave the boys a meaningful look as if they should know who Connolin Durga was, but all she got were blank stares. "Pah. You mean to tell me your mother didn't teach you any Hollish history? Well. You saw the statue in the courtyard, didn't you? The man on the horse was Connolin Durga, one of the great warriors of our land. He drove out the ridgerunners in the Second Epoch when they invaded and set fire to the Outer Vales. They infested the Hollows like groaches, creeping into homes and barns at night to burn them and scare us away. The house fires lit the trees, and a hundred miles of orchards were consumed. Whole acres of fruit, gone! Fruit!" She looked at the boys again to be sure they appreciated the gravity of the loss.

They pretended to be shocked, and she continued: "Connolin Durga was the only chief cunning enough to muster us in the chaos to defeat the ridgerunners and their allies. The Banick Durga is named after him, as is the Finnick Durga. The Durgan Guild is a fellowship of warriors and spies."

"Spies?" Kalmar whispered.

"Oy. For as long as we can remember, the ridgerunners have crept into our borders to steal fruit and animals and tools—but mainly fruit, the little swipers. They love it, and who can blame them? We actually do a bit of trading with them, under the strictest protocols, of course, and only at the border. But it seems there's no end to their appetite for sneakery. Our Durgans counter their efforts. Now, of course, it's more than ridgerunners we fight. It's Fangs and the cloven too."

As annoyed as Janner had been, he was warming to the idea of creeping through the forests with a company of fellow watchmen, sending signals by the light of the moon and chasing ridgerunners over hill and vale.

"That's Guildmaster Clout." Olumphia sniffed. "He's a despicable man. Arrogant, short tempered, and rude." She glared at him for a moment and muttered, "I'd marry the old rotbag faster than I could pluck a whisker. But he acts like I don't exist. Despicable man."

The guildmadam scratched at her bony jaw with one hand and twirled a lock of hair in the other. Janner imagined her as a young girl, lanky and outcast, spying on her more popular classmates from behind a hedgerow.

"Despicable or not, he's the finest guildmaster of Durgan technique I've ever seen. He'll evaluate you for two months, and if you can pass muster, you're in. You boys clear on that? Good."

Olumphia straightened and tugged at her sleeves as if to conceal her knobby wrists. She held her breath, plucked another whisker, flicked it into the bushes, and loped into the courtyard just as one of the two students in the ring got socked in the face by the other. The girl who got hit spun around once and crumpled to the ground. Olumphia crossed the courtyard with her hand extended, stepping over the groaning student without a glance.

When Janner and Kalmar approached the circle, the guildlings backed away and flanked the guildmaster, none of them bothering to conceal the look of disgust on their faces. They scowled at Kalmar and looked ready to pounce on him.

Janner felt his arms and shoulders tingle at the clear sense of danger. The last time he had felt his skin prickle like that was when the snickbuzzards swooped down at him and Maraly on the snowy peak of the Witch's Nose. It took effort to stand his ground and not grab Kalmar and run.

"Guildmadam Groundwich," said the man in a menacing voice. "It doesn't do to interrupt the Durgan Guild. We've spoken about this before. I require privacy and focus."

"Guildmaster Clout." Olumphia's dark tone equaled Clout's, but she seemed even more threatening because she stood at least a hand taller. And she had eight whiskers. "As head guildmadam of this institution I reserve the right to interrupt you as often as I please. If you'd like to have a tackle and smash to sort it out, I'm ready." She pushed up the sleeves of her dress, revealing her knobby elbows, and balled her hands into fists. When the muscles in her forearms flexed, she looked like a furless bomnubble.

"That won't be necessary," said Clout with a glance at his students. Janner suspected he didn't want to lose a fight in front of his guildlings. "What can I do for you, Head Guildmadam Groundwich? I hope you haven't come to enroll this scrawny lad and his pet."

The guildlings snickered. Clout hushed them with a wave of his hand.

"I've come to enroll Janner and Kalmar Wingfeather in the Durgan Guild. Janner is the Throne Warden of Anniera, and Kalmar the High King. Oy, you heard me right."

"But they're not old enough. If they're thirteen years old, I'm a basket of swipple berries. I won't allow it."

"They're eleven and twelve years old, and our long alliance with the Shining Isle demands that we be willing to make an exception."

"They'll be smashed up by the end of every day, guildmadam. I don't wish to incur the wrath of their mother."

"Nor their grandfather again, I'd wager," said Olumphia with a sneer.

"It wasn't a fair fight," snapped the guildmaster. "His peg leg might as well be a weapon."

"I only ask that you evaluate them for two months as you would any other guildling. Oy! I can tell from the older one's scars that he's seen more action than every one of these students. Janner, how many Fangs have you fought?"

"Ma'am? Uh, I don't know." Janner was startled to be introduced into the conversation. "One with a sword, several with arrows. Ten, maybe?"

Olumphia folded her arms and looked pleased at the surprise on the students' faces. "How many Fangs have your guildlings fought?" she asked Clout.

"You know the answer to that, guildmadam."

"How many?"

"None," Guildmaster Clout said through his teeth. "Fine. I'll allow the older one. But not the Fang."

Olumphia took a step nearer to Clout. "I forbid you to call the boy a Fang. I'll admit, he looks it. But his eyes tell the rest of the tale. That's no Fang. It's the High King, and he deserves your respect. Kalmar," she said, still holding Clout's gaze. "How many Fangs have you killed?"

"Twenty-seven," said Kalmar without hesitation. Janner looked at him with surprise. He knew Kalmar had shot a lot of Fangs at Miller's Bridge, but he didn't know he had kept count. Now the guildlings whispered among themselves. Their surprise turned to quiet excitement.

Guildmaster Clout sighed. "I'll evaluate them for two months. But if they're not ready by then, that's the end of it. I won't coddle them just because they're royalty. And you can't meddle. Is that understood?"

"Understood," said Olumphia.

"I wasn't asking *you*," said Clout. He stepped away from Olumphia and towered over the Wingfeather boys. "Is that understood?"

"Yes sir," the brothers said.

"Then it's settled," Olumphia said. "Janner, Kalmar, I'll send your mother to pick you up this afternoon. Guildmaster Clout, they're all yours." She nodded at Clout and loped away.

As soon as she was around the corner of the building and out of sight, Clout said, "Circle up!"

Janner and Kalmar followed as the guildlings created a ring and sat, awaiting further instruction.

"Brosa. Larnik," Clout said. The two biggest boys stood. "Janner and Kalmar, isn't it?"

They nodded and gulped in unison.

"Commence." Guildmaster Clout stepped outside the circle as Brosa and Larnik, with bone-chilling growls, leapt on the Wingfeather boys and let their fists fly.

21

A Late Caller

Janner's jaw hurt. He hadn't actually been punched in the face—Guildmaster Clout had forbidden it since they were newcomers—but the boy named Brosa had driven Janner's head into the ground with his knee. He had been kicked in the stomach by the other boy, Larnik, and had tripped over Kalmar and smashed his elbow. Even his hair hurt because, unfortunately, Clout *hadn't* forbidden hair-pulling, and Brosa had pulled it by the fistful.

Kalmar had fared better but only because Larnik was slower and had a hard time catching him. Even when Larnik managed to pin Kalmar down, he grimaced at the touch of his fur, as if Fangishness was a disease he didn't want to catch.

After fifteen minutes that seemed to Janner like fifteen hours, Guildmaster Clout waved a hand and the two brutes returned to the edge of the circle. Janner and Kalmar lay stunned, groaning, and out of breath in the center of the ring, trying to ignore the snickers of the other guildlings.

Once they picked themselves up, Clout lectured for an hour on the history of the Durgan Patrol between the years 230 and 262, when Ban Hynh had been involved in an illegal fruit-smuggling operation. As soon as Janner and Kalmar had caught their breath, though, Clout had all the guildlings running laps and jump-clapping.

The boys met Leeli at the entrance to the houndry, and Janner limped with his siblings to the statue of Connolin Durga to wait for Nia. In his miserable condition, he moved so slowly that they were the last guildlings to reach the courtyard. Nia greeted Leeli and the boys without any show of pity, which upset Janner all over again.

As they rode back to Chimney Hill in the wagon, Janner's insides felt as dark as the bruises already coloring his arms. For a fleeting moment before the class began, he thought Kalmar had chosen the better guild, but now he felt he had been treated unfairly and he wanted his mother, brother, and sister to know it. He chose to sit on the back bench of the carriage, where he slumped in his seat and pouted, hoping they would notice his silence, and all but dared them to speak to him.

Leeli, of course, was the one to do it. She turned around and said, "Is there anything I can do?"

It was the only thing she could have said that he couldn't answer with anger, which frustrated Janner even more. If she had asked what was wrong, he would have hurled a perfectly sassy reply right back at her. If she had told him to cheer up, he would have grouched something about how cheery he'd be if he had played with puppies all day. If she had tried to be silly to cheer him up, he would have barked that he was sorry he wasn't in the mood for games.

But "Is there anything I can do?" poured cool water on his fire. It told him that she cared. It told him that she saw he needed something, even if she didn't know what. It told him that she hurt with him.

He just said, "No. But thanks."

Kalmar rode beside Nia and showed no sign of being hurt or sore or worried. He pointed at various houses, listened to Nia talk about Ban Rona, asked her questions about her youth, and carried on in quite an unacceptable way, Janner thought, given how upset he himself felt. When Leeli turned to the front again, Janner slumped back into his sulk for the remainder of the ride home.

The carriage crossed the creek bridge and wound up the hill just as the sun shot its last rays across the countryside. Chimney Hill was beautiful, and the sight of it improved Janner's mood. As bad as school had been, the sight of the old stone house with its ingrown tree branches, splashed with sunlight and glowing with welcome, was a balm for Janner's bruises.

Freva emerged from the house with little Bonnie close behind. The maidservant bobbed her head like a bird as she took the reins from Nia, lifted her daughter up into the carriage, and led the horses to the barn.

"Where's her husband?" Kalmar asked.

"He died three years ago, just before Bonnie was born." Nia watched the young woman and her daughter disappear into the barn. "He was an apple salesman, traveling from city to city, when somewhere between Ban Rugan and the Outer Vales he was attacked and killed. By a cloven."

"That's terrible," Leeli said.

"Yes, it is," Nia said, "and it's been very hard on her."

Janner knew she was thinking about Esben.

When they entered the house, it smelled like a feast. Bonifer Squoon, Oskar, and Podo sat around the fire, roaring with laughter, each of them cradling a pipe in one hand and a mug of something warm in the other. Podo seemed to have aged ten years since that morning. He didn't look unhealthy; he just looked his age, like an old man happy to be surrounded by his progeny—not an old sailor fighting every day to stay young enough to carry his family through danger. He was like a setting sun, weaker and fading, but with a fitting beauty. The fire of his days was burning low, and Janner felt happy and sad for him at the same time. Podo cheered when the children entered, raised his mug in a toast, and then returned to his conversation.

"Get cleaned up, then come down for supper," Nia said.

Leeli hopped up the stairs, and Kalmar chased after her, growling like a puppy. Janner turned to follow but Nia pulled him close and squeezed. Somehow, she knew to squeeze just tight enough that Janner felt her love but not so tight that she hurt him.

"You're the bravest boy I know," she whispered. He felt the warmth of her breathing when she spoke. She kissed his head and sent him upstairs.

While he washed himself and changed into his nightclothes, Janner struggled to hold on to his anger but found in the end that he couldn't. He came downstairs to find everyone waiting for him at the long table, which was candlelit and heavy with henmeat biscuit pie.

"My favorite," he said with a smile that was reflected in every other face.

"I know," Nia said.

Over dinner Podo demanded to hear the story behind every bruise on the boys' bodies. He muttered unrepeatable things about Brosa and Larnik, winced at some wounds, and grinned at others. He asked Leeli about the puppies and about the O'Sally boys and roared with laughter when he learned that she had fainted with happiness.

Freva poked her head in from the kitchen. "Yer highness, if everything's set for now, I'll head to the barn and feed the animals. Still have to brush the horses down."

"We're fine, Freva. Thank you," Nia said.

"Come now, Bonnie. Let's leave these nice people to their food." Bonnie peeked over the back of the couch, where she'd been playing with a goat doll.

"She can stay here till you're finished," Nia said. "She's no trouble."

"I'll take care of her!" Leeli said, scooting over to make room on her chair. "Bonnie, come sit with me."

Freva relented and bowed her way out of the room while her daughter crept up to Leeli and leaned her head on her shoulder.

"Janner!" said Oskar, clapping his hands so vigorously that his jowls trembled. "I spent the most splendid day with Bonifer! We visited the library of Ban Rona. You won't believe it, lad. Bookshelves as far as the eye can see, desks where you can sit and work for hours undisturbed, galleries of maps, paintings, and murals—you're going to love it."

"Indeed," said Bonifer. "And there's a librarian who can help you find anything you like."

"If you're not afraid of her stinky eye, that is." Oskar shivered. "She gives me the spookies."

They finished eating and carried the conversation to the hearth, where the adults eased into chairs and the children (including little Bonnie) sat on the rug. It felt like the old days in Glipwood when they used to listen to Podo's tales of the sea—before they knew that their father had been a king, or that their grandfather was hunted by dragons, or that Gnag the Nameless was scouring the face of Aerwiar for the Jewels of Anniera.

There had been many times since their adventure began that Janner had wished things could go back to the way they were, but this night wasn't one of them. He had pleasant memories of his time with his family in the Igiby cottage, but there had always been, just beyond the door, a night haunted with prowling Fangs and a roving Black Carriage. Here in the Green Hollows they had the fire and the stories and the good food, and none of the fear. The Hollish distrustfulness, along with their tendency to use their fists, was a problem, but at least they didn't want to kill anyone or cart them off in a creepy carriage.

Janner lay on his back and closed his eyes, feeling the heat of the fire on his cheek and the soft fur of the rug beneath him. The sharp pain of his scrapes was gone, the dull ache of his bruises from school faded, and a belly full of henmeat biscuit pie made him drowsy as he listened to Oskar talk.

"Lad, Bonifer here was an invaluable help today. He convinced that frightful librarian to help me find what I need to complete my translation of the First Book."

Janner had all but forgotten about the First Book his father had left him. What little Oskar had already translated seemed to be a history of Anniera—it was mildly interesting, but Janner didn't have the energy to care just then.

Oskar rubbed his hands together. "Isn't it splendid? If things continue to go as smoothly as they did today, I think we could have the whole volume translated from Old Hollish in a month, maybe five."

"That's great," Janner said with a yawn.

"Indeed," said Bonifer, drawing on his pipe. "I'm happy to help in any way I can. I'm sure all manner of mysteries and histories lie in those old leaves. And it must be very important, or Esben wouldn't have risked everything to get it to you."

"What's important is that these children get a good night's sleep before school tomorrow," Nia said, and the children groaned. Janner's bed seemed miles away.

"Can Grandpa tell us a story first?" Leeli asked, scooting up into Podo's lap.

"A short one," Nia said with a hard look at Podo. "And I mean it. You can't keep them up all night, Papa. Not if you expect Janner and Kalmar to hold their own in the Durgan Guild."

"Aye, aye. A short one. What shall it be about?"

"Why don't you tell them about the time Esben and Artham raced from one end of the island to the other?" Bonifer said. "I seem to recall that it had something to do with a boat."

Podo chuckled. "Aye, that's a good one."

Janner shook away his sleepiness and sat up with his back to the fire. If the story involved his father, he wanted to hear it.

"Well," Podo began, "yer ma here had made a pot of bean and batter soup—yer pa's favorite. It also happened to be Artham's favorite. They got into a spat over who got to eat the last bowl. Yer father said he should get it because he was king. Artham said kingship don't matter when it comes to bean and batter soup, and besides, he was older."

"They were acting like children," Nia said, trying not to smile.

"Well, one thing led to another, and soon they were fighting over who was going to take the *Silverstar* out."

"What's the *Silverstar*?" Kalmar asked.

"Ah. The most beautiful ship in the sea," Podo said. "Sleek and graceful she was. But not a big boat, mind ye. Esben liked 'em small and fast. Fit for five or six passengers at most. One person could manage it, and Esben and Artham took turns sailin' her. Well, the next thing you know—"

A banging on the door interrupted Podo. Everyone in the room jumped. Podo and Nia looked at each other, wondering why someone would call so late. The banging continued, and Podo limped to the door. When he got there, he grabbed his legbone and said, "Who is it?"

"Open the door," said a deep voice.

"It's Rudric!" Nia called. "Papa, let him in."

When Podo opened the door, Rudric stormed inside, ignoring Podo's outstretched hand. He was dressed in black from head to foot, wore a cape, and looked so much like a giant version of the Florid Sword that Janner had to remind himself that Gammon was in Kimera, not the Green Hollows.

"Nia!" he said. "I'm glad you're safe. I had to make sure you were all indoors."

"What's going on? And why are you dressed like a Durgan?" Nia asked.

"I may be the Keeper, but I'm also head of the Durgan Patrol. Listen," he said with a quick glance around, "is everyone here? Everyone accounted for?"

"Yes—but why?" Nia asked.

"We just got word from the patrol at Ban Yurga. There's a cloven loose in the Hollows."

"This far west?" Podo hefted the cane and looked out the door. "How did it get all the way here from the Blackwood?"

"They've been chasing it since last night. It slipped past the Durgan Watch in the Outer Vales. They raised the alarm and gave chase and have been hunting it ever since. I just got word that it might be approaching Ban Rona."

"How big is it? What manner of cloven?" Bonifer asked.

"I don't know. I just needed to know you were all safe inside. The cloven have grown bolder in the last few years. This isn't as unusual as it once was . . . though the monsters have never come so far as Ban Rona."

"I'm glad you came, Rudric," Nia said. "Thank you. As you can see, we're all here."

Then Janner heard little Bonnie speak for the first time. "Where's Mama?" she said.

A scream split the air. It came from the direction of the barn.

"Freva!" Nia gasped.

22

A Cloven on the Lawn

Rudric was gone before the scream died. Podo limped out after him, already swinging the legbone and bellowing curses at the evil in the world. Janner and Kalmar were on their feet in an instant, but Nia ran across the room and slammed the door.

"Nobody goes outside. Boys! Get Leeli upstairs and into your room. Lock the door and keep away from the windows."

Janner and Kalmar knew better than to question her, so they each took one of Leeli's arms and bounded up the stairs.

While they ran, Janner heard Nia say, "Bonifer! Where are the weapons? There must be weapons here somewhere."

"In the kitchen closet, I believe. Maker help us!"

Janner locked the door to the boys' bedroom and wedged a chair under the door handle. Leeli curled up on Janner's bunk and sang to herself as Kalmar ran straight for the window. Janner didn't understand what was happening outside or why his mother had given the order, but Kalmar's disobedience woke his sleeping anger.

"Kal, *no!* Mama said to keep away from the window!" Janner grabbed him by the arm and jerked him back. "Why can't you just do what she said?"

"It's not locked!" Kalmar snapped. "We opened it last night, remember?" Kalmar threw back the drapes and locked the window.

Janner opened his mouth to apologize, but no words came. He felt like a fool.

Before the drapes settled back, he and Kalmar glanced out at the moonlit yard beyond the branches of the tree. In the shadow of the trees, they saw a shape, a lurching pile of a creature. It was taller than a man, and it snuffled and grunted. Though the window was closed, Janner caught a sharp odor that made him think of sweat and garbage. The thing was black with shadow as it hunched across the yard, but moonlight glinted off its lumpy, misshapen back—it looked to Janner like the monster's internal organs were growing through its skin and hanging from its flesh.

Just before the drape obscured the window, Janner saw the thing turn and peer up at them. Its eyes locked on Janner's, and a shock like a strike of lightning shook him so hard that he tumbled backward and sprawled on the floor, knocking his brother over. He felt Kalmar squirming beside him and heard Leeli singing, but both sensations were distant and dreamlike.

Janner's head swam, his vision blurred, and he saw in his mind a dripping, torchlit dungeon. He heard wailing and the clink of chains, and words formed in his mind. At first they seemed foreign, but they gathered themselves into something he understood, spoken in a monstrous voice—a deep, bubbling growl:

> *I'll find you.*
> *I'll prowl the face of Aerwiar.*
> *I'll sniff you out*
> *wherever you are,*
> *and when I do,*
> *I'll hold you fast.*
> *Forever.*

The word "forever" rattled Janner's skull, and the vision faded.

He sat up, blinking away the pain between his ears. Where was he? He heard a vague pounding but couldn't be sure what it was. He saw Kalmar lying dazed on the floor and Leeli sitting on the bed in the dark, staring. A steady *thud, thud, thud* pushed through his confusion. Someone was knocking. Janner remembered where he was, remembered wedging the door shut—

"Children! Are you all right?" It was Nia's voice.

Janner struggled to his feet, still unsure what had happened, still shaken as much by the sight of the horrid creature outside as he was by the voice that had dripped words into his mind. He pulled the chair away from the door and unlocked it. Nia burst into the room in a flood of lamplight.

"Are you all right?" She hugged Janner, pulled Kalmar to his feet, and knelt before Leeli, pushing her hair from her face. "I heard you cry out. What happened?"

"I saw it," Kalmar whispered.

"I *felt* something—a terrible sadness," Leeli said, "and . . . and something hot. Inside. Here." She pointed to her heart. "I don't know what it was, but it hurt."

"Janner?" Nia asked.

"I heard it. Words. I don't know if it was the creature—the cloven—or if it was Gnag the Nameless, or dragons again."

"What did it say?" Nia stood and put her arm around him. "Tell me what it said, son."

"It said, 'I'll find you. I'll prowl the face of Aerwiar.'" Janner paused. It wasn't that he didn't remember the words. He just didn't want to repeat them. "'I'll sniff you out wherever you are, and when I do, I'll hold you fast. Forever.'"

He finished and looked up to see Kalmar, Leeli, and Nia staring at him, all with the same mixture of surprise and fear.

"Come on," Nia said. "Let's get downstairs and talk with Rudric."

Rudric sat at the dinner table trying to comfort Freva. Her face was splotchy from crying, her bonnet sat crooked on her head, and her hair was frazzled. She held Bonnie in her arms. Podo, Oskar, and Bonifer stood nearby, whispering.

All the lightness that had filled the house only minutes ago had been replaced by gravity, and Janner told himself he would never be safe again. Every time he let his heart believe that they were out of danger, something dangerous found them. Every time. He ignored the quiet inner voice that reminded him that the Maker had sustained him, had brought him safely to Chimney Hill through more danger than most people saw in a lifetime.

"Any word?" Nia asked Rudric.

"No, highness. I'm sure I'll hear something from Danniby soon."

"The beast is gone, sir," said a man who, as far as Janner could tell, had materialized in the corner of the room when his name was mentioned. He was dressed in black, and stood as still as a statue. It took Janner a moment to realize it was the same Danniby who had led them to the Orchard Inn on their first day in the Hollows.

"Goodness gravy!" Oskar shrieked, jumping into what he thought was a fighting stance. "Where did he come from?"

"We're Durgan Guildsmen, Reteep," said Rudric with a chuckle. "Our business is sneakery."

"Some of us are sneakier than others," said Danniby, aiming a sly grin at Rudric.

Rudric flexed one of his gigantic biceps. "Only because our muscles get in the way."

"I don't care if you're guildsmen," Nia said with a roll of her eyes, "you're acting like children. Poor Freva is in shock and you're parading. Now tell us if we're out of danger. Has the cloven been caught?"

"No ma'am," Danniby said. "One of the men claims to have hit it with a spear, but it got away. I don't know how something that big can move so fast. But you can rest easy tonight. The Durgans are keeping watch in every corner of Ban Rona."

Rudric nodded and said, "Danniby and I will remain at Chimney Hill for the night. I won't sleep a wink, your highness." Janner noticed that Rudric looked at Kalmar kindly. "The cloven was wounded, so it will either scurry back to the Blackwood or find some place to die. This is the first time one has come this far west, probably only because it fled the patrol last night." Rudric patted Freva on the shoulder. "She came face to face with the thing. It's a wonder she wasn't killed."

Nia brought Freva a hot drink, and the young girl's eyes filled with tears.

"Don't make us go outside again tonight, yer highness!" she pleaded. "It looked me right in the eye! I tell you, ma'am, it weren't like no animal! When it looked at me, it *saw* me. Saw through me eyes all the way to the tips of me toes." She buried her face in Nia's neck and wailed. "Maker have mercy, it *knows* me now! I'm so scared, ma'am."

"You're welcome to stay here tonight, dear. Papa, can you get the children in bed? We'll let Freva and Bonnie have Leeli's room. Leeli, you sleep in the boys' room."

"That's a good idea," Leeli said. "They might need my protection." She whacked Kalmar in the leg with her crutch, and the tension in the room eased a little. Bonifer bade them good night and shuffled upstairs to his bedroom, and Oskar went to the kitchen to make a sandwich.

When the children were safe beneath their covers and the lantern was snuffed, Podo sat on the edge of Janner's bed and said, "Yer ma tells me something strange happened up here."

Janner frowned and nodded. "Yes sir. The same weird thing that happened before with the sea dragons."

"Only worse," Leeli said. "This time it hurt."

"So was it the monster?" Podo asked. "The cloven?"

"I don't know," Janner said. "The voice was like a monster's, I guess. It sounded sick and wet. It said that it would find us, that it would never release us. I thought it was the sea dragons at first, and then I thought it was the cloven. Then I thought it was Gnag the Nameless. Could the thing out there *be* Gnag? Could Gnag actually be a cloven from the Blackwood?"

"What if that was *him*?" Leeli whispered. "Gnag the Nameless, right outside our window!"

"That wasn't Gnag the Nameless," Kalmar said.

"How do you know?" Janner asked.

"I just know. I saw its eyes. It was . . . I don't know. It just wasn't Gnag the Nameless."

"What did ye see, lad?" Podo asked, and there was a long silence before Kalmar answered.

"I saw a dungeon." Kalmar's voice grew so quiet that Janner held his breath to hear it. "Spiders crawled up the walls. They were as big as mice. Snakes and worms were everywhere. I saw people in chains. They were crying. And there were monsters too. Monsters chained in the darkness, licking the floor for food. I think they're as scared of Gnag the Nameless as we are."

"That may be true, lad, but the cloven are still as dangerous as toothy cows. Worse even, to look at 'em. All I know is, I'm glad Rudric and his Durgans are keeping watch. Me old bones are tired, and I ain't fit for sittin' up all night watchin' for gobblers in the dark." He kissed Leeli's forehead and patted each boy on the cheek. Janner loved the feel of Podo's cool, callused hand. "Now sleep. You've got yer puppies to tend to tomorrow, and you boys have got to learn to duck at the proper time. In a few weeks I bet old Brosa and Larnik will be sorry they ever met the Wingfeathers."

Janner tried to sleep, but every time he closed his eyes he saw the monster in the yard and heard its ominous words. He knew Leeli and Kalmar were awake too, but no one spoke. Dogs barked in the distance, probably at the bitter scent of the cloven's passing, but from time to time Janner heard Rudric's voice drifting up to the window from the yard, and it brought him comfort.

When at last he drifted to sleep, his thoughts were of his father, and of Anniera, and of Sara Cobbler.

23

The Light He Left Behind

Sara Cobbler was starving. But she was used to that. She was cramped and sore, but she was used to that too. When Mobrik the ridgerunner opened the coffin and let her out, she no longer felt the hopelessness that choked the air of the Fork Factory. She'd once been just another of the weary children mindlessly doing whatever the Overseer told them to do. But not anymore.

Something had changed the day she saw a boy she recognized. A boy from Glipwood. His hands weren't yet blistered. His skin wasn't yet covered in soot. His name was Janner Igiby. His eyes shone with a sparkle of hope, and that faint light had rekindled something inside of her.

All the children thought of escape when they first arrived—Sara too. She had been defiant, though not with her words; hers had been a rebellion of silence.

The Fangs had kicked down the front door of her house and dragged her from her bed, and neither her mother's pleas nor her father's struggle could stop them. Sara could still feel their moist, scaly hands ripping her from her father's arms, could still smell the rot of their flesh, could still hear their hissing laughter. Nothing she had experienced since had been as awful as that night. She tried not to think about it, but when she was stuck in the coffin, it was hard to think about anything else. She kept picturing her parents' horrified faces shrinking into the distance as the Black Carriage creaked away.

In the Carriage, she had screamed until her voice left her, and she knew in the helplessness of her own silence that she was utterly alone.

When she was dragged from the Carriage the next morning and thrown at the feet of the Overseer, he asked her a single question: "What's your name?"

She opened her mouth to speak, but she no longer had any voice with which to answer. He demanded that she answer him, but she couldn't, and then she learned to fear the Overseer's whip.

That night she attempted to escape. She didn't have a plan. She just ran through the double doors, down the long corridor, and into the carriage room—where the Overseer was waiting. He had learned to recognize which of his new "tools" would attempt to flee, he said. That night she learned the full extent of his cruelty. She never again tried to escape.

Every child came to the factory clinging to defiance or hope, but the harsh sting of the Overseer's whip or the Maintenance Managers' chains or the long, lonely dark of the coffin eventually broke their will.

It was different with Janner Igiby, though. Like others before him, he had defied the Overseer and the Maintenance Managers, and he had been beaten and thrown into the coffin. But after he'd been punished multiple times, after he'd spent days in the awful coffin—he *kept* trying. That was what stirred Sara's waters. Never had another child shown such strength. Sara knew the Overseer had tried to make a Maintenance Manager out of Janner, had tried to lure him with power. But Janner had defied him. He was like a candle the Overseer couldn't snuff out.

And after Janner left, after Sara had weathered her punishment for helping him escape, she was surprised to find that some of Janner's candlelight still flickered in the Fork Factory. She noticed it reflected in the other children's eyes and in the way the ridgerunner watched her. It took her a few days to realize the light was coming from *her*. She was shining it. Janner Igiby had changed her. He was gone, but he had left some of his gift behind.

When Sara passed the paring station, she thought of Janner and imagined that flecks of light sprayed the ground where he had walked, like glowing paint splatters only she could see. When she sat at the table where they had talked about his escape, she imagined blurs of gold stirring the air where he had been, ghostly trails that helped her believe in the world outside these walls.

And so, without a plan, without purpose, and without even realizing it, Sara Cobbler became that light to the children around her. Because there was hope in her heart, there was courage too. Courage changed the way she moved among the other prisoners. Now she patted them on the back and smiled at them even when their eyes were blank. Now she tied her hair in a bun instead of letting it hang around her face like moss. Now she walked with a straight back and looked the Maintenance Managers in the eye when they bossed her around. It made them uncomfortable, and soon they stopped harassing her at all.

Before Janner came, she had suppressed the memory of her parents and her home. Before, she had found it easier to bear the long hours of work if she didn't think about the streets of Dugtown, just on the other side of the brick wall, where people still walked and talked and ate together, even if it was under the hateful gaze of the Fangs. But now, while she pared forks and swords, carted coal, cranked wheels, and stoked fires, she thought of her father's musty, pipe-smoke scent and her mother's bright laughter, of the books in her room and the bright mornings in late winter when spring stirred in the tall grass.

One day as she sat sipping her soup and thinking with pleasure of Janner's wild ride away from the Fork Factory, she felt someone tap her shoulder. She snapped out of the daydream with some difficulty and turned to see a little boy. He was so short he only came up to her shoulder while she sat. His face, like all the other faces, was dirty, and his teeth had begun to blacken. His fingernails were crusted with dirt, and his shirt was several sizes too big and hung from him like a rag on a clothesline.

But his eyes! They were *looking* at her. He wasn't a tool but a boy.

"Can I sit with you?" he asked, and his voice was as small and sweet as a piece of candy.

"Of course you can." She laughed. "I would be honored. What's your name?"

The boy looked around for the Maintenance Managers.

"Oh, don't worry about them," Sara said. "They leave me alone. You can tell me your name."

He leaned in close and said, "Borley. I'm seven, I think."

"It's nice to meet you, Borley. My name's Sara Cobbler." Sara smiled at him and motioned for him to sit. He placed his soup bowl on the table, climbed onto the bench, and scooted close to Sara. He looked up at her and smiled, and flakes of ash broke from his cheeks and fell to the floor. He put his head on her shoulder for a moment, and Sara felt in her heart a joy so heavy it hurt.

When Sara looked up, seven more children stood across from her, all holding their bowls, asking with their eyes if they, too, were welcome at the table. Tears spilled from Sara's eyes and left bright trails on her cheeks, and she nodded for them to sit, thanking the Maker for Janner Igiby and the light he had left behind.

So began the quiet revolution of Sara Cobbler.

24

A Carriage Ride to School

When Janner awoke, the first thing on his mind was the cloven. He wanted to know if it had been caught or killed, and he wanted to know if it could speak. If it was the cloven's voice he heard in his head, then it must have been delivering some kind of message from Gnag the Nameless. On the other hand, maybe the cloven was hunting for someone or something else, and Janner had listened in on the beast's inner thoughts.

There was also the possibility that the cloven had nothing to do with Gnag and didn't speak at all—maybe the strange flash of power and the voice in Janner's mind were caused by something else entirely. Every time it had happened before, Leeli was making music, but in Kimera, when they tried to get the power to work again, Leeli had played song after song and Janner had concentrated as hard as he could, to no avail. They couldn't make it work on their own. So why had it happened last night?

At breakfast, Janner was so deep in thought that Nia scolded him for not answering her greeting. He apologized and made sure he gave her cinnamon hotcakes an extra dose of praise. By the time Kalmar and Leeli joined them, Rudric had also come inside for breakfast tea and a plate piled with crispy, batter-dipped bacon. He sat at the table in his black Durgan uniform and gobbled it up, moaning about how delicious the bacon was. He had patrolled Chimney Hill all night, but he looked wide awake, especially when Nia passed through the room.

"No sign," he told Podo. "It's like the beast up and disappeared. My guess is that it grobbled its way back to the Blackwood when no one was looking. If it were still around, you'd smell its rot. Those things stink so bad we can't even use the dogs to track them. The best dogs in Ban Rona take one whiff and set to whining. So I mean it when I say you can rest easy. There's no cloven in Ban Rona."

"Will you send a guard for at least one more night?" Nia asked. "Just to be sure? I felt better knowing you and Danniby were standing watch."

"Aye, your highness. I planned on it. Danniby and I are at your service."

Janner just had time to wonder where Danniby was before he stuck his head out from a kitchen cabinet and said, "I'm happy to patrol, but I'll need a nap this afternoon. And a bibe. I'd love a bibe, your highness."

Nia thanked them both, then clapped her hands and announced that they had to leave or the children would be late for their first full day of school. "Put these on," she said and handed each of the children a jacket made of tough brown fabric. The outside was scratchy as a totato sack but the inside was lined with soft fur. The children's initials were embroidered inside the collars: JW, KW, and LW. "Those are from Freva," Nia told them. "She couldn't sleep, so she worked on them all night."

The children thanked Freva, who somehow blushed and yawned at the same time and said, "It's nothing, me lords and lady. They're lined with flabbit fur. They say monsters don't like to eat it, so keep 'em on whenever you go outside. And if you do get eaten, hopefully the creature will spit out the jacket, and we'll be able to tell which one of you it was by the initials."

"That's very thoughtful of you," Nia said.

"Oy," Freva continued. "Even so, the initials might be hard to find. We might have to piece the jacket back together if it gets all torn up. That cloven's claws were pointy. Oh, and we'll also have to wash the pieces, 'cause they'll be stained with monster spit and blood—"

"Freva! Let's just hope my children don't get eaten, shall we? Why don't you go see if Bonnie's awake?" Nia shooed her upstairs.

"You'll be fine," Rudric said to Janner and his siblings, brushing crumbs from his beard. "The monster's gone. Besides, I'm pretty sure we'd be able to tell who you were without the initials in the jacket, just from the bones and such."

"Rudric!" Nia snapped. "These children won't be eaten!"

"Of course they won't." He turned back to his food with a shrug. "These eggs are good."

"Don't forget these," Nia said and handed each of the children the well-worn packs she had made them in Glipwood. She had removed their adventuring supplies and filled the packs instead with the necessary school accessories: books, quills, ink bottles, paper, and a jar of gadbalm to be applied after their Durgan training.

When Janner hefted his pack over one shoulder and heard the familiar leathery creak and saw the dark, smooth spot on one strap where he had a habit of resting his hand, he smiled. He felt a quiet pride about the road he had traveled with this old pack—from Glipwood Forest, over Miller's Bridge, past the Stranders, to Dugtown, then back along the Strand, over the Barrier, up through the Stony Mountains, over Mog-Balgrik, to the Ice Prairies, then across the Dark Sea of Darkness. His anxiousness about another day at school shrank when he thought about how far the Maker had carried him. He may be scarred and worn in places, but like his pack, he believed he was better for it.

The morning was chilly with the coming winter. The sky in the east was brightening, but the sun hadn't yet risen over the Green Hollows. As the children found their seats in the carriage, Oskar stuck his head out the door and called, "Janner! Perhaps you can visit the library after school. Bonifer and I will be working on the translation of the First Book all day. In the words of Anjudar the Waif, 'I've nothing better to do. You should come by!'"

Bonifer appeared at the door and said, "Ah, but in the words of Gumphrey Half-Toe, 'If it's all right with your mother, of course.'"

Oskar adjusted his spectacles and looked at Bonifer with dumbfounded delight. "Too true! It was in *Morbidity, Fluidity, and Bile*! Not my favorite of his works."

"Agreed!" Bonifer said. "Not nearly as concise, necessary, or timely as—"

"*Glavinpoole's Gander*," they said in unison, then burst into chortles. Oskar's belly shook, and Bonifer's top hat nearly toppled off his head.

"It's fine with me," Nia said, knowing the two old men weren't listening, "as long as he finishes his T.H.A.G.S." Janner groaned, but Nia shushed him. "No complaining. I've been lax with all three of you, but now that we're here and your Hollish education is underway, it's time we focused on your Annieran studies too."

The carriage pulled away as the first sunbeams broke the horizon and bridged the land from hilltop to hilltop with gold. The trip to school that morning was very different from the previous day. This time there were children everywhere. Some rode with a parent, as the Wingfeathers did, and others stood in clusters at street corners, where they were picked up by a long community wagon pulled by a six-horse team.

The children on the carriages and wagons chattered and shoved and called to one another and laughed, but they stopped and stared when the Wingfeathers passed. Janner did his best to pretend he didn't notice the way they snickered and pointed and whispered. He couldn't wait to get away from all the school traffic.

But when they rolled deeper into Ban Rona, which bustled with activity of all kinds, the whispers and stares continued from the adults. Nia ignored them and wove the carriage among other wagons carrying fruits, bread, tools, rope, and barrels to the harbor market. Janner saw shopkeepers hanging Open signs in their windows while dogs bounded from storefront to storefront, carrying rolls of parchment in their mouths or in packs on their backs. There were men with wheelbarrows and women with donkeys, but as the Wingfeathers neared the Keep, they saw more and more guildlings, many of them with dogs of different colors and breeds, and all of them big.

By the time they reached the school, the Wingfeather carriage was one of many in a train that stretched from the gate of the Guildling Hall back around the corner of the Keep and down into Ban Rona. The carriages and wagons moved slowly, but they never stopped, even when they drove through the school gate and rounded the statue in the courtyard.

"Have a good day, children," Nia said. "When you hear the horn blow, you'll have three minutes to get to the main hall. Don't be late or Olumphia will waggle her whiskers at you." She looked each of them in the eye and smiled. "Remember who you are. I love you so."

Janner waited for her to stop the wagon, but she only slowed it and said, "Out you go."

With a stomach full of butterflies and a head full of bees, Janner hopped out of the moving carriage. Kalmar sprang to the ground. The boys trotted beside the carriage and helped Leeli down. In seconds, Nia's carriage washed away in the river of horses and wagon wheels and barking dogs.

Among hundreds of other children in the chaos of the courtyard, the Jewels of Anniera huddled together: a boy with scars, a girl with a crutch, and a little Grey Fang. They were surrounded by students, but the Wingfeathers felt terribly alone.

Before the first horn blew, Janner had his first chance to protect his brother.

25

Taunted by Grigory Bunge

I guess we should get this over with," Janner said, leading Leeli and Kalmar through the crowd to the door of the main building. Even in the bustle of students he felt conspicuous, and though he made a point of not looking at any of them directly, he knew that they were all staring at him and his siblings. He heard whispers, felt their eyes, and noticed the way the crowd parted as they passed.

All they had done was arrive, and already they were a spectacle. Janner told himself that it had to improve over time. They would get used to Kalmar, just as Janner had (though a voice in his mind reminded him that he knew Kal better than anyone and still had moments of doubt). Kalmar and Leeli followed Janner so closely that he worried their feet would get tangled and they would trip, which would *really* give the other kids something to laugh at.

"That's a good trick," someone said.

Janner was staring at the ground as he walked, so he wasn't sure at first who said it. He wasn't even sure it had been directed at him.

"I said, that's a good trick."

A few feet ahead stood a boy with shaggy red hair. His arms were folded, and Janner couldn't help but notice that they were big for a boy his age. Big and hairy. The boy's nose was flat, his forehead was flatter, and his jaw was square. On one side stood several other boys of roughly the same size and ugliness, and on his other sat a huge dog with a narrow black head. When it saw Kalmar, it curled its lips and growled.

"Did you hear me?" the boy said.

"I heard you," Janner said. He decided to try being friendly. "My name's Janner. And I don't know what trick you mean."

"Getting your dog to walk on two legs. And getting it to wear breeches and a jacket. It's a good trick."

Janner couldn't think of anything to say. He was wrestling with his fear of the boy's big, hairy arms and the big, hairy dog; his anger that the boy had insulted his brother; his worry that a fight in the courtyard with so many kids around would get out of hand; and his frustration that he hadn't even made it to the building before having to deal with a bully.

As it turned out, he didn't have to think of anything to say because Kalmar said it for him.

"I've got another trick I can show you." Kalmar growled and stepped in front of Janner. "How about the one where I warn you not to call me a dog ever again?"

"Oh! It can talk too!" said the boy.

Kalmar took a threatening step forward, and the boy's smile vanished. He made a clicking sound with his mouth, and the dog at his side raised its hackles and readied itself to pounce.

"If you take a step closer, I'll loose Graw on you. My pap warned me that I might see a Grey Fang at the Guildling Hall today and told me to defend myself from it however I liked."

"You don't have to defend yourself against anyone," Janner said as he stepped in front of Kalmar, trying to ignore the crowd that had circled around them. "We don't want to fight you or your dog."

Janner wasn't as worried about getting beat up as he was about looking like a fool in front of every child in Ban Rona. He wished they could slip to the back of the hall undetected and creep their way into class without anyone noticing they were there. But with every passing moment the dog and its owner looked closer to attacking, and the crowd grew in number.

"Oh, stop it!" Leeli said. She marched past Janner and walked straight up to the dog. She let it smell her hand, and then she scratched it behind the ears while she hummed a whistleharp tune. The dog's snarl vanished. It wagged its tail and rested its head on Leeli's chest.

"Graw, get him!" the boy said, but the dog ignored him.

"I said stop it!" Leeli snapped, and she whacked the boy in the leg with her crutch. "I don't know who you are, but you can't call my brother a dog."

The boy sputtered and looked from Leeli to his dog to Kalmar.

"What's this business?" said a welcome voice. Olumphia Groundwich appeared and the crowd dispersed, including the redheaded boy.

"Grigory Bunge! Come back here this instant."

"Yes, head guildmadam?" Bunge said.

"What just happened here?"

"Nothing, guildmadam. Just welcoming the new students."

"Ah! Good. I wondered who might be the first to volunteer."

"Volunteer for what, guildmadam?" Grigory asked with a wince.

"To show them around."

"No!" Janner said. "I mean, no, *thank* you, guildmadam. We'll be fine. We don't want to be any trouble."

Janner didn't want to spend another second with the boy. He didn't want to think about what would happen as soon as Olumphia turned her back. Grigory looked as worried as Janner felt but said nothing.

"Janner, that's very thoughtful of you," Olumphia said. "But I think Grigory would like to get to know you. You're to stay together until the

second horn, and then I want Grigory to escort you to lunch. Is that clear, Mister Bunge?"

"Yes, guildmadam," muttered Grigory Bunge.

"Is that clear, Wingfeathers?"

"Yes, guildmadam," they answered.

Olumphia left the Wingfeathers and Grigory Bunge to glare at each other in the now-empty courtyard. Grigory's dog wagged its tail and panted. Grigory appeared to be weighing the misery of escorting a Grey Fang against whatever punishment he would receive for disobeying the head guild-madam.

Finally, he shrugged and made for the main door. "Come on," he said, as if it sickened him to talk. "I'll just have to get you after school."

With that encouraging thought, Janner began his first day at the Guild-ling Hall.

Grigory Bunge and his dog led the Wingfeathers to Lectures and Learn-ing. It wasn't hard to find a place to sit, because as soon as Kalmar approached, the students scrambled away. Some looked mean, like Grigory, and others looked terrified. Janner was annoyed at them all. He wanted to stand on the dais at the front of the class and announce that Kalmar wasn't going to attack anyone, and he was actually considering it when the horn blew, signaling the start of class.

"Silence!" said a man behind a lectern at the front of the room. "Silence, guildlings!" The man was tall and thin, with a pale, narrow face. His mouth was drawn downward, and he looked out at them through half-lidded eyes.

"Today we shall learn," he said with a yawn, "about the War of 189. It was terribly"—he yawned again—"exciting."

Janner stifled a yawn, as did a hundred other guildlings.

"Imagine that you're on the battlefield armed with"—*yawn*—"arms. You're fighting someone, and they're fighting back. There's a big fight. That's what happened in the War of 189. It was, as I said, terribly exciting." The man looked at his notes. "Very well. Moving on."

In this manner they learned about the War of 189, the Famine of 235

("Imagine that you're very"—*yawn*—"hungry"), the Ridgerunner Raid of 274 ("Imagine some things to do with raiding, guildlings"), and the Apple Riot of 312 ("Imagine it," was all he said before informing them that they'd be tested on it next week).

Kalmar fidgeted. Leeli stared at the ceiling. Janner, since he enjoyed imagining, did his best to listen, but he spent most of the time studying the Hollish children who filled the room.

At last, when even Janner was ready to implode with boredom, a horn blew.

"Right. Well, that's Guildmaster Nibblesticks," said Grigory. His voice was dull and he didn't bother to look at the Wingfeathers, but at least he wasn't taunting them. "Next up is P.T., when the whole school is on the field."

"What's P.T. stand for?" Janner asked.

"Pummelry Training. It's when everybody's racing and wrestling and punching. The guildmasters can't keep an eye on everybody out there, so I might go ahead and beat you up then. Come on. Bring your dog."

"Hey!" Janner yelled, but Grigory kept walking.

Kalmar growled, and it took Leeli's sweetest voice to calm him down again.

26

Getting the Boot

As soon as Janner stepped onto the field, he was knocked to the ground.

To be fair, the person who smashed into him didn't mean to. She was hugging a boot to her chest and running from a riot of other guildlings. She yelled, "Sorry!" over her shoulder and left Janner to scramble out of the way of the stampede.

As Kalmar pulled Janner to his feet and brushed him off, a stocky man and a stocky woman approached, leading two stocky dogs.

"You'll want to keep a watch out for whoever's got the boot," said the stocky man, introducing himself and his wife as Guildmaster Pwaffe and Guildmadam Pwaffe. They seemed as wide as they were tall, but without an ounce of fat. Their arms were short and thick, their necks were as wide as their heads, and their fingers looked like sausages.

"Oy," the woman said. "That's basically all there is to Get the Boot. That's what we call the game. Get the Boot. Someone has the boot and everyone's supposed to get the boot. And when you've got the boot, everyone else is trying to get the boot. So you have to keep the boot. That guy over there is timing how long each guildling has the boot. Any questions?"

Janner had lots of questions, but before he could ask a single one, Guildmaster Pwaffe said, "Oy, guildlings. Off you go. Get the boot."

Janner, Kal, and Leeli looked at one another.

"Now?" Kalmar asked.

"That's what I said." The man pointed across the field at the herd of children still chasing the girl, who appeared to be having the time of her life.

"But what do we do when we get the boot?" Kalmar asked.

"Keep the boot. It isn't hard." Guildmadam Pwaffe shook her head sadly. "Not too smart, these, eh, Wimble?"

"The whole game is right there in the title," the man said. " 'Get the Boot.' That's it. So get the boot. Go!"

Kalmar ran and Janner followed. Leeli, without a word of complaint, flung her hair back and took after them as fast as her crutch would allow.

"Wait!" said Guildmadam Pwaffe. "Not you, lass."

Janner held back to be sure Leeli was all right.

"I can keep up," she said with fire in her eyes. "I'm used to it."

"Leeli's right," Janner said. "You wouldn't believe how fast she is."

"We've received instruction from Head Guildmadam Groundwich," the guildmaster said, pointing across the field to a track where another group of students were busy harnessing dogs to little wooden chariots. "You're to drive a houndrick."

"She said you had a way with dogs. Is that true?" the guildmadam asked.

"Yes ma'am," Leeli said. "I used to have one. He was as big as a horse."

"Sure he was," said the man. "Big as a horse. Did you hear that, Rosie?"

"Oy, I heard it, Wimble. I think this girl's *imagination* is as big as a horse."

"No, really! He used to be small, but we poured water from the First Well on him and he grew and grew. His name was Nugget."

"Water from the First Well," the man said with a glance at his wife. "Lass, the head guildmadam said you three had been through a lot. Sad to see it's affected your brain."

"Don't worry, sweetie," the woman said. "You don't have to lie here in the Hollows."

"But it's true!" Leeli folded her arms and glared.

"I'm sure it is," said the woman, laying a sausagey hand on Leeli's shoulder. "Now let's get to the houndricks. Is that all right? Can you understand the words I'm speaking? So sorry your brain is damaged."

Leeli looked to Janner for help, but he could only shrug as the guildmadam led her away. He turned to find the game of Get the Boot, but the game found him first. The girl with the boot was huffing straight for him, just an arm's length ahead of the mob.

"Here!" she cried and threw the boot.

Janner caught it without thinking, saw the students thundering straight for him, let out a yelp, and fled. He ran as fast as his twelve-year-old legs could carry him. He leapt over dogs and logs and barrels, skidded around younger guildlings, and didn't think once of abandoning the boot—not because he wanted to win the game, but because he'd forgotten he had it. All he knew was the thumping of feet on grass, the burning in his lungs, and the shouts of "I'm gonna get you!" and "Give me that boot!"

He saw a gray shape out of the corner of his eye. Kalmar jogged up to him, grinning out of one side of his mouth. "You want a break?" he asked.

It took Janner a moment to understand what he meant, and then he flung the boot at Kalmar as if it was a hot coal. Kalmar caught it, let out a happy howl, and sped ahead of him. Janner trotted to a stop and bent over, breathing so hard that he thought he might throw up.

Guildmaster Pwaffe appeared beside him. "Get the boot."

"Can't—run—anymore," Janner said, panting.

"Can't stop, either," the man said with a smile. "The game isn't over. Off with you. Get the boot."

Janner inhaled all the air his lungs could hold, straightened, and chased the boot. He spotted Leeli at the opposite end of the field, kneeling in one of the houndricks as a team of six dogs tugged it along at a trot. She held her chin high, and her hair swayed with the motion of the rick. Three other teams sped past her, snapping their reins, urging their dog teams faster. Guildmadam Pwaffe shouted at Leeli and gestured wildly, but Leeli showed no interest in winning. She looked like part of a regal parade.

By the time Janner caught up with the crowd chasing the boot, Kalmar was so far ahead of them all that he looked bored, and he stayed out front until Guildmaster Pwaffe blew a horn. The guildlings caught their breath and guzzled water from canteens. Kalmar and Janner stood apart from the rest, doing their best to ignore all the scowls and mutterings. More than once Janner heard the words "dog" and "mutt" and "Fang."

"You know the drill, guildlings!" said Guildmaster Pwaffe. "The winner of Get the Boot faces yesterday's Tackle Smash champion. Master Wingfeather, that means you get to face Grigory Bunge. Circle up!"

The guildlings gathered around a white ring painted on the grass.

"Maybe that wasn't the best way to introduce yourself," Janner muttered with an encouraging pat on his brother's shoulder.

"Yeah." Kalmar sighed. "Why'd you let me do that? Some Throne Warden you are."

"I could have caught you. I just didn't feel like it."

"What do I do now? Grigory the Red looks like he wants to eat me alive."

Grigory Bunge had removed his shirt and was flexing his hairy red arms for everyone to see. Janner thought for a moment. "Well, if you dodge him the whole time, it'll just make him mad and he'll get you later. And if you fight and win, it'll just make him mad and he'll get you later. I think your only way out of this is to let him eat you alive."

"Like I said, some Throne Warden you are."

"Kal, listen." Janner grew serious. "Don't use your teeth. Or your claws. You have to forget you have them. You can't give them any reason to call you a Fang. If you're going to fight him, you have to fight him on his terms. If you can help it, don't even growl."

Kalmar nodded.

The guildmaster blew his horn.

"Guildling Wingfeather, there'll be no punching in the head area, no kicking in the head area, and absolutely no tickling. The first one to leave the ring loses."

The boys stepped into the circle. Wimble said "Go!" and Grigory charged.

Time after time Kal spun away from Grigory's lunges, but every time he tried to shove Grigory out of the circle he was grabbed and tackled and thrown closer to the edge of the ring himself. Janner could tell that Grigory was getting tired, while Kalmar looked as if he could keep at it for hours if he chose.

After several minutes, Kalmar looked at Janner with a little shrug, moved in to push Grigory, and let himself be caught. Grigory grunted with triumph, spun Kalmar around, grabbed his tail, and slung him as hard as he could. Kalmar went tumbling out of the circle, and the guildlings cheered.

"Take *that*, Fang!" Grigory sneered, and many of the other students sneered with him.

Janner's stomach lurched. If it was his duty to issue a challenge every time someone called his brother a Fang or a dog or some other awful name, their time at school would be one never-ending fight. Was he supposed to say something? Was he supposed to dive into the ring and pummel Grigory, even if he got beat up or disciplined by the guildmaster? What would Artham have him do?

Fortunately, Guildmaster Pwaffe blew his horn for silence, marched into the ring, and grabbed Grigory Bunge by the nose. "You'll apologize to the Wingfeather boy or you'll be disciplined before the class. I'll have no dishonorable talk under my watch. I don't care if you fight a Fang or a ridgerunner, a ratbadger or a bloath, you'll not gloat over your victory. Win quietly or not at all."

"Snnnnry, gnnnndmsstr." Pwaffe released Grigory's nose. "Sorry, guildmaster."

"And to your opponent?"

Grigory could hardly conceal his loathing, but after a moment he said, "Sorry, *Kalmar*."

Janner helped his brother to his feet and whispered, "Nicely done, King Kalmar."

After that, the rest of the students took turns facing each other in the ring. Janner's opponent was a boy about his size and weight, so the match seemed to last forever. No matter how hard he tried, Janner couldn't push the boy hard enough to get him outside the ring, and neither could the boy budge Janner. In the end, Janner managed to twist the boy's arm behind his back long enough to push him, then gave him a good kick in the rump that sent him staggering out of the ring. None of the other guildlings cheered for Janner, but they didn't jeer, either.

When the horn blew for lunch, the guildlings and teachers dropped whatever they were doing and ran like mad for the dining hall. The dogs, which had already been unharnessed, barked and bolted for the houndry. Janner, Kalmar, and Leeli were the only ones left on the field. The boys were dirty and drenched with sweat, even in the cool air. Leeli was beaming.

"That wasn't as bad as I thought it would be," Kalmar said, wagging his tail.

"It was wonderful," Leeli said. She twirled her hair and watched the dogs bound away.

"It could have been worse," Janner said. "And how bad could lunch be?"

Lunch turned out to be much worse than Tackle Smash, and not because of the food.

27

Late for Guildmaster Clout

The moment they walked into the noisy dining hall, it fell quiet. It wasn't the same as yesterday, when Nia and Head Guildmadam Groundwich escorted them and provided some protection. Now there wasn't an adult in sight. The teachers chattered together in an adjacent room, oblivious to anything that happened in the dining hall, which was the domain of guildlings and guildlings alone. Janner would rather have faced twenty of their fists in the ring than several hundred of their eyes in the room.

"Come on," Janner said, making his way toward the food table at the front. The Wingfeathers crossed the hall in silence, and every eye followed. Janner had never wanted so badly to disappear. After an eternity at the back of the line, they reached the long table loaded with a giant bowl of fruit salad.

As they filled their bowls, Janner's neck tingled under the weight of all those eyes, and when they turned to find a table, no one moved an inch to make room for them. The Jewels of Anniera crossed to the back of the lunchroom and, with no other place to go, sat on the floor and leaned against the wall.

"Just eat," Janner whispered. "Ignore them."

He ate a few pieces of the chopped fruit, though he was too nervous to taste it. Leeli scooted around so her back faced the watching eyes and popped a grape into her mouth. Kalmar stared at his bowl of fruit without taking a bite. The students gradually lost interest in the Wingfeathers, and the noise of the dining hall rose to its initial pitch.

"You should eat, Kal," Janner said.

"I'm not hungry." Kalmar pushed the bowl away and leaned against the wall. "Not for fruit, anyway."

"What's wrong?" Leeli asked.

"Nothing." Kalmar scratched behind one of his ears, and Janner couldn't help thinking about how much he really did look like a dog. "I just feel bad that all this is happening. It's my fault that I look like this."

Janner didn't know what to say. It *was* his fault. Running to the Stranders was Kal's decision. And running to the Stranders was what got him kidnapped by Fangs.

"No it isn't," Leeli said. "The Fangs did this to you."

"I wish that were true." Kalmar gave her a sad smile. "But it isn't. This is my fault."

"Yeah, but you didn't know you'd be kidnapped by Fangs," Janner said. He ate the last bite of fruit, wiped a drop of cantalime juice from his chin, and asked, "Are you sure you aren't hungry? I'm starving."

Kal shook his head and pushed his bowl across the floor to Janner.

"You didn't know they'd send you into the Phoob dungeons." Janner crunched into an apple wedge. "The fur is the consequence of a bad decision. That's it. You didn't ask for it, so don't worry about it, all right?"

Kalmar looked like he wanted to say something but didn't.

The horn blew, and the guildlings cleared their tables and filed out to their respective guilds. Janner heard wisps of conversations about woodwrightery projects underway, cookery dishes the students planned to perfect, and even one student bragging about the quality of her latest book at the bindery. When he heard the words "book" and "bindery," he clenched his teeth to keep from complaining. *He* wanted to make a book. If he couldn't be at the library reading, he wanted at least to be around books, learning to work the leather and fashion the pages. Instead he was about to get another lesson in pummelry at the Durgan Guild.

As the Wingfeathers pushed their way out of the dining hall, they were elbowed and jostled often enough that Janner was sure it wasn't accidental. The students were making it clear that the Wingfeathers weren't welcome.

Janner glanced at Kalmar, the unlikely young king with whiskers and a tail, watching the floor in order to avoid the fear and hatred on every face that looked his way. Janner's anger faded a little. The students stared at Janner because he was a stranger, and maybe because of the bright red scars on his neck, but they stared at Kalmar because they thought he was a monster, something evil in their presence. Kalmar's was the heavier burden, and he bore it in silence.

The problem was, his silence wasn't just honorable—it was also impenetrable. More and more it seemed that Kalmar was hiding inside himself, which troubled Janner. He wanted to know what his brother was thinking and feeling.

"Leeli!" said a grinning boy whom Janner immediately recognized as Thorn O'Sally. His hair was slicked back, his thumbs were hooked under his suspenders, and he leaned against a post in front of the houndry, trying, Janner could tell, to look nonchalant.

"Hello, Thorn!" Leeli waved and limped over to him. They immediately fell into conversation about dogs and puppies and leashes and houndricks, and Leeli was so excited that she followed him into the houndry barn without a word to her brothers.

Biggin O'Sally, beard once again tucked into his belt, rounded the corner of the building with four puppies on leashes. They pranced along on either side, wagging their tails and sniffing at everything in reach. When one of the puppies pulled ahead, Biggin made a sound with his mouth—part whisper, part click, and part whistle—and the puppy held still and looked up at him.

Biggin bowed his head to the boys. "Good afternoon, your highness. Hello, Throne Warden. Your sister inside already?"

"Yes sir," Kalmar said. "With Thorn."

"She's good, you know." He stared at the houndry door and clicked again. The puppies sat and wagged their tails. "Real good."

"Good at what, sir?" Janner asked.

"Dogspeak." Biggin stroked his beard. "She never had any training?"

"No sir," Kalmar said. "She's always been good with animals."

"Real good," Biggin O'Sally repeated, then turned his attention back to the boys. "What about you two? Either of you speak dog?"

Janner knew Biggin wasn't being mean. The man hardly seemed to notice that Kalmar looked quite a bit like a dog.

When the boys didn't answer, Biggin said, "What I mean is, if you wanted these pups to lie down and roll over, how would you get them to do it?"

"I'd say, 'roll over,' I guess," Janner said. Then he tried it, in a high voice like he had heard Leeli use. "Roll over, puppies! Roll over!"

The puppies stopped panting and cocked their heads at Janner, but they didn't lie down or roll over. In fact, Janner had the feeling they felt sorry for him.

"What about you, highness?" Biggin asked Kalmar.

Kalmar tried waving his hand in a circle, and when that didn't work, he dropped to all fours and rolled over. The puppies wagged their tails and looked at him like children watching a clown at a carnival.

"I suppose not, then," said Biggin. "This is dogspeak, boys. Watch and learn." Without even looking at the dogs he made another series of sounds, and all but one of the puppies dropped to the ground and rolled over. The one who didn't chased his tail. "Still trainin' 'em, but you get the idea. Your sister could get them to do that and more. When she played that whistleharp yesterday, every dog in the houndry stopped what it was doing and would have knitted her a sweater if she'd asked. As I said, she's good. *Real* good."

Biggin O'Sally dropped the four leashes and swaggered into the houndry. When the door opened, whistleharp music drifted out, and the four puppies yipped and padded inside after their trainer.

"She's good," Kalmar said.

"Real good," Janner said, and they laughed. Then a horn blew and Janner realized there wasn't a student in sight. "We're late! Come on!"

The boys ran down walkways and dashed around hedges. They burst into the Durgan Guild courtyard and skidded to a stop. Guildmaster Clout stood glowering at the boys with his arms folded. The rest of the guildlings sat on the floor behind him, doing their best to mimic their guildmaster's look.

"Lateness won't be tolerated," he said.

The brothers nodded.

"Laps around the courtyard till I tell you to stop. Commence." He turned back to his class and began his lesson.

Janner's ears were hot. It was unfair that they were being punished for lateness when it was another guildmaster who had made them so. If O'Sally hadn't been talking to them about dogspeak, they would have made it in plenty of time. Janner clenched his jaw, shook his head, and began his laps.

He started out at a steady pace, conscious of Kal just behind him. He could hear his brother's claws scraping the flagstones with every step. Out of the corner of his eye, Janner watched Guildmaster Clout barking commands, lecturing the students, and demonstrating fighting stances. Now and then he called two students to the center of the circle to spar, stepping in from time to time to correct their technique.

By the seventeenth lap around the courtyard, Janner started to think Clout had forgotten about them. His lungs were on fire, and his pace had flagged to a trot. Kalmar whispered encouragement from behind and eventually moved to the front. He didn't look tired in the least.

Janner lost count of the laps. His legs felt like jelly. His feet felt like bricks. Kalmar edged farther and farther away until he was a half a lap ahead, running toward Janner on the opposite side of the courtyard. Kalmar gave him an encouraging nod when their eyes met, but it did no good; it only added frustration to Janner's exhaustion. He willed his legs to wake up. He was the older brother. He may not be able to outrun Kalmar in a sprint, but he had always told himself that endurance was his strong point. Now it was clear that he was outmatched again.

Guildmaster Clout ignored them, but the guildlings stole glances from time to time. Janner saw them pointing to Kalmar and whispering, and when he heard Kalmar's footsteps approaching from behind, embarrassment joined the other dark emotions.

The Wingfeather boys never joined the class that day. At one point Guildmaster Clout sent a guildling over with two canteens. The boys guzzled them dry, and then Clout ordered them to continue. They ran until the horn blew, signaling the end of school. By that time Janner could hardly put one foot in front of the other, and even Kalmar looked spent. The other students scattered, and Janner collapsed to the ground, feeling as if he would never walk again. Kalmar sat next to him and handed him another canteen.

Clout approached and studied them for a moment before speaking. "Don't be late," he said and strode away.

28

The Legendary Library
of Ban Rona

Janner didn't say a word the whole ride home. Leeli, on the other hand, talked the whole time. She told Nia all about the O'Sally boys, especially Thorn, who had taught her how to harness a dog to a houndrick, how to clean the kennel, how to prepare the dog food, and about the basics of dog-speak. She said Guildmaster O'Sally had spent most of the afternoon watching her interaction with the dogs, asking her questions about the various whistleharp tunes she played, and writing notes in a little book.

"I remembered how the whistleharp calmed the sea dragons, so I thought I'd try it out with the dogs," Leeli said. "I figured out how to—I don't know—*tell* them things with the music. It was easy. Guildmaster O'Sally said I was good," she finished with a blush.

Janner felt Kalmar looking at him and glanced up to see him mouth the words, "Real good." A hint of a smile pushed through all Janner's grouchiness.

When the carriage arrived at Chimney Hill, all Janner wanted was a long, cool drink of water and a nap. His joints protested when he lowered himself to the ground and limped inside after the others. Instead of a drink and a bed, however, he was greeted by Oskar N. Reteep standing just inside the door with a satchel full of books.

"Janner! I've cleared it with your mother. To the library we go! Bonifer's waiting." Reteep squeezed through the door and mounted the carriage.

Janner looked at Podo, asleep in front of the fire with his feet up, and at Kalmar and Leeli snacking on bread and jam at the table, then at Oskar waiting with the reins in his hands.

Nia called from the kitchen, "He's been looking forward to showing you his work on the First Book all day."

Janner heaved a sigh and grimaced his way back onto the carriage.

"My lad, you're going to love the library! In the words of Omrimund, King of Something, 'Get ready. It's better than you think.'"

They wound down the hill, over the creek, and back to Ban Rona, turning away from the Keep and heading west, toward the harbor.

Without Kalmar on the carriage for all to see, Janner felt refreshingly anonymous as they made their way through town. For the first time, he was able to watch the Hollowsfolk go about their business as usual. When they weren't scowling or cowering from a Grey Fang, they seemed pleasant enough—cheery, even. They greeted one another from front stoops, played with their dogs, chatted on street corners, and strolled the sidewalks in song. Janner's spirits lifted. Oskar even stopped at a snack stand and bought Janner a jellymuffin and a cup of ermentine juice, which gave him a burst of energy and allowed him to forget his tired bones for a while.

Ban Rona was much more enjoyable when Kalmar wasn't around, he thought, and as soon as he thought it, he felt guilty. *It wasn't Kalmar's fault,* he told himself. But it was true.

"Here we are!" Oskar said as he reined in the horses in front of a majestic building with fat trees shading the entrance. The building was of reddish stone, streaked with age, and beautiful. It was several stories high, and each level had a balcony where people sat in the shade with pipes and mugs of cider, reading books among the leaves.

Since Janner was a boy, and boys always think of climbing things, he noticed how easy it would be to step off the balcony and climb along the thick limbs—then he spotted several people doing just that. They strolled along the branches of the trees, deep into the overstory where platforms were attached to the limbs. Comfortable chairs perched on the platforms, and feet dangled over the edge where people reclined, lost in stories or studies. The more Janner looked, the more people he saw in the trees.

Janner dismounted without a thought of his soreness and followed Oskar through the main doors and into the library. His mouth hung open, and goosebumps tickled his arms. In every direction he saw another hallway lined with bookshelves. It was like Books and Crannies, only a hundred times bigger. In every corner of the room, stairs spiraled up to the next floor. Lanterns flickered on the walls. Cushioned chairs were tucked into nooks, and where there were no chairs there were desks.

In the center of the main room, "the hub," as Oskar called it, stood a signpost with arrows pointing to different sections of the library. Straight ahead were STORIES ABOUT CREEPY SOUNDS; another sign pointed a little to the left and read, STORIES WITH TREASURES; to the right were STORIES WITH BITTERSWEET ENDINGS AND TRUE STORIES (IF YOU DARE). The lowest sign read SIGNPOST NUMBER TWO and pointed to the far side of the hub, where another sign gave directions to a host of other sections.

"Can I help you?"

Janner spun around. A woman stood where a moment ago there had been empty space. She appeared to be a little younger than Nia and wore a pretty brown dress with flowers on the sleeves. Her hair was the color of toasted bread and was tied up in a bun.

Janner smiled at her. "No ma'am. This is my first time here, and I'd love to look around."

"Very well. My name is Madam Sidler. I'm the librarian. If you need me," she looked to her left and right, "I'll be around."

"Thank you," Janner said. He glanced at Oskar, then heard a rustle of movement, and when he looked back, the woman was gone.

"She does that," Oskar said. "It's creepy. Come on."

They climbed the stairs to the third floor and walked past corridor after corridor of books with sections like HISTORIES OF PIRACY IN THE SYMIAN

STRAITS and HISTORIES OF PIRACY BY PIRATES' WIVES and HISTORIES OF COUNTRIES YOU WILL NEVER VISIT, and finally under an archway to a wing of the library labeled DEAD LANGUAGES.

There were no windows, so even with the lanterns on the walls the place was shadowy as a catacomb. It was quieter, too, without birdsong or breeze or the hushed voices that flitted about in the rest of the library. Bonifer Squoon sat at a desk poring over a pile of notes.

"Can I help you?" said a voice. Madam Sidler stepped into the lamplight, and Janner jumped.

"No ma'am." Janner gave her a fake smile. "I'm with Mister Reteep."

"Thank you, Librarian Sidler. We're *still* fine. Still researching the same thing we were researching yesterday."

"Nothing at all, then?" she asked hopefully.

"I assure you," Oskar said.

Another rustle of her dress, and she vanished into the shadows.

"She's very helpful, as you can see," said Bonifer with a chuckle.

"Creepy," said Oskar, palming his flop of hair to his head and squeezing into a chair next to Bonifer. "Janner, come look."

The table was heavy with books. Most of them were thick, with tattered black covers and yellow pages. Leaves of parchment were scattered over every empty space. A candle guttered at the corner of the table, with a cascade of wax hardening around it.

At the center of the desk lay Janner's book—the First Book. Janner felt guilty that he hadn't shown much interest in it lately. Try as he might, he wasn't as excited about translating it as Oskar and Bonifer seemed to be, especially with everything else going on. But his father had given the book to him, so it was important.

The book was written in Old Hollish, a language even Nia barely knew, and as far as Oskar could tell, it was a history of sorts. It contained writings about Anyara, the ancient spelling of Anniera, and even the written music of "Yurgen's Tune." The song had saved them when Yurgen himself, the ancient sea dragon, had risen out of the Dark Sea to kill Podo. Leeli had played it on her whistleharp and quieted the dragon's rage. So even if they never translated another letter of the book, it had already saved their lives.

But now, when Janner looked at the thousand pages of handwritten script, his heart skipped a beat. What other mysteries lay in those pages? Why did his father risk his life to get it for him? Thank the Maker for Oskar N. Reteep, Janner thought, or the book would have been nothing but an old souvenir, a keepsake to remind him of his dead father.

Bonifer put down his quill and rubbed his eyes.

"Janner, my boy, it fills my heart with joy and sadness every time I see you. You look so much like your father. Indeed, you even talk like him."

Janner pulled up a chair and smiled at the old man. He didn't know what to say, so he turned his attention to the book. "Have you made any progress today?"

"A little. The script is sloppier in this section. As if the author wrote it in a hurry."

"But we managed to get a few sentences yesterday." Oskar snapped the candle free of the wax and held it over the page. "Read it, lad."

Deep, deep, deep in the world, under rock and river, under shadow
of shadow, the Fane of Fire, where stone and water wake the walker,
there descends the Maker, and the king alone may come.

"What does it mean?" Janner whispered, because it seemed right to whisper in the wake of the ancient text.

"I wish I could say," said Bonifer. "But I don't believe we'll know until we translate the whole of it."

"It will take us months." Oskar giggled. "Months! Between Bonifer, myself, and this wealth of books, we'll be able to get every letter of it right. I feel as though I was born for this." Even with his bald head and white wisps of hair, Oskar seemed to have grown years younger—especially next to the ancient Bonifer Squoon.

"I'm not a librarian," Janner said, "but can I help you?"

The old men shook with phlegmy chortles.

"Indeed!" said Bonifer when he had collected himself. "I need to reference the seventh volume of *Old Hollish in Daily Use,* which you should be able to find right over there."

Janner lifted a lamp from the wall and ran his fingers over the old books until he found it. He removed it from the shelf, blew off a layer of dust, and laid it on the table among the others. Oskar and Bonifer were already huddled over the First Book, discussing the curve of a certain character, comparing it to a similar one on a previous page.

Janner wished he could be more useful. He kept looking out of the Dead Languages archive at all the books in the other rooms until Oskar glanced up from the desk.

"Lad, I think we've got what we need for this page. Why don't you go have a look around? And keep out of trouble, or that Madam Sidler will scare you silly." Oskar put a hand to the side of his mouth and lowered his voice. "She's everywhere."

"Can I help you?" said Madam Sidler from the corner of the room. Oskar jumped with such violence that his spectacles clattered to the floor. "I heard you mention my name and thought I might be of assistance."

"Good heavens, woman!" Oskar exclaimed. "We're fine!"

"Very well," she said and sank into the shadows again.

Janner smiled as he stood at the top of the stairs, trying to decide where to go first.

A Lineage of Kings

Janner had never seen so many books in one place. He wandered from room to room, perusing books that struck his interest and others that didn't. He couldn't resist pulling them from the shelf to smell them, to feel their pages, and to skim their contents, no matter what the books were about. He read a few disturbing poems by Adeline the Poetess in a collection called *An Anthology of Maniacal Verse;* he browsed through pages of illustrations by someone named R. Smackam, mostly of fairies and witches and gnoblins; he found a biography of Connolin Durga, which he tucked under his arm for later; and to his delight he found a whole section of Annieran history.

One of the books, titled *A Lineage of Kings,* had page after page of genealogies along with portraits of various members of the Annieran court. Janner stood in the aisle, ears ringing and skin tingling, turning pages with trembling fingers. Here, among all these books, was one about *his* family—and it wasn't just a list of names hung on a family tree. Each name was listed with the date and place of birth and a short biography, and some included a gallery of portraits.

Janner slid to the floor and gazed for a long time at drawings of his ancestors. Some of them, he thought, looked remarkably like Kalmar, and some of the women looked like Leeli. The Wingfeathers had sat on the throne for generations—Throne Wardens, High Kings, High Queens (in the event that the secondborn was a girl), Song Maidens (or Song Masters in the event that the thirdborn was a boy), and Lore Wains (which, Janner learned, was the title for each child born after the third). Lore Wains were weavers of tales who traveled the kingdom telling stories to every village in order to keep Anniera's histories and myths close to the hearts of the people.

Janner held the book up to the lamplight and studied the faces of a royal family from the year 67. There was a bearded king, a short woman with a sword (who was the queen, according to the text), a tall girl who must have been an apprentice Throne Warden, a young prince, a toddler boy sucking on a whistleharp, and an infant in the arms of a nurse. It was a big family, and the artist had captured so much personality in their faces that Janner felt as if he knew them. At the bottom of the page were the words, "High King Bormand Quickfoot and Family, 67–92, Third Epoch."

Janner flipped to the end of the book and found, with a pinch of disappointment, that it had been written before his father's time. He ached to see another picture of Esben, even as a baby. But the last page read, "Jru and Nala Wingfeather." He couldn't be sure, but he thought he remembered those were the names of his grandparents. There was no picture, but on the previous page the branches of the family tree included name after interesting name, such as Samwell Durbin and Tumnus Button—names that sounded Hollish to him—and funny names like Tollers Greensmith, and noble names like Lander Wingfeather (his great-great-great-grandfather, as best as Janner could tell).

He felt as if he were glowing from the inside out.

"Do you need anything?" said a voice.

Janner had been wondering when the librarian would pester him again. But when he looked up and down the aisle, he couldn't find her. He shrugged and turned back to the bookshelf and almost jumped out of his skin when he saw her face peering at him from the slot where he'd removed the book.

"Anything at all?" she asked.

"No, thank you," said Janner, and she vanished into the shadows. He pulled a few more books out and saw only the back of the bookshelf. He tapped it with his knuckle and could tell it was hollow. "Secret passages," he said to himself. "Spooky."

He wandered the library till he saw the gold rays from the sunset angling through the windows and gilding the walls. Twice he saw the librarian swoop up behind other people to see if they needed help, and twice he saw the people jump. He climbed the steps to the third level and found Oskar and Bonifer straightening papers into stacks, capping ink bottles, and gathering their things.

"How did you do?" Janner asked.

"Another page!" Oskar said. "I tell you, lad, at this rate we'll be finished in no time."

"If by 'no time,' you mean eight months, then you are correct," said Bonifer with a sniff. He placed his top hat on his head and stood with some effort. "Janner, would you mind fetching my cane there by the wall? It seems so far away at the moment."

Janner handed Bonifer the cane and showed him the book of Annieran history.

"Ah! What's this?" Bonifer said, squinting at it through a monocle.

"It's a family tree." He flipped to the last page. "I wanted to ask if you knew Jru and Nala Wingfeather."

Bonifer winced. He put a hand on Janner's shoulder and looked over his spectacles at him. "My lad, those are your grandparents."

"I thought so," Janner said. "Did you know them?"

Bonifer laughed. "Of course I did. Jru's father, Ortham Greensmith, was one of my finest friends. He and I grew up together right here in the Hollows! When Madia Wingfeather came to the Hollows as a young maiden to watch the Banick Durga, Ortham fell in love with her. They married, and he took the name Wingfeather. He left for the Shining Isle and took me with him as his advisor. I've been close to the Wingfeather family ever since. Indeed, I was with him every moment of his reign."

"So you knew my great-grandfather?"

"Indeed." Bonifer smiled. "And your grandfather Jru. I was on the other side of the door when Jru was born, as I was there when Esben was born. This may surprise you, lad, but I was one of the first people to hold you too."

"How old *are* you?" Janner asked.

"Eighty-seven."

Janner was pretty sure that made Bonifer Squoon the oldest person he'd ever met. He knew Bonifer had been his father's advisor, but he didn't know his friendship with the Wingfeathers went all the way back to his great-grandfather. "What was my great-grandmother like?"

"Madia? She was lovely." Bonifer patted the book, lost in thought. "We should head back to Chimney Hill. Your mother told me she was making mushroom and potato chowderstew tonight, and that makes even these old bones want to hurry." He turned to Oskar. "Don't forget the pages we've translated, my friend. It would be a shame to lose all that work."

"In the words of Boonta Nood—"

"'I've got them right here in my sidebag,'" Bonifer finished.

"Just what I was going to say!" Oskar jiggled with delight and slung the satchel over his shoulder.

They descended to the first floor again as dusk settled and cast the interior of the library into a gloomy shade. Hollowsfolk stood in line at the desk while a teenage boy entered the titles of the books they were borrowing into a ledger. Janner couldn't see the librarian, but he could tell where she was by the occasional gasp when she appeared before some poor reader to ask if they needed help.

Janner approached the desk when it was his turn and placed his books before the boy.

"Name," the boy said.

"Janner Wingfeather."

The boy looked up from the ledger. "The Throne Warden. You've got a tough job, don't you?"

"What do you mean?" Janner asked, prepared for a cruel remark.

"Just that it's hard enough being a Throne Warden—from what I've read, I mean—without having to deal with a bunch of angry Hollish kids picking on your brother."

"Yeah."

"These are due back in two weeks. And I'd make sure I was on time if I were you, unless you want *her* after you." The boy pointed at the librarian as she startled someone else.

"That's something I definitely don't want," Janner said.

"My name's Owen. See you around."

Janner smelled the salty harbor air as he boarded the carriage. The sky in the west lit the water with the last light of the day, watergulls called in the air, dogs barked, and Hollish people strolled the street in happy conversation. Ban Rona seemed less threatening than it had only a few days ago.

"What are you so happy about, lad?" asked Oskar.

"I just had my first normal conversation in the Green Hollows."

"With the librarian's assistant?" asked Bonifer. "A good lad. You know, I could put in a good word with Librarian Sidler, if you like. She might like another bookish young man on her staff."

"Really?" Janner said. "What do I have to do?"

"Nothing at all. You just have to be in the bookbindery guild."

Janner slumped in his seat.

"What's wrong?" Oskar asked.

"I'm not in the bookbindery guild."

He no longer felt like talking, so he tried to read the first pages of *Connolin Durga: Serving a Bowl of Pain to Ridgerunners,* but there wasn't enough light. He shut the book and tossed it aside. Owen was wrong. It wasn't hard being a Throne Warden. It was annoying.

It was dark and chilly when they got home. Rudric sat on a bench in the front lawn of Chimney Hill talking and laughing with Danniby. When the carriage stopped and Freva came out to lead the horses to the barn again, Rudric hurried over and took the reins from her.

"Freva dear, you're as pale as the moon," he said.

Freva mumbled and looked at her feet. "Oy, that barn is dark, me lord."

"The cloven is gone, I assure you."

"Me lord, I hated going in there at night even before I seen that beast."

"That's all right. You help Mister Squoon inside while Danniby and I tend to the horses. Run along."

Freva thanked Rudric profusely and offered Squoon her arm as he eased his way down from the carriage.

Rudric smiled at Janner. "Oy, lad. You look like you've been ridden hard."

Janner had all but forgotten about his exhausting run that afternoon, and Rudric's reminder woke up the ache in his joints. "Yes sir. We were late for the Durgan Guild today."

Rudric let out a low whistle. "Oy, that's a bad one. Late is one thing. Late for Guildmaster Clout is another. I doubt you'll be late tomorrow, eh?"

"No way on Aerwiar," Janner said, and Rudric laughed as he led the horses away.

It was good having Rudric around, especially now that Artham was gone. Rudric was no flying Throne Warden, but he was as big as a mountain and laughed like thunder. With a cloven lumping about, Janner was thankful to have the Keeper of the Hollows nearby.

After a dinner during which Leeli chattered about her favorite dogs at the houndry and Oskar and Bonifer exchanged weird quotes from weirder books, Janner could hardly hold his eyes open. Kalmar seemed as happy as ever, which put Janner in another foul mood.

He ate without speaking and asked to be excused. Nia kissed him on the head and sent him to bed without clearing the table. Once in his room, he didn't bother lighting the lantern on the wall. He didn't bother reading his books. The soft bed welcomed him with a pile of warm blankets, and he was asleep in minutes.

But when Kalmar came to bed, he was noisy. Janner groaned and pulled the covers over his head when the lantern flared to life.

"Sorry," Kalmar whispered. "Didn't mean to wake you."

"Well, you did," Janner grumbled.

He felt Kalmar sit on the bottom bunk at his feet. Janner lowered the covers and squinted at Kalmar. His whiskers drooped, and his wet, black nose caught the lamplight.

"What is it?" Janner asked, sounding meaner than he meant to.

"I'm sorry about the Durgan Guild thing. I know you'd rather be making books." Kalmar scratched his chin, but not like a person would; he raked with his claws in a quick, doglike motion. "I just don't know what you want me to do. Say it and I'll do it. I hate feeling like you're mad at me all the time."

Janner sighed. He felt a stone in his heart beginning to move, but he didn't want it to. He wanted to stay angry so Kalmar would know how much it cost to be his brother. "I'm not mad at you. I just—I just wish I could do *one* thing I want. One thing."

"You went to the library today."

"Yeah, but—"

"And *you* actually stand a chance of making friends. I don't. I messed up. Messed up really bad. And now I have these." He held out his claws. "I'm stuck with these awful things. Stuck with this face." Kalmar hung his head.

The stone in Janner's heart moved a little more and teetered on the verge of rolling away. He sat up on his elbows. When he saw a tear run down the length of Kalmar's snout, dangle at the end of his nose, and drip to the bed, the stone went with it.

"It's not your fault," Janner said. "The Fangs did this."

"You don't understand." Kalmar wiped his nose. "I'm a terrible king. I'm a terrible boy. That's not the Fangs' fault."

"What are you talking about? Are you saying you *wanted* to get kidnapped?"

"No."

"Are you saying you *wanted* to get thrown into the Black Carriage?"

"No."

"Are you saying you *wanted* to turn into a Fang?"

Silence.

"Kal?" Janner sensed a coldness in the room. Kalmar had stopped crying and stared at the floor. "Kal?" Janner repeated.

"Yes," Kalmar whispered.

"Yes, what?"

"Yes, I wanted it." Kalmar wiped his nose. "It only works if you want it. That's what she said."

"What who said?" Janner felt afraid without knowing why, afraid of the answer. With every word Kalmar spoke, Janner felt as if he was inching his way farther into the maw of a black cave.

"The Stone Keeper. She had such a beautiful voice. They told us in the Carriage that we could be powerful. They told us we would know strength and speed and skill, and all we had to do was sing what she told us to sing."

"And you sang it?" Janner asked in a quiet voice.

Kalmar nodded.

Janner was afraid to ask, but he did anyway. "What happened? What did it feel like?"

"It felt good. And it felt like dying," Kal said after a moment. "Like my heart had shriveled up in my chest. But I wanted it. She said the song wouldn't work unless my heart was in it. And it was." Kalmar's voice cracked and he looked away. "I'm so sorry."

"Then how did you come back?" Janner asked. "Can any of the Fangs come back like you?"

"I don't know. Uncle Artham told me he kicked down the door before the Stone Keeper named me. He said names have power, and he got to me before the change was complete. I don't know how it works. I'm just glad he found me. I don't want to be a Fang, Janner. But today when we were running, and when I wrestled Grigory on the field, I felt like it was still in me. Still in my blood. I wanted to let it loose."

Kalmar's eyes met Janner's, and a cold shiver ran down Janner's back. The air between them tingled. Kalmar's eyes were still blue, but Janner thought he saw flecks of yellow at the edges. He couldn't remember if they had been there before. Maybe it was a trick of the lamplight.

"I thought I was lost, Janner. I never thought you would find me again. They told me I could either sing the song and fight in Gnag's army, or die in a cold, dark dungeon. I was scared. And I didn't want to be king. I *still* don't want to be king. I don't know how." Kalmar had a knot of the blanket between his claws and was twisting it as he spoke. "I'm not smart like you are. I don't know poems and histories, and I don't dream about Anniera like you do. I just want to be left alone."

Janner felt the need to comfort his brother, but for some reason he didn't want to touch him. "You know what Mama would say?"

"What?"

"She would tell you that you were the king whether you liked it or not. She would tell you our papa's blood runs in your veins, and that it's stronger than you know. She would tell you your name. Your true name. Kalmar Wingfeather."

"I know that already."

"Well, you're the king. Don't forget it." Janner forced a smile. "I certainly can't. Every time I turn around I'm having to protect you from something or someone."

Kalmar let go of the blanket and looked away. It was ripped to shreds. Janner saw bits of cloth under his claws. "Can you protect me from myself?"

Kalmar crossed the room and blew out the lantern, then bounded silently up to the top bunk.

"Kal?"

But the little Grey Fang didn't answer.

Janner lay awake for a long time, unsettled and scared. Through the window he saw a flash of lightning in the distance, and sometime before dawn the sound of thunder marched over the Hollows to rattle the window.

30

Borley and the Dagger

For days, Sara could hardly keep from smiling. She worked every hour thinking about the next meal, which was the only time she could talk with the younger children without drawing unwanted attention.

Talking with the other tools—*children,* she reminded herself—helped her believe she wasn't crazy. Whenever the drudgery of her labor began to numb her mind, she remembered that in a few hours she would be like a normal girl, whispering with other normal children. Sometimes when the meal whistle blew, she was surprised at how the hours had flown. Other times she spotted, among all the dirty faces, one of the children she had befriended, and she would watch for him or her to pass again as the hours trudged by.

The ebb and flow of time was a welcome change from the numbness and monotony her life had been before Janner Igiby. Her mind was awake, and it was sharp, and that meant there was hope.

Now she noticed things. She noticed that once every several days, the Overseer was joined at the top of the stairs by Fangs. She noticed how the Overseer seemed agitated, angrier at the Maintenance Managers when weapon production was slow. Once she saw one of the Fangs grab the Overseer by the collar and shake him. She couldn't hear what the Fang was yelling, but after they left, the Overseer had straightened his top hat, uncoiled his whip, and marched down the stairs to scream at every child he saw. Sara noticed the way he and Mobrik the ridgerunner paced the factory floor more than ever, and she saw the worried looks they exchanged whenever Fangs arrived.

After Janner's escape they had no longer acted like the rulers of their domain, but like two more tools, just a step above the Maintenance Managers. This made Sara wonder who Janner Igiby was. It seemed odd to her that the Fangs would care so much about an ordinary boy's escape. She spent hours greasing cogs on the rattling coal machine, asking herself over and over what it was about Janner that made him so special. She even went so far as to imagine that he was a prince from some faraway kingdom, and that he would one day return to rescue her.

On the third day after she first spoke with the little boy named Borley, Sara chose a seat in the mess hall and waited for him to arrive, eager to find out more about him and her other new friends. Borley sat across from her and grinned as if he wanted to tell her something. He beckoned for Sara to come close.

"What is it?" she whispered.

From under his shirt, Borley pulled a hunk of metal so black and jagged that it took Sara a moment to realize it was a dagger that hadn't yet gone through the polishing or sharpening process.

"Borley, cover that up!" she hissed, looking from side to side to be sure none of the Maintenance Managers were watching. "You could get in *big* trouble for having that."

Borley's shoulders slumped. "I thought we could use it to get out."

"It doesn't work like that, dear," she said. "We can't just fight our way out. The Overseer would stop us before we started."

By then several other younger children had arrived. A little girl with big brown eyes and black hair asked, "Then what do we do, Sara Cobbler?"

"Nothing, Grettalyn. We do nothing. Right now the best thing we can do is talk. I'm sure someday we'll get out of here, but we have to be *so* careful, do you hear? It would be terrible if the Overseer or Mobrik caught Borley hiding the knife and put him in the coffin, wouldn't it?"

The children's eyes grew wide, and they all nodded solemnly.

"Borley, will you give me the dagger?" Sara asked.

He handed it under the table, and Sara concealed it in the sleeve of her shirt. She would have to hold onto it until her next shift and then sneak it onto a passing wheelbarrow.

Then she heard a voice that made her jump so badly that the dagger nearly slipped out of her sleeve.

"What's going on over here?" said Mobrik the ridgerunner. He stood at Sara's shoulder in his usual top hat and ratty black coat, the tails of which dragged on the floor.

The children at the table lowered their heads and sipped their soup in silence, acting sad and sleepy, as Sara had told them to behave when the Maintenance Managers passed. Though her heart pounded and Mobrik's face was inches from hers, she felt a measure of pride in her friends' steely nerves.

"What do you mean, sir?" she asked in the dullest voice she could manage.

"I saw you talking. Were you talking?"

"Maybe I was, sir. Other tools have accused me of talking to myself. I don't realize it's happening." She slouched so low her chin nearly touched her bowl. "I'm just so tired," she said and yawned for effect.

"It's you again," Mobrik said, inching closer. "You're the tool who helped the boy escape."

Sara held still and gave no answer. The dagger was slipping. She bent her arm a little to keep it from falling out, and the point poked through a hole in her sleeve.

Sara wondered whether she should do something now, before Mobrik spotted the dagger, or wait and hope he didn't notice. She was as tall as he was, so she stood a chance of overpowering him. Or if she threatened him with the weapon, she might be able to keep him quiet. Or she could run, but she knew how that would turn out—with the Maintenance Managers swinging about from the rafter chains, no one ever made it far. Still, for a wild moment she thought it might be her only chance. She was surrounded by allies, she had a dagger, and the Overseer was nowhere to be seen.

Then she remembered how patiently Janner had planned his escape. He had spent days in the coffin waiting for the perfect time; he had help from Sara; he had the apples for bribing the ridgerunner—and even then he had nearly been caught. She also remembered how awful her punishment had been for helping him, and she knew she couldn't put Borley or Grettalyn or any of the others through the same. No, if she was going to make a move, it had to be on her own terms.

She prayed to the Maker that Mobrik wouldn't notice the little black point of metal jutting out of her sleeve. He narrowed his eyes at Sara, and she was certain he would see it. If she wanted the advantage of surprise, she was running out of time. Her heart thundered in her chest.

Then Borley burped.

Mobrik looked at him and said, "Rude." Then he skittered away.

Borley kept his head down till they were sure the ridgerunner had pushed through the door, and then they all snorted with laughter.

Sara planned to get rid of the dagger at her first opportunity, but that night when she lay down, she tucked it in the corner at the foot of her cot instead. A plan was forming in her mind, one she thought even Janner Igiby would be proud of.

She wondered where he was and whispered a prayer for his safety as she sank into a fine sleep in which she dreamed of a castle and a river and a horse on a grassy hill.

31

Olumphia's Warning
and Bunge's Game

The next morning it rained and rained on the Green Hollows. Nia and the children boarded the carriage in hooded raincoats that did little to keep them dry. The creek at the bottom of Chimney Hill was a roaring rapid, so high that foamy waves lapped over the bridge. When Nia drove the carriage across, Janner voiced his worry that it might wash away, but Nia reminded him that the bridge had stood for hundreds of years and had weathered many such storms. Kalmar was quiet, which had become his usual manner, especially in the morning.

They joined the train of carriages plodding toward the Guildling Hall, and once again Janner felt the heat of the other children's eyes. Even with Nia present, they hardly concealed their looks of loathing and distrust. Janner didn't understand why his mother chose to remain silent; she seemed impervious to both the rain and the hatred. When she rounded the statue in the courtyard, she bade the children good-bye, said, "Remember who you are," and rode on.

Janner, Kalmar, and Leeli had no trouble making their way through the children to the school because wherever they walked a bubble of space opened before them. Guildlings shuffled out of the way with hisses and whispers and mutterings of "don't let it touch you" and "they smell like dogs."

Janner stared at the soggy ground and thought about how nice it had been at the library without Kalmar around; for a few hours he had almost believed he was an ordinary boy. He was still troubled by what Kal had told him the night before, he still felt rumblings of frustration about the book-bindery guild, and worst of all, he was afraid, afraid to look his own brother in the eye. He was afraid he would see those yellow spots creeping into the edges of the blue—because if they were there, it meant something that Janner didn't want to imagine.

As they crossed the threshold out of the rain and into the school, Grigory Bunge stuck out his foot and tripped Kalmar. The floor was slick already, so when Kal fell, he jarred Leeli enough to take her down with him. Her crutch slid away and she sprawled on the wet floor. Grigory didn't seem to mind that he had caused Leeli's fall and made no move to help her. The floor was filthy from all the wet boots, and Leeli's dress was covered in mud.

Janner helped her up and brushed her off, trying to control his anger and decide whether to fight or yell or calmly find a teacher and let him or her discipline the Bunge boy.

Kalmar, though, had already made his decision. He crouched on all fours, bared his teeth at Grigory Bunge, and growled.

The sound stilled the room. The children in the hall backed away with fear in their eyes. Even Grigory Bunge looked scared. Janner hardly recognized his brother. The way his snout curled made his fangs seem longer, and the fur on the back of his head and neck was raised and quivering.

"Kalmar, don't!" Janner said.

He stepped between Bunge and the wolf, realizing as he did so that he was afraid of Kalmar too. He remembered his scars, the bright fire of pain in his shoulders, legs, neck, and back when Kalmar had fought him in the water. His senses told him that this was no longer Kalmar in front of him—this was a Grey Fang, all the way down to the marrow.

"Kalmar, it's me!" Janner said. "Calm down!"

But Kalmar's eyes remained locked on Grigory's. Leeli limped forward and in a trembling voice hummed a melody in Kal's ear.

The wolfish growl faltered and one ear twitched. He looked away from Grigory and focused on Janner, blinked a few times, and in an instant he was

Kalmar again. Janner took him by the hand and stood him up, and the tension seeped from the hall.

"Keep your dog on a leash, Wingfeather," Grigory sneered.

"It's hard with all the rats loose in the hall," Janner said.

Grigory Bunge grinned wickedly and raised his fists. Janner prepared himself for a beating.

"Oy! What's going on here?" Olumphia Groundwich pushed through the crowd, and in seconds the guildlings dispersed. Her hands were on her hips and her whiskers trembled. She looked at Leeli's muddy dress and gasped. "Bunge! Did you do this?"

"I didn't mean to, guildmadam." Bunge put on a look of concern. "Leeli, isn't it? Are you all right? I'm really, *really* sorry that happened."

"Then why didn't you help me up?" Leeli asked.

"I was scared of the—the—of *him*." Grigory pointed at Kalmar and pretended to be afraid. "He was growling at me, guildmadam! I thought he might attack."

Olumphia pointed her long arm down the hallway and said, "Get out of my sight, Bunge. You'll be late for lectures."

"Yes, guildmadam. Sorry, guildmadam." Grigory hurried past Janner and flashed him a look of dark glee.

"Come on. We don't want to be late again," Janner muttered. He hefted his pack to his shoulder and made to follow Grigory to the lecture hall.

"Stop right there, guildling," Olumphia ordered. "To my quarters, Wingfeathers. We need to talk."

As they followed her to the office, Janner's blood boiled. Once again, he was in trouble, and once again, it wasn't his fault. Why wasn't Grigory getting punished?

Olumphia slammed her door behind the children and told them to sit. She sat at her desk and looked long and hard at all three of them. Janner was determined not to apologize, so he busied himself counting the guildmadam's whiskers. He almost laughed when he realized the ones she had plucked on their first day had already grown back.

"Your mother," Olumphia began, her voice choked with emotion, "is in great danger."

Janner's stubbornness vanished. "What do you mean?"

"Is it the cloven?" Leeli asked. "Is it back?"

Kalmar said nothing. He stared at the arm of his chair and scratched the claw of his forefinger against the wood grain.

"No, it's not the cloven. I'm talking about something even worse. Oy! I'm talking about you, Kalmar."

He looked up and narrowed his eyes at her. "I'd never hurt my own mother."

"Not directly," Olumphia said.

Kalmar folded his arms. "Not at all."

Olumphia took a deep breath and seemed unsure what to say.

"Head Guildmadam Groundwich," Leeli said, "I don't mean any disrespect, but you're wrong. Kalmar wouldn't hurt her. Not ever."

"You don't understand, guildlings. I love your mother, but she did something foolish."

"What are you talking about?" Janner demanded.

"*Turalay.*" Olumphia's chin quavered. "At the council. Her blood is on the great tree. She declared before the council and the seven chiefs that she vouched for you, Kalmar. Do you understand what that means?"

"That if I break the law, we'll both be punished," Kal said. "But I'm no criminal. I'm not going to break any laws."

"Ah, child," Olumphia said, shaking her head. "It's not that easy. I knew when you first arrived that it would take some time for the guildlings here to get used to you. To be honest, I knew it would take me some time as well. If you weren't my dear friend's son, I'd be as suspicious of you as the rest of them." Kalmar gouged the arm of his chair with his claw. "Understand, Kalmar, that you're up against nine years of hurt and anger. Even before the Great War came and the Fangs killed our sons and daughters, the Green Hollows was less than welcoming to outsiders. For good or ill, it's in our blood."

"But if Kalmar doesn't break any laws, how is Mama in danger?" Janner asked.

"My ears are still ringing from being screamed at by the parents of these guildlings. I've had to listen to it every day since you arrived. They're upset that I've allowed you to come to school at all. They think I've put their children in danger, and they're determined to do something about it."

"What will they do?" Leeli asked.

"Well, for starters they'll tell their kids to provoke you. That's Grigory Bunge's game. His father wants to see you kicked out of the Guildling Hall. If you fight his boy, he'll claim a Grey Fang tried to kill a Hollish child. If you so much as leave a scratch on that Bunge boy, the council will believe him. They'll throw you into the dungeon for years."

Janner gulped as the implication unfolded in his mind. Kalmar didn't have to steal a horse or damage city property. If the Hollowsfolk wanted to lock him away for good, all he had to do was scratch one of their children.

"And if you're thrown into the dungeon, lad," Olumphia said in a strained voice, "your mother goes with you. Dear Nia will be chained in the dark, cold and alone. Do you understand? If you had attacked the Bunge boy just now, that would have been the end of it."

Janner and Leeli looked at their brother. Kalmar stared at Olumphia, stunned into stillness.

"That means no fighting for you, Kalmar, except in class," Olumphia continued. "Even then, you *must* restrain yourself. No teeth. No claws. Don't give them any reason to bring a charge against you."

"Yes ma'am," Kalmar said. "I'm sorry. I didn't realize—"

"Hush," she said, waving a hand. "No need for that. You've done nothing wrong. It's these Bunge fools who ought to apologize. And you two," she turned to Leeli and Janner, "are to keep watch at all times. Leeli, if you see Kalmar on the verge of a fight, play that whistleharp or throw yourself between them or something. Oy! Janner, you're a Throne Warden so this is going to be hardest for you. You're used to protecting your brother. Now I'm asking you to protect buffoons like Grigory Bunge *from* him. There's one more thing," Olumphia said, leaning forward and tapping her fingers on the desk. She pursed her lips, which made her whiskers jut out at new angles. "I beg you not to say anything about this to your mother. At least for a while."

"Why? We don't keep secrets from her," Janner said.

"That's good. And this is no secret. It's just that I'm afraid if she gets wind of these rumors, she'll light up like a bonfire and storm the city until she finds the culprits."

"What's so wrong with that?" Kalmar asked.

"The last thing your family needs is more trouble. Some of the Hollowsfolk who aren't happy about you—Nibbick Bunge, for instance—are powerful people who happen to think that Rudric should have refused you refuge here. They think you'll bring Gnag and his whole army upon us."

"But Gnag doesn't know we're here," Leeli said.

"Not yet, he doesn't. Either way, it doesn't matter what you or I think. It's what the Hollowsfolk think. I know your mother as well as you do. Maybe better, even. She's fierce when it comes to those she loves, and she'll come after anyone who's out to get her son. If Nia sticks her nose in their faces, which she just may do, they won't just fight back with their fists. They'll gather support from their friends and make things in Ban Rona even worse for you. If you think things are bad now with all this Grey Fang business, wait till they make outcasts of the whole family."

"I'm not lying to Mama," Janner said.

"You're a fine lad," said Olumphia with a proud smile. "Nia did well with the three of you. I'm not asking you to lie. I'm just asking you, Kalmar, to stay out of any scrapes for as long as it takes for these Hollowsfolk to realize you're not going to start gobbling up their henpecks and hogpigs in the middle of the night. That's all. And the less your mother knows about boys like Grigory Bunge, the better. Your mother's freedom—and maybe her *life*—depends on it. Yours too." Olumphia studied the children to be sure they understood. "Now get to lectures. You're learning the history of the Watercraw today. One of Guildmaster Nibblestick's favorite topics."

The rain stopped in time for P.T., but the field was a muddy mess. It should have made Get the Boot and Tackle Smash more fun, but now that Janner knew there were students out to provoke Kal, he was more uptight than ever. He kept close to his brother, telling him over and over to ignore the taunts, to remember his name, and to keep his claws under control.

The Wingfeathers sat on the floor again at lunch, and they ate without speaking. The brothers dropped Leeli off at the houndry without encountering Biggin O'Sally, so they arrived at the Durgan Guild courtyard in plenty of time.

Guildmaster Clout greeted the boys with a nod and treated them no differently than the other students, though they were all at least a head taller than Janner and two heads taller than Kalmar. Clout had them wrestling along with the others. He critiqued their moves and suggested various holds and blocks, and by the end of the day Janner began to enjoy it in spite of himself.

Every time Kalmar was in the ring, though, Janner tensed, ready at every moment to step in if he heard any growling or saw any teeth. But he had no need to worry; Kalmar allowed himself to be outwrestled in every match, even though it meant he was hurt more than once.

When the horn blew at the end of the day, the boys ran to get Leeli from the houndry and found her with a puppy in her arms. It was already as big as Nugget (Nugget before the water from the First Well, anyway), but it still had the soft brown and white fur, cute face, and high-pitched yip of a puppy. Thorn O'Sally sat beside her on a bench at the houndry door, tickling the pup behind the ears.

"Hey, there," he said. "Got your sister a pup. You'll get one too, if you like. As soon as you're ready." He fished a comb from his pocket and slicked his hair back. "Leeli here already knows as much dogspeak as I do, and I've been here my whole life. She's real good, you know. Show 'em."

Leeli blushed and put the puppy on the ground. Just like Biggin O'Sally, she made a series of quick, whisper-click-whistle noises with her mouth, and the puppy turned in a circle, stood on its hind legs, and barked three times.

"Tell him to bark seven," said Thorn.

Leeli made another sound and the puppy barked exactly seven times. Janner and Kalmar clapped and shook their heads in amazement.

"Aww. Did she learn dogspeak from her dog brother?" said a voice.

Janner turned to find Grigory Bunge towering over him. He had brought a gaggle of friends, all of whom were bigger and stronger than Janner and Kalmar.

"Let's see if we can teach the mutt to play dead, eh, boys?" Grigory said.

The gang howled and barked and laughed in Kalmar's face. Janner pushed himself between them.

"Get out of here!" Leeli jabbed Bunge with her crutch. "Leave my brother alone!" But the boys only howled louder. "Thorn," she said, "go get your father. Quick!"

"He isn't here. He's out on a houndrick for a training run. Won't be back for an hour." Thorn didn't look scared, but the way he was eyeing the bullies told Janner he knew they were in trouble. "Janner. Kalmar. There's nine of them and just three of us. I don't know that now's such a good time to brawl."

Grigory silenced his gang with a wave of his hand. "I've got no quarrel with you, O'Sally. Just the dog here. And his brother if he's fool enough to jump in." He leaned over and put his face in Kalmar's. "Are you angry, dog boy? You stink like you're angry."

"Yes, I'm angry." Kalmar met Grigory's eyes. Then came a growl from deep within his throat.

"Leeli, play something, quick," Janner said. "Kalmar, this is what they want, remember?"

The growl continued, and Grigory grinned wider, eager for the attack.

"Grigory, please," Janner said. "Leave us alone. We don't want to fight you or your friends."

Then Janner heard another clicking sound—dogspeak—and out of the houndry came Thorn's older brother, Kelvey, along with a pack of dogs.

Leeli abandoned her whistleharp tune and whistle-clicked something to the dogs. They growled and circled the gang of boys: fifteen huge dogs, ready to pounce.

"A word from me, and they'll attack." Leeli limped over to Kalmar. She made another sound and the dogs barked in unison; several of the boys jumped at that, and Leeli couldn't help but smile. "Now leave me and my brothers alone."

"No need for anybody to attack anybody." Grigory shrugged. "We're just here for our dogs, is all."

"They're in the kennel," said Kelvey, who leaned against the houndry doorframe. "Be quick about it or my pa will have words with the head guildmadam."

Grigory shrugged and led his boys inside, and every one of them made sure to bump into Kalmar as they passed.

"You'd better get gone," said Kelvey. "They'll be back out in a minute, and they'll have their dogs too. Things could get awful, and quick."

Kalmar and Janner thanked Thorn and Kelvey for their help, and the Wingfeathers hurried to the courtyard, Leeli's puppy at her heels.

"Sooner or later that's going to happen and we won't have any help," Janner said. "What do we do then?"

32

A Discovery in the Vale

If Janner wasn't sure about telling his mother about their conversation with Olumphia Groundwich, one look at her told him he should wait. For the first time in a *long* time, Nia was in a fine mood.

She greeted the children with a smile that made her seem ten years younger, and then she drove the carriage past the Keep and pointed at Ban Rona and the distant harbor. The clouds had broken open to reveal blue sky, and sunlight painted the hills a vibrant green in contrast to the blaze of color in every treetop. Smoke rose from chimneys, ships rocked in the quay, and the sun was warm in the chilly air.

"This city has always been so beautiful in the fall," Nia said, taking a deep breath. "I never thought you'd see it, you know. The Maker is full of surprises." With a sigh, she shook the reins and the horses heaved on.

When they got home, Rudric was waiting. He sat on a huge horse, hands folded on the saddle horn. Next to him stood another horse, saddled and stomping the grass. Bonifer, Oskar, and Podo reclined in garden chairs, dozing in the sunlight with pipes dangling from their mouths. Janner supposed there were no plans to visit the library that day; Oskar and Bonifer had been working for two days without a break, and the weather seemed to have lulled them to sleep.

"Ready when you are," Rudric said to Nia without even a glance at the children. He grinned at her in a way that made Janner feel a little embarrassed, though Nia didn't seem to mind at all. She let out what Janner would have called a giggle if he didn't know any better. Nia Wingfeather didn't giggle. But without a word to the children, she mounted the horse and the two of them trotted down the hill.

Leeli led her puppy inside, cooing to it about finding some food and asking what its name should be. She left Janner and Kalmar on the front lawn.

"Come on," Kalmar said, dropping his pack at the front steps. "I want to show you something."

He didn't wait for an answer. Janner tossed his bag aside and ran around the house to catch up.

In a flash, he went from mulling over Grigory Bunge, Rudric, Olumphia, and a host of other worries to thinking of nothing at all but the bright, wet grass and the wide openness of the afternoon. Kalmar jogged across the back lawn, past the barn and the goat pen, to the open prairie beyond. Fields and hills and wooded valleys spread out as far as Janner could see.

Kalmar turned to be sure Janner was following, then whooped and sped off. Janner couldn't catch him, but he could see him up ahead, always over the next rise or around the next bend, pausing now and then to make sure Janner was coming.

Janner vaulted a wooden fence, surprising a family of wild goats and sending them running. He followed Kalmar's trail down a wagon path overgrown with prairie grass, passing a ramshackle skeleton of a barn where a rooster perched on a rafter.

Just after the old barn, the land dropped away and Kalmar disappeared from view. When Janner got to the last spot he'd seen his brother, he skidded to a stop, lungs aflame. The field fell away down a grassy slope so steep it might have been a gully. Janner reminded himself that there were no gargan rockroaches in the Green Hollows, according to Pembrick's *Creaturepedia*, anyway. At the bottom of the hill was a pond with green algae at the edges, surrounded by weeds—but no Kalmar.

"Kal!" Janner called between breaths. "I know you're down there!" Janner half expected to see him come up from under the water, soaked and covered in green goo. He scanned the vale again, more slowly this time. He was certain Kalmar had come this way. But other than the pond there was nowhere he could hide. "Kal, where are you?"

"Right here," said Kalmar. He sounded close, but his voice was muted.

Janner edged his way down the slope, bracing himself for Kalmar to jump out and scare him.

"Getting closer," Kalmar said, taunting him.

Janner made his way to the pond, sliding on his rump in the steepest places. He turned in a slow circle until he was facing the way he had just come. Then he saw it.

At the bottom of the hill, overgrown with weeds, was the mouth of a cave

from which a trickle of water ran, feeding the pond. The hillside sloped out over the entrance so that it was hidden from anyone not standing at the bottom. Kalmar's head poked out among the weeds.

Janner grinned. "How did you find this?"

"What do you think I did while you were at the library—stick my nose in some book?" Kalmar waved Janner over. "I found it yesterday. I wanted to show you."

Janner crawled through the soggy weeds and ducked under the grassy overhang. He smelled wet earth and a sharp, foul odor like mildew or mold, but he couldn't see more than a few feet into the gloom. He waited for his eyes to adjust and soon saw that, a little way ahead, the ceiling rose enough so that he could stand. Janner wiped his muddy hands on his pants and looked around.

"How far back does it go?" he whispered.

"Why are you whispering?" Kalmar whispered back.

"I don't know," Janner whispered, and they laughed.

The brothers crept deeper into the cave, sidestepping the little creek, until the green tint of light at the entrance seemed uncomfortably far away.

"I wish we had a lantern or something," Janner said. "I can't see a thing."

"I can see fine. It goes several more steps back, then turns a corner. I'm going to check it out."

"Wait!" Janner said, not because he was worried but because he wanted to go with him. But it was too late. Janner could hear Kalmar scraping his way ahead, calling back from time to time about how high the ceiling was, or about a pincherfish swishing through a puddle. Janner didn't want to be a Fang, but he certainly wouldn't mind being able to see in the dark. He leaned against the damp wall and waited for several long minutes. He didn't mind the dark so much, but he didn't like being alone. Kalmar had gone out of earshot, and the stench and the dripping silence were unnerving.

"Dead end," said Kalmar, right in front of Janner's face.

Janner jerked with surprise, his foot slipped, and he landed on his rump in the puddle. Kalmar doubled over with laughter, and then Janner laughed too, and the cave echoed with it—perhaps for the first time since Aerwiar was made.

When they crawled out, the sun was sinking in the west, casting a shadow on the little valley. They were wet and muddy, but neither boy noticed, nor would they have cared if they did. They had gone caving, which was far better than cleanliness.

At the top of the hill the sun smiled on them and dried their clothes on the walk home. They talked about little things like their favorite meals, how much they wished they knew dogspeak, and techniques they had learned that day in the Durgan Guild. By the time they arrived at Chimney Hill, Janner forgot that his brother was a Grey Fang. Kalmar was just Kalmar.

When they walked inside, caked with dried mud, Nia gasped and shooed them upstairs to clean up and change. She didn't ask where they'd been or how they'd gotten dirty, and Janner was pretty sure he knew why. All her attention was on the big man visiting with Podo at the hearth. Rudric stayed for dinner.

Janner went to bed that night with a lightness in his heart that battled with his frustration at his brother. He heard Leeli in the next room, singing her puppy to sleep. Kalmar must have heard it too, because he was snoring in seconds.

Janner's mind was working too fast for him to sleep, so he got out of bed. He found the matches, lit the lantern, and fished his journal and quill out of his pack. He hadn't written in a long time, and he had a lot of things to think about. Sitting at the desk and writing was the best way he knew to sort them out.

He still wasn't sure what to make of his conversation with Kalmar the night before about his transformation in the Phoob dungeons. He knew Kalmar had an impulsive nature. He knew he was prone to rash decisions, which were also typically *wrong* decisions. But there was a difference between wrong and evil, wasn't there? Kalmar hadn't just made an incorrect judgment; he had willed something very dark into his heart. He had *meant* to do it. When Kalmar sang the song in the Phoob dungeon, he had not just given up on the possibility of rescue, but he had chosen to open a deep part of his heart to a powerful blackness. Janner had told Kal that Esben's blood was stronger than that blackness, but now he wasn't sure. Was that still true even if Kalmar had invited the blackness in?

Janner also wondered about the song the Stone Keeper made Kalmar sing. He had seen power before in music, in Leeli's power to still the dragons, to speak to the dogs in the houndry, and, strangest of all, to awaken whatever magic bound the Wingfeather children together and allowed Janner to hear the strange voices. It made sense, then, that there could also be music that carried dark power—music dark enough and powerful enough to change a boy into a Fang.

If that was true, it meant that every Fang had been a regular person once—and those people hadn't had it forced upon them, either. They had chosen it. Kalmar said that the Stone Keeper told him it only worked if he wanted it to. So the Fangs were people who had welcomed it in, embraced the transformation, put on lizard skin or wolf's fur like a costume they could never remove.

Then what about Uncle Artham?

Janner thought back to when he had first met him as Peet the Sock Man. Peet was as crazy as a loonbird and wore socks up to his elbows to hide the talons his hands had become. If the transformation came because of Artham's willingness not just to sing some black music but to *mean* it, then he understood his uncle's insanity a little better.

But only Peet's hands had changed. Did that mean he had only *started* to sing the song? Had he changed his mind? That didn't seem bad enough to make him go crazy over it. There must have been something else, some deeper wound that drove the mighty Artham P. Wingfeather mad. Maybe it was the thing he feared in the Blackwood. If it was a forest populated with creatures as scary as the thing that lurched through the yard that night, Janner could see how someone would go insane if they were lost in it, wandering about in the dark with all those lumpy, hungering monsters.

Still, he couldn't make sense of the Artham he knew now—the Artham with the span of bright wings. For some reason, when he rescued Kalmar in the Phoob dungeon, he had grown into something more and not less. That meant that the power Gnag the Nameless and his Stone Keeper had unlocked in the music could do more than just warp and deform. It could do more than destroy.

It could change something twisted into a flourish.

It could take what was bent and make it beautiful.

It could heal.

Janner turned from the desk and looked at his brother, snoring in his bed, sleeping peacefully for a few hours before he had to face another day of stares and mockery and cruelty. Janner was humbled and saddened all at once. Whatever wounds his heart bore because of Kalmar's betrayal, whatever wounds his flesh bore because of Kalmar's claws and teeth, whatever loss of freedom he bore as the Throne Warden, they were dwarfed by his brother's burden. Kalmar's was the heavier load by far, one that he clung to even as it hurt him: shame.

Janner heard Artham in his mind, saw him as he leapt into the rockroach den, one word pulsing in him like a beating heart: *Protect. Protect. Protect.* And what had Janner done? *Complain. Complain. Complain.*

Janner gritted his teeth. He didn't want that to be his story. He didn't want that to be the word that defined him. He wanted to shake free of it and put on something better. He didn't know how, but he had to find a way to stop the trouble at school. He was a Throne Warden, and he had to stop Grigory Bunge and anyone else who threatened the High King of Anniera.

Janner woke sometime in the night with his head on the desk and his quill in his hand. His heart was heavy as a stone, because a solution to their problem at the Guildling Hall had come to him. He could see no other way. He blew out the lantern and crawled under his covers without noticing that Kalmar's bed was empty.

33

A Reckoning
for the Bunge

The next morning, Kalmar slept through breakfast. Nia sent Janner upstairs to fetch him, and after much shaking and pinching, he finally woke and stumbled out to the carriage with his pack.

Leeli had named her dog Baxter after a boy in one of her favorite stories, and she rode in the carriage with the puppy in her lap. All the way to the school she spoke to it, and Baxter seemed to understand her. She tried to teach Janner how to dogspeak the command "sit on my lap," but no matter how he clicked his tongue, the dog ignored him.

"Kal, you want to try?" Leeli asked. "I bet you'd be great at it."

"What's that supposed to mean?" Kalmar snapped.

"Just that—you've always been good with dogs. I don't know."

"Kal, don't talk to your sister like that," Nia said from the front. "You know she wouldn't make fun of you."

"Sorry." Kalmar slouched in his seat and turned to face the road. Janner knew his brother was hardening himself for the day ahead. They hadn't even arrived at the Guildling Hall and already the struggle had begun. When they encountered carriage traffic, and with it the stares of children and adults alike, Kalmar hunched even lower, as if he could fold himself and become invisible.

Janner knew Kal's restraint couldn't last. Anyone would break if a whole school of children pushed hard enough. And Kalmar wasn't just anyone. His

Fangness made him strong enough to outmatch any bully at the school—any guildmaster too, perhaps—which would make it even harder not to fight back.

Janner knew what he had to do, and he dreaded it. He wasn't impulsive like Kalmar. He had to think things over. The problem was, thinking was exactly the wrong thing to do in this case. If he thought too much, he'd never follow through.

"Out you go," Nia said as she rounded the statue. Janner hopped to the ground just after Kalmar, and the brothers lifted Leeli and Baxter over a puddle and handed her the crutch. "See you this afternoon, children. Remember who you are."

As soon as she was gone, Janner heard Grigory Bunge's laughter.

"Oy!" said Grigory. "Good morning to the nursemaid, the dog boy, and the girl who can't walk."

Lightning flashed and a chilly rain fell.

Janner's heart shrank. He had hoped there would be at least a little time before he had to act, but Bunge was waiting. Janner looked around for help, but Guildmadam Groundwich was nowhere to be seen. The parents driving carriages through the courtyard looked everywhere but at the Wingfeathers.

"I'm talking to you, Fang," Grigory said.

Janner sighed and dropped his pack. The time had come.

Before Grigory knew what hit him, Janner spun around, roared something unintelligible, and dove headfirst into the boy. It was like diving into a wall, but Janner heard the air wheeze from Grigory's lungs, and the two of them toppled over. Janner swung his fists wildly, grunting like an animal. He took several punches, which he hardly felt, and threw several back.

He prayed for strength even in his rage, for he swung not in his own defense but his brother's, his sister's, and his mother's. He fought not over a petty insult but for their honor and even their freedom. Grigory Bunge, whether he knew it or not, was doing more than bullying—he was waging war with the Jewels of Anniera, children of the king.

Janner knew nothing but a white-hot anger for a while, and then he felt Kalmar's claws dragging him off the bewildered bully. A crowd had gathered and stood in the rain watching Janner writhe in his brother's grip.

"Leave my brother alone!" Janner shouted. "I don't want to fight you, but I will if I have to, Grigory Bunge! And that goes for the rest of you!" Janner hurled his defiance at every guildling in the courtyard. He shook loose of Kalmar's grip and strode forward, beating his chest with a fist and shouting, "I'm the Throne Warden of Anniera, and Kalmar is my charge. Do you hear me? I've battled Fangs and trolls! I've walked the Stony Mountains and sailed the Dark Sea! I've stood in Yurgen's shadow and looked the dragon in the eye!" Lightning scraped the clouds as Janner stood in the rain and screamed. He flung a finger in Grigory's terrified face. "The Maker has brought us safely this far, Grigory Bunge, and I will fear no *guildling* of the Green Hollows. If you insult the High King or the Song Maiden, you will reckon with the Throne Warden. Do you understand?"

Grigory glanced at the other children.

Janner leapt forward and put his face in Grigory's. He knew that the boy could beat him into the mud if he had a chance to gather his wits, so Janner's only weapon was his madness.

"*Do you understand?*" Janner said through clenched teeth.

Finally, Grigory nodded and stammered, "Y-y-yes."

"Yes, *Throne Warden Wingfeather,*" Janner growled.

"Y-y-yes, Throne Warden W-Wingfeather."

Janner pushed away from Grigory and walked back to Kalmar and Leeli. His knees trembled so violently that it took all his willpower to stand. Leeli's face came into view, and she spoke words that were like cool water poured through his veins. The horn for school blew and in a rush Janner felt the rain again, heard the chatter of students shuffling inside, and realized his nose was bleeding. Grigory was gone.

Janner didn't know why, but he felt like crying. He wiped his nose with his sleeve and tried to avoid looking at his siblings, but he couldn't because

Kalmar and Leeli were standing right in front of him, heedless of the rain. Leeli held one of Janner's hands.

Kalmar and Leeli hugged him, and he could hold in his tears no longer.

After that, things seemed to go better. When word spread about the fight with Grigory, the guildlings' attitude changed toward the Wingfeathers. Where before they had stared and muttered, now they ignored the three of them completely. It would have been nice to be treated with kindness, but indifference in this case was just as good. The bond between Leeli, Kalmar, and Janner strengthened. The more they leaned on one another, the stronger they were.

The lecture that morning was as boring as the one the day before, but Janner passed the time writing in his journal, and P.T. was a giant game of tackleball, an activity that always improved his mood, however foul he felt. Leeli ran houndricks up and down the field while Janner and Kalmar played. The Jewels of Anniera sat on the floor again at lunch, but for the first time, the room didn't go silent when they entered.

At the Durgan Guild, things went even better. It was a smaller class, and the brothers were quick learners. Guildmaster Clout was hard but fair, and soon the other guildlings treated them with respect. They still seemed uncomfortable when they wrestled Kalmar, but none of them liked being outmatched, so they learned to get over it if they wanted to win.

That was the way of things for weeks.

Olumphia Groundwich kept watch over the Wingfeathers. Janner spotted her from time to time, peeking in at lectures or glancing at him in the hall while she spoke with other guildmasters in hushed tones. Sometimes she winked or waggled her whiskers at him. As for Grigory Bunge, he avoided the Wingfeathers, and Janner sometimes went days without seeing him.

When he happened to pass him at P.T. or in the mess hall, Grigory gave him a stiff nod and moved on.

Most days, Janner visited the library after school and sat in the corner reading or working on his T.H.A.G.S. while Bonifer and Oskar translated line after tedious line of the First Book. Janner asked them about their progress, but he was far more interested in books like *Terrible Tales from the Woes of Shreve* and *Omer and the Moondragon,* both of which were recommended by Owen the Archival Apprentice, and both of which Janner devoured in a matter of days.

After several weeks in the Green Hollows, the Wingfeather family at last began to settle into a routine. It had been months since their lives in Glipwood had turned upside down, so the change was welcome. Nia and Freva prepared a scrumptious breakfast each morning; Podo took a morning nap; Nia drove the children to school and often bought vegetables at the harborside market while she was out (one day she returned with the news that the *Enramere*'s mast had been repaired and the Kimerans were sailing back to Skree); Bonifer and Oskar spent hours upon hours in the library; and Rudric found reasons to come to Chimney Hill as often as possible. It wasn't long before they all realized the Keeper of the Hollows had his eye on Nia Wingfeather.

It took Janner a while, but he eventually warmed up to the idea of his mother courting. He wasn't sure how all the politics worked (Would Nia still be the Queen of Anniera if she was married to the Keeper of the Hollows? Was she the queen, anyway, since Kalmar was technically the king now?), but he liked Rudric, and he believed that even his father would want Nia to find a good husband.

With each passing day, Chimney Hill felt more like the home Janner had always wanted. He thought of Anniera less and less, partly because of Nia's strong ties to the Hollows and partly because, well, Anniera was a smoldering ruin. On certain days when the wind was right, he could smell it. He had assumed it was some neighbor's chimney until Rudric told him otherwise. He said the scent was different, sharper, as if the island itself, not just the trees, were burning. Soon Janner could tell the difference. It troubled him when he smelled it, but the wind came from the south seldom enough that it was rare for him to think of Anniera at all.

The weather turned cold, and Janner at last allowed himself to believe that he had found a home where he was safe from Green Fangs and Grey Fangs and toothy cows and bomnubbles and anything else *with* fangs.

That was when the first of the hogpigs went missing, and rumors passed from home to home that another cloven was loose in the city.

34

Palaver in Gully's Saloon

A man named Paddy Durbin Thistlefoot went out to feed his hogpigs one morning and found his gate open and another hogpiglet missing. The other animals were asleep, and once again there was no sign of an intruder or attack. The sowpig snorted contentedly, as if she hadn't noticed that another one of her brood was missing.

Paddy counted the seven remaining hogpiglets over and over, just to be sure, and he even slogged into the pen and kicked at every lump of mud in case the hogpiglet was dead and covered in the slop. His last measure was to check with his wife, Ooma, to be sure they had indeed owned eleven hogpiglets and not seven. He *was* bad at math, and with seven goats, four horses, thirty-two sheep, eighteen hens, five dogs, and eight children in his care, it was possible that he had miscounted the hogpiglet litter.

He had found one less hogpiglet each morning for the past four days, and now that the number was down to seven, he was suspicious. The thought formed in his feeble mind that something was amiss.

The first frost of the year lay on the ground as Paddy Durbin Thistlefoot tromped into Ban Rona, still wearing his slop boots, to report at least *one* missing hogpiglet to the Durgan Patrol. He wasn't sure, but it had to be at least one.

Podo Helmer had begun riding to town after his after-breakfast nap to "gnaw the gristle," as he called it, with the locals at a tavern called Gully's Saloon. He told Nia he went for the company and the news, but she knew it was because he loathed her bean brew. He had politely encouraged her to darken it up, but she could never get it strong enough for Podo's taste.

Early one morning before dawn she caught him in the kitchen in his nightclothes, spooning black powder into the brewer by candlelight. "Just didn't want to bother ye," he said. "Er, I was up, so I reckoned I'd make it meself today."

She didn't bother telling him that he had gotten into the pepper instead of ground brewing beans. She watched with amusement as Podo stirred the pepper into the water, could hardly contain herself as he waited for it to steep, and woke the house with her laughter when Podo raised the mug to her health, took one sip, and spewed peppery black sludge all over the wall.

Podo had ridden to Gully's Saloon every morning since, and Gully's Saloon was right across the street from the offices of the Durgan Patrol. Podo was sipping thick black bean brew and half listening to his new friend Lennry Gardensmith blab about the superior quality of his wife's apple crunch recipe when he saw Paddy Durbin Thistlefoot emerge from the patrol office. Thistlefoot marched across the street, fists pumping, and burst into Gully's Saloon, demanding bean brew.

"Strongest you got," he said, kicking his muddy boots off at the door.

"What's got you all sizzled?" asked Lennry.

"They don't believe me, that's what." Paddy pulled up a stool at the table where Podo and Lennry sat. "They said my math was bad. I said that may be true, but I didn't think it could be bad four mornings in a row. They thought that was pretty funny." He took a long, noisy sip of his bean brew and shook his head. "But the more I think about it, the more certain I am that I had eight hogpiglets yesterday. And the day before I had one more than that. Ten!"

"That's not right," Lennry said.

"Eh?" Paddy counted on his fingers and moved his lips.

"You said you had eight yesterday, and the day before you had one more than that. That makes nine, not ten."

"Not true," said Paddy. "Look at my fingers. One, two, three." He counted to eight, then held out one more finger. "Eight plus one. That's ten. Ten hogpigs."

"You forgot nine," Lennry said.

"What's nine?" Paddy asked.

"It's between eight and ten."

Paddy furrowed his brow and nodded slowly. "Nine. You're right. Plumb forgot about that one." He and Lennry raised their mugs to math and sipped. "The point is, I'm missing hogpigs. The Durgan Patrol said it wasn't their business if there wasn't proof and I couldn't count. But I tell you, for four days now my hogpiglets have been shrinking."

"They're getting smaller?" Lennry asked, shocked.

"No, they're roughly the same size. The *number's* getting smaller. I had eleven. Now I have seven."

"Ah! Good. I thought the world was getting weird."

Podo listened to all this with vague interest until Paddy Durbin Thistle-foot leaned forward and lowered his voice. "You know what I think? I think it's a cloven."

"In Ban Rona?" Lennry scoffed. "They don't come this far west."

"One did this fall. Remember?"

"Oy, that's true. But they ran it off. If there was a cloven loose in Ban Rona, it would be doing worse than just stealing your hogpiglets. Those things can gobble a horse. My cousin lives in the Outer Vales and saw it happen once."

"If you're so smart, what's taking my hogpiglets?"

Lennry shrugged. "Could be wolves."

Podo felt them glance in his direction at the word *wolves*. It took him a moment to understand why. It had been a while since he had heard of any trouble with Kalmar in the Hollows, and he'd assumed they had finally stopped worrying over the boy's fur. It wouldn't do for these two Hollish gabbers to start any new rumors.

"Pah," Podo said. "Wolves run in packs. They don't slip into pens and swaller a hogpiglet whole. Was there any sign of struggle?"

"None," said Paddy.

"Footprints?" Podo asked.

"Hard to tell in the slop."

"Well, then, I'd say you've got snickbuzzards."

Lennry gasped. "Snickbuzzards?"

"What's a snickbuzzard?" Paddy asked.

"I don't know," Lennry said, "but they sound mean."

"Aye," Podo said. "They are. Terrible mean. Razor-sharp beaks. Talons like daggers. And the worst part?"

"Yes, yes?" Lennry and Paddy said.

Podo sipped his bean brew and raised a bushy eyebrow. "Belly button."

"No," said Paddy with a shiver. "Not on a bird."

"Aye. On a bird. Fleshy, bald belly just like my mammy used to have, and right there in the center, a belly button starin' at you like a wrinkly eye. It'll keep you up at night, I tell ye."

Lennry narrowed his eyes. "If it's a snickbuzzard, why haven't we seen one before now? And what makes you so sure that's what's taking Thistlefoot's hogpiglets?"

"Who knows? It's a strange time in Aerwiar, ain't it?" Podo peered out at the sky through the window. "Could be a new migration pattern or something. I was a pirate, if you recall. I know all about migration patterns and birds and such."

Podo knew this made no sense, but it worked. Lennry and Paddy squinted out the window as if a snickbuzzard would crash through it at any moment.

Podo continued, "And ye said there were no tracks, right? No commotion? Whatever took them hogbabies had to swoop in and pluck it out without a sound. Only a snickbuzzard could do that."

"Oy," said Paddy. "Only a snickbuzzard could do that." He paused. "And you're sure they have belly buttons? Absolutely certain?"

"Aye," said Podo.

"That's weirder than shrinking hogpiglets," Lennry said.

"I don't like this," said Paddy, leaving a coin on the table and draining his bean brew. "Not one bit."

Podo bade his friends farewell and rode home with a kernel of worry in his gut. The hogpiglet count wasn't the only thing shrinking lately. The number of hens in the coop at Chimney Hill had been decreasing too.

35

A Lesson in Sneakery

Durgans!" said Guildmaster Clout. "The best way to outsmart ridge-runners is to think like them. Your job today is to sneak an apple from this tree without me knowing."

Janner and Kalmar sat in the dark with the other Durgan Guildlings, dressed in black. It had been two months, and Clout had granted the Wingfeather boys the honor of full status in the Durgan Guild by giving them uniforms. It hadn't been easy, especially for Janner. He had never run so much or done so many chin-ups, sit-ups, or throw-ups in his life. His arms felt stronger, facing bigger students in the ring had made him a fine fighter, and he was even able to keep up with Kalmar when they raced.

Guildmaster Clout's refusal to allow anything less than excellence was frustrating at times, but on the rare occasion when he gave a word of approval—and the even rarer occasion when he smiled—Janner's heart swelled with pride. All the Durgan Guildlings loved their guildmaster, even when he punished them with laps or labor. When students from other guilds voiced their distaste for Clout, the Durgan Guildlings voiced their loyalty and challenged them to sanctioned wrestling duels (which no student was fool enough to accept, because they all knew the Durgans were the best fighters in the school). The Durgan Guildlings carried themselves with pride, and anytime it turned to arrogance, Guildmaster Clout disciplined his students without hesitation.

"I want you all to spread out beyond the courtyard and hide," Clout instructed. "Pretend you're ridgerunners trying to relieve me of my hard-earned fruit. I'll guard the tree, just like the Durgan Patrol at the Outer Vales. All you have to do is sneak past me, pick an apple, and deliver it to that basket over there. If I catch you, you're out. The first guildling to get an apple to the basket in the center of the courtyard without me whacking you with my staff won't have to run laps with the others. Also, you won't have a bruise from my staff—and you get to keep the apple. Clear?"

The guildlings nodded and fidgeted, eager to begin. Guildmaster Clout had begun holding one night class per week for the guildlings' sneakery training, and on those days Janner and Kal got to wear their uniforms and practice Silent Sneaking, Shadow Climbing, and General Night Stalking. Kal wore no boots, but he and Janner both had black outfits, complete with gloves, a cape, and a cowl. It felt like an elaborate game of night zibzy.

The guildlings' capes flapped in the wind of early winter as they waited for Clout to give the signal.

"I'll give you two minutes to choose a position. Commence," he said, and he turned his back while the guildlings scattered.

Janner sprinted across the courtyard and hid behind a low wall. He lowered his hood and peeked over the edge. He could barely see Clout's shadowy figure under the dark shape of the apple tree as he lifted the horn and blew. Janner looked around to see what the other guildlings' strategies might be. Something thwacked nearby, and he heard a muffled cry. One of the guildlings had already been caught by Clout and was rubbing his thigh as he crossed the courtyard and sat near the basket to wait out the rest of the game.

Clout was nowhere to be seen. The apple tree was unguarded but seemed impossibly far away. There was no way to cross the courtyard without being seen.

Janner crept forward to peek around a shrub and came face to face with Morsha MacFigg, a fifteen-year-old girl with a pretty face. It didn't look so pretty now because she had smeared it with mud.

"Get out of here, Wingfeather!" she whispered. "This is my spot."

"Sorry," Janner said, backing away.

He bumped into someone else—Churleston James, a fourteen-year-old. "Shoo, Janner! I've got a plan and you aren't a part of it."

"Sorry," Janner said again.

He scurried away from the low wall to one of the stone buildings that bordered the courtyard. As soon as he was safe in the shadows, he heard two quick whacks and saw Churleston James and Morsha MacFigg moping across the yard to sit with the others who had been caught. Guildmaster Clout had come and gone and Janner never saw him. By now Janner counted six children who had been staff-whacked and every few seconds he heard someone else say, "Ow!"

"Psst."

Janner looked up.

Kalmar was on the roof of the building, two wolf ears poking over the edge. "What should we do?"

"I don't know," Janner whispered, "but I think we stand a better chance if we work together."

"That's what I was thinking," said another voice from behind a prickly bush at the corner of the building.

"Who's that?" Janner whispered.

"Joe Bill," came the answer.

"It'll only work if one or two of us is a sacrifice," Janner whispered. "We need to distract Clout and let the other one get the apple."

"But I don't want to get whacked!" Joe Bill said. "That sounds like it hurts."

"You're going to get whacked either way," Janner said. "Look, *you* can be the one to get the apple. Kalmar and I will be the distraction. All right?"

"I'm not as fast as Kalmar," Joe Bill said after a moment.

"Nobody is," Janner said.

"Hush! Here he comes!" Kalmar hissed.

The three boys held their breath as a shadow passed, quiet as smoke and low to the ground.

When Clout had gone, Joe Bill said, "Aw, Kalmar should do it. It's either him or nobody, the way I see it."

"I agree. Kal?"

"All right, if you're sure. What do I do?"

"Joe Bill and I will flank the apple tree. I don't think Clout will expect anyone to come straight across the courtyard. When he comes after us, make a run for it."

"A *sneaky* run," said Joe Bill.

Janner waited till he heard another whack from farther away, and said, "Now!"

He and Joe Bill crept around the perimeter of the courtyard in opposite directions. Janner inched forward, listening so hard that all he could hear was the ringing in his ears. When he reached the end of the low wall, just a stone's throw from the apple tree, he braced himself to run.

"Ouch!" someone said from the opposite side, louder than the others. "I'm Joe Bill, and that hurt, guildmaster!"

Janner sprang. He knew Clout would catch him before he got to the apple tree, but he didn't mind if it meant Kalmar made it through. Just as he expected, Clout's cloaked form rose up as if from nowhere. Janner tried to dodge the staff but was too slow.

He felt a sting on the back of his leg, and Clout whispered, "Take a seat, Janner."

Janner saw the faintest movement near the tree and knew that Kalmar had crossed the courtyard and climbed up into the branches. Now he just had to get the apple to the basket. Janner sat with the other guildlings and watched to see what would happen, smiling in spite of the throbbing in his leg.

"Good work, Joe Bill," Janner whispered, and Joe Bill's smile showed in the shadows of his hood. By Janner's count, there were only two guildlings left. He couldn't fathom how Clout had managed to tag almost every one of his students and guard the apple tree at the same time, all without making a sound.

After what seemed like a long time, Clout caught someone in the dark just behind the tree, and Janner's heart fell. But instead of Kalmar, Quincy Candlesmith emerged, downcast from having come so close to the tree only to be staff-whacked. Janner studied the dark branches and finally spotted a smudge of black, barely moving. Kalmar was still there, and Clout had no idea.

After another long silence, Kalmar made his move. He dropped from the limb with only the tiniest ruffle of his cape and scurried toward the basket. Janner was ready to leap to his feet and congratulate Kalmar when a whisper of movement came from behind. Kalmar dove for the basket and threw the apple, but Guildmaster Clout swung his staff and whacked the apple away at the last moment in an explosion of juice and chunks of fruit.

Kalmar landed in a crouch and punched the ground. The students stood as the guildmaster approached.

"Up, Kalmar," said Clout, and Kalmar joined the others. "That was the weakest attempt at sneakery I've seen in all my years as guildmaster. I caught most of you in the first two minutes of the lesson."

The guildlings shuffled their feet and hung their heads.

"If you mean to be in the Durgan Guild, you'd better learn to control your breathing. Keep your joints from cracking—especially you, Larnik. It sounded like you were frying bacon. You need to know when to statue and when to creep. Pathetic display, the lot of you." Clout shook his head at the guildlings and watched them squirm. "Kalmar! Janner! Joe Bill! Step forward!"

Janner approached with the other two, wondering what he had done wrong.

Clout's voice was menacing. "Why don't you tell the class what you did back there?"

"We, uh, came up with a plan, sir," Janner said.

"A plan." Clout glared at Joe Bill. "What do you have to say, boy?"

"It was Janner's idea, sir."

"And what was this plan, Janner? Tell the class. Go on."

"I thought our only chance of getting the apple was to team up. Divide your attention. I figured if we were all going to get tagged, we might as well get tagged for a reason, sacrifice ourselves so at least one of us could succeed. Kalmar is the fastest of us, so Joe Bill suggested he be the one to get the apple."

"What do you have to say, Kalmar?" barked Clout.

"It almost worked, sir."

"Do you want to know what I think?" asked Clout. No one spoke, so he said, "Class! Do you want to know what I think?"

"Yes sir," they all said.

"I think it's pathetic," he sneered at the guildlings. "Pathetic that in twenty years of teaching this guild, no guildling has ever come as close to getting the apple into the basket as Kalmar Wingfeather." A smile broke over Clout's face. It always surprised Janner how different the man looked when he wasn't scowling. "That last approach to the basket was one of the finest sneaks I've ever seen in a guildling. And it only happened because these three boys worked together. It's not unusual for guildlings to figure that out after two or three games, but *never* the first time—and in less than two minutes!" Clout patted them each on their backs, which Janner had never known him to do. "Outstanding, lads. You're dismissed for the night." Then his smile vanished. "The rest of you? Pathetic! Twenty laps! Go!"

After they bade farewell to Joe Bill, the boys waited for Nia in the courtyard. But instead of a carriage, a horse thundered through the gate and whinnied as it rounded the statue, blowing steam from its nose in great bursts. Rudric towered in the saddle and smiled through his beard at the brothers, who still had occasion to be awestruck by the giant man. He wore his full Durgan Patrol uniform.

"Oy, Wingfeathers! Those are fine-looking outfits you're wearing. Hard not to look handsome in black, isn't it?" Rudric whipped his cape around and winked. "Your mother sent me to fetch you. Dinner will be hot and ready when we get back. Up you go!"

Rudric pulled Janner up as if he were a stuffed doll.

"Why are you wearing your Durgan outfit?" Janner asked as Kalmar sprang up behind him.

"The council met today to discuss the missing animals," Rudric said. "It's worse than anyone thought."

"How bad is it?" Kalmar asked. "I heard it was just ratbadgers."

"If it's ratbadgers, there are hundreds of them," Rudric said. "Farmer after farmer came forward and reported their missing animals. You wouldn't believe it. Hogpiglets, flabbits, hens. Some people reported missing goats."

"Goats?" Janner asked. "It seems like a goat would be too big for a ratbadger."

"Oy," said Rudric. "It also seems like a ratbadger would leave some trace. Whatever's taking these animals is sneaky. Your grandfather thinks it's snickbuzzards, according to Paddy Thistlefoot."

"There aren't any snickbuzzards in the Green Hollows," Janner said. "Grandpa knows that."

Rudric flashed a look of surprise. "Oy? Well. Maybe Thistlefoot heard him wrong. Either way, we're going to solve this mystery. That's why the Durgan Patrol is on watch. We have to hunt it down before every animal in Ban Rona gets eaten. And speaking of food—" Rudric wheeled the horse around and spurred it into a gallop. "Your mother's dinner is waiting."

Janner gripped the folds of Rudric's coat and thrilled at the speed and strength of the horse, the cold air, the surety with which Rudric rode. The boys' capes popped in the wind as they sped through Ban Rona and over the hills. The air of early winter brightened the stars and stung Janner's hands.

They arrived at Chimney Hill and ate dinner, and then Danniby arrived in his Durgan uniform and informed Rudric that the patrol was gathered at the Keep and awaiting orders.

"Wish us luck, Wingfeathers," Rudric said as he excused himself. "We have a flying ratbadger to catch tonight."

"I tell ye," said Podo with a belch, "it's a snickbuzzard. You'll see."

That night, something woke Janner. He sat up in bed, heart pounding, afraid without knowing why. He shook the sleep away and listened to the creaking house, the stir of the wind outside, the scratch of bare branches on the window. They were eerie sounds, but not unusual. Still, something wasn't right, and he couldn't figure out what.

He looked at the window and remembered the voice he had heard that night when the cloven had seen him: *I'll sniff you out wherever you are. And when I find you, I'll hold you fast.* Janner shuddered and curled under his covers again, trying to figure out what it was that unsettled him.

The next morning while he gobbled his hotcakes and eggs, he noticed two things: Kalmar looked exhausted, and Kalmar wasn't eating. That he looked tired wasn't all that surprising. With the T.H.A.G.S., school, chores, and now the night classes of the Durgan Guild, both boys were worn out. Janner had a hard time getting up every morning too.

But Kalmar was *always* hungry. Wasn't he? Now that Janner thought about it, he couldn't remember the last time Kal had asked Leeli for the rest of her soup or snuck a biscuit when Janner wasn't looking or been caught in the pantry with a mouthful of muffins.

That was when Janner realized what had troubled him when he woke in the night. It wasn't a sound but a silence. He hadn't heard Kalmar snoring.

Janner didn't know what it meant, but he didn't like how it made him feel.

36

Snaphounds and Snowfall

That day at lunch, the Wingfeather children sat with Joe Bill, Morsha, and Quincy, their friends from the Durgan Guild, along with Thorn and Kelvey O'Sally. A fire roared in the hearth at the head of the room but did little to ease the chill in the rest of the hall, so the guildlings ate with their coats on.

As soon as they had thanked the Maker for the food, Morsha said, "Did you hear? Last night the patrol figured out what's been taking the livestock."

"What was it?" Janner asked, stopping mid-chew with a mouthful of henmeat casserole. "A ratbadger?"

"Worse," Morsha said with relish.

"I heard too, but I don't believe it," Thorn said as he crunched into an apple. "Doesn't explain the sheep."

"Sure it does," said Kalmar.

"How do *you* know what it was, Kal?" Janner asked, annoyed that he seemed to be the only one at the table who hadn't heard.

Kalmar shrugged and popped a sausage link into his mouth. "Someone told me earlier."

"I heard about it in the hall after lectures," Leeli said. "I'm with Thorn. I don't think it sounds right, either."

"Somebody *please* tell me what you're talking about," Janner said.

"My ma says she's seen one up close," Morsha said, "and it could definitely kill a sheep."

"ONE OF WHAT?" Janner shouted.

All the guildlings at the table leaned back and raised their eyebrows at him, including Leeli and Kalmar.

"Somebody's cranky," Joe Bill muttered as he slathered strawberry sweet sauce on a biscuit.

"A dog," said Thorn.

"Not just a dog," said Morsha. "A snaphound. Much bigger. Longer teeth."

"They're not *that* big," Kelvey said. "And besides, snaphounds hunt in packs. There was only one set of tracks."

"They found tracks?" Janner asked.

"Oy," Kelvey said. "Pa told me the Durgan Patrol found a pile of feathers and chicken parts outside of Waverby's hen coop, along with clear pawprints leading away. They tracked it for miles and miles, clear into the wooded vales, before they lost the trail."

"But they didn't catch it?" Janner asked.

"Not yet, they didn't." Joe Bill slurped the strawberry sauce where it had dripped on his hand. "But they will. The Durgan Patrol are the best trackers on Aerwiar."

"Oy!" said Morsha, clinking her mug of ermentine juice against Joe Bill's. "Durgans!"

"I still don't think a dog could do all that," said Leeli.

"You don't know everything about dogs," Kalmar told her. "I don't see what's so strange about a wild dog eating a hen."

"Easy, Kal. I think she's just saying that *one* dog couldn't eat that much livestock," Thorn said. "And a whole pack of wild dogs sneaking in and taking chickens and hogpiglets and even sheep, all without leaving a trace—well, it's highly unusual. I've never heard of anything like it."

"Well, I'm just glad it's over. They figured it out," Kalmar said as he cleared his plate, "and now everybody can get back to whatever they were doing before."

That day in Durgan Guild, Clout took a look at the sky and said, "Snow."

About thirty minutes later, the sky grayed, the wind picked up, and the first flurries of the year came down in whirls.

Clout led the guildlings to one of the buildings adjacent to the courtyard and fished a key from one of his pockets. "Snow means it's time for the next part of your training," he said as he fit the key into the lock, turned it, and swung open the door. He led the guildlings inside, then slammed the door behind them and plunged them into darkness. "Brosa! Come!"

"Yes, guildmaster." Brosa stumbled through the dark, stepping on toes and bumping other students as he tried to find Clout. A match flared to life, illuminating Guildmaster Clout's scowling face, which was nowhere near where Brosa stood.

"I'm over here, boy! Take these matches and light the sconces. You'll find ten of them. Hurry up about it." As Brosa lit the lanterns and revealed more and more of the room, Clout said, "Welcome to the Sneakery. Built two hundred years ago by the stonewright and woodwright guilds, it's been the winter training ground for the finest Durgans the Green Hollows has ever known. Here you'll learn not just to outsmart ridgerunners but also to climb walls, surprise your enemies, gather information, and creep through the Hollows—all without making a sound."

Guildmaster Clout folded his arms and surveyed the guildlings, allowing them time to take in what they saw. There were platforms and passageways, low walls with windows, and ladders that led to rope bridges high above. One of the walls was fitted with pegs and little outcroppings for climbing. Everywhere Janner looked, there were ropes, poles, platforms, and a thousand other ways to break an arm or a leg. It was beautiful.

"Chewbing! Climb to the top of that wall and bring me your weapon of choice. Don't fall, or your mother will never forgive me." Chewbing gulped and ran to the wall. "Larnik! You and Morsha head into the tunnel maze and find the exit. The first one there will have half as many laps. Janner! Grab a slingshot and stand guard in the perch up there while the rest of you try to sneak past him. Kalmar! Joe Bill! Ambush whichever of Larnik and Morsha comes out of the tunnel maze first. Try to pin them down and tie them up with that rope over there."

Clout gave orders and the guildlings obeyed, unable to conceal their smiles. Janner fetched the slingshot, thinking how silly he was to have ever wanted to join the bookbindery guild.

The Durgan Guildlings climbed and crawled for an hour under Clout's supervision before he ordered the same drills with the lights out. In the darkness of the windowless Sneakery, guildlings tripped, slipped, and ran into one another so often that in the end they were all scared to move. Janner couldn't remember the last time he had had so much fun.

When the horn blew and school ended for the day, Janner and Kalmar emerged from the Sneakery to find that snow had covered the ground. The Green Hollows had turned white.

They met Nia at the snow-covered statue and waited in the snow for Leeli. When the courtyard had emptied of carriages and Leeli still hadn't shown up, Nia asked Janner to fetch her from the houndry.

Just as he hopped down from the carriage, Leeli arrived with a train of dogs harnessed to a houndrick. The wheels had been replaced with runners that glided over the snow with a pleasant hiss. The cart was decorated with ornate swoops of purple and white and bore Leeli's name in a graceful script. She was rosy cheeked from the cold and bundled in a brindleskin coat with the hood pulled so tightly around her face that her cheeks bunched up when she smiled. Baxter yipped and stood in the cart beside Leeli with his front paws on the rail.

"What's this?" Nia asked.

"My houndrick." Leeli clicked her tongue, and the six dogs sat.

"*Your* houndrick?" Nia climbed down from the carriage to inspect it.

"Thorn and Biggin O'Sally commissioned it from the woodwrightery last month, just for me. It was finished today. They want me to train the houndrick dogs." She blushed and played with a button on her coat. "They said it was time I had my own rick. They said I was real good."

"*Really* good," Nia corrected, kicking the runners on the little sleigh to test their strength. "Not 'real' good."

"That's just how they talk," Leeli said.

"That's fine for them. Not for a Song Maiden." Nia mounted the carriage. "It looks solid. Well made. The woodwrightery guildlings did a *really* good job of it. Now," she said, making sure the boys were seated, "let's see how fast it is. Hya!"

Janner and Kalmar nearly tumbled off their seats when the horses lunged forward. Janner looked over his shoulder at Leeli and waved as they sped away. She looked shocked for a moment, and then Janner saw her mouth move and heard the dogs bay. The snowfall was so thick that Leeli disappeared in swirling curls of white as they passed through the gate, but he could hear the dogs and knew Leeli was close behind.

Nia laughed as the carriage careened through the streets. Kalmar whooped and crouched on his seat, nose into the wind, howling at the snow. He looked more like a wolf in that moment than Janner had ever seen him, and Janner loved him for it, because in that moment Kalmar didn't care a hoot what the Hollowsfolk thought.

The horses were winded by the time they crossed the bridge at the foot of Chimney Hill. Nia reined them in and turned in her seat. "Do you hear her?" she asked, and they all listened. Janner heard nothing but the wind and the trickle of water in the creekbed. Nia's face fell. "I should go back for her."

"Look, Mama." Kal pointed at two parallel lines in the snow that ran over the bridge and up the hill. "She beat us."

When they rounded the bend and climbed up to the front lawn, they found Leeli loosening the straps of the last dog and scratching it behind the ears. Freva greeted Nia and the boys, then led the carriage to the barn, muttering about how much she disliked snow.

Nia calmly stooped and gathered a pile of snow into a ball. She aimed it at Leeli and let it fly. It hit Leeli in the back and exploded, and she spun around with her mouth hanging open.

"That's your prize for winning," Nia said. She threw another snowball. "And that's for no reason at all."

Kalmar, Janner, and Leeli exchanged a confused look. Janner had no idea what had gotten into his mother, but he sensed that it was a rare moment, one that should be taken full advantage of.

Kalmar and Leeli were already throwing snowballs at Nia by the time Janner cocked his arm. He paused, struck by how beautiful his mother was. Nia's bright red scarf was dotted with snowflakes and matched the rosy blooms of her cheeks. The lines at the corners of her eyes were creased with laughter instead of worry, and her teeth glistened while she laughed. He had never seen his mother so fair or so playful, and he doubted it would last. It was a glimpse of who she had been before his father died, before her home had been set on fire, before her kingdom had fallen and her children were hunted. He told himself to write this moment down so he would remember it. Then he hurled the snowball.

When the four of them were winded and the cold had crept into their boots and collars and sleeves, they sat on the front lawn among the snow-happy dogs.

"Will the whole winter be like this?" Leeli asked, leaning against a gray hound she called Bounder. "Like Kimera?"

"No. This much snow is a rare surprise in Ban Rona. Farther east, closer to the mountains and the Blackwood, it sticks to the ground for weeks at a time."

"Well, I hope it stays," Leeli said. "The houndrick is a lot faster with runners than wheels. I don't think I would have beaten you with the wheels on—not as badly anyway." She poked her mother's arm and laughed, but Nia didn't laugh along. Janner could already tell the moment of lightness was passing.

"Children," Nia said, "I need to speak with you about something."

The children sat up when they heard the somber tone in her voice.

"What's wrong?" Janner asked. "Do we have to leave again?"

"No, no. Nothing like that." Nia smiled, but her eyes were strangely sad. "I need to tell you about Rudric and me. We've been courting."

The three children looked at one another, then at Nia, and burst out laughing.

"Did you think we didn't know that?" Kalmar said. "You hardly know we exist when he's around."

"And he's *always* around," Leeli said.

Nia laughed and shook her head. "I forget how smart you three are. But there's more." Her smile vanished and she looked each of them in the eye. Janner thought for a moment that she looked frightened, but then he discounted that idea. Nia Wingfeather was never frightened. "He's asked me to marry him."

In the silence that followed, Janner was surprised to feel a stab of pain in his chest. He knew he should be happy for her. He liked Rudric. But for some reason, when Nia said those words, Janner heard something very different. He heard his mother say, "Your father really is dead." He heard her say, "I'm letting him go." He heard, "We're never going home. Let Anniera burn. It's over."

Tears leapt into Janner's eyes. He felt his mother's gaze on him, and it burned his skin. He heard himself sob as he staggered to his feet, and then he ran.

He ran blindly into the snow, not knowing or caring which direction. His heart erupted with anger and sadness and embarrassment and hurt that he had to put somewhere. So he ran. His cheeks ached with cold. His nose dripped, and he hated the way he sounded, blubbering words that made no sense. He wanted his father to be alive, to love his mother, to make her young again, the way she had been just now. He fell to the ground and convulsed with sobs, heedless of the snow on his face.

He wanted to be alone, and he wanted to be found. He wanted his family to ignore him, to show their indifference and feed his anger, and at the same time he pleaded to the Maker that they would come and lift him from the frozen ground. And in the middle of it all, he felt the Maker's presence so palpably that the very wind seemed to be his breath and the snowflakes his touch. Janner knew he was not alone, nor could he be, however far he ran.

Then he felt hands on his back and arms, and he heard Kalmar's voice in his ear, saying, "I'm here."

Kalmar lifted him to a sitting position and studied Janner's face with eyes that were moist and sad. Janner saw no trace of yellow there. Only blue. "She doesn't understand, you know. To her, he's been dead for nine years. But it's like we just found him this summer, in Uncle Artham's tree house. And now it's like he's dying all over again."

Janner wiped his nose and nodded. He was grateful that he didn't have to explain a thing to his brother. "I just miss him," he said. "And I know that sounds dumb, since I'm too young to even remember. But he's so real in my mind sometimes, it's like he's still around. Watching over us."

"I know," Kal said. "But he's not. And Mama's been alone for nine years. *Nine years.* Janner, I like her when she's like this. Lighter, I mean. I think she needs Rudric. He's like medicine or something."

Janner wiped his nose. He cringed at the thought of facing everyone with his snotty face and puffy red eyes. "I should probably go apologize."

"Yeah."

Janner shivered as a gust of wind cut through his coat and reached every spot that was damp from either tears or snow. "Come on. Aren't you freezing?"

Kalmar looked at the flurries as if he had forgotten he was standing in the snow. "I don't really get cold anymore, Janner. Just hungry."

To Janner's great relief, the main room was empty except for Leeli and Nia. They sat together on the couch, staring at the fire. Janner said, "Sorry," and another tidal wave of tears came, but this time they were better tears, wept into his mother's arms.

The three children and their mother talked for a long time by the fire. After a subdued dinner, Janner collapsed into his bunk, thinking about Rudric and his father and how things could hurt and heal at the same time.

Late that night, Janner woke to the muted sound of someone knocking at the front door. He slipped out of bed and cracked his door to listen and be sure everything was all right. He could tell that everyone was in bed, but the downstairs glowed red from the embers in the fireplace.

He heard Rudric's voice outside, followed by a brief howl of wind when Nia opened the door to him. Janner heard the murmur of their voices and the warmth of their tone and the rightness of it, and he knew his mother was telling Rudric about what had happened. He heard the words, "I'm sorry, Nia," and she said, "It's going to be all right."

After several moments, Nia asked, "What are you doing out so late?"

"I came to say good-bye."

"What do you mean?"

"I'll be gone for a few weeks. Word came from the chief of Ban Hynh that there's trouble in the Outer Vales. The ridgerunners are active, and there's rumor of something worse."

"What?"

"Fangs. Two children reported spotting a Grey Fang in their back pasture last night. Farmers all across the hills are scared and angry. They're demanding action. I've mustered my best men, and they await me at the Keep. I hate to go. It's not always easy, you know, being a Keeper of the Hollows."

"Nor is it always easy to love one," Nia said, and Janner heard a rustle that told him they were embracing. "Be careful, Rudric. Come back soon. We have a wedding to plan."

Janner heard a long silence and suddenly felt like he was intruding. He tiptoed back to bed and noticed once again that Kalmar wasn't snoring. He stood on his bunk and peered into the dark, listening. He saw Kalmar's form under the blankets but heard no breathing, so he reached out and nudged his brother.

But his brother wasn't there. Janner ripped back the cover and found a quilt wadded up as a decoy. Kalmar was gone.

Janner rushed to the window and threw back the curtain, whispering,

"No, no, no, no, no." He opened the window and cringed at the cold. The snow had stopped, and the hills were crusted with a pristine spread of white, like icing on a cake.

Footprints, vivid under the bright moon, led from the snowdrift below the window, out past the barn, and into the night.

37

Sara's Army Makes Ready

Tomorrow is the day," Sara Cobbler whispered to Borley. He turned over in his cot and smiled. His eyes were bright against the soot on his face. "Just wait for my signal. All right?"

"I'll be ready," said Borley.

Sara weaved through the beds in the bunk hall to another cot and squeezed the toe of a little girl. "Hello, Veera."

"Hello, Sara Cobbler," the girl whispered.

"Sleep well. Tomorrow's the day."

"Is it going to be scary?" Veera whispered. She tucked her blanket under her chin.

"Yes," said Sara. "But I think it's going to work."

"Me too," said Veera, and she closed her eyes.

Sara wondered if she believed her own words. Did she really think it was going to work, or was she acting out of desperation, putting the lives of so many young ones in danger? She had worked for two months now, so it wasn't a rash decision. She'd had plenty of time to turn back, to rethink the plan, to talk herself out of it, or to be caught. But as far as she could tell, neither the Overseer, nor Mobrik, nor the Maintenance Managers had noticed that she and her little band of children had been stealing daggers, swords, and even forks.

The idea had struck her the night Borley showed Sara the dagger he had stolen. He had asked why they couldn't use it to escape, and she had lain in bed asking herself the same question for hours. It wouldn't work if just one person tried. She knew that. But what if all the children took up arms? Would the Overseer have time to get help? Would Mobrik?

She had hidden Borley's dagger in her bunk and watched the Maintenance Managers for two days before she swiped another. Managers were stationed at the ends of the conveyor belts and at each station, and they were supposed to keep count of the blades and inspect them for flaws. But Sara noticed that even the older, meaner ones were usually too distracted to do their jobs well. They talked to one another and were always watching for Mobrik. They knew they didn't have much time before the ridgerunner informed them that they'd been promoted out of the factory (as the Overseer put it), so they cared less about their jobs and never saw when a sword or dagger went missing.

Even the Overseer's regular appearance on the factory floor worked to Sara's advantage. The evil man in the fingerless gloves would stomp through the aisles and machines, cracking his whip and spitting curses at the children. Sara kept her head low when he was nearby, but as she sharpened or pared or polished at her station she watched the Maintenance Managers. She saw how frightened they were of him. She saw how their eyes darted and how they only pretended to count the blades in the barrels.

Sara refused to let her little army take any weapons. She couldn't bear the responsibility of them being caught and beaten or thrown into the coffin. So she took one blade a day. When she caught glimpses of Mobrik on the far side of the smoky room, skittering about on rafters or the tops of metal shelves, and when she was certain the Maintenance Managers were preoccupied, she slipped the jagged hunks of metal up her sleeve.

At first she had been terribly nervous and convinced herself over the course of her shift that she had been seen and that the Overseer would spring out from behind a pile of coal with his brownish teeth and bloodshot eyes. Her hands shook as she worked and continued to shake right through her meal until she got to her cot and slid the dagger beneath her pillow.

After the first week, she grew in confidence, but she was more careful than ever for one good reason: she had run out of room to safely hide the weapons in her bunk and had made the difficult decision to hide some in Borley's as well. He had been eager to help.

"You can't tell *anyone*, Borley," Sara had whispered over their bowls of soup. "And you can't play with them. Just pretend they aren't there, all right?"

He had nodded and said, "Anything for you, Sara Cobbler."

When the edges of Borley's cot had been lined with weapons, carefully hidden beneath the mattress and in the folds of his blanket, she had asked Grettalyn to help, and in a few more weeks, Veera. Soon she lost count of how many names she knew.

Sara hadn't recruited them. They had come to her, quietly, innocently, drawn by something Sara couldn't name. All she knew was that before Janner Igiby came, she hadn't thought of escaping because she hadn't thought of anything at all. Her mind had become numb. Any hope of escape was killed by the overwhelming futility of it. How could any child escape when there were boys and girls with chains to beat you, an Overseer with a whip, a ridge-runner spy, and only one way out? But Janner Igiby had proved that it was possible, and something that had fallen asleep in Sara Cobbler's heart was awake now.

Many of the children sensed it and came to her and were comforted. But some of the slaves ignored her. She smiled at them when they passed and sometimes asked their names, but they only looked at her blankly and moved on. She tried to wake them, but she couldn't reach them all. They cowered from the Maintenance Managers and shuffled to their cots in silence, no matter how many times Sara tried.

But the others, the ones who dared to believe, smiled back. They followed her. They winked from across the sharpening station or as they passed with wheelbarrows of coal. She told them at the mess table to stay quiet, to hold their tongues whenever any Maintenance Manager was around, and never to speak to one another on the factory floor. And once they promised her on the Maker's name, she leaned forward, looked to her left and right, and told them stories.

She told them of Janner Igiby's daring escape. She reminded them of the sunlight, which was so easy to forget in the smoky darkness. She reminded them that they had names. They weren't tools in a factory, she told them, but sons and daughters, brothers and sisters. They were Borleys and Grettalyns and Maddies and Yerbiks, children who had to fight to remember there was a world outside the Fork Factory, where the sun shone. The Overseer wanted them to forget, she said. That was how he controlled them. If they remembered, they were strong, Sara told them.

She asked them about their parents, about their houses, about their friends before they had been taken by the Black Carriage or kidnapped by the hags and beggars in Dugtown. The children didn't want to remember at first, but Sara kept asking, in spite of their tears and their loneliness for their parents and homes. She taught them that the homesickness was good, because it helped them remember the world outside the factory.

And now the time had come. Sara slipped from cot to cot, watching for Mobrik and the Maintenance Managers. Her next shift was about to begin, so she whispered to each of the children in bed to be ready. She told them that tomorrow was the day—that yes, she thought it would work. She knew her friends were many, but that night she was surprised by how many cots she visited and how many names she knew.

A boy with a bell marched through the room, announcing the next shift. It was time for Sara to face another night at the sharpening station. As she grabbed her gloves from her bunk, it occurred to her that there was no turning back now. There would be no way to spread the word to her little army if the plan changed. It was going to happen tomorrow, no matter what.

She turned from her bed and bumped into one of the Maintenance Managers.

"Excuse me," Sara said, pretending to have just woken up.

"I've been watching you, tool," said the boy. He was a head taller than Sara, skinny but strong, with a missing front tooth. He held a chain in one fist and swayed it back and forth. Sara quickly looked at the floor. She had to remind herself to act like a factory tool, not a girl. "I've been watching you for a long time."

"Excuse me," she repeated and tried to walk around him. He stepped sideways and blocked her path.

"Look at me," he said.

Sara couldn't slip by him, and she couldn't look at him. She was afraid if he saw her eyes, he would know in an instant that she was up to something. He would report her to Mobrik and that would be the end of it. If she was thrown into the coffin or punished, the children wouldn't know what to do. Borley was bold enough and foolish enough to try to do it without her, and she couldn't let that happen.

"I said *look* at me." The Maintenance Manager grabbed her face and forced it upward.

Sara could pretend no more. She looked into his eyes, but not as a factory tool. She decided not to hide her awakeness but to pour it into him. If he saw the light in her, maybe it would wake some compassion in him and he would let her go. It was a terrible risk, but she didn't know what else to do. She willed him to see her as a girl, as someone he might have known before the Fork Factory, someone he could have been friends with. If she carried any of Janner's fire, she prayed it would cross the few inches between them and make its way through his eyes and into his soul.

He looked ready to raise an alarm or to hit her, but after a while he let go of her and said, "Get to work, tool." Then he walked away.

Sara panted and struggled to control the trembling in her legs. Then she pushed through the doors, crossed the dining hall, and entered the roar and clank of the factory floor for what she hoped was the last time.

38

Wolf Tracks in the Snow

Even with gloves, a scarf around his face, an extra layer of underclothes, and his Durgan uniform, Janner cringed at the cold when he landed in the pile of snow below his window. He crouched there for a while to be sure no one in the house stirred, but all he heard was his breathing and the hoot of a fleck owl in one of the trees.

He thought about Guildmaster Clout's lessons on sneakery: *always keep your joints from cracking; listen before you move; be patient; pay attention to night creatures—if they move, you move.* The owl told Janner it was safe to sneak. Doing his best to step in Kalmar's footprints, he edged out from the shadow of the house and into full moonlight.

Janner's footsteps were deafening in all that snowy silence, and he felt exposed, especially wearing so much black. He was a splatter of ink on a blank page. Surely there were white Durgan uniforms for snow sneakery, he thought, but he had no choice. These were the warmest clothes he had.

The tracks were easy to see, though a dusting of fresh flakes softened their outline. That meant it had still been snowing when Kalmar left. Janner followed the tracks past Freva and Bonnie's little cottage to the barn. The door was open wide enough that Janner was able to squeeze through without a sound. He stood in the hay-scented darkness for a moment, listening. "Kal!" he whispered, but the only answer was a snort from one of the horses. He crept past the stalls and found the back door standing open. A small drift of snow had blown in, and Kalmar's footprints led through it, out past the goat pen and the kennel where Leeli kept her houndrick dogs. The dogs woke and wagged their tails when Janner approached, but they didn't bark.

Janner stopped every few steps to listen. He didn't know how long Kalmar had been gone or how close he might be. It was possible, after all, that Kalmar was only slipping out for a romp in the snow. It was a beautiful night, and maybe he couldn't sleep, maybe he snuck out the window because he didn't want to wake anyone. But Janner knew somehow that this wasn't the first time. What about all the other nights?

Beyond the barn, the tracks turned left and circled back around to the front of Chimney Hill. They followed the lane, but a stone's throw to the right of it, angling from tree to tree as they descended the hill. Janner could see where Rudric's horse's hooves had pocked half-moons in the snow on his ride to and from the house. At the bottom of the hill, Kalmar's trail led not to the bridge, but down the creek bank. Janner was thankful for the bright moon, or he wouldn't have been able to spot the stones Kalmar used to hop across.

As soon as Janner set foot on the opposite bank, he heard a rumble in the distance. His heart skipped a beat and he saw a large, dark, steaming shape crest the hill coming from Ban Rona: horses. The thunder of hoofbeats grew in volume as they sped toward Janner. He scrambled along the creek bank and hid in the shadow of the bridge just as they shot past. Janner counted at least twenty horses, their riders garbed in black, sword hilts and hammers rattling and glinting in the moonlight. It was Rudric and the Durgan Patrol, on their way to the Outer Vales. They were gone as fast as they had come.

Janner eased out of the shadow of the bridge, still shaken by the passing of the horses, and found Kalmar's tracks again. He didn't walk on the road but kept off to the right, on the opposite side of the creek, all the way up the big hill and out of the valley. Janner crested it and saw Ban Rona below, every rooftop soft and white, every tree branch outlined with snow. Kalmar's trail led down the road and turned left, into the city.

The sneak into town was less difficult in some ways—there were plenty of hiding places, for one thing. Kalmar's tracks zipped from bush to hedge, from park bench to stone fence. Janner followed in bursts, just as the tracks indicated Kalmar had. But creeping through the city was harder in other ways—every window facing the street was like an eye watching him pass. Janner sensed the sleeping presence of people in the houses. He wondered how he would explain himself if he were caught. And where was he going? The farther Janner followed his brother's trail, the more his dread loomed. He was terrified of what he would find at the end.

He ducked through a front yard, paused behind a fat tree, then tiptoed to a garden table at the edge of the yard, where Janner half-expected to find Kalmar hiding. Instead, the trail cut right, between two houses and into a dark alleyway. Janner's ears tingled, but he heard nothing. He saw no tracks coming back out. He was scared to go on, not sure he wanted to know what waited at the end of the alley. But he had to know. He had come this far. It was too late to turn back.

Janner stepped into the shadows of the alley and waited, listening, trying to pay attention to every one of his senses. He heard little other than the creak and thud of ships rocking in the harbor. He smelled a tinge of chimney smoke but little else; the cold and the snow hid the usual scents of mud and horse and the ocean's salty breath. When his eyes adjusted, he inspected the alleyway and saw nothing unusual: refuse bins, crates, a broken old wagon wheel, something made of wire mesh in a wood frame, rakes and shovels hanging from the stone walls on either side—everything dusted with snow.

At the back of the alley was a structure of some kind, but Janner couldn't tell what. Kalmar's footprints led straight to it.

39

What Janner Found
in the Alleyway

Quiet as a whisper, Janner placed his feet in Kalmar's tracks, one at a time, nearer and nearer to the rear of the alley. When he was halfway in, he saw that the structure was a hen coop. It had nine small, square doors with a wire mesh window framed in the center of each. The coop stood a few feet above the ground on four legs, and beneath it was an open space where old planks of lumber were stacked beside some empty milk canisters.

Janner could hear his own heartbeat as he crept closer. He struggled to control his breathing. Why was he so afraid? It was only Kalmar.

Janner reached the coop without a sound. Kal's footprints led beneath it. A blood-spattered pile of white feathers littered the snow, as if someone had emptied a pillow and sprinkled berry juice all over it. Janner clenched his teeth against the sudden urge to vomit.

Just as he gathered the courage to peek into the shadows beneath the coop, Kalmar's hand shot out and grabbed Janner by the leg. His claws dug in, and Janner fell. The little Fang snarled and leapt on Janner. He thrust his snout into Janner's face and bared his teeth. Little feathers were stuck in his dark, wet whiskers.

Janner froze in fear. He tried to see past the black nose and the blood and the terrible teeth. He tried to see Kalmar's eyes in the dark. He needed to see their color and depth, to know if the thing attacking him was a Grey Fang or Kalmar Wingfeather. One of Kalmar's wet hands was on Janner's forehead, holding him to the ground, and the other was wrapped around his throat. All Janner heard was a growl made more monstrous by its controlled softness.

"Kalmar," Janner whispered. "K-Kalmar, it's me. It's Janner."

After a moment Kalmar's hands flew to his mouth to quiet a whimper. He flung himself backward, beneath the coop again, knocking over the milk canisters. Janner scrambled to his feet and wiped the hen blood from his face and neck. He could smell it now, like metal and burnt soup. Kalmar's tail protruded from the shadows, trembling in the snow. He was crying.

"Kal? What's going on?" Janner whispered. He edged forward, as if he were approaching a wounded animal. "What are you doing?"

"I'm sorry," Kalmar whimpered. "I didn't mean to."

"It's all right. I'm coming in with you. Can I do that?"

Kalmar nodded from deep in the shadows. Janner could just make out the glint of his eyes. He eased under and sat beside his shivering brother, trying not to think about the hen bones scattered beneath him. He couldn't think of anything to say, so he put his arm around Kalmar and whispered his name. As frightened as Janner had been, it was Kal who wept.

Finally, Kalmar sat up and wiped his eyes. "I messed up. I didn't think the snow would stop so soon."

"What do you mean?"

"When I left, it was still snowing. I thought it would cover my tracks. But by the time I got here it stopped. I started to leave and saw my footprints, and I realized they'd lead straight to Chimney Hill, and they'd know it was me. It would ruin everything."

Janner froze. *Turalay.* When they caught Kalmar, they caught Nia. Janner had been rubbing Kalmar's shoulder to soothe him, but he pulled his arm away. The implications screamed in his mind. Nia would go to the dungeon. They would lose Chimney Hill. They might be exiled from the Hollows. Nia wouldn't be able to marry Rudric. All because Kalmar was hungry for raw meat. All because he couldn't control his impulses.

Kal was right. He had ruined everything.

Janner knuckled his forehead and ground his teeth, trying to think, trying to stay quiet, trying most of all not to unleash his temper on Kalmar—partly because he was afraid to wake the wolf again. He knew that was a fight he couldn't win.

"I didn't know what to do. I've been here for hours, asking the Maker to help me. Asking him to fix me. I don't want to be a Fang anymore, Janner. I just want to go home."

"You can't go home. They'll follow the trail."

"But what do I do?"

"I don't know." Janner hung his head and tried to think. "So it was you, then? All those animals?"

"Yes."

"But there were hundreds! Were you really that hungry?"

Kalmar was silent for a moment. Then he said, "I didn't eat them all."

"What does that mean? Did you kill them just for fun?" Janner wished there was more light so Kalmar could see his face. He wanted Kal to know he was disgusted with him. Then he remembered that his wolf eyes *could* see in the dark. Good.

"I didn't kill them for fun. You won't understand unless I show you."

"Show me what?"

"Will you come with me? Please?"

"Where? Why?"

"Please," Kalmar said.

"What can it hurt?" Janner muttered. "You've ruined everything already."

"I know," Kalmar whispered, and he slipped out from under the coop with a dead hen in one hand and waited for Janner at the corner of the house.

40

Bones and Bones

Janner no longer bothered to walk in Kalmar's tracks. It didn't matter anymore. In the morning, whoever owned the chicken would discover the bloody mess in the coop, call the Durgan Patrol, and follow the footprints straight to Chimney Hill. It wouldn't be hard to figure out that they were Kalmar's tracks, and then things would unravel.

Janner wished it would snow again, enough to wipe the trail clean, to erase the knowledge of Kalmar's terrible hunger—but there wasn't a cloud in the sky. In fact, the sky was clearer than Janner had ever seen it. The stars vied with the moon for brightness and seemed close enough to pluck out of the heavens like apples from a tree. The boys could try to cover their tracks, but the Durgans weren't stupid. It would be obvious that someone had disturbed the snow.

Janner also thought about running away. But of course that would make it even more obvious, and it probably wouldn't save Nia from the dungeon. Even if she weren't arrested, her boys would be fugitives and she would never see them again.

There was nothing to do but carry his grieving heart through the snow to whatever Kalmar had to show him. Every step was a silent farewell to Chimney Hill, and every minute brought him closer to the end of the peace he had found there.

Kalmar said nothing. His head hung low, and the dead hen left vivid specks of blood in the snow. He led Janner back the way they had come, and when they crested the last hill on the outskirts of the city, Janner could see the steep, snow-white roof of Chimney Hill in the distance. Kalmar paused and looked out at the moonlit valley.

"It's so pretty," Kalmar said. Frost clung to the tips of his ears and dusted the fur that framed his face; steam clouded out of his snout in little bursts; his black Durgan cape caught the moonlight; his brow shadowed his eyes with mystery; his back was bowed as if he carried a great weight, and Janner sensed his fight to bear it and his sorrow that it had to be borne. Even with the dead hen drooping from his claw, he shone with a kingly grace. He smiled, and Janner had the sudden urge to bow.

Janner's emotions swung like a pendulum between anger and awe, grief and confusion. One moment he was mourning his father's death and the next he was happy for Rudric; one moment he was frightened and the next he was angry; and now he was awestruck by the undeniable truth of Kalmar's kingship. He could do nothing but hold his tongue and follow.

The boys followed the road to the creek, crossed the bridge, and climbed up to Chimney Hill, where Podo, Bonifer, Nia, and Leeli slept. They crept past the house, and for one baffling moment Janner thought Kalmar was going to bring the dead hen inside. But they passed Chimney Hill and slipped past Freva's cottage and the barn. Leeli's dogs stirred at the scent of henmeat and watched the brothers creep over the fence and down into the pasture.

It wasn't long before Janner lost his bearings, especially with the snow repainting the landscape. He had the sense that they were heading east, but he couldn't be sure. Kalmar sniffed the air and strode ahead without hesitation, and now that they were in the sparseness of the prairie neither of them bothered to keep quiet.

Soon the rickety skeleton of the abandoned barn loomed ahead, and Janner recognized it. He remembered seeing a rooster perched in its rafters, but now the rooster was gone, like so many of the animals in the Hollows. A stone's throw beyond the old barn, the land fell away to a pond, an unfrozen black oval in the valley's white bowl.

Kalmar was taking him to the cave.

Janner imagined it in the earth under his feet, dark and dripping, an empty place secreted from wind and sunlight and every good thing. He felt its hollow presence beneath the hill. Janner had read about dens like this, places where monsters made their homes, places where rockroaches lured animals to gobble them up, places where bomnubbles sucked the marrow from wolf bones and slept in the stench of decay. Now, he supposed, it was Kalmar's den.

The little wolf bounded down the slope and looked up at Janner from the bottom. Janner wanted to run away, back to Chimney Hill, duck under his blankets, and pray this was all a nightmare. Whatever Kalmar had to show him in the cave was something Janner didn't want to see.

He found himself staggering down the hill without meaning to, as if his legs knew his need for answers and drew him on in spite of his dread. He reached the bottom as Kalmar ducked through the entrance. Janner saw his tail disappear into the dark. He took a last look at the pond, the sinking moon, and the quiet stars, and then he crawled into the cave.

As soon as he cleared the low ceiling and stood, he was slammed with a terrible stench. He gagged and staggered forward and felt things snapping under his boots. He heard a sound like the breaking of twigs, and he knew there were bones everywhere he stepped. Janner's vision starred in the utter darkness, and he fought to keep his feet. The last thing he wanted was to fall to that sordid floor.

Kalmar grabbed Janner's elbow to steady him and said, "You look like you're going to throw up."

Janner twisted out of Kal's grip and bent over with his hands on his knees.

"It smells terrible in here," Janner panted. "How can you stand it?"

"You'll see." Kalmar took Janner by the elbow again. "I'll guide you. A few more feet and you'll have to step over the little creek."

Janner straightened and pulled the collar of his cape over his mouth and nose. It helped a little. He stepped over the water and let Kalmar lead him deeper in. The smell worsened, as if it were getting wetter and warmer. He blinked away tears and said through the cloth over his face, "What have you done?"

"The only thing I could think to do," Kalmar replied. "Turn right and duck a little. We're almost there."

Janner fumbled around the corner and ducked, still crunching bones with every step.

Then he heard it.

41

What Janner Found
in the Cave

Somewhere in the darkness, something was breathing. But it wasn't ordinary breathing. It rattled and bubbled and wheezed, and now that Janner heard it, his mind wouldn't let him hear anything else.

"Stay here." Kalmar let go of Janner's elbow and crept deeper into the cave.

Panic sizzled in Janner's chest, and he would have run if he knew which way to go. He may as well have been at the bottom of the ocean or buried in a tomb. If he dropped to all fours, he might have been able to navigate his way out, but that would mean crawling on the slick, bone-rotten floor.

Kalmar murmured a few indistinguishable words, and the rhythm of the thing's breathing changed. It grunted and snuffled. Kalmar said something else, and the thing gurgled something close to a word. Then Janner felt Kalmar's hand on his elbow again. "Ready?"

"Is that what I think it is?"

"What do you think it is?"

"A cloven," Janner whispered.

"Not just *a* cloven," Kalmar said. "It's the one we saw. From the window."

Janner tried to remember how long it had been since they'd seen it. Two months, at least. Not long after they had arrived.

"I found it in the cave," Kalmar said. "It was wounded."

"Wounded? How?" It was hard for Janner to clear his mind enough to remember details from that night so many weeks ago.

"The Durgan Patrol. Remember Rudric told us that they hurt it? He said it would either run back to the Blackwood or find someplace to die." Kalmar paused. "Well, this is it. I showed you the cave, remember?"

"And this thing was in here that day?"

"Yes. I wanted to show you, but—I got scared. I thought you would be mad at me."

"You should have told someone, Kal."

"But if I told anyone, they would come in here and kill it. I couldn't let them do that. I saw its eyes. That night from our window, remember? I saw something in its eyes that scared me worse than anything." Kalmar swallowed, then whispered, "I saw myself."

The cloven grunted. Janner heard bones crunching and a sound like the stirring of noodles in a pot, and he realized the thing was moving, crawling closer.

"I couldn't just let it die, Janner. And I couldn't let them kill it. What was I supposed to do?"

"It's coming," Janner said.

Bones snapped. The cloven huffed and mewled from just a few feet away. Janner felt its breath on his face. He imagined sagging flesh and twisted fangs. He saw it in his mind, lurching closer with its knotty jaw drooping open.

"I had to take care of it," Kalmar continued. "It started with wild animals. It wasn't hard to hunt down a flabbit or a hen out on the prairie. No one noticed. I even found a few wild goats. I thought I could help it get better and convince it to go back to the Blackwood. But it was hurt worse than I realized. There was a spearhead lodged in its back. I pulled it out and tried to bandage the wound, and I even used some of that gadbalm Mama gave you. But for days it bled and bled. I thought it was going to die."

Janner heard it sniffing just inches away. He knew if he reached out, he would feel the moist skin of its face as it smelled him. Janner wanted more than ever to flee, but he knew it was useless.

"But it didn't die. It's still hurt, but it got a little better. And the better it got, the hungrier it got. I hunted all the way to the wooded vales, near Ban Yorna, but I couldn't find any more wild animals. I know it was wrong, but you have to believe me, Janner. I couldn't let it starve. And I couldn't let them kill it."

Janner felt something moist and cold touch the side of his face. It was all he could take. He screamed and careened backward, crashing into the wall and then to the ground. The cloven moaned and withdrew to the rear of the cave. Janner sat on the muck of the floor, panting, wiping his cheek with the back of his glove.

"Kalmar, I want to get out of this place. Now."

Kalmar sighed. "We can go. I just wanted you to know why I took the animals. I'm sorry about all this."

"Please, Kal. Get me out of here."

Kalmar spoke to the cloven. "I have to go. No one is going to feed you anymore. You're well enough now, so it's time to go back to the Blackwood."

The monster grunted.

"Do you understand? I have to go. I can't come back."

It grunted something that sounded like a question. Surely the thing couldn't understand what Kal was saying. Could it?

"Please, just go back to the Blackwood. They won't hurt you there, and there's plenty of food. It's almost morning, so wait until tonight and go back. Please." Kal's voice trembled with emotion. "Good-bye."

The cloven howled mournfully and approached, and Janner knew that Kalmar was hugging it, crying into its shoulder. The monster's howl turned to a pitiful wail, and the cave seemed to shake with the sound of sadness.

Janner heard Kalmar pull away, and then the little wolf took Janner's hand and pulled him to his feet.

When the boys turned the corner, a hint of pale blue light was visible a little way ahead. The cloven wept and wept, but by the time they reached the exit, the monster was barely audible.

Janner dropped to his hands and knees, so glad to leave that he didn't care about the bones on the floor anymore. He scrambled out, gulping clean air as if he'd been underwater. A moment later he realized the light wasn't from the moon at all. A band of gold showed in the east. Dawn had come to the Green Hollows.

Kalmar appeared, his face slick with mud and tears, and sat on his haunches.

"I always took a dip in the pond. To wash off the smell," Kal said, looking out at the cold water.

The boys sat for a moment in the silence of the waking day. Janner could think of nothing to say. He didn't blame Kalmar. He was only eleven years old, after all. It was hard enough to survive, even without Gnag the Nameless and Fangs ruining your life at every turn. Janner tried to imagine what he would have done in Kalmar's place, and he doubted it would have been much different. What was done was done. Now they had to get home and tell Nia. She would know what to do.

Janner said, "Come on, Kal. Let's get back to Chimney Hill while we still can."

Kalmar bowed his head and rested it on his forearms, still sniffling. "What's going to happen?"

"The Maker only knows." Janner saw a flicker of movement at the top of the hill. "But we need to get home right now."

He heard the snap of a twig in the weeds beside the pond. The Durgan Patrol had found them. If it wasn't the Durgans, *someone* had found them. It was over.

As the first ray of sunlight reached the top of the hill, Janner saw a face he recognized, stretched with wicked satisfaction: Grigory Bunge.

The boy stood, and Janner saw that he held a bow with an arrow already nocked on the string. Movement flitted somewhere to the left. That meant at least three people. Probably more.

They were going to ambush Kalmar, and Kalmar was going to fight. If that happened, the Durgans would kill the Grey Fang in their midst. Not only that, if the cloven heard and came to Kal's rescue, there was no telling what would happen.

There was only one thing he could do.

"Kalmar, don't fight me."

Kal lifted his head and narrowed his eyes. "What is that supposed to mean?"

"Now!" someone screamed, and Hollowsfolk rushed down the hill.

42

Sara and the
Maintenance Manager

Sara should have been exhausted at the end of her shift. She had been standing at the grinding tool in a spray of sparks for eight hours, with few breaks for water and food. Her back ached, her hands were numb from the constant vibration, and she was so dirty she felt like she was made of soot and grime. But as soon as the bell rang and children began filing in and out of the doors, she trembled with anxious excitement.

She had asked herself a thousand times during the shift if she was a fool, and a thousand times she answered herself, yes, she was a fool, but she would rather die a fool than live a half-life in a hopeless, helpless fog. And she was willing to risk the danger to the children who trusted her. She wanted them to know it was better to fight and lose than to sink away into nothingness under the Overseer's evil grin.

She joined the line of slaves and walked to the dining hall. Instead of eating, though, she continued on to the bunk hall, straight to her cot. But something was odd. Four Maintenance Managers leaned against the walls with their chains and pipes, watching the children with suspicion. The boy who had stopped her earlier was among them, and Sara pretended not to see him. She didn't have to look to know he was staring at her.

She passed many familiar faces: Borley, Veera, Grettalyn, and the others, all of them staring at the floor like good tools ought to do. She prayed none of the children would say anything to her. But like professional spies, they passed without a single glance to betray them. She was terribly proud of their courage, especially knowing they all had weapons stashed in their clothing.

Sara reached her cot and stretched as if she was going to lie down. She had planned to sneak into the bunk hall, grab her dagger, and follow the next shift out to the factory floor without anyone noticing. But with the boy watching, she couldn't.

She lay down on the cot. There was her dagger, just where she had hidden it. The rest of the weapons in her bunk were gone, taken sometime during the shift by her little army. She slid the dagger up her sleeve and peeked over her pillow at the boy against the wall. He had turned his back to Sara to talk to another of the Maintenance Managers, and she knew it was her only chance.

She crept out of bed and fell in step beside another boy, who yawned and rubbed his eyes on his way to his station. She imagined the Maintenance Manager's eyes on her back, imagined him staring at her, imagined that he could see through the sleeve of her shirt to the dagger hidden there.

Just before she and the sleepy boy pushed through the doors to the food hall, she risked a glance over her shoulder. The door swung shut on the sight of the Maintenance Manager standing in the middle of the aisle, chain in hand, staring right at her.

It was all she could do to stifle a scream. There were no Maintenance Managers in the dining hall, and no Mobrik, so she sprinted for the doors to the factory floor. If the boy raised an alarm, there wouldn't be time for Borley to do what had to be done, but she had to try.

Just as she reached the factory door she felt a hard grip on her elbow. She spun around and came face to face with the Maintenance Manager. He was out of breath from chasing her down and his lips were curled back to reveal his missing tooth.

"I knew it!" he breathed.

"I don't know what you're talking about," Sara cried.

"What are you up to?"

The dagger slipped from her sleeve and clanged to the floor.

43

Muzzled and Bound

Janner saw a blur of bows and swords and spears, all of them aimed at Kalmar, all in the hands of bloodthirsty Hollowsfolk. Some of the men wore the black uniforms of the Durgan Patrol, and others were farmers who had lost livestock. Kalmar bared his teeth and spun in every direction, his tail whipping a circle in the snow.

In seconds, their hands would be on Kalmar, and if he fought, they would happily put their weapons to use.

"Please, Kal, don't fight," Janner said, and he dove on top of his brother. He didn't think the Hollowsfolk would hurt a regular boy, and he hoped Kalmar wouldn't hurt him, either—but even if he did, Janner had survived Kal's teeth and claws before; he could live with more scars if it saved his brother's life.

The little Grey Fang twisted in Janner's arms. The hands of the mob fell upon the boys and tried to pull them apart. Kalmar fought to get loose and defend himself while Janner struggled to hold him tight and protect him, even though in a way it wasn't just Kalmar he was trying to protect—the Hollish mob was in danger of Kalmar's claws and the cloven that might try to help him.

One of the men shoved a muzzle over his snout and cinched it tight. When Kalmar's arms and legs were bound, Janner heard the sound of swords and daggers snapping back into sheaths and saw disappointment on several faces, and he knew that he had just saved his brother's life.

Kalmar lay in the snow, huffing and twisting against his bonds. Someone jerked Janner to his feet and tied his arms behind his back. Janner scanned the mob for Danniby, or Guildmaster Clout, or even Rudric, but of course Rudric was gone. He had set out for the Outer Vales and had taken his best men with him. There would be no help among the scowling crowd.

"So this is where the Grey Fang's made his den, is it?" said a voice Janner recognized. Nibbick Bunge, Grigory's father, stepped forward and threw his cape over his shoulder. Janner hadn't realized that Grigory's father was a Durgan Patrolman. "Grigory! Duck in there and tell us what you see."

With a cruel smile at Janner, Grigory crawled into the cave.

"No!" Janner said. "Don't go in th—" Someone punched him in the stomach, knocking the wind from his lungs.

"Quiet, you!" snapped Grigory's father. "As far as I'm concerned, you're as guilty as that mongrel brother of yours."

Janner didn't like Grigory Bunge, but that didn't mean he wanted the boy to be killed by the cloven. He tried to regain his breath so he could warn him, but before he could muster a word, Grigory wriggled out of the cave, gagging and waving a hand in front of his face.

"It reeks in there!" he said, sputtering.

"What did you see, boy?" asked Nibbick Bunge.

"Bones, Pa. Bones everywhere."

"You was right, Nibbick," said one of the other Durgans. "It was the dog boy all along. And Rudric wouldn't believe you."

"Oy, Sackby," said Nibbick Bunge. "And it's a shame the fool isn't here to see me proven right. Take him—*it*—to the Keep. Send word to the chiefs. Time to muster the council."

Janner wanted to tell them everything, but one look at his brother stayed his tongue. The little wolf's eyes pleaded with Janner not to say anything. And even if Janner had wanted to, he lost his chance when Nibbick Bunge pulled a strap of leather out of his pocket and gagged him.

The biggest of the men heaved Kalmar over his shoulder, and they shoved Janner back up the hill, past the old barn and Freva's cottage, and straight to Chimney Hill. When they arrived, one of the men timidly approached the front door.

"Go on, then," barked Bunge. "We don't have all day!"

Sackby banged on the front door and waited. The sun had broken over the horizon, and Janner knew Nia would be awake and making breakfast with Freva. He couldn't imagine what she would do or say when she answered the door. She thought her sons were asleep in their beds. She had probably woken happy, with wedding plans on her mind.

The door swung open and there stood Podo Helmer, squinting in the sunlight with a biscuit in one hand. He shaded his eyes and said, "Mornin' to ye, Sackby. What brings you out this early?"

"We're, er, here for—for her highness." Sackby cleared his throat. "Queen Nia Wingfeather is under arrest. *Turalay,* Podo. I'm sorry."

Podo looked past Sackby at the mob, then at his grandsons. His eyebrows shot up and he roared, "WHAT DO YE THINK YOU'RE DOIN' WITH ME LADS? IF YOU THWAP-GROUNCING SISSIES DON'T UNTIE THEM, I'LL POUND YE DEAD!"

Sackby scampered back to the protection of the mob while Podo limped out into the snow, swinging his legbone.

Nia appeared at the door.

"Get her!" said Nibbick Bunge. Two men stepped out of the mob and seized her.

Nia looked at Janner with confusion as they bound her wrists and led her down the steps. "Papa, drop that bone! There's been some misunderstanding." Podo gave one last swipe with the legbone and trembled with rage as Nia descended the front steps and looked over the gathered crowd. "Who's in charge here?"

"Nibbick Bunge, at your service." The man gave a mocking bow. "I think you know my son, Grigory. One of your boy's victims, remember?"

"You're a fool, Nibbick. As soon as Rudric returns, this will be set right. You know that." Then she saw the smear of dried blood on Janner's forehead and Kalmar beside him, muzzled and whining, and doubt washed over her face.

"It's me who's setting things right," said Nibbick Bunge. "We caught the Grey Fang in the act. Tracked him all the way to his den of bones. Seems he prefers raw goat to your cooking."

He laughed, and Podo leapt forward and shoved him so hard that he landed on his back in the snow. The mob fell on Podo and bound him too.

"For our protection," Nibbick said, brushing himself off as Podo's ropes were tightened. Then he turned to the crowd. "Take them to the Keep!"

Leeli appeared in the doorway. "What's going on? Mama! Grandpa!" Her dog, Baxter, stood at her side.

"It's going to be all right, dear," Nia told her. "Where's Freva?"

"Making breakfast. Bonnie's still sleeping."

"Go wake Oskar. Tell him what's happened. We'll be at the Keep."

"I'm coming with you," Leeli said.

"No," Nia said. "Stay here and wake Oskar."

"But you're going to need me," Leeli said in a matter-of-fact tone as she put on her boots.

Bunge shrugged. "Bring the limper. Might as well."

Leeli took Baxter's face in her hands. She whispered something to him in dogspeak, then grabbed her crutch and joined her family. Baxter didn't follow. He barked once, then bounded around the corner of the house.

As Bunge and his mob marched the Wingfeathers down the hill, Janner saw the tracks he and Kal had made the night before. The things he had seen and the secrets he had learned in the last few hours made him feel old and ill of heart. He wished he had never woken in the night. He wished he hadn't climbed out the window and followed Kalmar to the hen coop. But if he hadn't, there was a good chance that his brother would have been killed already, slaughtered like a hunted beast. Janner wouldn't have been there to protect him from Nibbick Bunge and the bloodthirsty gang; no one would have stopped them from putting a quick end to the monster in their midst.

It was still early, so few people were on the streets of Ban Rona to see the procession. But those few stopped and stared, then ran to spread the word that the Grey Fang had been muzzled and bound.

When the Wingfeathers got to the Keep, they passed into the great hall where the ancient tree loomed, bare of leaves or fruit. Bunge led them through another set of doors and down to the dungeon. It looked like every dungeon Janner had ever read about: iron bars, dripping ceilings, shackles hanging from walls.

Bunge held a torch in his hand and smiled at them. "We'll muster the seven chiefs and hold the council at sundown. In the meantime, you get to spend the day in our finest quarters."

Nibbick Bunge led them down a stone corridor and stopped at a low iron door. Sackby withdrew a ring of rusty keys from his coat and with a lot of rattling and wrenching managed to unlock it. The door creaked on its rusty hinges as Bunge shouldered it open. He pushed Kalmar inside.

"Leave it tied up," Bunge said. "This isn't an inn."

Janner was relieved that he would finally be alone with his family. With some time to talk they might be able to come up with a plan, or maybe some old friend of Nia's would break them out. At least they would be together.

But Janner was wrong. Sackby slammed the door behind Kalmar, locked it, and moved on to an identical door beside it. In went Podo, despite the old pirate's well-aimed barrage of insults. But the door was thick; as soon as it slammed shut, the sound of Podo's voice was cut off. Nia was next, then Leeli, and finally Janner. They removed his gag and pushed him in. Nibbick

Bunge smiled at him, slammed the door, and with a resounding click, locked him up.

The cell was featureless and dark. A faint light filtered down through a grate near the ceiling. Janner didn't poke around for more than a minute before he knew there was no hope of either communication with his family or of escape, so he sat on the damp floor and waited. His eyes drooped, and he felt the weariness of the long night seep into his bones. With his arms still tied behind his back, he curled up on the floor and went to sleep, thinking, for some reason, about his father, Esben, and the picture of him on a sailboat, handsome and young with his face to the wind.

44

The Case Against Kalmar

When he woke hours later, his neck hurt, his arm was asleep, and he was hungry. There was no way to tell what time it was, but there seemed to be less light than before. His mind was full of cobwebs, as dull and musty as the cell itself. He felt as if he should be worried, but he was too groggy.

Finally, he heard the key in the lock, and the door swung open. Torchlight stung his eyes, and he was yanked out by none other than Grigory Bunge, who looked pleased that his father had put him in charge.

"Oy, is that dog boy brother of yours in trouble." Grigory spat on the floor. "Let's get the murdering mutt out of its cage." The guards looked mad enough to explode as Grigory unlocked Kalmar's door.

Murdering? There was a big difference between stealing hogpigs and murdering someone.

The guards readied their weapons and nodded at one another. Grigory shoved open the door and ducked out of the way as the men rushed in. Janner heard bone-crunching thuds and Kalmar's muzzled screams.

"Stop it!" Janner cried, and he lunged for the door.

Grigory Bunge pinned him against the wall. "You can't help him now. And I can't imagine why you would want to."

The guards emerged with Kalmar. Janner could tell from the way his head lolled back that he was unconscious.

"Why are you doing this?" Janner screamed. "He's not going to hurt anybody!"

"You don't know, do you?" Grigory said.

"Know what?" Janner cried.

Grigory laughed. "You'll find out soon enough. Come on."

The guards collected the rest of the Wingfeather family and marched them up the stairs to the great hall. Janner tried to speak to Nia and Podo, but the guards quieted them with dark looks.

Night had fallen. Fires roared in the hall. Torches lit the walls. It seemed that every soul in Ban Rona was crammed into the Keep. As the Wingfeathers filed toward the mound at the root of the great tree, the crowd whispered to one another. Janner heard them murmur things like "I knew it all along" and "I can't wait to be rid of the Fang" and "I hope they deal with the wolf sooner rather than later."

Oh, how he wished Rudric were here. If anyone could talk sense into the Hollowsfolk, Rudric could. But on their first day in Green Hollows, even Rudric had been unable to stop Kalmar's arrest. And at the council, he lacked the authority to free Kalmar without the chiefs' approval. If the Hollowsfolk wanted Kalmar to pay, even the Keeper's presence might not be enough to stop them.

Grigory Bunge led the Wingfeathers to the tree under Nibbick's gaze and, giving Janner a demeaning shove, ordered them to sit. The guards carrying Kalmar shook him till he woke and sat him beside Nia. She whispered to him and rested her cheek on his head.

The branches of the great tree no longer brightened the room with leaves and dangling fruit—the limbs were bare, and the room was cold and gray. Even with the great hall crammed full of people and fires lit in the four hearths, a chill haunted the chamber. The only color seemed to be the dry, rusty smudge of Nia's handprint on the tree.

Nibbick Bunge posted four men to guard the Wingfeathers and conferred with Sackby and a few other townspeople in a far corner of the room. Leeli told Kalmar to turn around and began to unbuckle his muzzle. When one of the guards stopped her, she whipped her head around and gave him a look to melt stone.

"We can't allow it, lass. Too dangerous."

"He is *not*!" Leeli seethed and continued loosening the straps.

"I'm afraid he is," said the guard. He grabbed Leeli by the arm and sat her down.

Podo glared and curled his lip. "Keep your hands off me granddaughter, Galvin."

"Sorry, Podo. You can work those eyebrows all you want, but the wolf is going to meet his judgment today. The Grey Fang is guilty. You know the law."

Podo was too angry to speak, and his face turned red as a fireberry.

Bunge stepped up to the mound and raised his hands. "Hollowsfolk!" he cried. The crowd hushed and sat on the floor. "I call the council to order." Grigory stood beside him with his arms folded. "Let the ambassadors from Ban Hynh, Ban Rugan, Ban Yorna, Ban Finnick, Ban Verda, and the Outer Vales come forward."

"You forgot Ban Soran!" someone shouted as the chiefs approached.

"Oy! Ban Soran too." Bunge cleared his throat. "The Keeper is absent and may be gone for weeks, but the situation demands action now, not later."

"And what situation is that?" said a voice from the back. Olumphia Groundwich pushed through the crowd to the front.

"Ah! Guildmadam Groundwich," said Nibbick with a smile.

"Nibbick Bunge, you'd better think long and hard about what you're doing," Olumphia said. "Whatever happens to the boy happens to the Queen of Anniera. And that's on *your* head."

Bunge rolled his eyes. "There is no Anniera. She might as well be the queen of my fireplace. Sit down, Olumphia, and don't interrupt the council again." He spread his arms wide. "All of you know we've been losing animals. Most of you have lost some portion of your precious livestock. Well, you'll be pleased to know we've discovered the monster in the Hollows."

"Oy!" cried several people at once, and many frowned at Kalmar.

"You're telling me this lad is responsible for the deaths of *hundreds* of animals?" Olumphia wheeled around, whiskers atremble. Her hands were on her hips and her eyes roved the room, just as she did when students got too rowdy at the Guildling Hall.

"That's exactly what we're telling you," said Bunge. "Madigan Olliver, are you here?"

"Oy!"

"Tell the council what you found at your chicken coop this morning."

"I found a pile of feathers and two hens missing. Blood everywhere."

The crowd gasped.

"That's not all," Madigan Olliver continued. "I found tracks. Tracks in the snow leading right out of my alley and up the lane."

"And what did you do?" Bunge asked.

"I ran straight to the Durgan Patrol office. Told Sackby here what had happened."

"That's right," Sackby said. "I alerted Bunge, and we followed the trail. Brought along several others, just in case."

Bunge paced the mound. "And where did the trail lead?"

"It led to Chimney Hill."

"*Past* Chimney Hill," Bunge said. "Right past the servant's quarters, correct?"

"Oy. Straight into the prairies."

"Tell them what we found," Bunge said.

"We found the Wingfeather boys in a cave."

"Correction!" shouted Bunge. "You found *one* Wingfeather boy." He pointed at Kalmar. "And one Grey Fang!"

"Tell them about the bones, Pa!" said Grigory.

"Oy!" Nibbick said. "The cave was full of bones!"

The crowd erupted in shouts.

Olumphia waved her hands for order. "I've had this young man in the Guildling Hall for months, and I've not seen a single instance of misbehavior! All three Wingfeathers have been exemplary guildlings—better than most of your children!"

"I agree with Olumphia!" Guildmaster Clout moved to the front of the room and stood beside Olumphia, who blushed and pulled the sleeves over her lanky wrists. "That boy you call a Grey Fang has outperformed every student in my guild. He's the finest Durgan Guildling there is." Guildmaster Clout smiled at Kalmar. "Just days ago he pulled off one of the finest sneaks I've ever seen."

"Exactly," said Bunge with a triumphant laugh. "Only your finest snooper could steal so many without a trace."

"Then—then what about the snaphound tracks?" Olumphia said. "You followed them all the way to the wooded vales!"

"A decoy," said Sackby.

"Impossible," said Clout. "The wooded vales are fifteen miles away."

"And who's the best runner in the Guildling Hall? Who of your guildlings can run for hours on end without trouble?" asked Nibbick Bunge.

Clout and Olumphia exchanged a worried glance.

"Please! Tell the council."

"Kalmar Wingfeather," Clout muttered.

"Thank you, guildmadam and guildmaster. You've left us with little doubt." Bunge turned to the crowd. "The infractor is obviously the Grey Fang."

"Lies!" bellowed Podo. "These boys were asleep in their beds!"

"Were they?" Bunge looked at Podo and grinned. "Don't take my word for it, Helmer. Why don't you ask them?"

Podo blinked. He seemed unsure that he wanted to know the answer. "Janner, is what they're saying true?"

"Janner," Leeli said, "tell them! Tell them Kal didn't take all those animals. He would never do such a thing." Leeli looked at Kalmar. "You wouldn't, would you?"

Kalmar's answer was a heavy sigh. He looked at Janner, pleading with his eyes, and Janner knew he was asking him not to tell them about the cloven. Why was he willing to risk so much for the monster? Why would he give up his freedom—and his mother's freedom—for the twisted thing in the cave?

But Janner knew the answer. *I saw something that scared me to death,* Kal had told him. *I saw myself.* Kalmar was the only person in all of the Hollows who would show mercy to a cloven, because only he knew how a cloven felt: hungry, outcast, and alone.

"There must be some explanation," Nia said.

Even if Janner told them that Kalmar had done it all for a cloven, it wouldn't change a thing. They'd still throw Kalmar and Nia in the dungeon, and then they'd hunt down the cloven and kill it. The Hollowsfolk had been looking for a reason to rid themselves of the Grey Fang, and now they had it. The cloven didn't matter.

"Janner," Nia said quietly, "is it true?"

"Yes ma'am." Janner couldn't meet her eyes. "Kalmar took the animals. All of them."

"He swiped my goatlings!" someone shouted.

"And my flabbits!"

"And my seven, or possibly four, hogpiglets!" said Paddy Thistlefoot.

"Yes," Janner said. "All of them."

A silence fell over the great hall.

"But that's not all," said Bunge. His eyes raked the crowd for a moment, and then he motioned to a guard near the side door. "Bring in the servant girl!"

The doors opened and Freva entered, wailing into the chest of one of the guards. When she saw Kalmar, she tore out of the guard's arms and raced across the room at him, screaming, "What have you done? *What have you done?*"

She landed on Kal and beat him wildly until Janner, Podo, and Nia managed to put themselves between them. One of the guards pulled Freva away and led her to Bunge's side.

"Shall I tell the assembly," Bunge said in a sickly gentle voice, "or would you like to, dear?"

"Oy, I'll tell 'em." Freva took a deep, trembling breath and raised her voice. "Me daughter is gone! Dead! Eaten by the Fang!"

45

The Plan

Sara closed her eyes. It was over. The dagger lay half on the floor and half across the toe of her shoe. The Maintenance Manager let go of Sara's arm, and she waited for the pain from his chain or fist or the sound of his voice as he shouted for his fellow managers. She thought of Borley and the others who had followed her, of all the precautions she had told them to take, and the bitter irony that it was her who had spoiled everything.

The Maintenance Manager lifted the dagger from the floor. "What's this?"

Sara shrugged, suddenly tired from the night's work. "It's a dagger. What does it look like?"

"You're Sara, right?" the boy said.

Sara's head snapped up. "How do you know that?"

"I've been listening. Paying attention. You think you're being pretty sneaky, but it hasn't been hard to tell that you're planning an escape." Sara's cheeks flushed. "What do you plan to do with this dagger?"

"Why should I tell you?" Sara said, looking away.

"Because," the boy said quietly, "I want to help."

"What?"

"Name's Wallis. I'm sick of this place. I'm sick of the Overseer. And I want out. Several of us have been talking and waiting for the right moment to do—something. We just didn't know what so few of us could do. But there are a lot of you, aren't there?"

Sara nodded, still not sure what to think of the toothless boy.

"What's the plan?" Wallis asked.

Before Sara could answer, she heard shouting on the factory floor. The boy kicked the door open and pulled Sara after him.

She saw little Borley standing near the iron-bellied machine as it rattled and roared for more coal. Two Maintenance Managers had him by either arm while another shouted at him.

"You think you can throw a hunk of coal at me and get away with it, tool?" shouted the bigger boy.

Borley looked scared. But when he saw Sara watching him from the doorway, he found his courage. He smiled up at the Maintenance Manager and nodded.

Another friend of Sara's, a girl named Trilliane from a village in the Linnard Woodlands, calmly walked over to a pile of coal, picked up a piece, and threw it at the same Maintenance Manager.

"Ow!" he said, rubbing his head. "Somebody get her too!"

Four more Maintenance Managers swung down from chains and dragged her to where Borley and the others stood.

"What's going on here?" demanded the manager.

Borley and Trilliane shrugged. The Maintenance Manager answered by unfurling his chain and whacking it on the floor. Sparks flew, and the two children jumped.

Then Grettalyn threw a piece of coal too. A moment later she was dragged over with the others, and Sara counted seventeen Maintenance Managers around them, drawn by the commotion. Meanwhile, the rest of the slaves in the factory continued their work as if nothing was happening.

"*That's* the plan," Sara said. "Get all of you in one place. Surround you. Wait for the Overseer to show up."

"Then what?" asked Wallis.

"Then we attack."

"What if there are Fangs?"

"I've been praying to the Maker that there wouldn't be any. They haven't been around for a while, so I figured now was as good a time as any."

The double doors at the top of the stairs banged open. Mobrik and the

Overseer appeared, but they weren't alone. Three Fangs of Dang slithered through the door, tongues flicking and teeth bared. Sara thought for a moment that the Fangs looked strangely frightened—there was something jittery about the way they moved.

Borley, Trilliane, and Grettalyn looked at Sara with wide eyes. Borley's hand slipped up his sleeve, where she knew his dagger was hidden.

Sara shook her head at him and mouthed the words, "Not yet."

"What's going on in here, tools?" shouted the Overseer. He motioned to the Fangs and they followed him and Mobrik down the steps.

She had thought it might be possible to overcome the Maintenance Managers and even Mobrik and the Overseer. But three Fangs? Jittery or not, it was too dangerous. One bite and the children in her care would die.

"It's over," Sara said. "I have to stop the children from doing anything."

"Don't," said Wallis. "This is the closest I've come in three years to getting out of this place. Let me worry about the Fangs." He hopped onto a barrel, swung up by a chain, and disappeared into the maze of rafters.

The Overseer approached Borley and the others while the Fangs stood a little way beyond him, snarling at the nearest children. Everywhere Sara looked, she saw her friends looking to her for guidance. They peeked from behind counters and glanced at her while they wheeled carts. They didn't know what to do. But neither did she.

Sara calmed her nerves and thought about it. The plan seemed to be falling apart, but it didn't have to. Yes, there were Fangs. She had hoped that wouldn't happen. But there was also the surprise appearance of this boy named Wallis and his friends. She wasn't sure if the two developments balanced each other out, but it didn't matter. Sara and her army still had the advantage of surprise. The Overseer had no idea the factory floor was full of armed children—not just armed, but armed and ready to attack. If she gave a signal to abort the mission, poor Borley, Grettalyn, and Trilliane would be punished severely. The Overseer would discover their hidden weapons too, which would probably lead to a discovery of the whole revolt.

Sara thought about Janner Igiby, riding into the night on the Overseer's carriage. She wanted that for these children. They may not make it far into Dugtown before the Fangs caught them, but she was sure at least *some* of them would escape. And the rest would know a few moments of freedom. If Janner's escape had kindled her hope, then maybe what she was about to do would kindle even more in the rest of the slaves, and eventually the Overseer and his wretched factory would be no more.

Sara took a deep breath, clutched the dagger in both hands, and screamed, "Now!"

46

Freva's Accusation

At Freva's pronouncement, every soul in the hall gasped. They clamored for justice and Fang blood. The room shook with the outrage of Hollowsfolk. Kalmar whimpered and hid behind Nia. Even Clout and Olumphia looked at him with shock.

"Kal, what are they talking about?" Janner shouted over the din.

Kalmar shook his head in a panic. He tried to talk but the muzzle made his words unintelligible.

"This is going to get out of hand, and fast," Podo said under his breath. He stood and bellowed, "WHAT PROOF HAVE YE? LET THE WOMAN SPEAK!"

Bunge blew a horn and calmed the crowd. The people quieted, but they simmered on the verge of a boil.

"Freva, have you the strength to speak?" Bunge put his arm around her and patted her shoulder. Freva buried her face in his chest and shook her head. "It's all right, lass. Many of you know Freva's been employed at Chimney Hill these last months, living in their guest quarters and raising her daughter—in the vicinity of the Fang." The crowd seethed again. "Just this morning, not an hour after we arrested the dog and its brother, she found her daughter's bed empty and footprints in the snow! We tracked it from Olliver's coop to the monster's den. We can only assume that among the bones in the cave were the remains," Bunge's voice cracked, "of her daughter."

Janner struggled to his feet. "That's a lie! He would never do that! I followed him to the coop and straight to the cave. We never set foot inside Freva's house!"

"Then you snuck out with the Fang?" Bunge asked.

"Yes. Well, no, not exactly," Janner stammered. "I followed his tracks to Olliver's coop."

"And those tracks led past Freva's quarters?"

"Yes, but—"

"Then how do you know the Fang didn't slip inside and steal the child first? Did you notice if he had already been to the cave that night?"

Janner had no answer. He *hadn't* paid attention to the tracks on the way to the cave; his mind had been elsewhere. He knew Kal hadn't taken Bonnie—but he was too flustered to sort it out, especially with all the eyes watching him. All he could do was look at Kalmar.

"Sit down, boy," said Bunge with a wave of his hand. "The council has already taken this evidence into consideration. We've decided that, given the brutal nature of the Fang's crimes, it will be treated like every other Fang that has crossed our borders to kill and destroy our people."

"Execute it!" someone shouted, and the rest of the Hollowsfolk took up the cry. "Execute it! Execute it!"

Freva wiped her nose and joined them: "Execute it!"

"Janner, what are they talking about?" Nia asked.

"It wasn't him, I know it. They're setting us up or something. Kalmar, tell her! It wasn't you."

Kalmar cringed at the voices screaming hatred at him. The crowd was on its feet, chanting, "Execute it! Execute it!" Those who had weapons shook them in the air.

The guards posted in front of the Wingfeathers cast nervous glances from Bunge to the crowd to one another. If something didn't happen soon, the Hollowsfolk would riot and carry out the sentence themselves.

47

The Fingerless Glove

When Sara Cobbler gave the signal, a hundred and twenty-two children drew weapons and screamed. They charged the center of the factory where the Maintenance Managers, the Overseer, Mobrik, and three Fangs of Dang stood in confusion.

Wallis and four other boys dropped from the ceiling onto the Fangs. Wallis swung his chain around one Fang's neck and pulled with all his might while the other four boys attacked with pipes and fists.

The Maintenance Managers who had seized Borley, Grettalyn, and Trilliane held up their hands and backed away from the many sharp points of steel aimed at them. Children who knew nothing of Sara Cobbler and her army saw what was happening, grabbed forks and swords from their workstations, and joined the revolt.

The Overseer cracked his whip and shouted orders at his Maintenance Managers. Mobrik's eyes shot in every direction, looking for a way out, but Sara's army advanced too quickly. In seconds, Mobrik and the Overseer disappeared beneath a pile of their own slaves.

Sara rushed toward the remaining Maintenance Managers and shouted, "Drop your chains! Drop them or we'll attack!"

One of the bullies sneered and advanced on Sara, but Borley appeared and stood between them with his dagger raised. The manager laughed and shoved the little boy out of the way, but five other children placed the points of their weapons against the manager's neck.

Sara smiled. "I warned you."

The manager dropped his chain and raised his hands just as the last of the Fangs fell with a papery scream. Wallis's arms were scratched and bleeding, but he and his friends clapped one another on the back and laughed with amazement that they were still alive. Mobrik and the Overseer both struggled against the throng around them until Sara spotted the whip on the floor and ordered the children to tie up the Overseer with it.

"Tie up the ridgerunner, too," she said, then turned to the Maintenance Managers. "Are you with us, or do we need to find another use for your chains?"

Most of them stood with Wallis and his friends. The few who didn't were wrapped in their own chains and placed on the floor with Mobrik and the Overseer.

It was over.

Sara stepped past the decaying Fangs and climbed the stairs to the platform where the Overseer had stood so many times to watch his slaves do his bidding. She looked out over the factory floor, now strangely still and empty of its captives.

Borley took Sara's hand. "It worked, Sara Cobbler."

Sara smiled at him. "Yes, Borley, it did."

"Can I go home now?" Borley asked.

Sara's smile fell. The truth was, she doubted Borley still had a home. Sara didn't even know if *she* had a home. Who knew what had happened outside all these months? There could be an army of Fangs on the other side of the door waiting to snatch them up. "I don't know." She stroked his hair. "But I know we're getting out of this place. Come on."

Sara led the children down the long hallway and paused at the double doors that led to the main room where the Overseer's carriage had unloaded each of them over the years. She hadn't seen the room since the night she'd helped Janner escape. She motioned for the throng of children clogging the hall behind her to keep quiet so she could listen. When she was sure it was safe, she pushed through the doors and led the children out of the darkness and into the light.

Thick beams of sunlight angled through high windows and lit the floor.

The children held their hands up to the light as if it were the first time they'd ever seen it. The moment of awe was quickly broken, however, by squeals of delight and celebration. The children of the Fork Factory danced and ran and tumbled across the floor. They found water in a trough against the wall and splashed it on their faces, rubbing the soot away and meeting one another, in a way, for the very first time.

Sara leaned against the wall by the doors and smiled. It brought her great pleasure to stand apart from them and see their joy, and she was content to be the last thing on their minds.

Then the door to the hallway cracked open, and a hand wearing a fingerless glove slipped out and yanked her back inside. The jubilation of the other children was so loud that none of them heard Sara scream.

48

The Chumply Amendment

As the Hollowsfolk chanted for Kalmar's death and his family huddled around him, there came a commotion from the back of the room. The crowd parted and someone pushed forward, interrupting enough of the chant that it fell apart and was replaced by shouts of annoyance. Janner spotted a top hat and after it a shiny bald head.

Bonifer Squoon and Oskar N. Reteep made their way through the crowd and approached Nibbick Bunge. Bonifer wore his suit coat with long tails and a bowtie. Oskar was dressed in a scarf and a fur coat and carried a thick leather satchel over one shoulder.

"What's the meaning of this?" shouted Nibbick Bunge. "Outsiders aren't allowed a voice in the council."

"Indeed," said Bonifer, "but I've as much right to speak as you, Bunge. I was born here. My accent may be Annieran, but my blood is as Hollish as yours."

Bunge shook his head with impatience. "What do you have to say?"

"Oskar N. Reteep and I have spent hours in the library, as you may know. And we wanted to be sure you were upholding article seven of the Chumply Amendment."

Bunge blinked. "Er, what in Aerwiar is that supposed to mean?"

"In the words of Chumply himself," said Oskar, "'You can't just execute *royalty*, you piggish brute.'"

"We can execute anyone we like," Bunge growled.

"Not true," said Bonifer. "You may only banish them. Article seven of the Chumply Amendment of the year 115 of the Second Epoch clearly states that in cases concerning royalty, even in cases of kidnap and murder, you may exile but not execute."

"Lies! I've never heard of such a thing."

"How surprising," said Bonifer dryly. "This is such a common situation, and your knowledge of Hollish law is *so* extensive since you've been the Keeper for—what is it, twenty hours? Forgive me, I meant to say the *temporary* Keeper for twenty hours. When Rudric returns, you'll be just another Durgan Patrolman under his command. In the meantime, it would behoove you to obey the laws of the Hollows, would it not? Mister Reteep, please show the *temporary* Keeper the document."

"Gladly." Oskar handed a wrinkled parchment to Bunge, who hardly looked at it. Oskar winked at Janner. He had smudges of ink on his fingers and a devious look in his eyes.

Bonifer hobbled around to face the crowd. "Since the *true* Keeper is absent *and* since the little girl has not been found and since the laws of this land clearly forbid it, I think it is in your best interest to stay this execution in favor of banishment. Deliver the Wingfeathers to me, Bunge. I have a skiff waiting at the harbor."

Bunge thrust the parchment at one of the council members. The seven chiefs from the seven districts looked it over, then shrugged at Bunge. He sighed. "Very well. Banishment is just as good."

Bonifer bowed his head and smiled. He was ancient, but he had managed to change Kalmar's fate with just a few words. If Janner's arms weren't tied, he would have hugged the little man.

"No!" cried Freva. Her voice was ragged from weeping. "That thing killed me baby! What's become of us, to let a Grey Fang in our borders, to let it go to our school, to let it loose in the city? And *see what happens!*" Freva was mad with grief. All her sadness had turned into a red-faced fury. "That monster will eat your young, as it did my Bonnie! Execute the beast!"

"Execute it!" the crowd roared, louder than before.

Bonifer's face paled.

Nibbick Bunge smiled at the Wingfeathers. He took the parchment from the council, tore it to pieces, and threw the tatters in Bonifer's face. "Raise the gallows!" he shouted, and two men who looked like sailors pushed through the crowd with coils of rope slung over their shoulders.

Bonifer looked at Bunge, then at the ropes, then at the Wingfeathers— then he snatched the satchel from Oskar and ran.

He moved faster than Janner thought a man in his eighties could move. His top hat bobbed among the crowd as he dashed for the exit. The chanting Hollowsfolk ignored him.

Janner had no time to wonder where the old man was going, because all his attention was on the nooses the men were fashioning out of the ropes— nooses that would soon kill Nia and Kalmar.

While he watched, several other men disappeared through a side door and reemerged with planks, hammers, and stakes. Bunge sat on Rudric's throne and watched with a look of satisfaction while the builders assembled the structure. The wood was dusty with disuse, and the men argued with one another and turned the planks this way and that, trying to remember how it fit together. However bloodthirsty the Hollowsfolk were now, it seemed a formal execution wasn't a regular occurrence.

Podo roared and strained against his ropes, and Janner thought he might actually break them. He bellowed and kicked at the guards as they held him down, until Bunge gave the order for him to be gagged and tied with more rope. It took eight men to subdue him. When Podo's strength was gone, he slumped in his seat and fought to breathe. With his hair unkempt, his gag foamed with spittle, and his tunic drenched with sweat, he looked like a madman. Nia leaned against him and kissed his cheek, and Podo wept.

Oskar hurried over and knelt in front of Nia. "Your highness! I don't know what to do!"

"It's all right, Oskar," Nia said. "Will you loosen the king's muzzle?"

The guards were busy keeping the crowd at bay and making room for the gallows, so if they noticed, they said nothing. Oskar threw the muzzle aside.

"Kalmar," Nia said, "I don't believe you took little Bonnie."

"Thanks," he said in a small voice.

Nia smiled. "I don't know what happened, but this isn't the time to talk about it. We don't have much time left. I just want you to know that I love you. I love you and I don't regret vouching for you. I'd do it again." Nia kissed him and turned to Podo, Janner, and Leeli. "Papa, children, if they go through with this, please don't blame them. The Hollowsfolk are just decieved. It's Gnag who's to blame. His poison has embittered them, and it will take great mercy to undo that. I know you're going to want to leave here, but stay. Your presence will remind the people of this treachery and will convict their hearts in the years to come. They must remember what happens here today and reckon with it and be humbled. Only then will their hearts soften. That's what your father would have you do."

Leeli wept and put her arms around Nia and Kal. Janner and Nia were still tied and could only lean on each other as the gallows took shape.

The chanting abated, and though most of the city was crammed into the great hall, the room was silent except for the hammering of pegs and stakes into the structure. The nearer the platform was to completion, the heavier the air in the room felt, and it seemed to Janner that the Hollowsfolk were only now considering that they were executing not only a Grey Fang but the Queen of Anniera too. But a reawakening of conscience was not enough to stop what was set in motion. The Hollowsfolk had pushed forward a judgment and were unwilling to withdraw it.

At last, one of the guards climbed the rickety steps and raised the trapdoor that stretched beneath the two nooses. The platform creaked and wobbled, but it was strong enough for a little wolf and his mother. Nibbick Bunge and the seven chiefs stepped forward with grave expression and looked out at the Hollowsfolk.

Nibbick spoke. "Citizens of Ban Rona, the council has decided to bring judgment on the Grey Fang before you. For the charges of animal thievery, unlawful animal slaughter, and"—Bunge glanced at Freva—"murder, we sentence you to death. May you suffer greatly, Grey Fang. When you turn to dust, I look forward to sweeping you from this hall." Janner felt Kalmar trembling as Nibbick spoke. "And you, Nia Igiby Wingfeather, because you have invoked *turalay*, you are to be executed with him. He was yours to keep, and your failure resulted in the death of Freva's daughter."

Bunge gestured at the guards, and they pulled Nia and Kalmar to their feet. Podo moaned and tried to stand, but another guard pushed him to his seat. Janner scanned the crowd for Bonifer, hoping the old man had come back, hoping he had concocted some new plan to rescue them. But the top hat was nowhere to be seen.

The guard cut the bonds around Kalmar's ankles and pointed him up the gallows steps. Janner heard Nia whisper, "Be strong, my love."

They reached the top, and one of the guards positioned them over the trapdoor. He draped a noose over Kalmar's head, then Nia's. Bunge climbed the steps after them with a dark look, and Janner thought he saw a flicker of uncertainty in his eyes. Perhaps he was thinking of Rudric's return and the fury that was sure to descend upon him.

Bunge stood between the condemned and cleared his throat. "Have you anything to say, Fang?"

"His name is Kalmar Wingfeather," Nia said.

Bunge spat. "His name is murderer. Fang, have you anything to say?"

"I took the animals," Kalmar said in a small voice.

"If you're going to speak, son, speak up," Nia said.

Kalmar cleared his throat and spoke in a clear voice. "I took the animals. I'm sorry about that. But I didn't take the girl! I thought Bonnie was wonderful, and I'd never hurt her. Or anyone else. Someone else took her, and for that matter she may not be dead. I hope when you're finished with me, you'll look for her. I'm sorry about the animals."

"And have you anything to say, your highness?" Bunge said.

"Your actions condemn you. The Maker sees all." Nia's gaze swept across the room, and then she nodded at Bunge. "I'm finished."

"Then by the authority of the seven chiefs of the council, and for crimes

against the citizens of the Green Hollows, I give you over to execution."
Bunge reached for the lever to release the trapdoors.

"Please, sir," Leeli said, limping up the steps with her whistleharp in one
hand.

Bunge rolled his eyes and sputtered. "What is it now?"

"Please, sir. Let me play a song for them."

49

A Vision, a Voice, and a Villain

Into the silence of the great hall, Leeli played. Her eyes were closed and she stood beside her mother, swaying with the melody.

Janner knew the moment she spoke that if she played, the strange magic would awaken. And he was glad, though he couldn't imagine what good it would do them, with Bunge's hand on the lever that would send Nia and Kal plunging to their deaths. Except for the time it had assuaged the sea dragon's anger, the magic had never really done them any good; the words and visions that filled Janner's mind mainly left him confused.

Still, he welcomed it. His heart was black with despair, so the Maker's magic was most welcome. It helped him believe there was power pulsing behind the veil of the visible world, pulsing like blood through the world's veins, sending life and light coursing through everything, surprising and confounding at every turn. When he remembered this, the darkness glimmered with goodness.

He was surprised to find that he was smiling. "Play, Leeli," he said, and her song lifted into the hall and swooped among the boughs, echoed off the ancient walls, and fluttered among the crowd. It seeded the soil of many hearts, and only the stoniest rejected it and held to their murderous yearning. The rest, though, felt themselves believing, as Janner did, that the world was bigger and more terribly beautiful than they thought.

Janner expected it, so as soon as the air before him swirled, he leaned into it; he listened for whatever words would be spoken, whatever visions would emerge. The great hall faded into the periphery, and before him he saw many things: Artham Wingfeather, marching rain-wet streets before an army, screeching defiance at an enemy invisible to Janner; deep caverns with glittering walls, and beneath, as far below as the earth from the heavens, a glow as warm as a setting sun; a bright sail under a full moon, backlit by the thousand lights of a great city.

But more than the vision, which was blurry as if he were peering through sleepy eyes, he heard words:

> *I found the girl.*
> *Now I'm coming for you.*
> *I'll sniff you out.*
> *And when I do,*
> *I'll hold you fast*
> *forever.*

The words jarred Janner's mind and shot through the vision like an arrow through smoke. *Who? Who will find me?* He didn't know if it would work, but he hurled his own words into the vision like stones into a lake.

Who are you? What do you want from us?

Janner felt the asker—whatever it was—choke with surprise, as if it hadn't expected to be answered.

I am . . . I am . . .

The speaker faltered, and Janner sensed that it was too shocked to form a sentence. Janner wasn't sure if the voice was the cloven in the cave, Gnag the Nameless, or something else, but he threw more words, desperate to know the answer.

Why are you after us? What do you want?

"Enough!" Bunge cried. He took a step toward Leeli and smacked the whistleharp away from her mouth. The vision vanished, and Kalmar raised his head and loosed a long, mournful howl. Bunge reached for the lever that would open the trapdoor and let Nia and Kalmar fall.

But before he could pull it, a mighty pounding shook the giant doors at the back of the hall. The crowd turned in time to see them fly open.

In the shadows of the doorway stood the cloven. Janner knew it by its hunched silhouette. Like a wave, the odor of the beast washed into the room. People gasped and scrambled away, covering their faces and gagging.

"No!" Kalmar screamed. "Go back!"

The cloven cowered for a moment, pausing in the safety of the shadows, and then it stepped through the doors and into the light. The beast was as tall as a man, but it stooped. Matted brown fur clung to it in patches, and where there was no fur, its skin was gray and bubbled, as if its muscles had melted and slid down to grow in the wrong places. Its face was like an animal's—but not just any animal's, Janner realized—a bear's. Its jowls hung low, and tendrils of slobber dangled from its black lips. Its ears were small, ragged half circles, and its eyes were deep set and hidden in shadow. The limbs were grotesque and twisted, so that it moved with a pitiful lurch, twisting and swinging and grunting with every difficult step. Its shoulders were broad and muscular, but one hung lower than the other so that one of its hands dragged the floor. It stopped and cocked its head when it spotted Nia and Kalmar on the gallows.

"Mama?" said a tiny voice. Janner thought for a baffling moment that it was the cloven who spoke, but then he realized that it held something in one of its arms. "Mama?" said the voice again, and a little face peeked out from the beast's fur.

"Bonnie!" screamed Freva, and she rushed across the hall past the dumbfounded crowd.

The cloven grunted again and lurched forward, loosening its grip on the little girl enough so that she climbed up on its arm where everyone in the hall could see her.

"It's got the girl!" one of the men shouted, and the spell of silence was broken. The hall erupted in screams of terror and screams of anger.

The thing held Bonnie out to Freva, and its face broke into a horrible smile. Bonnie leapt into Freva's arms with a squeal of joy, and someone shouted, "Shoot it!"

Arrows plunged into the cloven's back and shoulders, and it slogged forward a step, then fell to one knee. Kalmar struggled against his bonds and howled indecipherable words, more concerned for the cloven than the rope around his neck. Men and women grabbed weapons from the outer walls and advanced on the beast while Freva ran with Bonnie to a nook in the roots of the great tree and held her tight. The cloven fell forward and lay motionless. Those bearing weapons stood over it, ready to strike if it moved.

"Nibbick Bunge," Nia said, "the girl is alive. You no longer have grounds to execute anyone. Remove the rope from my son's neck."

Bunge looked from Nia and Kalmar to the council to the cloven.

"Remove it *now*," Nia commanded.

Bunge shrank before her and lifted the noose from Kalmar's neck, then Nia's. Kalmar crumpled to the floor, exhausted and sobbing. Janner and Podo climbed the gallows, and though their arms were bound they did their best to hug Nia and Kalmar.

"You ought to be ashamed of yourself, Bunge," Olumphia shouted. "You were ready to hang a daughter of the Hollows for a murder her son didn't commit! You're no more suited to be our Keeper than that dead cloven is."

"It was the cloven all along!" said Guildmaster Clout. "Nibbick Bunge is the only one here who's guilty of trying to kill anybody."

Several other Hollowsfolk shouted their agreement. Bunge, in a daze, cut Nia's bonds. He descended the gallows steps without a word, sat next to Grigory on the mound, and hid his face. The seven chiefs stared at the floor. The stealing of the livestock seemed to matter little in the wake of Bunge's humiliation.

Nia stepped to the front of the gallows and gazed out at the assembly. "Hollowsfolk! We have been met with suspicion and hatred since we set foot here." People squirmed as if she were looking at them each alone. "You're so proud that the Green Hollows has withstood Gnag the Nameless all these years, but I tell you he has conquered you as surely as he conquered the Shining Isle. Your fear of him has poisoned your hearts so that you have lost the ability to see with anything but your eyes. Your borders may be fortified, your

Durgans may be ruthless, and your precious fruit may be safe, but your fear has left you as twisted as that beast on the floor. We came to you for refuge! We came to you because we had nowhere else to go. And you would hang us from the great tree without evidence, without a thought in your head—without even a day to learn the truth! I tell you, today you lost your love for truth and fled into the arms of fear."

"Indeed!" said a voice from the back of the room. Bonifer Squoon hobbled into the hall on his cane. He removed his top hat and wiped sweat from his forehead. His cheeks were flushed, and he was out of breath. "A fine speech, your highness. I'm glad to see the council came to their senses. I don't know what I would have done if they had hanged you."

"Thank you, Bonifer," Nia said. "I'm glad to know *someone* here hasn't lost his mind."

"Not at all, highness! Not at all. Oh!" he said when he saw the cloven in the center of the floor. "A beast! Much has transpired in the few minutes I've been gone, I see."

"Yes," Nia said. "And the missing girl has been returned to her mother. It was the cloven that took Bonnie."

Squoon chuckled. "Was it?" Then he laughed so hard that he doubled over his cane and wheezed. His wheeze became a cough, which turned into more laughter. It was the only sound in the hall. He placed his hat on his head and wiped the corners of his eyes. Bonifer collected himself and patted his stomach with a sigh, then folded his hands over his cane.

"The cloven, you say?" Bonifer's eyes twinkled.

"Yes," Nia said. "And if you'll forgive me, I don't see why that's so funny."

"It's funny, your highness, because the poor cloven only happened to find the girl. It didn't take her."

"Then who did?" Janner asked.

Bonifer bowed. "I did, Throne Warden."

50

Retribution and Rescue

Y ou're as rotten as that boy," whispered the Overseer into Sara's ear. His breath smelled of onions, and the hand over her mouth smelled of sweat. "So I'm going to let you rot."

He dragged Sara down the dark hallway and through a side door. She struggled, but his grip was unrelenting.

"You have to try harder than that to tie up a ridgerunner," Mobrik said from somewhere beside her as the Overseer dragged her down a set of stone stairs. Her mind was blank with terror, and she kicked until her feet hurt.

A match flared, and Mobrik lit a torch in the wall. Sara screamed through the Overseer's hand when she saw the two long boxes lying on stone slabs. She was in the coffin room.

"I've learned a few things over the years about controlling tools," snarled the Overseer as he shoved her toward one of the coffins. "If you get rid of the troublemakers, you get rid of the trouble." He grinned his yellow-toothed grin. "In you go."

Sara fought with all the strength she could muster.

"Get her legs!" the Overseer shouted at Mobrik.

Sara kicked her feet as if she was running in midair, and one of the kicks caught Mobrik in the face. He crashed into the wall, crumpled to the floor, and lay still.

The Overseer growled with annoyance and jerked Sara closer to the coffin. He let go of her with one of his arms and flipped open the lid. Sara brought her heel down on the Overseer's bad foot—the one Janner had driven the carriage over the night he escaped. The Overseer howled with pain. He clutched his foot and hopped in place. Sara grabbed the Overseer by the leg and lifted with all her might. He tumbled backward into the coffin.

"Tool!" he screamed, and the lid fell shut. Sara leapt on top of the coffin and fought to latch it while the Overseer pushed from inside. His fingers poked out and wriggled like worms.

Sara rode the bouncing lid like a horse in full gallop while the Overseer screamed, until at last the lid shut long enough for her to jam the latch into place and lock it tight.

She knelt on all fours on top of the coffin, trembling and out of breath. The Overseer beat the inside of the box and screamed, but he sounded far, far away.

Sara climbed down and stepped over Mobrik. She thought about throwing him into the other coffin but changed her mind. It was tempting to lock them both up and forget they ever existed; it would be an appropriate punishment for the years of anguish they had put the children through.

But Sara wasn't interested in punishment right now. She was too tired. She just wanted freedom. By the time Mobrik woke and released the Overseer, she and her army of children would be long gone.

As she staggered up the stairs, she heard Borley and Wallis calling her name. They found her in the dark hallway and carried her out into the main room. The celebration died when the children saw Sara and heard what had happened.

"I'm all right," Sara told them. "I just want to get out of here."

"But what's out there?" Trilliane asked.

"Where are my parents?" a little girl named Peasley asked.

Sara sighed. "I don't know, dear."

Now that she was on the verge of freedom, she was frightened of it, and so were the other children. Were they really going to stroll out of the Fork Factory and into a city full of Fangs and expect everything to work out? She hadn't given it much thought. She wished she had another plan, but she didn't. All she had was a dagger and a few hundred scared kids.

Then she heard shouting outside.

The wooden gate to the portcullis was closed, so she couldn't see what was happening. Then she heard the clink of chain and metal as the portcullis was forced open from the outside. After everything she and the children had accomplished, the Fangs were coming to get them anyway.

"Wallis!" Sara cried. "Lock the gate!"

Wallis and a few of his friends ran to the gate and dropped the beam into the brackets on the door. There was more shouting, then pounding. Then something heavy slammed into the gate and the children screamed.

"What do we do?" Borley cried. The gate shuddered with another blow.

"Just be brave, Borley." Sara squeezed his shoulder. "Ready your dagger and follow me."

Sara strode through the panicked children with Borley at her side. As she passed, they quieted. They lifted their weapons and were drawn into the wake of her bravery. Sara stood at the front of the host, facing the gate as it shook on its hinges. The children cringed with every bang, but they held their ground as long as Sara Cobbler stood with them.

In a final, splintering blast, the beam split in two and the gate swung open. The children screamed.

Out of the dust pounced a man dressed in black from his boots to his cape to his mask. He ran down the corridor into the Fork Factory,

whipping his sword in the air while Sara and the children watched in stunned silence.

"Aha!" he shouted. "Filthy Fangs, be thou warned, for the Florid Sword hath arrived!" The man blinked, waved the dust away from his face, and said, with disappointment, "Avast! Be thou gone alreadyest, vile villains? Aha! I seest only children in the sights I see with mine seeing eyes!"

"Gammon!" someone called from outside. "I can't hold this open forever."

"Aha! Sorryeth am I about that."

The man in black sprinted back down the corridor and, after some grunting and clinking of the chain, secured the portcullis. Sara peered through the gate and saw a crowd of men carrying away a log as thick as a barrel.

"I don't know what to make of it," the man in black said to someone beside him as he walked back through the shadows to the chamber. "Children everywhere and not a Fang in sight."

When the two figures emerged from the corridor,

the children gasped. Beside the man in black was a creature that was half man, half bird. Bright wings rose from his back. He had reddish arms and white hair, and Sara had the strange feeling, when she saw his eyes, that she recognized him.

"Are you going to hurt us?" asked Grettalyn.

The birdman smiled, and Sara knew they were safe. "No, dear. We've come to save you. This man in the ridiculous black costume—"

"It art not ridiculous, thou pigeony person!"

"—is the Florid Sword. Or you can call him Gammon, like I do. My name is Artham Wingfeather, and we're here to help." He studied the children's faces for a moment before his eyes fell on Sara. "You look like you're in charge here."

"No sir," Sara said. "I'm just a girl."

"She's our queen!" said Borley, stepping forward and folding his arms. "Queen Sara! She set us free."

The winged man raised his eyebrows and glanced at the Florid Sword, then knelt before her and bowed his head. "Queen Sara, I offer you my service. I'm the Throne Warden of the Shining Isle of Anniera." Artham smiled at her for a moment. "You're Sara Cobbler, aren't you?"

She nodded.

"I was sent to find you," Artham said.

"By whom?" Sara asked.

"By the son of the High King of Anniera."

Sara tilted her head, confused.

"He told me you saved his life."

Sara was breathless. All she could muster was a whisper. "Janner Igiby?" she said.

Artham nodded.

"The son of a king?"

Artham nodded again.

Then Sara Cobbler's legs stopped working. Artham caught her up and carried her out of the Fork Factory into the open air over Dugtown.

51

A Name Is Spoken

Bonifer Squoon looked like a giddy boy in an old man's skin. His eyes shot around the room from face to bewildered face as his words echoed in the hall. "I did!" he cackled. "I didn't want her to die, of course. Indeed, that would have been cruel of me."

"Bonifer, this isn't funny," Nia said. "What are you talking about?"

"I slipped into Freva's cottage while she cooked your breakfast this morning and took the girl! After you were arrested I rode out to the cave, tied her up, and threw her in! Of course, I assured the Hollowsfolk that I searched it *thoroughly,* and found only bones." The old man tapped his cane on the floor and danced. "They were so angry, it took little to convince them that the wolfboy had eaten her up! If there's one thing certain about Hollowsfolk, it's that they act before they think. It all worked just as I planned! Until that Bunge idiot decided to hang you both, that is. I only meant for you to be banished. I underestimated his hatred. Indeed, I underestimated the hatred of *all* the Hollowsfolk." He waved his cane at the crowd. "But it makes no difference now. I've worked everything out."

"Bonifer—" Nia's voice was thick with dread.

"What are you talking about?" Oskar asked. "This is no time for games."

"Indeed, it is not, Oskar N. Reteep." Squoon's face darkened. "Not the time for games at all. Now is the time for action." He whacked his cane on the floor. "General Swifter!"

A Grey Fang appeared in the doorway behind Squoon. It was dressed in battle gear and clutching a sword. The creature's fur was almost white except for a stripe of black that came to a point at its snout.

The wolfman smiled. It barked out a signal, and behind it appeared a host of Grey Fangs. They poured into the hall with snarls and howls of laughter. The Hollowsfolk were so shocked they had no time to muster an attack. The side doors crashed open, and more Fangs appeared to block the exits.

"Fight if you wish!" growled the Fang at Bonifer's side. "There are a thousand of us outside these walls, eager to slaughter the lot of you."

"Indeed, it would be foolish of you to raise arms, Hollowsfolk," said Bonifer. He bowed to the Fang. "General Swifter, as promised, I have delivered to Gnag the Nameless's mighty hand the Green Hollows, the Jewels of Anniera, and"—he opened the flap of the satchel—"the First Book."

General Swifter took the satchel from Bonifer and slung it over his shoulder. "Good. The Nameless One will be pleased."

"That's not all!" Squoon said, holding a finger in the air. "Thanks to Oskar N. Reteep, the First Book has been translated into the common tongue, from the first page to the last. Its secrets await His Nameless's perusal."

The Grey Fang nodded. "You've redeemed yourself, Squoon."

"Indeed!" Bonifer clapped his hands.

General Swifter pointed at the Wingfeathers huddled together on the gallows. "Get them. Just the children. We have no use for the others."

A company of Fangs marched forward and seized Janner, Kalmar, and Leeli. Two of them held Nia and Podo fast while the others led the children across the hall. Janner heard Nia crying their names, heard Podo and Oskar struggling, but more and more Grey Fangs filed into the room and stood between the Jewels of Anniera and those who loved them most.

Janner's mind was numb. He could make no sense of what was happening. The sudden sight of Grey Fangs in the Hollows, Bonifer Squoon's dark delight at the revelation of his treachery, the cloven's arrival with the little girl—all of it filled him with too much anger and too many questions. He could do nothing but put one foot in front of the other and try to keep calm.

When they walked past the hulking body of the cloven, Janner heard a faint huff of air. The thing was still alive. He glimpsed the beast's eyes, tucked in the shadow of its brow like jewels, and his heart skipped a beat. He saw something there that lodged a sudden lump in Janner's throat, some flicker of meaning hidden in the madness that stopped him in his tracks.

A Fang pushed him, and Janner threw himself to the floor. Some deep instinct compelled him to look into the creature's eyes. Janner lay beside it on the blood-slick floor, knowing he only had moments before the Fang yanked him to his feet again. He saw the thing's terrible bearish face, flecks of blood on its lips and blood puddled around its head. Its black nose—just like Kal's, Janner thought—flared as it struggled for another breath.

Then it spoke. Or it seemed to. It grunted, but there was a form to the grunt, as if it were trying to say a word. Janner felt the Fang's paws pulling him up, but he squirmed out of its grip. He didn't know why, but he had to know what the thing was saying, had to catch another glimpse of the light in its eyes. The thing huffed again and tried to lift itself from the floor. Its strength failed, and its head lolled sideways. It wasn't dead, but it was dying.

"What is it? What are you trying to say?" Janner pleaded.

The monster's eyes locked onto Janner's. They shone in the shadowy depths of its brow like a circle of sky at the end of a tunnel. They were blue, flecked with gold, and deep as the sea. The cloven drew another shuddering breath. It spoke again in a wrecked voice, a word heaved out rather than breathed.

"Janner," it said.

Then the Fang dragged Janner away. When he lost sight of the cloven's eyes, he felt a searing pain in his chest, as if an invisible cord had been ripped out of his heart.

And then he knew. He knew by the voice he had heard, by the glimmer in the cloven's eyes, and by the words it had spoken: *I'll find you. And when I do, I'll hold you fast. Forever.*

Janner screamed and bit at the Fang, whipping his head to and fro and straining at his bonds. He was mad with desperation. General Swifter was shouting, the Hollowsfolk were shouting, and somewhere across the hall, too far away for Janner to see, Podo and Nia were shouting. In the clamor the Fang dragged Janner away from the cloven, and a single word tore from Janner's throat.

"Papa!"

His voice was lost in the pandemonium, but there was one, at least, who heard.

The cloven rolled to its side, snapping off the shafts of arrows lodged in its flesh. It grunted, and though the sound was garbled and weak, Janner heard it again—his name. It spoke his name.

"Janner."

"Papa," Janner wept. "It's me."

Kalmar gazed at Janner, then down at the cloven, wonderstruck. Then he snarled and howled, fighting with renewed fury to free himself from the Grey Fang that held him.

"One of you, kill the beast," General Swifter barked, eyeing the raucous Hollowsfolk. "Bring the children!"

A Fang stepped forward, sword raised. The cloven lifted one of its deformed arms to shield itself from the blow. Leeli broke away from the Fang that held her and threw herself upon the cloven. The Fang drew up short, snarled with annoyance, and slung Leeli away. Her crutch clattered across the floor.

Then the Hollowsfolk found their courage. They brandished their weapons and inched closer to the nearest Fangs, bellowing taunts and curses. Bonifer Squoon's shifty eyes scanned the room for an exit as the tension rose in the great hall.

That was when Leeli's dog arrived. Baxter darted between the legs of the Fangs clustered at the door, yipped, and licked Leeli's face. The hall fell strangely quiet.

Leeli hugged Baxter and looked hopefully around the room. "Did you find him?" she asked, laughing through her tears. "Where is he? Did you find him?"

Baxter wagged his tail and looked up.

"Oy, Leeli," said Rudric. He crouched in the boughs of the great tree with an arrow on the string. "He found me."

Rudric loosed the arrow. It sang through the air and buried itself deep in the chest of General Swifter.

52

"My Love Has Gone Across the Sea"

The tree teemed with Durgans. More crept into the boughs from the upper windows.

Janner spotted Danniby dangling by his legs from a narrow limb, a dagger between his teeth and a drawn bow in his hands. He let the arrow fly and killed another Grey Fang before General Swifter hit the floor. Then Danniby dropped, twisted in the air, and landed on all fours beside the cloven, as graceful as a cat. In the heartbeat of silence before the chaos erupted, he winked at Janner.

Then the Fangs howled for battle, and the Hollowsfolk rushed to meet them. Rudric and the rest of the Durgan Patrol skittered through the trees, shooting into the mayhem until their arrows were spent, then dropped one by one and joined the fray.

Janner, Kalmar, and Leeli gathered over the dying cloven, heedless of the battle clamoring around them. Danniby and several other Durgans created a perimeter of protection, but Janner knew they didn't have long.

"Is it him?" Leeli asked. She scooted around beside Janner and leaned over to look the beast in the eye. But it had spent its strength. Its eyes were closed, and its breath came in ragged gasps. A thicket of arrows sprouted from its back and shoulders.

"He said my name," Janner told her. "And I saw his eyes."

Kalmar lay on the cloven with his head on its shoulder, whispering to it as Leeli worked to untie Kal's wrists.

"Kal, did you know?" Janner asked.

"I only knew he was hungry and wounded. And alone."

Leeli freed the little wolf's arms, and Kalmar lifted the cloven's head and rested it in his lap while she freed Janner. Janner pressed his forehead against the monster's shoulder and clamped his eyes shut.

If it was true, if it was really his father hidden somewhere in the dark of the monster's heart, Janner needed him to live. He prayed to the Maker in a hopeless groan. He knew better than to pray that the cloven would transform in a whirl of light into Esben Wingfeather, young and handsome and whole. Those things only happened in stories. So Janner pleaded simply for each beat of the beast's heart. *Please, please, please,* he begged, and the heart beat and beat and beat. But with each pulse, blood leaked from every wound.

"Leeli, sing," Kalmar said.

She wiped her cheeks. "What do I sing?"

"It doesn't matter," Kal said. "Just let him hear you before he dies."

Amidst the clash of swords and the shouts of battle, Leeli Wingfeather leaned her head on the gray shoulder of what was left of her father and sang.

> My love has gone across the sea
> To find a country far and fair
> He sailed into the gilded west
> And lo, my heart will never rest
> Until my love returns to me
> Or I set out to find him there.
>
> Come home, come home! I sing to thee
> My love, come home and rest thy head
> I'll watch for you the winter long
> And sing for you a summer song
> And if you can't return to me
> Then I will sail to you instead

Through tow'ring wave and shriek of gale
I'll aim my vessel ever west
And steer it by the cord that bound
My heart to yours, until you're found
And should you find my body pale
And wrecked upon the loamy shale
Rejoice, my love, and call me blessed!
In death, my love, I loved you best

The cloven lifted an arm and lowered it around Leeli and Janner. It squeezed them close, and the voice spoke in Janner's mind again, gentle and rich. *I found you,* it said. *And now that I have, I'll hold you fast.*

Janner didn't understand any of it, and he didn't care. He didn't understand why his father was a cloven, or how he ended up with Freva's little girl. He was only grateful that his father was still alive, and even though he was deformed and he stank, even though they sat on the floor of the great hall in the middle of a battle, and even though he knew the moment would be over all too soon, Janner was bright with gladness. He felt a deep magic swirling about them. He looked into his father's blue eyes and listened to the words that echoed again and again in his mind: *I found you, I found you, I found you.*

"Get them!" Bonifer cried. His eyes were wild and wheeling as he ducked beneath swinging swords with a speed unnatural to his aged frame. Danniby and the Durgans had lost their position in the chaos of the battle, and the circle of safety around the Wingfeathers broke.

Squoon grabbed Leeli and thrust her at a Fang as two others seized Janner and Kalmar. They struggled, but the Fangs were mighty with the fever of battle. Though the children screamed and reached for their father, they were swept away from him.

"Papa, help!" Leeli cried.

Esben moaned and lifted himself a few inches from the floor, but then he collapsed again and lay still.

The three Fangs dashed from the Keep with the children over their shoulders. Bonifer scooted behind them as fast as his old bones could carry him.

"Onto the carriage, you fools!" Bonifer cried. The Fangs threw the children aboard and climbed on as the horses galloped toward the harbor.

53

The Liberation of Dugtown

Sara clung to the strange man's neck as he flew over Dugtown. She saw houses burning and groups of men and women tossing Fang armor into piles. The sun was bright in the chilly air, but it was muted by smoke and a strange musty powder floating in the wind. Most of the streets were deserted, but in a few open courtyards and along the river there were multitudes of soldiers standing in formation, marching through the streets or mounted on saddled birds as big as horses. Townspeople crowded the walkways, and even from her height Sara heard their cheers.

"Are they gone?" Sara asked. "The Fangs, I mean."

"Not yet," Artham said. "But we've driven them out of Dugtown. It's only the beginning, but it's a victory. Look."

He angled a wing and they turned southeast, toward the Mighty River Blapp. Far across the muddy water was Torrboro and its catlike castle. It used to be Dugtown's cleaner, wealthier neighbor—in fact, Sara and her parents had lived in a house on the southeastern edge of the city before the Fangs had taken her. Now it was green with Fangs. They clustered and slithered at the riverfront in a way that made Sara think of worms in garbage.

"Getting the Fangs to abandon Dugtown was the easy part," Artham said. "Torrboro is where the fortress lies, and Fangs from all over Skree are mustering there. It's going to be a difficult fight."

"What about the people there?" Sara asked.

"Gone. Either they've fled or they've been killed."

During her time in the Fork Factory, Sara had come to believe her parents were gone forever. But seeing her city overrun with snake men made her stomach feel as if someone had just put a heavy stone in it. She shuddered with grief.

"I'm sorry, dear," Artham said.

"Where are you taking me?" she asked after a moment.

"Someplace safe."

"What about the other kids? Borley and Grettalyn—"

"Don't worry. They're in good hands. I'll take you back to see them after you've had a bath and a good meal. You're their queen, after all."

Sara smiled. A bath sounded wonderful.

Artham flew lower, over a hill on the north side of Dugtown where a handsome house stood. Two horses were tethered to a fence out front. When Artham landed, the front door opened and a girl about Sara's age stepped onto the porch. She was dressed like a boy and held a leg of half-eaten henmeat in one hand.

She burped, wiped her mouth with her sleeve, and asked, "That her?"

"Aye. This is Sara Cobbler," Artham said with a laugh as he set Sara on the grass.

"Wanna play tackleball?" the girl asked.

"What's—what's tackleball?" Sara took a hesitant step forward.

"Maraly," Artham said, "there will be time for that later. Why don't you find her another hunk of henmeat, and maybe some soup?"

Maraly shrugged and went inside.

"Thank you, Mister Artham," Sara said.

When Artham didn't reply, she turned to find him squirming on the ground, clutching the sides of his head. His eyes were clamped shut, and his wings were bent and crooked beneath him.

"Mister Artham, what's wrong?"

Artham loosed an earsplitting shriek.

"Help!" Sara cried. "Somebody help him!"

54

Treachery

Why are you doing this?" Janner screamed. He struggled in the Fang's grip as the carriage clattered out of the courtyard.

"Indeed, why does anyone do anything mad?" Bonifer arched an eyebrow at Janner. "For love, boy. You wouldn't understand."

"You kidnapped Bonnie!" Leeli cried.

Bonifer rolled his eyes. "Oh, relax. Someone would have found her sooner or later. And someone—or some*thing*—did. I arranged everything just so. I spread the rumor of Fangs in the Outer Vales to get rid of Rudric. Bunge was to banish you, and then I was going to sail you out past the Watercraw and safely deliver you to one of the Fang ships that waited in the dark outside the gate. When they lowered the chain, the Fangs were going to invade." Squoon glanced back at the Keep in the distance and pointed his thumb. "But that fool Bunge tried to hang you and your mother, even after I threatened him with article seven of the Chumply Amendment." Squoon chuckled. "That was a good ruse, eh? Old Bonifer worked it all out, though. I just had to ride out to the gatehouse at the Watercraw, kill the guard, and lower the gate to let in the Fang ships."

"You—you killed a guard?" Janner said. He couldn't imagine Bonifer Squoon doing much of anything besides reading and shuffling around.

"It had to be done, lad. Since you hadn't been banished, I wasn't going to sail out of the harbor with you. And if I wasn't going to sail out with you, the guards weren't going to lower the chain. I had to let the Fangs into Ban Rona or Kalmar would have been hanged. Gnag the Nameless would have been most displeased with me. Indeed, now that I think about it, tonight wasn't so different from when I opened the portcullis at the Castle Rysen nine years ago."

"It was you?" Janner said, aghast. "You led the Fangs to our castle?"

"Indeed."

"But why?"

"I already told you." Bonifer looked up at the moon. "For love."

"That doesn't make any sense!" Leeli said.

"Of course it doesn't. You're only nine years old."

"Which is young enough to know when something's evil," she said.

"Indeed. I suppose I believed the same thing when I was nine." Bonifer steered the carriage around another corner and began the descent to the harbor. His voice turned bitter. "But as you grow you'll find that even your dearest friend can betray you. If you're weak, he'll steal the thing you love most."

"Which is what you're doing right now," Kalmar said.

Janner had no idea what Bonifer Squoon was talking about. Nor did he care anymore. The old man was crazy. Janner wanted to jump off the carriage and run back to his father. He wanted to be sure Nia and Podo were all right. "We trusted you," Janner said.

"Indeed!" Bonifer chuckled. "As has your family for three generations."

"But our family was good to you!" Leeli said.

Bonifer rounded on her and grabbed her wrist. His face was red and his flesh trembled. "Your family *ruined* me. And do you know the worst of it? None of you has any idea." Bonifer took a deep breath and released Leeli. He adjusted his top hat and turned back to face the road.

"I've known Gnag since he was born. I loved his mother dearly, and so I have done my best to help him however I can."

Janner was dumbstruck. Bonifer Squoon loved Gnag the Nameless's mother? Janner hadn't known until that moment whether Gnag was a troll or a Fang or a dragon. But a human? And Bonifer Squoon knew him? Janner wanted to push Bonifer off a cliff, and at the same time he wanted to ask him a thousand questions.

"But he destroyed Anniera," Janner said. "He's killed thousands of people."

"Ah, but he's *created* many thousands too. Where do you think the Fangs come from? The Maker? No, Gnag has made improvements on the original design, wouldn't you say, soldiers?" The Fangs laughed. "Wait till he discovers how to meld us with snickbuzzards! With trolls! Wait till he melds me with a *dragon*. Now *that* will be something to see." Bonifer sighed. "The possibilities are endless, children. But only with more of the holoré and the holoél. Only with the stones from the deep places."

"The deep places?" Leeli asked.

"Caverns where the walls and ceilings glow with the light of the making stones. If Gnag the Nameless can make an army of Fangs with but two of the stones, think what he could do with a city of them! And do you know how to get there?" Bonifer raised his eyebrows at the children. "No? I'll tell you. *The Castle Rysen*. That's right! Your father knew. He had just begun to decipher the First Book, and he told me of a long-forgotten passageway beneath the castle. A chamber that leads to the deep places, where the Maker walked with the First Fellows. The river that feeds Aerwiar runs there, between mountains paved with holoél." Squoon shrugged. "Or that's what your father told me, anyway. It could all be made up. But Gnag doesn't think so. The holoél and holoré had to come from somewhere, did they not?"

"Then why does he want us?" Kalmar asked. "He already destroyed Anniera. What's keeping him from digging up the stones and doing whatever he wants with them?"

"Because your father learned just enough from the First Book to know that it takes special gifts to open the chamber."

"What gifts?" Leeli asked.

"Word, Form, and Song."

"T.H.A.G.S.," Janner said.

"Indeed. But not just anyone can open the chamber. It only works with the three of you, born of the High King of Anniera. No amount of fire or digging or hammering has been able to open it in nine years. Gnag needs you, children. And *I* need you." Squoon's voice dropped to almost a whisper. "He's going to turn me into something beautiful and strong and young again. I think I want to be a spider." He waggled his fingers at Leeli and she cringed. "But I couldn't just show up at the Castle Throg when I had allowed you to escape Anniera with the First Book! The Nameless One was angry with me, and I knew it. I've been hiding here ever since. I tell you, I could hardly believe my good fortune when you arrived in the Green Hollows and came to live in the very same house as I! It was perfect. I could keep watch and plan. I knew you were sneaking out, Kalmar. You'd be surprised how lightly an old man sleeps. I thought at first that your escapades would foil my plans, but then I realized they would play into them perfectly. I was going to sail the three of you out of the harbor with the Hollowsfolks' blessing. All I had to do was wait until that fat fool finished translating the First Book."

Bonifer reined up the horses at the harbor. By the light of the moon Janner saw at least ten Fang ships. More Fangs marched onto the pier with bows and swords in their paws, on their way to join the battle. Bonifer bowed as they tromped by.

"Bind them," Bonifer told the Fangs. "And gag them while you're at it. I don't want them making any unnecessary noise."

The Fangs tied the children's wrists, gagged them with strips of cloth, and then pulled sacks over each of their heads.

Howls echoed through the streets of Ban Rona.

55

Artham and the Deeps of Throg

When Leeli sang over the cloven, her song rose from the depths of her heart and sent a burst of shimmering cords into the matter of the world. They sizzled from her in a million strands, like a spiderweb of lightning bolts. They shot through Janner and Kalmar and Esben, waking something bright in their bones, and each of them felt it differently. The music's power was invisible to everyone around them, even to Nia; for her and the others it was just a pretty song amidst the clamor of warfare. But for the Jewels of Anniera, who bore the blood of their ancestors, the music reached into secret places and did wondrous things. Janner heard voices, Kalmar saw pictures, and Leeli's tender heart coursed with the rivers of emotion swirling in those near her, opening her to the deep, unutterable mysteries of their souls.

Esben, lost in a vast darkness, saw a golden light.

The strand of song burned through the bedrock of the Green Hollows, through a thousand miles of molten stone and layered rock laid by the Maker at the speaking of the world, past the black depths of the Dark Sea, coursing unnoticed through the blood and marrow of massy, eyeless beings asleep on the ocean floor, till the cord was weakened by distance into a quivering rustle of cells lifting invisibly from the ground where Artham Wingfeather stood with Sara Cobbler. It reached weakly up and up, through his flesh and into the well of his heart, and drank deeply from its waters. The strand revived and thickened and crackled back through the earth to where Esben the Cloven lay dying.

Artham felt his old shame awaken. It screamed at him. He was at once able to see in his mind Janner, Kalmar, and Leeli, huddled over a broken thing, a cloven, and he knew it was Esben. His brother, whom he was born to protect.

His brother, whom he had abandoned.

His mind shrank and he could form no thoughts, only memories. He thrashed at Sara Cobbler's feet as he remembered when he and Esben had been captured in Anniera and thrown into the dark, wet horror of Gnag's dungeons in the Deeps of Throg. He had tried to forget the wicked, sweet voice of the Stone Keeper, the woman who every day coaxed them to sing for power and their own freedom, coaxed them to deny their homeland and swear allegiance to Gnag the Nameless.

Artham had been so strong. Even chained to a wall and starving in the blackness, he would spit at the Stone Keeper and defy her temptations and her tortures. He had resisted the voices that seemed to come from outside himself but shrieked in his mind nonetheless. He had fought to ignore the song that was always singing, always singing, always singing, and closed his eyes on the glowing shards of stone and the hawk in the cage beside him.

Every night for a thousand days he had refused Gnag and the Stone Keeper and the voices. And then one day, he could no longer tell which of the voices in his head was his own. He couldn't separate them. And he couldn't quiet them. They rose in volume and wrath and convinced him that it was better to sing the song for power than to die alone.

But Esben! he had screamed. *I cannot leave him!*

And the voices laughed.

Then one day, from the cell where he was shackled, Artham saw Esben. The king's head dangled between his outstretched arms, and he was chained beside a hulking and wretched old bear. Patches of fur sprouted from Esben's shoulders, and Artham knew.

His brother had lost his fight with the Stone Keeper. She had won. The change was upon him. Esben had broken. And that meant one thing: Artham Wingfeather, Throne Warden, Firstborn of the Shining Isle, had failed the High King of Anniera.

The voices hounded him, told him it was better to stop fighting. *Just sing the song,* they said. They told him it was too late. *Just sing the song. You'll be so powerful. You'll be able to fly away from here.*

And one dark night, through tears, while his misshapen brother lolled his great ursine head and watched and the Stone Keeper whispered, Artham began to sing. He felt the tingle in his arms as the hawk jittered in its nearby cage. The tips of his fingers burned and contorted into claws, and he was glad the fighting was finally over.

Then he looked up to see Esben's face, haggard and stretched, bearded with a scruff of fur. He looked on Artham with such sadness, such pleading—and such unbearable disappointment.

Artham clamped his eyes shut and stopped singing. The pain in his hands abated, and in an explosion of strength he broke his rusty shackles. The Stone Keeper fled, shrieking down the dungeon corridors.

Flee! screamed the voices. *Save yourself!*

Artham saw the cell door standing open, and he ran. The voices in his mind cackled with glee. He held his deformed hands over his ears as he screamed down the corridors that veined the depths of the Killridge Mountains, and the talons cut his cheeks and ears and mocked his cowardice. He ran past chamber after chamber of muttering prisoners, mad with the music and the endless night.

For hours he ran, until he forgot his name and his brother and his kingdom. He crawled through tunnels where insects nested and slithered in shallow pools, and he swam through ponds of living sludge, trying to escape the song and the voices and the memory of the one he had abandoned.

Then, suddenly, he emerged from the Deeps of Throg into a forest at the foot of the mountains. He lay for a long time at the mouth of the cave, looking up through towering trees at the sunlight that filtered faintly down.

He wandered for weeks, eating leaves and fruit and creeping things. And one day he stumbled into a clearing where stone pillars, covered in vine and mildew, rose like the bones of giants. At the center of the ring of pillars lay a pool of water as still as glass. The trees whose roots drank from its water were thick as houses, and Artham heard enormous things thudding through the foothills, behemoths calling to one another in a language as old as the world. He woke that night beside the pool and saw the shapes of ancient, beautiful beings, not seen by men since epochs long forgotten, lapping up its water.

In some distant part of his mind, he knew he had found the First Well, though he had no words for it. He wondered if the water might heal him, might remove the terrible red talons, maybe even quiet the voices. He found on the forest floor an empty brown shell as big as a bowl—the husk of a seed fallen from the towering trees—and he scooped up the water.

He raised it to his lips, aching to taste its power, wanting so much for it to kill the voices in his mind. But he couldn't drink. He remembered his brother in the Deeps of Throg, still chained to the wall. How could the Throne Warden be whole when the High King was broken?

So Artham Wingfeather wandered the old forest for days, seeking the way back into the Deeps where his brother languished, carrying with him the water for Esben's healing. Where it spilled, the ground burst with flowers and green things, and Artham longed to drink. But he kept it from himself.

Many days he sought the cave. He cradled the water as the seasons passed, and it never steamed away and hardly diminished, so careful was he not to spill it.

Artham encountered monsters in the woods, and he knew them to be like him: half-made beasts, bent things, Gnag the Nameless's abandoned mistakes, who had either escaped from the Deeps or been cast out. They snuffled and rooted and lurched through the forest, and some who could speak begged Artham for a taste of the water. He refused them, finding that he could hardly speak a sane word. He told them in his gibberish that it was for the High King of Anniera, and they laughed. Some attacked him, so mad were they for respite and healing, but always he kept it safe for Esben, for Esben, always for Esben.

But the cave, the entrance to the Deeps of Throg, eluded him.

After many moons fattened and diminished, blinking in the night sky like the Maker's all-seeing eye, Artham emerged from the Blackwood. He found a vial in an abandoned farmhouse, emptied what was left of the water into it, and swore, with what was left of his mind, to find his brother's children and keep watch over them in Esben's stead. Long he sought them, listening through the dark voices to a single bright one that he knew told the truth.

Cross the Dark Sea, the bright, quiet voice whispered to him, and he knew it was true because the other voices told him not to. He stowed away on a Fang ship, nearly starved in the hold, but set foot at last on the shores of Skree. He found Glipwood, the town Podo Helmer was from, and one glad day he saw three children who looked, in different ways, like Esben Wing-feather. Artham watched the Jewels of Anniera from afar, always ready to ward and protect them, since their father, the High King, was lost.

Or is he? screamed the voices in the night as Artham tossed in his tree house.

And the more he wondered, the louder the voices grew.

As he writhed on the grass, while Sara Cobbler and Maraly Weaver knelt over him, calling his name, he knew.

Esben is alive.

His heart tore in two. He had begun to believe—to hope, even—that Esben had died. That he suffered no more. That Gnag the Nameless had not managed to break his spirit and make a monster of him. Nine years was too long to dangle from a dungeon wall with that incessant music screeching in his mind. But he saw his brother now, bulging and bent, a lost thing. And it was Artham's fault. He had fled when he should have fought.

Oh, Esben! Artham wailed in his mind. *I'm sorry.*

His words pulsed through the earth, carried by the cord of Leeli's song, and spoke in Esben's mind. As Artham writhed in Dugtown, he saw the Grey Fangs in the Hollish Keep, saw the children huddled over the cloven and the arrows in its back. He saw the battle and knew the jewels were in great danger.

Sing the song, Artham said into the cavern of his cloven brother's mind. *Sing it for them. Sing it to save, not to be saved. Sing it for love, not power.*

Artham? said Esben's voice.

"Esben!" Artham said aloud through clenched teeth.

Sara and Maraly, kneeling beside him, looked at each other helplessly.

"What's wrong with him?" Sara cried.

"Yes, it's me, little brother." Artham was crying. "Please listen to me. Sing the song of the ancient stones! You must remember it! But do it for them. Not for the Stone Keeper! You can't let Gnag get to them! *Wake up, Esben!*"

Artham clung to the connection between them, willing his words to find their way deep, deep into the cloven body where Esben's heart still beat. Artham pleaded with him, but his mind seemed so far away.

SING IT! he told his brother as he saw Bonifer Squoon racing through the Fangs and Hollowsfolk to grab the children.

Then the connection broke. The vision vanished. Artham Wingfeather curled up on the grass and wept, unable, yet again, to help the king.

Sara Cobbler and Maraly Weaver helped him inside and tended to his sorrow, though his only words were gibberish.

56

The Queen and the Cloven

Nia heard Janner scream, "PAPA!" But she didn't understand why.

A Grey Fang stood behind her with one arm around her neck and the other pressing the point of a dagger against her ribs. Podo was beside her, held fast by three Fangs. She saw Janner fall, saw him look into the cloven's face, then sensed a crackle in the air, like a silent flash of lightning in a distant cloud. She didn't know what it meant, but it sent Leeli running to the monster's side to block the Fang's sword. The Fang yanked Leeli away just as her dog, Baxter, darted into the hall. Nia looked up to see Rudric, the man she loved, poised on a high limb, just as he shot the Grey Fang leader and ignited the battle.

Rudric and his Durgan Patrol swarmed the branches of the tree with bows and arrows, felling Fang after bewildered Fang. The wolfmen holding her and Podo tensed and dragged them farther back into the great tree's roots. She caught a glimpse of Oskar N. Reteep comforting Freva and Bonnie as he peeked from behind the tree, but try as she might, she could no longer see her children in the chaos.

Grey Fangs and Durgans and Hollowsfolk roared and growled and hacked in the wildness of war, and somewhere among them were Janner, Kalmar, and Leeli—and the cloven. Why had Janner been talking to it? And why did the cloven have Freva's daughter? And why, oh why, was Bonifer Squoon, her husband's closest advisor, leading the Fangs of Dang into the Green Hollows?

Nia's thoughts were interrupted by the faint but unmistakable sound of her daughter's voice, singing from somewhere in the mayhem. Leeli, at least, was alive. The melody she sang unlocked itself in Nia's mind; it was an old Annieran sailor's tune called "My Love Has Gone Across the Sea," a song Leeli had first learned years ago in Glipwood.

The song was cut short, and for a moment the battle parted enough for Nia to see three Fangs and Bonifer Squoon hurrying out of the Keep with the children.

Moments after they were gone, she heard another sound cut through the clamor—another melody. This one was odd, and garbled. She thought at first that it was some son or daughter of the Hollows in the agony of death, so sad and eerie was its music.

Then the air shimmered as with the heat of a fire, and a light flashed in the room. The Fangs cringed and the Hollowsfolk gasped. It only lasted a moment, and then the battle raged on. But from the center of the room, a new commotion began, and Nia heard a ferocious snarling as the Grey Fangs intensified their attack.

The Fang behind her grew agitated and said to one of the wolfmen holding Podo, "What do you think, Gergin?" Nia felt its breath in her ear.

"I think General Swifter's dead," said the other. Nia and Podo exchanged a worried glance. "And it looks like our fellow soldiers could use our help."

"Aye. The jewels are gone. I saw Feral and the others carry them out."

"Then what are we doing with these two?"

"Don't suppose we need them anymore, do we?"

Nia felt the muscles in the furry arm tighten around her neck. Podo squirmed, but with his hands tied and in the grip of the Fangs, he could do little.

Nia dug her fingernails into the Fang's forearm and felt the blade press into her side. She screamed Rudric's name again and again, but her voice was lost in the clash and bellow of the fight. She caught a glimpse of him on the opposite side of the room with a war hammer in one giant fist and a sword in the other, embattled with seven Grey Fangs at once. Rudric saw Nia and roared, but there was nothing he could do. He was too far away. Every Hollish fighter Nia saw was either dead on the floor or locked in combat.

She looked to her left in time to see Oskar N. Reteep heave himself onto one of the Fangs holding Podo. But even as big as Reteep was, the Fang kept hold of Podo's neck and kicked Oskar aside so hard that he slammed awkwardly into a nook in the root and lay motionless, his spectacles cracked and dangling from one ear.

"Enough with these two," the Fang called Gergin said. "I'm going to fight."

"Rudric!" Nia cried again, but it was hopeless. If she was going to die, she certainly wasn't going to stand still and let the Fang run her through. She struggled against the Fang and felt the blade cut through her dress and pierce her skin.

Then from the center of the skirmish, she heard a voice as deep as thunder. It was a roar, but it was more than that—louder and stronger, and it carried a word. Her name.

"NIA."

From the center of the mayhem rose the shaggy head of a bear. Its golden fur-covered body was shaped like a man, but a man so strong that even Rudric looked small by comparison.

It flung its huge arms outward and Fangs flew through the air, crashed into walls, and snapped branches of the great tree. The bear hunkered down, aiming its shoulder at the clot of Fangs charging before it. Fangs flattened beneath the bearish creature like grass in a thunderstorm.

Gone was the mottled gray skin. Gone were the twisted limbs and the lurching gait. The thing bore toward Nia with such power and speed that the very walls of the Keep would not have stood before it.

The Fangs holding Podo and Nia whined like puppies, released them, and scampered away, but the bear seized them each and hurled them across the hall into a muster of Fangs gathered at the main door.

Nia couldn't breathe. She stood rigid with terror, looking up at the beast. She sensed Podo to her left, picking himself off the floor. "Easy there," he said to the beast, inching between them.

The bear sniffed. Nia looked up into its face, trying to see the thing's eyes, but they were hidden too deep in shadow. Its fur was the color of cedar bark, and it smelled like a horse or a dog or fresh-turned soil. As the battle boiled on behind them, the world between Nia and the bear grew still.

It lifted one of its arms and opened its fist—a fist as big as a pumpkin—and placed its hand on Podo's head. For perhaps the first time in his life, Podo was too afraid to move. Nia knew the bear could pop his head like a berry if it wanted, but it only patted the old pirate twice and nudged him aside.

The bear knelt before Nia, and she was able at last to see its face in the torchlight. Its eyebrows trembled and raised enough to reveal two blue eyes that Nia had looked into a thousand times. She touched the bear's face with a trembling hand. "Esben?"

When her fingers brushed the side of its snout, it sighed and closed its eyes and leaned its cheek against her palm. Nia shook with a sob, then lost herself in the warm folds of the bear's embrace. She closed her eyes and heard a happy groan deep in her husband's chest, and she felt young and safe and holy with love.

"Esben," she murmured. "Oh, my husband."

"Nia," said the bear. She felt the word vibrate in the bear's warm chest. "My love." Nia looked up to see Esben's eyes gazing down at her. His damp black nose nuzzled against her cheek. "Nia," he said. "I'm sorry—sorry I wasn't stronger."

"Shh," Nia said, content to feel her heart entwined with her husband's again. She didn't know how he had changed or how he got there, and she didn't care. Podo knelt nearby, watching Nia and the bear with a childlike smile.

"I was lost . . . in the Deeps," said Esben. "He tried to change me, and for years, I tried to be strong. But they broke me."

"It's all right, Esben," Nia whispered. "You're here now, and you're alive."

"I got out, but I was alone in the Blackwood for a long time." Esben's voice softened with what sounded like wonder. "And one day I felt the children. I saw them in my mind, as if they were standing right in front of me. And I heard sweet music. I knew they were in Ban Rona, and so I came. Kalmar, he—he took care of me. He told me to go back, but I couldn't. I found the girl in the cave and knew that I—I had to help her. Then I heard the music again! Oh, Nia. I found you." Esben's voice was thick with tears. "Leeli's so beautiful! And the boys are so strong and handsome, even—even Kalmar. But what did they do to him, Nia? My boy!"

Nia stiffened. The children. They were gone, and they might not have much time. "Esben, listen. We have to get them! Bonifer—"

"Bonifer," Esben rumbled. He straightened and held Nia out before him. "He's here?"

"Yes," Nia told him. "And he took the children. I don't know why, but he betrayed us."

"He's done more than that," Esben growled. "He betrayed Anniera. He betrayed the Maker himself."

"How do you know? What do you mean?"

"Gnag told me." Esben lifted Nia into his arms and said, "Come, my love. The children need us."

Esben the Bear turned and took one step down from the dais just as Podo yelled, "Rudric, no!"

Rudric stood before them, his face and beard soiled with the spray and sweat of battle, his teeth bared and his eyes fierce.

Esben jerked to a stop, and Nia looked down to see Rudric's sword buried to the hilt in Esben's stomach.

57

A Bear in Ban Rona

Let her go, cloven!" Rudric wrenched the blade farther in.

Nia was too stunned to make a sound. A trickle of blood ran out from the folds of Esben's fur, down the hilt, and over Rudric's black glove. Esben swayed and grunted, and one of his big hands went to his stomach.

Nia finally let out a sob and shook her head at Rudric, her eyes a storm of sorrow and confusion and denial. When Rudric saw those eyes, his grimace faded into a frown of confusion, then, slowly, the horror of regret as he began to understand what he had done.

"Rudric," Podo said quietly. "It's Esben."

Rudric released the sword hilt as if it were red hot and stumbled back from the steps. He tripped over a dead Fang and landed on his back, shaking his head slowly. "I'm sorry—I'm sorry, I thought—"

Esben shook his great shaggy head and heaved and coughed. "Not . . . your . . . fault." He looked around the great hall, empty now but for the bodies of slain Hollowsfolk and empty Fang armor, blown with dust. "Where are my children?"

"The Fangs retreated," Rudric said. "Back to their ships."

Esben took a deep breath and withdrew the sword. It clanged to the floor as the great bear, with Nia still in his arms, lowered his head and ran. He bounded out of the Keep and into the streets of Ban Rona.

Nia closed her eyes and rested her head against his warm neck. She felt his great strength, his mighty arms holding her fast, and the rhythm of his stride as he hurtled down the snowy street, thundering like a warhorse into battle. His head slung to and fro with every step. The wind peeled the fur back from his face and revealed his desperate blue eyes. She looked behind them to see Rudric and Podo running after, unable to keep up, and a crimson trail of blood strung out like a ribbon in the snow.

"Hold fast," Esben whispered.

Nia turned to see them approaching the rear of the Fang retreat. Hollowsfolk pursued them to the waterfront, hurling spear and sword and dagger, and Fangs littered the streets, crisping into dust. Biggin O'Sally and his boys led a pack of armored dogs that snapped at the Fangs as they ran. Wisps of gray and white fur littered the air like foul pollen.

Esben pushed through the Hollowsfolk and into the retreating Fangs, slinging his free arm like a giant hammer. Grey Fangs crashed through windows or were trampled underfoot. They squealed like hogpigs and fled the Bear King of Anniera and his queen.

Esben burst through the knot of Fangs and raced ahead to the harbor. When he turned the last corner of the road that led to the docks, a wall of Fang archers waited, lining the pier, their bows drawn. The Fang commander shouted, "Now!"

Esben twisted his body as he ran and cradled Nia as more arrows thudded into his broad back. He roared with pain as he lost his footing and slammed onto his side. Nia's head crashed into the bone of his shoulder and her vision blurred. She felt Esben roll forward and launch himself through the wall of archers and onto the docks.

"Are you all right?" Esben panted. "I can hide you here until it's safe."

Nia tightened her grip and felt his strength around her. She shook her head. She was rattled, but she refused to spend another heartbeat apart from him.

"Good," he said, and he vaulted to the nearest ship and crashed to the empty deck.

Nia's heart sank when she saw the fleet of Fang ships, roped together and dark in the harbor. "They could be anywhere."

"I can smell them," Esben said as he ran. He leapt to the next ship and lifted his head to sniff the air. "They're close."

From behind a nearby barrel, a Grey Fang growled and lunged at Esben. Without turning, Esben flung the Fang into the water and jumped to the next ship, then the next, all the way to the last ship in the line. Esben finally stopped and hunkered over, struggling for breath. Nia heard a rattle in his throat.

He sniffed the air again, peered into the shadows, and said, "Squoon."

58

Escape

Nia saw no one. The ship creaked as it rocked in the tide and bumped into the vessel beside it. They weren't far from the waterfront, where the Hollowsfolk and the Grey Fangs fought, but the battle seemed strangely distant. Esben placed Nia on the deck and motioned for her to stand aside.

"Squoon, I know you're here," Esben rasped. He sniffed the air and limped forward. Some bone-deep pain wracked him and he shuddered, then slumped to the ground, trying to prop himself up on his elbows.

Nia rushed to his side, then heard something thump against the hull, followed by a faint splash. She ran to the ship's rail and saw a small boat in the water. The sail hadn't yet been set, but three Grey Fangs tugged the oars. She saw three shapes, bound and motionless in the bottom of the little boat, and she knew they were her children. Bonifer Squoon sat in the prow with his top hat and cane and waved at Nia as the boat floated away.

He removed his hat and bowed his head. "Ah, Nia! Farewell! I'll send Gnag your greetings."

"No!" she screamed and heard her children's muffled voices.

Bonifer hit them with his cane and said, "Quiet!"

Behind her, Esben's elbows slipped. He lay flat on the deck, struggling to raise his head. He tried to roar, but in his weakness it was only a moan.

Nia turned back to the water, torn between her dying husband and her stolen children. All that lay between Bonifer and the Watercraw was open water. Nia had to stop them but couldn't think how. Even if she could swim that far and fast in the frigid water, the Fangs would kill her as soon as she approached the boat.

Nia looked around for someone to help, but all she saw were Fang ships stretching back to the dock and the clash of battle beyond. She looked for another boat, or a bow and arrow, or something—*anything*. But there was nothing she could do.

She wanted to scream. There were so many blasted ships and no way to stop one little boat from escaping. Though she was terrified of the sea dragons, she prayed that they would rise from the water. She prayed for another of Artham's sudden, dashing arrivals, but she knew he was on the other side of the Dark Sea.

Nia's despair hardened into desperation. She took Esben's weary head in her hands and looked into his eyes. She saw by the moonlight that they were glazed over, but some life glimmered there yet.

"There's no one else, my love. I need you to get up. Our children will be lost if you don't. Can you hear me?"

Esben grunted.

"Get up!" Nia cried. She scooted underneath one of his arms, tiny beneath his girth, and strained with all her might. She gritted her teeth and pushed and said, "Get up!"

As her strength began to fail her, she felt his arms and legs move a little. The muscles in her own legs and back screamed for rest, but she willed them to push on and on as Esben fought to stand.

Esben's feet slipped in the pool of blood that had gathered beneath him, but he managed to straighten. He staggered back from the rail, looking down at Nia with a tired smile. Even in the moonlight Nia saw blood dripping from his nose and lower lip.

"Our children need you, my king," she said.

Esben drew a long, rasping breath. He heaved himself forward, tottered for a moment, and then, with a furious roar, leapt over the rail.

Nia watched him soar across the water, farther than she would have thought possible. She saw Bonifer Squoon's smile vanish and imagined what it would be like to see that hulking shape overhead, blacking out the stars, edged with moonlight. Just before Esben hit the water between the ship and the skiff, Nia heard Bonifer squeal with terror.

The shock of cold water seemed to awaken a new well of strength in Esben. He swam after the skiff with quick, graceful strokes, nosing through the water like a fish. The arrows spiked in his back bobbed back and forth as he cut nearer, and the Grey Fangs abandoned the oars and drew their swords. When he reached the boat, they hacked, and their blades struck his arms, but it did little to stop him. With a sad, strange calm, Esben took hold of the Fangs one at a time, dragged them out of the boat, and held them underwater.

Then there was only Bonifer Squoon. Nia saw him clutching the rails, trembling in his seat, staring with white-faced terror at the beast heaving itself into the boat.

"Bonifer," Esben said.

"I-I know your voice," Bonifer stammered.

"And you knew my father's voice, and his father's."

"Esben!" Bonifer whimpered. "But how?"

He didn't wait for an answer. Squoon took a frantic look around, then threw himself into the water and swam away, leaving behind his cane and the satchel containing the First Book.

Nia was sure Esben would pursue him, but when she looked at the skiff, the bear was huddled over the children, loosening their bonds. When she looked back, Bonifer had vanished. His top hat bobbed in the water.

Whether he had drowned or died of shock from the frigid water and the sight of Esben Wingfeather after all these years, it didn't matter. The monster in the Hollows was gone.

59

Beneath the Moonbright Heavens

Janner felt the boat rock, pitching so far to the side that he feared it would flip. Then with a splash and a gush of water the boat righted itself, and he felt his father's fingers pulling at the ropes around his wrists. When his hands were free, Janner yanked the sack from his head and pulled his gag away. The moon was directly overhead, so bright that it took a moment for his eyes to adjust.

Janner gasped when he saw his father, covered in fur but without the twisted limbs and the slick gray lumps of flesh. He knew it was the cloven by the arrows jutting from his back, but everything else had changed. Though Esben was wet and wounded and his face sagged with weariness, he seemed to glow with a regal strength. His arms and shoulders were sleek and muscular—and his voice! Though it trembled with pain, his voice was warm and resonant, as if he had spoken in an echoing royal hall. Gone was the cloven's gurgling mewl, replaced by the voice of a king.

Janner untied Kalmar's bonds while Esben loosed Leeli. "Papa!" she cried, and as soon as her arms were free she wrapped them around Esben's neck. When the three children were untied, Esben slumped back against the hull, snapping arrow shafts like twigs, his face and torso aglow with moonlight.

"Children! Are you all right?" Nia called. She peered down from the deck of the Fang ship. The skiff had drifted back and bumped against its hull, where a rope ladder hung.

"Yes ma'am. But—" Janner couldn't bring himself to say it. He saw the dark stain spreading from his father's wounds. He heard the weakness of his breathing.

Kalmar crawled over to him and said, "Papa?"

Nia climbed down and dropped into the skiff. Leeli, Janner, and Kal gathered around their father and whispered their love to him as they leaned on him and stroked his fur. Nia sidled under one of his arms and rested her head against his mountainous chest. Janner wanted to speak, but he couldn't. His throat was tight and refused to make a sound as tears sprang from his eyes. He could hear Esben's heartbeat and the rattle of his breathing.

I found you, the voice said in his mind. Janner wiped his cheeks and looked up to find Esben's eyes on him. *My son.* Then Esben's lips moved. He licked the roof of his mouth, swallowed once, and spoke in a voice as frail as it was rich.

"Kalmar, come closer so I can see you."

Kalmar wiped his eyes and sat up. Janner watched with wonder as the two of them looked at each other: the great bear and the little wolf; the High King and his heir; the lost father and his outcast son.

"Have they done to you what they did to me?" Esben asked.

Kalmar nodded. "I'm sorry, Papa. I wasn't strong enough."

"None of us are, lad. Me least of all." Esben smiled and took a rattling breath. "But it's weakness that the Maker turns to strength. Your fur is why you alone loved a dying cloven. You alone in all the world knew my need and ministered to my wounds." Esben pulled Kalmar closer and kissed him on the head. "And in my weakness, I alone know *your* need. Hear me, son. I loved you when you were born. I loved you when I wept in the Deeps of Throg. I loved you even as you sang the song that broke you. And I love you now in the glory of your humility. You're more fit to be the king than I ever was. Do you understand?"

Kalmar shook his head.

Esben smiled and shuddered with pain. "A good answer, my boy. Then do you believe that I love you?"

"Yes sir. I believe you." Kalmar buried his face in his father's fur.

"Remember that in the days to come. Nia, Janner, Leeli—help him to remember." Esben coughed and pointed at the mast. "Janner, raise the sail, would you? It's that rope there. Go on." Janner blinked away his tears and scooted over to unwrap the line from the cleat. "Kalmar, row us out a little way. Get us into the wind."

Esben guided the boys while Leeli and Nia leaned against him and wept. He told Janner when to pull the rope tight and draw in the boom, and he helped Kalmar steer the rudder. "Point us south," Esben whispered to Kalmar. "To Anniera."

A few minutes later they were well away from the Fang ships and the pier, cutting through the waves toward the center of the harbor and the Watercraw.

At Esben's request, Leeli played her whistleharp. Nia held her husband while the children leaned against him and looked up at the moonbright heavens arrayed above the full, white sail.

The Maker's magic swirled around them as they went, gleaming strands that connected the hearts of the children to their father, and their father to his grieving brother across the Dark Sea of Darkness. The sorrow in Leeli's heart opened a door to a greater joy than any of them had known before. She felt her father's affection in her secret heart and through her song communed with him there. Kalmar's mind swirled with glimmering images and sounds: Esben's deep laughter in a firelit room; Esben lifting a young Kalmar over his head and looking up at him with delight and pride and wonder. Janner heard his father's love sung over him in words tender and ancient and strong: "I am well pleased with you, my son."

The bear's heart beat slower and slower, and Nia and the children knew he was leaving them. Esben looked at Nia. "I love you, dear Nia. Thank Artham for me. For the song." He put one of his big, trembling hands on her cheek.

Then he turned to the children. "In death, my love, I loved you best," he said, and under a quiet moon in a steady south wind, wrapped in the arms of his wife and children, Esben Wingfeather, High King of Anniera, died.

In the days that followed, people watching from the waterfront that night claimed they heard a sweet music and saw a swirl of shimmering mist that surrounded the little boat. They said it glowed like a spirit and a tendril of it twisted up and up, clear to the moon. They claimed it was the Maker's own breath, sighed out over the Wingfeathers from beyond the veil.

The Keeper and
the High King

Without a word between them, Janner and Kalmar turned the boat around and sailed back to the port. When they arrived at the quay, a multitude of battle-weary and wounded Hollowsfolk welcomed them home in respectful silence. They beheld the Bear King's body—not crumbling to dust, but majestic and peaceful in the cradle of the boat—and they murmured prayers of grief and contrition.

The battle was won, and not a Grey Fang had survived. Fang armor and weapons were strewn in the street and on the pier, and behind the throng, houses blazed.

Rudric stood at the front of the crowd. Nibbick Bunge was nowhere to be seen, but Janner saw Danniby, Olumphia, Guildmaster Clout, Joe Bill, Morsha, and other friendly faces, along with the O'Sallys and their brave dogs. All were dirty with soot, mud, sweat, and blood. Their clothes were torn, and their shoulders slumped with fatigue. Podo and Oskar pushed through the crowd and stopped short when they saw Esben's body.

Podo helped Nia out of the boat, and she stood on the pier looking over the multitude. Everywhere her gaze fell, the Hollowsfolk looked away. Rudric stepped forward and lashed the skiff to the dock. When he passed Nia, his face contorted with grief, but he swallowed it quickly and turned to the crowd.

"Some of you might say it was the Wingfeathers who brought this battle to our shores. Some may say it was Bonifer Squoon and his treachery. Some may say it was Gnag the Nameless. But I say it was none of these things!" Rudric glared at them, then pounded his chest. "We bear the guilt, Hollows-folk. It is we who have hidden behind the Watercraw these nine years while Gnag the Nameless has ravaged the breadth of Aerwiar. It is we who let fear speak louder than courage." Rudric stepped onto a crate so he could see the whole crowd. His face was fierce in the firelight. "We have abandoned the Shining Isle. We have betrayed its king and forsaken a long alliance. Our cowardice in this matter is made the more shameful by our great strength. No more." Rudric jumped down from the crate and knelt before the skiff, so low that his beard touched the dock.

Nia didn't have to say a word to Kalmar. He climbed out of the boat and stood straight and sure before Rudric, cape flapping in the harbor breeze. The

Keeper of the Hollows removed the bloodied war hammer from his belt and laid it at Kalmar's feet.

"High King Kalmar," Rudric said, loud enough that all could hear him, "as Keeper of the Hollows, I offer you our allegiance. And we ask your pardon."

Janner expected Kalmar to look to Nia or Podo for guidance. He expected him to fumble for words and stammer. But instead Kalmar put a hand on Rudric's shoulder and said in a loud voice, "Rise, Keeper." Rudric stood and looked down at the little wolf in the Durgan cape. "Your allegiance is accepted. And I gladly give what little pardon I owe."

Rudric nodded, then turned to his people and mounted the crate again.

"Countrymen! If there is evil in the world, it will find its way into the Green Hollows, no matter how vigilant our watch. If there is evil in the world, should not the warriors of the Green Hollows meet it?"

As Janner listened, Rudric changed the Green Hollows forever.

The histories of the Third Epoch tell how at the harbor of Ban Rona that

night, Rudric ban Yorna and the Wolf King of Anniera mustered the Hollowsfolk to war. Word spread throughout the land that the Durgans were readying for battle. Dogs carried messages to the Outer Vales and the cities of the hills and all the villages between, calling for arms and anyone brave enough to wield them against Gnag the Nameless and the Fangs of Dang.

As winter fell, weapons were forged, timber was harvested, ships were built, and food was stored. Among the fields and hills of the Green Hollows, an army prepared for battle. They gathered their strength, and they waited. In the fullness of time, when the winter faded and the spring brought the thaw, the free people of Aerwiar would go to war.

And the Jewels of Anniera would lead them.

Appendices

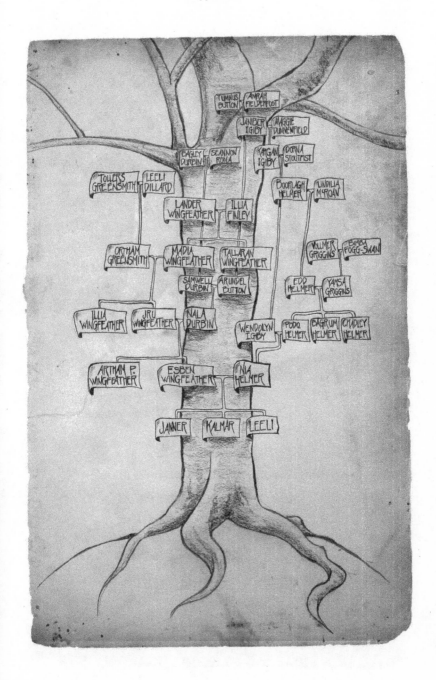

Omer, second son, hearken to me.

I fear your brother broken by the shadows of the world. He seeks not light, but light's power, and thus has come to love the darkness. When I walk the streets, I see in my people a fear they cannot name, a new and wicked presence in the world that steals their joy. They fear the hungering dark. They fear the very fact of the sullied and sundered nature of the world now that Will has chosen to defy me and the Maker. Cast off has he the yoke of wisdom and seeks he now dominion.

But he cannot walk the Fane of Fire. He must not! Omer, my boy, your brother is wild with rage, and his armies batter my gates. I beg you, keep safe the way to the Heart of the World. Wide runs the river there and gold with goodness glow the walls. If he finds the way beneath Anyara, the world will be forever wrecked. The Maker meets me there, and has told me so. You ask if the Maker is powerless against it, and indeed, I asked the same. But trust this: in his presence a king knows how little a king knows. The Maker fears not the doings of Will. He weaves and wends the tale of the world, and watches o'er its endings. He has bid me bear my courage. He my fear has long assuaged. Even as he warns me of my rebel son's ambition, even as his shining eyes are lined with grief in joy, I sense, my son, a mighty love for me and each of us, his children, and I am fain to trust his voice. He means to make his subjects merciful and wise; sorrow and struggle bringeth both. We will, he tells me, grow by grieving, live by dying, love by losing. The heart itself is the field of battle and the garden green.

The deep of the world awaits you and your progeny. The way is shut to all but heirlings, they who carry holy fire. The limning speaks, the shaping shines, the melody is light in time, and then the portal opens that the king may downward climb the stair into the Fiery Fane, the gilded city where remains the holy burning heart of hope. The way is in our keeping. Let none—

And that is the last of the written words of Dwayne, the First Fellow. His son, Ouster Will, slew him, killed the king, my father. He, the eldest son, hungered for power and dominion, and was not content with his lot. When the dragons sank the mountains and the way to the Fane was closed to him, he turned his wits to the destruction of Anyara and the delving of her secrets. I shall seek the aid of Yurgen, Dragon King. I will ask him to trench the sea and cleave Anyara from the bosom of the land. The Kings, Wardens, Song Maidens, and Lore Wains will be safekeeping the new-made Isle of Anyara from the wiles of Ouster Will, that the Fane of Fire may ever keep the world alive with light.

I go now to Yurgen, though I fear my death is certain. Maker help me.

Omer, Son of Dwayne,
Secondborn and King of Anyara

—From the final pages of the First Book, as translated by Oskar N. Reteep in the library of Ban Rona, with the unfortunate aid of Bonifer the Treacher.

About the Author

Andrew Peterson is a critically acclaimed recording artist and songwriter, as well as the author of the award-winning Wingfeather Saga. He's also the founder of The Rabbit Room, an organization that fosters community through story, art, and music. He and his wife, Jamie, make their home in Nashville.

Visit www.andrew-peterson.com for more information about Andrew or www.wingfeathersaga.com for more information about Aerwiar and its woefully dangerous creatures.

DON'T MISS ANY *of the* BESTSELLING SAGA!

FIND OUT MORE AT

WWW.WINGFEATHERSAGA.COM
WWW.HODDERFAITHYOUNGEXPLORERS.CO.UK

www.hodderfaithyoungexplorers.co.uk